REUNIFICATION

ADAM WEISSBURG

Reunification
by
Adam Weissburg

ISBN 979-8-9921874-0-3

For my brother, Marc,
For letting me read his books

For my daughter Michaela,
For giving me the courage to try

and

For my wife, Francie,
For never letting me give up and sharing this journey

BASUL

ONE

Truth. What is it? Do we know it when we hear it? Can we see it when it is right before us? Who can we trust to tell us the truth?

These are the questions of a child looking for simple answers to the quandary that many of us spend our lives trying to resolve. Few of us will ever be rewarded with satisfying conclusions. We must not forget that each of us has a child within, and it is the vision of the child—always asking "why?"—that keeps us ever watchful. Truth can be trusted, but one never knows if the messenger has told the truth. Too often, the victors manipulate the facts to suit their purpose, sacrificing the truth. We must all retain our inner innocence and keep asking questions.

The Teachings of the Prophet, 5:5

For Tuac Acira, it was a glorious season. Stara's Journey celebration was a few days away. He was twelve months away from his fourth turn and ready to devote the next year to figuring out what position he would take in his society. All across Mia, children Tuac's age used the year leading up to their fourth turn to explore career opportunities. That process culminated in the annual Journey festivities, when each child would announce their choice. For some, the decision was made for them.

His sister Rea had just passed her fourth Turn and would be participating in this year's Journey. As with all New Ones, it was time for her to leave the city of Stara to create her own name and to expand the wealth of Tuac's family. For the first time, Tuac would have his parents to himself.

The Journey daunted him. Upon reaching four turns, roughly sixteen years in the Royal Landing Calendar, a young person became a full member of Mian society. Tuac's coming year, called the Prophet's Probation, prepared him to embark on life in a different city, never to return home.

School did not explain the origin of the Journey tradition, but Tuac had learned much by eavesdropping on his parents' conversations with Rea. The original Terran settlers of Mia had left their home world with enough colonists, but many died on the trip. Worse, few of those colonists lived through their first turn. To ensure the survival of the Terran population, the colonists agreed to divide into small groups and settle across the planet. All of them encountered native peoples, joined them, and established the four Realms. The Realms stayed in close contact through the efforts of the Terrans, as the Mians had previously kept to themselves. With Terran intervention, the Mians realized they were stronger as a collective than on their own. To bind the Realms together, they sent their young adults to other Realms, and The Journey festivities enshrined the practice. When the Emperor united the Realms, the Journey formed the lynch pin of Mian governance. As the Prophet wrote, there was only one Mia and the Journey preserves the peace and unites the Realms.

Tuac believed this story was a myth, though he would not deny the Prophet's teaching aloud. He had too much mischief to make in this last year before his fourth turn. True to this purpose, Tuac slipped out of the house and set out for the market district, where merchants hawked their goods to families planning Journey celebrations. Almost everyone in town was either planning a going-away party or attending one. They needed to be dressed in the newest fashions and to stock their pantries for guests.

Colorful banners rippled over the market stalls and the scent of grilling meat and baking bread made Tuac's mouth water. Buyers argued with sellers, children chased each other, weaving among the stalls, and bards played and sang as they strutted through the crowd. Tuac spied two adjacent merchants, a fabric peddler and silversmith. Brushing up against the display of gleaming vases and bowls, Tuac moved a small candlestick to the fabric seller's table. He placed it on a batch of stunning red silk, bright against the rich darkness. In seconds, the silversmith snatched the candlestick back, cursing the silk merchant under his breath. The fabric peddler barked back at the silversmith. Their voices rose and the first fist flew. Tuac snickered, which was his undoing. Hearing the boy, the two combatants realized they had been played and hollered for the guards.

Tuac bolted around the corner and tore down the street deeper into the maze, shouldering his way through the throng. He almost collided with three constables responding to the alarm he'd caused. Not wanting to press his luck, Tuac decided to return home to his parent's alchemy shop. It was long past sunset and Tuac should have been home by now. He may have survived his mischief, but he was going to be in a world of hurt from his parents for missing another curfew.

His parents' business was called the *Stara Ki Mirro Tuac* or

Stara's Well For The Seekers. They had named their only son after their profession, hoping for the Prophet's blessing and nudging Tuac toward the alchemists' guild. The Aciras came from peasant stock yet had risen to positions of respect in their chosen field. Tuac was a seeker, his curiosity insatiable. He annoyed his teachers and parents with constant questions, like "Where did these formulas come from?" or "How do you know that will work?" His father grumbled but Tuac knew his father loved to share the intricacies of his business with his son. Tuac loved his father Cisrena, but Tuac longed for a more exciting life. He knew his father would see this yearning as a rejection, so Tuac kept his feelings to himself, though he suspected that his father could see restlessness in Tuac's eyes.

Tuac snuck back into his house through the kitchen door, surprised to find it empty. Loree, Tuac's mother, should have been busy making one of her mouth-watering stews for the holiday meal. Although he was disappointed that he wasn't able to taste test his mother's golden roasted vegetables, Tuac thanked the Prophet no one had detected his absence. His father was not in the adjacent laboratory where he mixed his curatives. His parents must be in the storefront helping a customer with an emergency. Most businesses closed ahead of the Journey festivities, but Tuac's parents stayed open right up to the celebratory feast.

Cisrena had often told Tuac, "Boy, so many customers wait until the last minute before coming to see me. If it were not for those last-minute orders, you would be wearing rags. We eat when *all* of the customers have gone home." Tuac would roll his eyes at his father's work ethic, but Loree never begrudged Cisrena's devotion, even if she wished he would raise his prices during the holiday season.

Tuac started to go upstairs but heard soft voices and realized that his parents had guests in the dining room adjacent to the storefront. Through the window he saw two majestic snow-white hursas outside. Only a few professions maintained stables, as most of the hursa population had not survived the Great Destruction. Other than The Emperor, only the army and the University had more than a dozen hursas. These two looked splendid. Their size, color, the absence of any weapons, and the quality of their tack told Tuac that mages had come to his parents' shop.

He peered into the dining room, hoping not to attract attention. He sensed the tension in the conversation.

Of course, Tuac thought, *the mages must be here for Rea. She's going to attend the University!* He studied the guests. Both had long, white hair, and wore flowing white robes. The taller one's robe had a bright crimson lapel, and the shorter one's lapel was greyish white. Tuac inched closer to listen.

The tall Mage said, "The University will take care of all of your concerns. Rea will get the best education available in the Four Realms and she will have a well-paying profession. If she becomes the mage I expect her to be, I see no limits to what she will be able to accomplish."

Tremendous! My sister will wield the power of the elements. They had always known that Aced—the god of magic and Mother Mia's mate—had blessed Rea. Only magic could explain how she could control small fires. Tuac had not known if her skill was enough to win her University admission. He studied his parents to see if they shared his excitement. His father looked stoic. Tuac could tell from his mother's frown that she was not enamored with the proposition that Rea attend University. In the weeks before the Journey, guilds invited New Ones to join. The University's invitations were rare, and no one turned them down.

Watching the negotiation, Tuac was struck by his father's

strength and bearing. His hair had thinned in recent years, and his body reflected Loree's fine cooking and his years in the sun. He was an imposing figure, respected by his neighbors and his guild. The only person not intimidated by him was his wife. Cisrena reserved his warmth for his family. Tuac loved his father's hugs. His mother, the outgoing, affectionate member of the pair, balanced her husband in their home and business life. A tad shorter and delicate, her face brightened a room. But you knew when she was angry, as she was now.

"But you have not told us what would happen if Rea cannot become a mage," his mother said. Tuac did not think Rea would fail, but their mother never took chances and prepared for all possible outcomes. He valued her planning skills, though sometimes he felt smothered by her endless attention to detail. The mages were not going to bully his parents.

The short one responded, "We *rarely* make mistakes in our selection. In the unlikely event Rea does not flourish at the University, she will be amply compensated for the time she has been detoured from the Journey and we will find an appropriate profession for her. Indeed, many productive members of society, *including many alchemists*, have gotten their start as a result of such detours." Tuac flinched at the disdain in his voice.

"Enough Ki'lel," the tall one interjected. "Please excuse my tactless colleague. We have been away from home for some time and Ki'lel's manners suffer when he does not sleep in his own chambers. Suffice it to say, Mr. and Mrs. Acira, the University selects only a few New Ones during each Journey. We carefully assess our candidates and your daughter has shown tremendous potential. In the unlikely event that your daughter is unable to reach full mage status, the University will provide her with a comfortable livelihood in one of the many professions that assist us in protecting the Realms."

Tuac's father startled him by gesturing him into the room. Without missing a step, Tuac's father introduced the mages.

"Tuac, this is Meiach and this is Ki'lel. They're from the University and have come to offer an invitation to Rea. Rea is packing, go help her." Tuac heard the certainty in his father's voice. The decision was made.

As he went up the stairs, the conversation turned to financial compensation for the Aciras' permission for Rea to attend. Tuac knew that money did not influence his parents' decision and wondered why the Mages offered what amounted to a bribe.

***

Meiach checked his hursa's girth. They had two more candidates' families to visit before evening.

Ki'lel snarled at him, "You should not have cut me off like that. I'm sick and tired of sniveling little shop keepers and farmers who impugn the integrity of the University."

"Stop moaning." Meiach said. "You and I know that with the shortage of young acolytes, we cannot take the chance that any potential mage turns down the University. When you and I had our Journeys, one had no choice but to accept the University's solicitation. We no longer live in that age. It is only because they are tradesmen, a status that you chose to insult, that the Aciras did not put up a fight. A more sophisticated family from Tushman would have realized that they did have an option and demand more compensation for the girl." Meiach swung up into the saddle. "We cannot take chances and waste opportunities with the ranks of mages thinning every turn. And you know that she is special. One more outburst and I'll report you to the Archmage."

Meiach urged his hursa into a full gallop, knowing that Ki'lel was not settled on his beast. Ki'lel swore as his mount lurched.

As he turned onto the road to their next appointment, Meiach hoped that that Rea would become a full-fledged Mage. Expulsions were never pleasant.

"Rea, you're going to be a mage!" Tuac said as he surprised his sister in their room behind the storefront. Startled, Rea turned away from the window. Tuac could see from the tidy packed bundle of her belongings that Rea was ready to go. Tuac studied his sister. Rea was disheveled from her harried effort to pack, her red hair tangled and covering her face. To his surprise, Tuac saw tears in her crystal blue eyes. He was confused by her reaction, but he did not want to say anything. Tuac thought Rea would be thrilled about attending the University, but seeing the sadness on her face, he realized that she was thinking about leaving home.

Tuac wanted to hug his sister, but he felt uncertain. Comforting his sister felt foreign. He realized he had never been his sister's protector. Rea had looked out for him, not the reverse.

"I am obviously excited," she said, "and don't think I have any choice in the matter. I have been blessed by Aced and now I have to assume my chosen role. Everyone knows what happens if you turn down the University." Rea tucked her hairbrush into the outer pocket of her knapsack.

Tuac could feel the lump in his throat. Every child in the city had heard about the misfortunes of Tsa Triacis. Tsa's magical ability had shown itself in her first turn. Count Triacis was a member of the local gentry and believed he could refuse the

University's invitation. He had a grand scheme to marry Tsa into another family to build wealth. From the day that Count Triacis made his decision, his family suffered horribly. First, Tsa suffered a strange illness that could not be diagnosed or treated and, ultimately, she died. Next, Countess Triacis went insane with remorse, blaming her husband for the loss of their daughter. After the Countess was committed, the Count mysteriously died. There was a suicide note but no one believed he had killed himself. The Count was too much of a coward. Rumor had it that the Mages were responsible for all the Triacis' misfortunes and had made an example of them.

Now that Rea's Journey was upon them, Tuac felt conflicted. No one considered the sorrow of younger siblings as they lost their brothers or sisters. Even though he had longed for Rea to be out of the way so he could have his parents' complete attention, now he wished he had more time with her.

While there was no rule that said siblings could not journey to the same city, other than the rare visit or family gathering, Tuac knew that he would have little contact with Rea after she left for the University. That was the way of the mage: solitary, loyal to only the University, seeking truth with no family connections that could be used against them.

"Come on, Rea, let's go out and cause a little mischief! The Journey starts the day after tomorrow and we won't have another chance." Tuac wanted his last moments with his sister to be memorable. He pulled at her hand, and while Rea was taller than Tuac, she could not resist him.

"Okay," she said, tousling his hair. "If you get into trouble, I'll be there to bail you out one last time. And if I get in trouble, there's really not that much anyone can do. After all, I am an acolyte of the University!" They laughed and set out.

First, the two went to the stables where they found a couple out for a late-night tryst.

"I always thought people were supposed to be a little more discrete than that." Tuac said and hatched a brilliant scheme. "Rea, do you think you could grab that rope over the stalls?" Rea caught on to Tuac's mischievous plan. He snuck up on them and slipped a noose around their feet. Rea threw the rope over the rafters. Tuac slid the noose tight and Rea pulled hard, lifting the struggling couple up to dangle half-naked a few inches above the floor, screaming and swearing.

Now for the finishing touch, Tuac thought. He said, "Rea, now that you're an acolyte, you might want to brush up on your skills before you arrive at the University. It's gotten rather chilly tonight, and mama always tells us we need to be mindful of those less fortunate that us—like these two, who might catch their death of cold. I think you should light a small fire in the farrier's brazier to keep them warm. Aced and Mia would certainly smile upon you for being so charitable."

Rea looked around the dim stable. "I'll need some kindling. Those clothes over there will work now that our friends won't be needing them." Rea concentrated. Sweat appeared on her brow and the clothes ignited. After making sure that the fire could not escape the forge, they left. In minutes, they heard shouts from the staff who had seen the smoke from the chimney. Shortly thereafter, the two heard laughter and it was clear they had accomplished their goal.

"I can't figure out how you get away with the things you do," Rea said. "I know those folks were distracted, but they should have noticed you."

Tuac grinned and shrugged.

They headed for their local pub to find their next victims. They performed several kinds of pranks on the unsuspecting patrons. Rea kept putting out the tavern's fire. The siblings stifled their laughter as the barkeep struggled to figure out what the problem was. He slammed the flue open and shut, shoved the logs around on the andirons, and added more kindling, but nothing worked. The patrons shouted suggestions and encouragement. Tuac sauntered throughout the taproom posing as a water boy and managed to dilute many pints. He would drop a napkin or a knife, and while bending to retrieve it, tie together the bootlaces of several customers. It was not quite *magic*, but fun nonetheless. He tingled with glee every time one of his victims tripped as they got up. Usually, their tablemates teased them for being inebriated until the person discovered Tuac's sabotage. All in all, Tuac and Rea felt rather proud of themselves.

Then the proprietor noticed Tuac. "Hey, you two!" Pointing at them, the innkeeper abandoned the fire and shouted. "You Aciras are always causing problems. When I catch you I'll turn you over to your father!" He lunged for Tuac, who dodged and ran. A few patrons joined in the chase. Tuac and Rea bolted for the door. Those with tied laces tumbled and those who were deep in their cups fell over them, turning the pursuit into a pile-up. Only two of the patrons made it out of the inn with the barkeep.

The siblings ran hard, knowing that they could not afford to get caught. Tuac was so scared he could feel his heart race. He glanced at Rea and Tuac sensed she was scared, too.

If only we could distract them, I know we could escape, Tuac thought. At that moment, the bartender stumbled and had to stop to keep his balance. The two men behind him crashed into him, and all three fell, swearing. That was all Tuac and Rea needed. The siblings slipped through a narrow gap in one of the street walls and ran, taking a circuitous route home to shake any pursuers.

When they arrived home, Tuac knew they had escaped. Then they walked into the kitchen to find the furious barkeep confronting their parents. He had come directly to the house as Tuac and Rea were perfecting their evasive maneuvers. Their furious parents were waiting for them. Cisrena dragged them by their ears to the livery and made them apologize to the staff and to the young couple now draped in hursa blankets. Tuac offered to replace the couple's burned clothes, but the lovers waved him off, asking everyone to forget what happened. Next, they went to the inn to apologize to everyone and clean up the mess they had caused. It was early morning when the two Aciras returned to *Mirro Tuac*. Loree banished Rea and Tuac to their bedrooms. Tuac was relieved that his father had not taken off his belt and walloped them.

Tuac's room was right above the kitchen, and he could hear his mother and father chuckling as Cisrena related everything their errant offspring had done.

Two

To ensure that we will have a future, we must be strong individually and we must be strong as a collective. Diversity is the key. To obtain diversity, we must sacrifice our most treasured possession—our children.

The Teachings of the Prophet, 6:12
Opening Benediction for the Journey

Tuac had hoped to spend much of the remaining time until the Journey with Rea. However, he ended up doing both his chores and most of hers. The days flew by, and she was often gone in the evenings. Tuac resented having to do so much extra work, though he knew that Rea had things to accomplish before she left, including last-minute shopping and goodbyes to her friends.

The Aciras planned a lavish celebration for Rea's big day. She had been considered gifted at school, and Tuac's parents wanted the entire town to know that the University had recruited her.

Tuac was proud of her, but he also wondered if he could meet or surpass Rea's accomplishments. He knew he would miss her, but he was also angry and anxious. She had set such a high standard for him to meet.

Tuac knew he would have to comfort his parents, which felt overwhelming. Indeed, since the magicians had extended an invitation to the University, Tuac's parents had been on edge, fighting with each other and snapping at him for minor infractions. The Aciras had minor spats like any family. But for some reason, everything triggered an argument right now, whether it was Cisrena not cleaning up after himself, Tuac being distracted, or Loree nagging someone to do something that did not need to be done. Tuac loved his sister, but these were difficult days.

The day of the Journey, Tuac woke when Mia's main sun rose. The rest of his family appeared shortly after first sunrise, and by that time Tuac had dressed in a simple shirt and matching pants. Passing his sister's open doorway on his way downstairs, he stopped and studied her as she braided her hair. She looked tense but radiant. She was ready.

Tuac realized that he was not. She was leaving and his contact with her would never be the same. Tradition emphasized the joy of Journey, but now he knew how much sorrow wove through the pageantry and beauty, the colorful banners flying from windows and across streets. The city teemed with emissaries from the various guilds, the Emperor's military, and the Church. Everyone wore their finest clothes. This was the first time Tuac felt no joy or excitement during the Journey celebration, only pain and sorrow.

His family did not eat together that morning, as each of them was coming to grips in their own way with the day's events.

Tuac stifled his tears. His mother's voice broke the eerie quiet as she urged them all to hurry. When she saw what Tuac was wearing, she barked at him.

"Tuac, I told you what to wear! Go change. We're ready to go. We can't be late."

"Yes, mother," he bounded up the stairs to obey her.

As the Aciras headed to the ceremony, Tuac studied the other families. Many wore bright, flowing gowns and crisp, new trousers. The wealthy families wore clothing decorated with ornate embroidery and lace. Most strode proudly toward the town center, but Tuac now noticed the grief of the parents whose children were departing. He saw the sacrifice and hardship that the Journey imposed upon Mians. He also saw sadness in the eyes of others, because the festivities were both a reminder of losses from prior Journeys and a harbinger of Journeys to come.

The only people who showed no pain were the local gentry, who were exempt from the Journey's requirements. The gentry had convinced everyone that they served the Journey's true intent by keeping their children and training them in governance so they could fill those positions in their home city. As the bureaucracy rarely admitted anyone from outside of the local gentry, the same families ruled for generations, their children inheriting their wealth and positions.

The Aciras and the dense crowd of other celebrants reached the town center just in time for the opening benediction by Stara's mayor, Micha Suare. Both of Mia's suns were near their apexes and all New Ones, who would start their Journeys today, stood with him on a platform so everyone could see them.

Tuac considered Mayor Suare a comical person. He was rotund, had a receding hairline, and florid cheeks. He shuffled as he walked. Yet on the day of the Journey, his outfit and bearing changed. He stood taller, walked with dignity, and his flowing white gown gleamed in the bright suns' light. Suare looked the part for this holy ceremony.

The mayor raised one hand and settled the crowd. He bellowed the Opening Benediction that Tuac had heard on every Journey day.

"The Prophet commands us to remember the folly that caused the Great Destruction: isolation. Once, each Realm was a kingdom unto itself. There was no trade among the Realms, no exchanges of emissaries, no communication. Each Realm thought itself better than the others. Each thought itself self-sufficient, able to withstand the forces of nature and time.

"For many turns, the isolation of Realms did not endanger Mia. Then Nabes, whose evil followers numbered more than the pebbles on Mia's shores, amassed an army and sought to control all of Mia. Nabes took advantage of the physical and political distance between the Realms. In only a few turns, the southern Realm fell to Nabes' control and the battle for Mia's soul began.

"Nabes' forces advanced and all seemed hopeless. Then the Prophet arrived. Traveling through each of the Realms, the Prophet forged alliances that stopped the Nabes contagion. Before long, the Prophet had confined Nabes' evil to the south. After raising an enormous army, the Prophet struck directly at Nabes' stronghold. So many lives were lost and bodies littered the battlefield. But the Prophet and the forces of good had prevailed.

"After the Great Destruction, the mages and the leaders of the military forces convened in Shalla, the site of the greatest and final battle. There, surrounded by the carnage of the Great Destruction, they started to rebuild Mia. The Prophet stayed out of those conversations, leaving governance to those who knew how to govern.

"The leaders of each of the Realms did not support a central-ized government, arguing that they needed to heal their own territories. Yet others who had fought and suffered in the war wanted to found a single government that would keep the peace across all of Mia. Despite several days of negotiations, the parties could not reach agreement. Just as Mia was about to fall to another wave of isolationism, the Prophet intervened. He confronted the delegates: 'Your foolish prejudices and petty differences have brought Mia to the brink of destruction. And for what? We are all Mians. Nabes took advantage of these prejudices and it was only by uniting as a people that we were able to defeat him. We must fashion a society based upon that unity, not one that continues the division.

"The leaders of the Realms recognized the Prophet's wisdom. As he had united them to defeat Nabes, so the Prophet brought them together to rebuild Mian society. The leaders created the triumvirate, a plan to share power. The great city of Tushman became the capital of an Empire, the seat of the central government lead by the Emperor who would protect Mia. Each city retained much of its independence while respecting laws that governed everyone. Taxes would support both the local and imperial governments, and the Empire would limit the size and capacity of its military. A separate Church, led by a wise Charge, would oversee the spiritual and moral wellbeing of Mia's people. The mages would construct their University, led by an Archmage, which trained gifted youngsters in the Arts. The leaders of the three branches would share governance of the planet, advising one another and balancing their power equally.

"The leaders told the Prophet of their resolutions. He approved, but told them that they needed to ensure that no Mians were so isolated from the others that they would be willing to wage war upon them. He wanted Mians to embrace their shared culture and not prioritize their differences. For this reason, the Prophet devised the Journey.

"The Prophet commanded that all children four turns of age were to set out from their birthplace and build their lives in other places. They would travel on their Journey for at least two weeks. In this way, Mians would spread between Realms and across the planet. The Journey forbade each New One from visiting their birthplace for four turns, and they could never live there again. New One would build their own family away from the place of their birth, and by mixing of the peoples of all Realms, the walls that separate Mians would disappear.

"The Prophet knew that all parents, siblings and friends would feel great loss. He believed that this shared grief would also unite us, and that by sharing our children with those in distant places we would thrive. As we bid farewell to friends and loved ones today, so do others elsewhere on Mia. And as we welcome others from all over Mia into our cities and our homes, so, too, do other Mians welcome our children.

"It is thus that culture, music, news, and skills, indeed our very families, travel the planet, intertwined for the benefit of all. Mians are never stagnant, never complacent, and never alone. The Journey is not about casting out, but about weaving the great tapestry of Mia that shelters us all." Dabbing his eyes with his handkerchief, the mayor concluded the benediction.

The crowd called out the traditional response: "It is with the Journey, as with all of life, that the parts become one. For only as one people can Mians survive."

On cue, a New One, in this case Tuac's friend, Kanella, daughter of the head of the local printers' guild, stepped forward and proclaimed her acceptance of the Journey.

"As the Prophet proclaims, so will I do. The survival of all depend on the Journey. Willingly, I go to fulfill my duty to family, to Mother Mia, and to the Prophet." Each of the New Ones repeated the words spoken by Kanella.

One by one, the mayor clasped their hands in his, saying, "It is done. We keep the promise."

When the final New One had spoken, the crowd erupted in joy, cheering and hugging one another. The sadness that Tuac saw when he arrived was still there, but veiled. The shared experience had an uplifting effect, even on Tuac.

Next, the New Ones started the process of selecting their professions. Parents did their best to ensure that the New Ones embarked on successful, lucrative livelihoods. Advance scouts for the University, the Emperor's military, the Church and the major guilds had selected their acolytes. Just as the mages Ki'lel and Meiach had invited Rea, the scouts had visited each family's home, extended their invitations, then awaited the New One's choice. The power and allure of the Military and Church were persuasive, and the guilds found willing students. Most of the New Ones had been picked by a scout. Seldom did more than one profession invite the same New One, although the heads of the various professions denied that the guilds worked in unison. For most Journeys, the guilds selected all the New Ones. In the rare instance where a New One was not selected, they would strike out on their own. It was a daunting task to leave your home and hope for the goodwill of another village. But each community had to contend with the same issue, and it was common throughout Mia for unattached New Ones to become day laborers. They served a valuable role wherever they settled. Over time, they would find sufficient work to survive and even thrive.

For Rea, the period of Selection was a time to say goodbye. Tuac watched Rea hugging her friends. They were not likely to see each another again.

"Come on, Tuac," Loree said. "Rea needs to sign her admission contract." Tuac and Rea accompanied their mother to the University's booth, staffed by the two mages Tuac had seen earlier. Seven other families waited in line for their contracts and their compensation. Mian society feared the power of the mages but most welcomed an invitation to the University given the generous compensation they received. Compensation for all families was framed in terms of the lost wages the New One would generate, and the magicians would often pay as much as one month's average wages. In contrast, none of the other guilds, the Church or the Empire offered more than a week's wages.

Rea was now at the front of the line. Meiach placed a contract in front of her, and she stared at her family. Cisrena nodded and Rea signed it. The shorter mage passed Tuac's father a bag with his compensation as Tuac was hugging Rea.

Tuac's parents, who wanted to leave the crowded square, pulled him away from the booth. When he resisted, his mother glared at him. Tuac decided not to push the issue. As they walked home, he heard his mother and father whispering to each other.

"There must be some mistake," Loree said. "This is two months' compensation!" The two stared at each other, and then at a Rea. Tuac realized that Rea's was no ordinary invitation.

Rea departed for the University the next day. She got up early hoping not to have to say goodbye to her parents and her brother and was stunned to see that she was the last one up. The table was set with warm bread, eggs and fresh coffee. No one said anything during the meal and, after the dishes were put away, Rea picked up her bags to walk out.

"I'm leaving now. I'll write as soon as I'm able." Everyone gathered around her, and Tuac kissed her on the cheek.

"Don't screw up. I may want to follow in your footsteps, and I don't want you wrecking it for me." With a smile that did not hide his pain, Tuac left the room so that his parents could say their goodbyes. Rea's mother had been crying since Rea came into the kitchen. Loree caressed her daughter's hand.

"I love you," she said, holding her daughter's gaze.

Rea, who disliked emotional displays, hugged her mother for several minutes, fighting the discomfort of the moment. She smiled and said, "And I love you." Rea looked down, rubbing at a spot that had been on the table for years.

The hardest part was to come, and not wanting the awkward moment to go on longer than it had to, Rea looked at her father.

"Dad," Rea said, "are you okay?" Cisrena got up and for the first time Rea realized that he was shorter than she had thought. Rea had always looked up to her father. What she had taken for physical height was the strength of his presence and his love. Now, on the verge of becoming an adult in her society, she saw her father as a person for the first time—his hunched back, his balding head, the lines in his face. When had her hero become so normal? Rea stared into her father's eyes. He stared back, his gaze thoughtful as though her father was seeing his daughter as an adult for the first time too. Cupping her face in his hand like he used to do when she was a child, he smiled.

"You know, my sweet daughter, I look at you today and all I can do is remember the day you were born. I held you and looked at your little face, counted your little fingers and toes and wondered whether you would love me as much as I did you. You have always made me the proudest father any person could ever be. You are my heart and my soul, and I will always be with you."

Rea had never seen her father cry. She embraced him and, in

a rare moment, cried as well. She clutched her father's hand and kissed his palm.

"Papa, I will always be your little girl." Not wanting to be disheveled for her trip, she sniffed and wiped her face, then reached for the door.

"Not so quickly, little one" her father said. Rea turned around and noticed that he held a simple box with a bow. She opened the box and found an ornately designed pen and matching ink well. "You can't write if you don't have a pen." He smiled, kissed her on her forehead, and let her go.

Rea turned and did not look back.

THREE

We react defensively to the danger of today. With time, the danger passes. Unfortunately, we often forget to take down our defenses and eventually the reasons for our actions become distant memories. Unjustified defenses, more often than not, pose even greater threats to survival.

Logs of the Watcher

Outside of town, Rea met up with a mage named Kir. He wore the robes of the order, but his mantle was yellow. His long silver hair gleamed against his dark skin. Rea tried not to stare. Starra was a small town and she had never met anyone from Tushman, the capital city. Kir ignored Rea's reaction and explained that they were waiting for another Mage who was collecting two New Ones. They would rendezvous at First Noon a few miles from Stara. When Kir handed Rea the reins to the hursa she would ride, she grinned. The big animal made her nervous, but she had always wanted to learn to ride. He helped her mount, instructed her in the use of her legs and the reins, and they set out.

They soon met up with the rest of their group. A second mage named Figan who wore robes similar to those Ki'lel had worn. Though he was overweight, he sat on his hursa with ease. His bald head shone under the first noon sun. He introduced Rea to Tia, a lean, muscular young man, and to Su, a small woman.

Rea had expected more of a procession to the University and was disappointed by the lack of pomp for herself and her traveling companions. Rather than traveling with a huge caravan comprising all of the Realm's new apprentice mages, she was accompanied by a small motley group.

Figan chattered constantly, a trait Rea found annoying. At the same time, Figan and Kir seemed much nicer than the Mage scouts who had visited the Acira's house, and based upon Rea's discussions with other New Ones, nicer than the scouts who had visited their cities too.

Tia hailed from Scri Choua, a small fishing village to the north. His body reflected a life of arduous labor. He was about the same height as Rea and had imposing tattoos, one on his right forearm and several interwoven images covering his left arm. Though Rea had no interest in courting, she considered him handsome. Tia explained that his family had not participated in prior Journeys because the local officials declared the operation of the cannery an administrative role, allowing them to opt out of the process of selecting a profession. He had expected to take over his family's business until the arrival of two mages altered his destiny. Rea suspected that Tia was relieved that he would not have to spend his life packing fish.

Su came from the Pri'an region to the west, near the Sea of Glass. Her olive-green complexion was normal for those residing in the forest region, though in the desert Su looked out of place. Rea had heard about Pri'ans, but none of the rumors proved true. Contrary to those tales, Su did not sleep with her eyes open and bathed as regularly as the rest of the party. However, Su's skin color did vary with her surroundings. When the party camped in the woods, Su's skin shifted to deep forest green. On the royal highway, she became first olive green, then golden brown.

Figan explained, "Pri'an was settled by magicians known as Gaeists, who practice nature magic that gives them a particular affinity for communing with flora and fauna. The settlers of Pri'an were particularly headstrong, almost cultish, in their desire to master their craft and felt that they should learn to change their skin tone to match the environment. Over time, the entire population of Pri'an, even those without magical ability, inherited this skill. Magicians from Pri'an are almost always Gaeists." Rea wondered how Figan knew that she was interested in Su's ability.

Figan continued, "Deary, I am a telepath and reading your thoughts is the least of my powers." He smiled at her then pressed his hursa into a trot so he could join Kir.

Rea found it exciting to be surrounded by people who could wield magic. It had never occurred to her that magicians specialized in particular areas. She had naively thought all magicians could do any form of magic. After watching Kir and Figan, she realized that was not the case, and suspected that her affinity for fire indicated her calling. The more she thought about the future, the more eager she was to be on her way to the University, though like most New Ones, she did miss her family. She had never ventured more than a few hours away from her home.

It was the beginning of the spring thaw, the roads were clear and not muddy, and though the countryside was still barren, it stirred with new life. Birds were returning from warmer regions and the rest of the local animal life emerged from winter hibernation. The group made slow but steady progress through the countryside. Figan frequently pointed out this tree, or that flower. It was almost as if he hated the sound of silence. Su described flora and fauna of her homeland for him. Rea did not pay much attention to their banter. Every morning the group woke to the smell of freshly brewed coffee and harken buns, a specialty of the Northern Realm where Kir was born. He made them for the group's breakfast.

By the seventh day, Rea's delight in the novelty of her experiences waned. She did not sleep well on the ground, and Kir's food was bland and monotonous. The eighth day, they camped outside of Shi'Bo Coula, which was only one day from the University. She wondered why the troupe did not stay in town and, as if on cue, Tia approached Figan.

"Will we find an inn here?" he asked.

Figan looked at Kir, who nodded. Figan dismounted and dropped his bags.

"This is your first lesson. Mages must be careful when associating with other Mians."

Tia, Su, and Rea exchanged glances.

Figan continued. "The Prophet observed that the natural order includes those who have power and those who crave it. From this, the Prophet ordained two rules that guide all magicians: Magic must not be used for personal gain. And mages must avoid being used by those who do not follow the Prophet's First Rule.

"As simple as they are, the Prophet's Rules are difficult to follow. In the early days of the University, most accepted the

Prophet's teachings, but some did not. Their reasons varied. Some craved material things. Others viewed magic as a divine right to take what they wanted. Yet others had a more altruistic stance—they believed that we should use magic to help our fellow Mians. The Great Destruction had to be repaired, they argued, and magicians should be focused on the end goal and not the means to reach it. The University's founders had survived the Great Destruction, when the misuse of magic nearly ended our society. They wanted to restrain the use of power according to the Prophet's directives. They expelled those that refused to follow the Prophet and the University policed their conduct to ensure that their arrogance harmed no one.

"The first thing we all learn are the strict limitations on the use of magic. All New Ones travel with a telepath like me. My job is to screen each candidate and determine if they are capable of adhering to our most sacred principles. Those individuals whom we deem unlikely to follow our Council are denied an education at the University. As a result, the unenlightened, as we call them, never reach their true potential and can only practice wild magic akin to what each of you has exhibited." He paused to let his words sink in and then smiled, "Don't worry. You all passed the test long ago."

Rea let out a breath that she didn't know she had been holding, and she saw that her two companions did the same thing. Everyone chuckled in relief.

Then Kir said, "Unfortunately, while the University's restraint on power protects Mians from renegade mages, this does not protect magicians from Mians. Often, when magicians interact with the ungifted, they ask the magicians to do something. Some tasks can be neutral, like repairing a wall, but power raises expectations. Healing a child is admirable, but healing a despot or a criminal boss presents a moral dilemma.

The only way to ensure that magicians are not pulled into the affairs of Mians is for magicians to distance themselves from the rest of the population. We work with rulers and the church, but only in limited circumstances bound by strict rules. In this way, we can protect Mages from the greed and thirst for power of a groa seeking to manipulate the true gift of Aced."

Figan's cavalier use of "groa" shocked Rea. It meant a heap of hursa dung and was used as a pejorative for those who refused to follow the wisdom of the Prophet. The term was a serious insult. Unsettled by the topic, Rea asked a mundane question.

"Shall we set up camp for tonight?" Everyone dismounted and started unpacking the animals. While Rea expected to see travelers going to the city, none passed their camp.

The next day they rose with the dawn. Only a few towns-people were awake at this hour. Rea noticed these folk looked upon their party with both fear and awe. Outside of town, they started ascending a formidable mountain called the Prophet's Peak. The Border Mountains separating the Western and Northern Realms lined the horizon. It took several hours to reach the summit. They arrived at first noon and stopped for lunch. Rea looked down at the valley below and saw a huge complex.

Kir smiled and said, "That's our destination and your new home."

Rea noticed a huge wall surrounded the University. Within the fortifications Rea saw multiple buildings constructed with a metal that she had never seen before. It glistened in the light of Mia's two suns. There were six large compounds arrayed around a huge central building like the spokes of a wheel.

As the party descended from Prophet's Peak and approached the University, Rea realized distance had dwarfed the magnitude of complex. Each of the main buildings in the six compounds was bigger than the Prophet's cathedral in Stara, which had been the largest building she had ever seen. The central building was as large as the entire city of Stara. Each compound had its own training facilities, dormitories, and stables.

At second sunset, they arrived at the main gate. She noticed the symbol of the University--the two Mian suns in convergence, with six rays, three on each side, extending from the smaller sun to the larger sun. The Prophet designed the sigil to remind Mages that, while blessed by Aced, they were part of a greater Mian people.

To her surprise, Rea could not see any guards at this great gate. No one asked them to identify themselves, they passed through with the routine traffic. Figan saw her raised eyebrows.

"Who would storm our gates?" he chuckled.

The Mages escorted the New Ones to the center complex.

"You will stay here until the end of Fourth Week." Figan said. Three individuals clad in grey approached the New Ones. "Go with them. These memas serve the mages and the University, and they will be your guides until you are assigned to your Art."

For the first week, Rea was confined to her chambers. Her mema brought her food and led her outside twice a day, to shower in the morning and exercise in the afternoon. Her room was stark, but larger and cleaner than her room at her parents' house. There, she had had to cope with her father's tendency to store shop inventory in her room. Here, she had her own space which featured a bed, a water basin, a dresser filled with the white attire of an acolyte, and a small bookcase. Her room opened into a cozy common area with a fireplace.

Five other rooms, including Tia's and Su's, adjoined it. Rea felt both strangely comfortable and homesick in this new environment. Tia and Su also missed their families so the three bonded over their collective loneliness. Rea, a private person, surprised herself by opening up to strangers in this new environment. Their shared experience formed the building blocks of what would be Rea's new family. Two other New Ones joined them at week's end, but by this point Tia, Su, and Rea shared a special bond. On the first day of Second Week, after her normal afternoon visit with Tia and Su, Rea noticed a thick tome, *Complete Annals of Basul,* in her bookcase. Although she was not a skilled reader because teachers were scarce in Stara, Rea found the book within her abilities. Rea realized that Basul was the ancient name for the University. The book was a compendium of its history from the days of the Prophet. The book's cover featured the same two-sun image that Rea had noticed on the gate. Someone had inscribed the first page: *From mentor to acolyte. All must remember the history of Basul, for knowledge loses its power if the source is forgotten.* She stretched out on her bed and it was not long before Rea was spellbound by Basul's colorful history.

Four

Prologue from the History of Basul

People from a planet called Earth visited Mia in turn 978 of the First Millennium. The Terrans, as they called themselves, came in a silver ship that moved through time and space. Their ship, Curiosity, crashed and many of the crew died.

The surviving Terrans brought powerful magic with them. With the wave of a hand, Terrans were able to move objects, bend metals, heal the wounded and many other things. They were the first magicians. Mians struggled with the fact that they were not alone in the Divine Universe, and that their god Aced, beloved mate of Mother Mia, had chosen to empower others with magic.

Unfortunately, the Terrans also brought conflict with them. That is not to say that Mia was without strife prior to the Arrival. But as most lived in isolated communities, Mian disputes had been small, border skirmishes resolved after a few casualties.

The Terrans changed that. A few Terrans had wanted to use Terran magic to enslave the native Mians. The Terran's leaders refused to embrace a strategy of conquest. The few Renegade

Terrans who wanted power over the native population left the main Terran encampment and headed toward distant parts of the planet. But their departure did not solve the problem created by this early divide. The tensions between the Renegades and the other Terrans grew until it threatened the soul of Mia.

Most of the records of those first Renegades were lost in the Great Destruction. What is known is that the Renegades established small fiefdoms, enslaving the native population. Those that remained at the crash site isolated themselves from the Mian population, engaging only in the trade necessary for their survival, and occasionally providing magical medical intervention to the local Mians.

During the first turn after the Arrival, many Terrans died of strange diseases. Within fifteen turns, the only remaining Terrans were those born on the Curiosity, and they started to form families with Mians. The Terrans, now part of Mia with no hope of returning to Earth, also started to teach Mians how to practice magic. Children with both Terran and Mian parentage proved highly adept at magic and could accomplish more than their Terran parents.

The Renegades also took Mian spouses, and their children fought among themselves with the Mians as innocent bystanders. If they were lucky, they were killed. The second-generation mixed-blood Renegades were more violent than their parents, and they enslaved, raped, and tortured survivors of their conflicts. Occasionally, Renegades would attack the Mians around the Curiosity crash site. The remaining Terrans allied with the local Mians and together they repelled the attacks.

This situation lasted until Nabes rose to power.

Rea gasped. She had only heard Nabes' name in whispers. He was evil incarnate, responsible for leading forces against the Prophet. Finally, she was going to learn his story. Rea's heart beat faster and she turned the page.

Although his true identity was never verified, Nabes is believed to have been the bastard son of a Renegade, born in the Fcha Province near Shalla and raised in a brutal Renegade enclave. His inherited magical skills manifested in a dark manner. He was able to call forth fire and he could stop a man's heart with a simple touch.

At the modest age of four turns, and only eighteen turns after the Arrival, he murdered his father and took control of the enclave. Then he turned his attention to neighboring Renegade settlements. He called his army the Dark Tide and recruited other mixed-breeds skilled in magic. Nabes taught them the same dark magic that came naturally to him. His legions were formidable, and his power grew with each victory. When Nabes brought all the Renegades under his banner, he turned his attention to the rest of Mia, demanding that they submit or die.

In early battles, Nabes carried out his merciless ultimatum. He publicly tortured anyone that did not submit, using them as examples of what would happen to those who resisted. Within two turns, the Nabes' Dark Tide gripped most of Mia in a gauntlet of terror and death. Nabes anointed himself ruler and announced that Mia had entered the Second Age.

Mian society appeared to be lost, enslaved by the lunatic Mage. Then a force rose to counter Nabes' iron grip over Mia: the Prophet. The Prophet was also mixed Terran and Mian blood, and was similarly skilled in magic. Yet where Nabes embodied all that is dark, the Prophet served light. His strength of character galvanized a formidable resistance made up of half-breeds who resisted Nabes.

The Prophet and Nabes assembled their forces. Though outnumbered, the Prophet and his allies had one weapon that Nabes did not: a cause. Nabes fought for power, and his allies and troops fought out of fear Nabes' wrath. The Prophet's allies and troops fought because they knew that Nabes had to be stopped or Mian civilization would end, replaced by a reign of terror. This conviction gave the Prophet and his allies strength to endure defeats and to stay focused after a victory. That cause was the deciding factor in the Prophet's victory at the Great Destruction.

Basul was the first city built after the Great Destruction. The Prophet knew that Nabes came to power because few people had a working knowledge of magic. The Prophet decided that Mia needed protectors who would ensure that another Nabes never came to power. Mia could not afford to repeat that history. To do that, Mia needed a center for magical study, research and training.

There would be only two rules for Basul: magic was to be used solely for the greater good and magicians must stand against the dark. Those who followed the Prophet's rules would share in a common purpose. Those that did not would forever be prohibited from using magic.

A voice startled Rea.

"So, you've only read the introduction. I had thought that you would be farther along by now."

Snapped out of her trance, Rea realized one of the magicians had come into her room. She recognized him as one of the two who had visited her family in Stara. She sprang up from her bed and faced him.

"My name is Meiach. You and I met when Scout Ki'lel and I identified you as a possible mage. I will be your tutor for the next two months. After we have completed your initial training, I will make a recommendation to the Archmage as to your field of study, although I suspect that has already been ordained."

Rea said, "I would have been farther along had the Annals of

Basul been given to me earlier. Of course, I am certainly willing to get an oral history to make up for lost time."

She held his gaze without blinking.

"Ha! Your fire presents itself in interesting ways. All right Rea, we will begin your lesson tonight with a short history of Mia and Basul." He settled himself in her desk chair and waved her to sit on her bed. He cleared his throat and began.

"After the Great Destruction, the Prophet determined that changes must be made to Mian society to prevent another civil war. The Prophet concluded that Nabes was able to amass his troops because Mian society was fragmented, allowing regional prejudices to fester. He created the Journey, and ordained that at the age of four turns, each Mian child would migrate to another town to start their own career. Because of this diaspora, every Mian knows that a war in any part of this world will result in a relative being killed. Families are mixed, blood blended. We are all one. Thus, we all strive for peace.

"Only the members of the Ruling Council have a limited exemption. The Ruling Council directs Mian society. The Prophet believed Mians needed a stable government, so he assigned the royal families from each of the Four Realms to form the Ruling Council. To ensure stability, the royal lineages needed to stay intact. They were allowed to steer their children toward local governance. The Ruling Council selects the Emperor, an office rotated among the Realms so that all of Mia is represented over time."

Meiach continued, "Mages do not participate in the Journey. It is not that they are exempted, but that they are not permitted to have families. Magicians dedicate their lives to serving Mia, without the joy of parenthood. Once you accept your true Art, Rea, you will be prohibited from having children."

This sacrifice stunned Rea. She had never given much

thought to whether she would have a family, but she always had assumed that she would. For the first time, she wondered whether being a Mage was a blessing or a curse.

Meiach did not say a word as Rea considered this cost of becoming a mage. After some time, Rea nodded.

Meaich resumed the lesson. "Basul was established to teach and nurture Mia's magicians, and the Prophet decided its physical construction should reflect this purpose. Thus, Basul was built with six outer compounds called the Vessels of the Arts, and an inner circle called the Prophet's Domain. Each Vessel houses one of the six distinct areas of study at Basul: nature, water, wind, fire, water, and telepathy. Each compound is the same size and distance from the center, no Art being more or less favored.

"You and all of the other New Ones are currently in the Prophet's Domain. In addition to the New Ones' dormitory, the Prophet's Domain also contains facilities in which representatives from each of the Arts meet to chart the course of Basul. We also host guests here, though rarely. Finally, it also contains the central library, which is open to all Mages after they have received and passed basic training.

"That's the summary of the structure of Basul and I've spared you hours of dry reading."

It was a lot to digest. Meiach stood, but Rea raised a hand to halt him.

"Meiach, I have a few questions, if that is permitted. First, what about healers? They've come to our villages from time to time, and the things they did defied explanation—are they not practicing magic? Second, what if I want to study more than one form of magic or what if my initial training does not reveal my true Art?"

Meiach raised an eyebrow. "You are an inquisitive one. I did say that this was to be your first lesson, and I do try to answer my students' questions."

"Healers are definitely not magicians and to call their skill 'healing arts' is far too generous. Their skills come from the rudimentary study of the body and herbs. While what they do may appear magical to the uninformed, it is not. Early in Basul's history, the Archmage thought it would be beneficial to have healers learn some of the basics of magic and they were given quarters in the Prophet's Domain. Over time, others resented the healers, who demanded that we consider their work a True Art. But memorizing herbal recipes is not the same as magic. About one hundred turns after the founding of Basul, the Archmage realized that healers did not belong at Basul. You would do well not to ask that question of others.

"As to your second question, it is not possible to learn more than one Art. Only the Prophet was able to control all of the Arts. We learned that not only was it impossible to practice more than one Art but trying to learn more than one actually impedes a magician's proficiency in their calling. As to determining your true Art, our methods have been perfected over time and are rarely wrong. Basul employs three phases in the testing, each with different observers, to ensure an accurate determination."

Meiach continued, "As you know, Figan is a telepath. What you probably did not know is that he excels at sensing the skills of others. You completed the first test during your journey here as Figan probed your nascent Art constantly. Before visiting you, I reviewed his detailed report. I have just given you the second test. Based upon what our observers and Figan told us, we believe you are Fire Walker like me. I was sensing the flame within you, and while you have one more phase to complete, I believe it burns quite brightly. All Fire Walkers share a bond, and members of the other Arts also have a unique bond. The final test measures your aptitude, not your calling.

"Rarely, a New One needs to be re-evaluated early in their training. If we were wrong, we can correct the New One's assigned Art. Though the Arts are different, and no one can master more than one, the foundational principals for all magic are the same. Any more questions?"

"How will you know that I have sufficient aptitude?"

Meaich laughed. "Truly, I will enjoy teaching you." He nodded at her and left.

The Watcher knew the Dark's hunger was insatiable. It controlled a significant portion of the Southern Realm. All human life—indeed, all forms of life—had perished there during the Great Destruction. The Watcher had no way to warn the Mian people of the approaching danger.

The Watcher travelled into the barren Southern Realm to observe. Knowledge, though not a weapon, was a kind of power. The Watcher mourned the loss of sentient life in this place. This was no mere desert like the Eastern Realms in the dry season, where emptiness was natural. This land had been poisoned. The Southern Realm's emptiness deprived the Dark of sustenance. This total emptiness saddened the The Watcher. The Watcher could only help the Reunifer grow.

The Watcher returned to where it all had started—Castle Shalla. This was the epicenter of the Great Destruction, where the Prophet had faced down the evil that threatened all of Mia. This was also where the Prophet made the mistake that could end all life on this planet. The lake beside the ruin shimmered like a mirror. No insect chirped or flew. Then the Watcher saw movement within the castle. Could the mages feel that? A huge crack opened in the center of Shalla's grand courtyard, and out of it stepped the shape of a man, black as a void. Its voice hissed across the dry wind.

"Who am I? I have been asleep too long and my memory has dimmed. Do I have a name?

"Where am I? Wait—I remember: there was a Great Destruction. One in white defeated me with his mass of followers."

The Watcher recognized the beginning of the end.

The Dark continued, "I am Nabes. I will not be defeated again.

FIVE

All are gifted, only the nature of the gift is different. Some are meant to be leaders, some followers, and still others challengers of our teachings. As society ages, leaders become memories, followers become the leaders, and challengers either become revered or vilified for their opposition. There is only one constant pattern—change is survival, and stagnation is death.

The Teachings of the Prophet, 2:1

As Meiach hurried down the long halls to the Council meeting room, he reflected that every Journey followed the same pattern. Basul would find qualified New Ones. When they arrived, Mentors confined acolytes to their rooms for constant observation. Mentors considered everything: an acolyte's demeanor, their dreams, and their personal habits. The Council reviewed the Telepaths' reports and the Mentors' observations not only to determine the Art of each New One, but also to filter out any dangerous candidates. A lapse could create a rogue mage.

At the end of the second week, acolytes received a copy of the Annals and their Mentor conducted a casual, but thorough, interview. Meiach was adept in this evaluation, able to connect with every one of his students' flames without alerting them. He could discern the contours of the flame, its appetite, its rage, and its chaos. Few were better at determining if a potential Fire Walker had a dark streak and did not merit formal training.

Meiach tired of the theatrical aspect, and his inevitable pangs of remorse and guilt when a student learned that their Mentor had probed them without permission. Mentors needed the trust of their students, yet the process began with this violation because Mia's safety depended on the accurate assessment of New Ones. If a potential student was angry or power-hungry, their Mentor could recommend that they be denied the magical teachings of Basul. Instead, they would be offered a lay job assisting Basul's administration. Basul filtered out those who might use magic in violation of the Prophet's two rules. The Mentor's decision was final, but there were times when Meiach wondered if the decisions were always fair.

At the next staircase, Ki'lel joined Meiach.

"Still agonizing over your duties?" Ki'lel asked.

"You know I am," Meiach said. He and Ki'lel had been in the same group of New Ones when they started at Basul, and each valued the other's skills. Ki'lel served Basul by finding New Ones to study the Prophet's Way. Scouts were typically telepaths, able measure the strength and predisposition of another magician. Ki'lel was one of the strongest telepaths in recent history. Normally, he would have been more involved in the governance of the Telepathic Arts. However, he had identi-fied so many New Ones that Ki'lel attracted the attention of his supervisors, and they appointed him Arch Journey Scout. It was an honor he deserved.

Originally, Scouts worked alone to find new magicians. More recently the Council paired Scouts with a potential Mentor to confirm the initial assignment of the New One. If a child might be either an Air Rider or Water Sculptor, two Mentors had to recommend them, as the basic skill for these two Arts was similar. For example, if a child had changed the temperature of a room, the question was whether she did so by moving air or freezing the water in the air.

In Rea's case, a Scout had made an initial determination that she was a potentially powerful Fire Walker. For this reason, Meiach got the assignment of going with Ki'lel to invite her to Basul. Meiach could also tolerate Ki'lel, which was itself something of an art.

Together Meiach and Ki'lel entered the Council chamber. Meiach loved this room's beauty. A commanding etching of the Mian suns similar to the carving on the main gate of Basul decorated the ceiling. Here, however, the rays of light featured inlayed materials representing each of the Arts: brown clay for the Stone Movers, pale gold for the Wind Riders, blood red topaz for the Fire Walkers, blue diamonds for the Water Sculptors, emeralds for the Gaeists, and ground plat—a metal whose gray surface sheen reflected a rainbow of colors—for the Telepaths.

Meiach thought plat was appropriate for the School of Telepathy, as this Art did not control elements but, rather, the building blocks of all that exists. Meiach wondered why the Gaeists had named themselves after a Terran god instead of connecting themselves with Mia's animal and plant life. Perhaps Gaeists wished to avoid implying that they were favored by Mother Mia.

Meiach noticed that all of the other Mentors were in attendance. In addition, the Archmage and the six Acetos, heads of each branch of the Arts, had taken their seats. They were finishing with the preliminary information when Meiach and Ki'lel entered.

The Archmage Ba'al addressed the assembly. "Once again, Basul opens its gate to New Ones. As always, we must ensure each student finds their proper Direction," Ba'al had accomplished much in a short period. She had ascended to Acetos of the Stone Movers, and then five years ago, the Council appointed her Archmage. During her leadership only five students needed to go through the Direction evaluation twice, and all but one were successfully redirected. The last one now worked within Basul.

Ba'al had not seemed a likely candidate for Archmage. She expressed her emotions more than was appropriate for a magician, let alone the Archmage. The Prophet taught that emotion tainted a mage's skills, so Basul counseled its magicians to avoid letting their feelings cloud their judgment or their Art. The ungifted did not understand the necessary social distance required of mages, often considering them cold and distant because they refused to intervene in conflicts. But magicians understood that questions of right and wrong were often a matter of perspective, and usually the perspective of the most powerful won. The magicians' neutrality tried to prevent this kind of injustice.

Ba'al resisted emotional restriction and had ascended the ranks of Basul while retaining her open compassion. She felt empathy for those less fortunate and, in private, she would often vent her frustration at the Emperor and his amorality. The way that the Emperor indulged his impulses and neglected his responsibilities added to Ba'al's ire. She was circumspect in public, but a fire smoldered beneath her stoic composure.

Her willingness to assert Basul's rightful role in governance and in restraining the Emperor was the reason for her rapid ascendency to Archmage. The Acetos knew that someone needed to stand against the Emperor and only Ba'al had the temperament to do so.

Ba'al smiled at Meiach. There was a bond of mutual respect between the two. After the opening remarks Ba'al turned to the issue at hand—the New Ones.

"In the next two weeks," Ba'al continued, "please devote your attention to the Direction. We all know the problems that result when we fail the Prophet. Any questions?"

"Archmage, I do have a question." Ki'lel stepped up to address Ba'al. "I seek guidance from the Council. One of the New Ones comes from a family in Stara, the Acira family. As we all know, usually Mages are the only child. This family has two children, the younger is a boy named Tuac. I request your permission to watch this one. I also suggest that we pay partic-ular attention to his sister, Rea." Ki'lel said.

The room fell silent. Meiach was so focused on Rea that he had not considered that she had a sibling. It had been over one hundred turns since two mages had come from the same parents. The bond between siblings was powerful and, espe-cially if they were close in age, could impair a magicians' duty to remove themselves from society. Ki'lel was right to bring this to the attention of Ba'al. However, dedicating resources to a prolonged observation of a single candidate would tax the Scouts.

After due consideration the Archmage said, "Ki'lel, you have once again proven why you are Arch Journey Scout." Ba'al looked at the rest of the Council. "Unless anyone objects, I would suggest that Ki'lel personally observe this Tuac."

Meiach smiled at Ba'al's shrewd decision. Normally, the Arch Journey Scout was given some time off after each Journey to review the other Scouts' reports and progress. By appointing Ki'lel, Ba'al had bridged the gap between two mutually exclusive concerns: observation of the boy and conserving the Scouts' resources. Meiach sensed fuming at the loss of his deserved break. Meiach decided he could not let his friend Ki'lel suffer the burden alone.

"Archmage," he said, "I am the mentor for Tuac's sister. I should have raised this issue earlier since I was also there when Rea received her invitation. I can sense that Rea is very bright and, if history is any guide, Tuac could truly be a formidable mage. Given my lapse of judgment, I feel honor-bound to share this task with Ki'lel. Even if Tuac is not a Fire Walker, I may provide some insight given my relationship with Rea."

Ba'al considered Meiach's suggestion. Scouts traditionally identified candidates. Involving a Mentor would be unconventional. But Meiach was one of Ba'al's most valued advisors. She trusted his instincts and she nodded in agreement. With that, the meeting ended.

Over the next weeks, several mages conducted extensive interviews with Rea. The pace frustrated her, especially since the process felt scripted. Each session started with the mage introducing him or herself. Then the mage asked Rea to close her eyes, imagine a peaceful place, and describe her surroundings. Rea's image was consistent: she was in a small cabin, next to a lake. There was only one room, with a fire in the hearth, a bed, a desk, and scattered personal possessions—her Annals of Basul, her favorite blanket and the ink well and pen that her father had given her when she had left for Basul. Depending on her mood and that of the interviewer, there might be small changes in the scenery. Sometimes the fire was only embers and other times it was raging. But her possessions and the fire were always present.

At the end of her fourth week, the interviews were finished, and she learned that each of the mages testing her were either Fire Walkers or Telepaths. Meiach had told her that she was a Fire Walker, and these interviewers were testing her strength. At the end of this period, the Mentors formally directed her to the Arts of Fire.

In her class of twenty-two, there were four students each in the Arts of Fire, Water, and Telepathy. Five students entered Air, one Earth, and three joined the Gaeists. The remaining student was Su. She did not have sufficient skill to continue in the Arts, but Basul offered her the opportunity to learn to be a healer. Though healers were not magicians, Basul maintained a comprehensive infirmary and medical staff as a logical extension of its educational role. Much to Rea's surprise, Su was not disappointed as she received lifetime room and board, an education in reading and writing, and instruction in basic alchemy. It had been two turns since a healer joined Basul's staff, so it was a perfect solution for all.

Rea moved into her new room in the dormitory for students of the Art of Fire. She had a new wardrobe with grey robes that looked similar to those worn by other mages, though without the crimson band that denoted her Art. A neutral robe indicated that she had been identified but had just begun her training. There were about one hundred other mages in the dormitory.

Rea's early lessons taught her that magic was the ability of one's mind to control the energy that flowed through Mia. Every person and animal had nascent magical ability. The strength of one's innate connection to Mia's lifeblood determined one's magical proficiency. With training, those gifted with magic could develop competency and power just like an archer's skill grows with instruction and practice. Basul ensured that a magician reached their full potential and also avoided the consequences of raw potential going untrained. Mia's history was littered with stories of unfortunates gifted with magical proficiency who failed to get the proper education. For these people, magic would accumulate until it found its own path out, causing severe mental damage. The lucky ones died quickly. Those less fortunate suffered insanity and paralysis.

A magical education included both fundamental principles and exploration. Professors did not impart tricks of the trade, but rather techniques for controlling the Arts. There were books with spells, describing principles of the process and explaining different aspects of control. Spells were not simple recipes, rather, they offered guidelines one adapted to one's gift. True magic emerged from the magician's personality and how their desire shaped what they created with their Art.

The mundane introductory steps bored Rea and she could not wait until she was permitted to explore her limits. For the most part, she studied the calming and breathing techniques that focused her Flame. Her initial mental exercises used the qualities of fire, but she could see how the same lessons could be transposed to fit the other Arts. She wondered if she could do the impossible and master another area of magic.

Rea's first training specific to being a Fire Walker started a few months after she entered Basul. On her first day in the class, she sensed that this session would be different. The New Ones settled down and Hala, the professor, started his lecture.

"Today, New Ones, I will teach you to become one with your Flame."

Rea felt her stomach tighten at the implications. She had waited so long to for this moment. Rea noticed her fellow classmates were equally excited by the prospect of applying their magic.

"Your Flame has its own spirit, its own soul," Hala said. "No two Flames are the same. For you to be one with your Flame, you must allow your soul and that of your Flame to mesh, to mingle. Once you have accomplished this, the next steps allow you to grow with your Flame and become a Fire Walker. Close your eyes and start your mental focus exercises. Today, we will take them farther. Today, you meet your Flame."

The New Ones closed their notebooks and began the familiar meditation.

"Close your eyes. Calm your breath. Visualize the air coming into your body and then let it flow out. Feel your body, every muscle, your blood, your heartbeat."

At the beginning of her training, Rea had found relaxation difficult. Now meditation was second nature to her. Her heart slowed. Her breath was so controlled that she could not hear it. In earlier instructions, the New Ones stayed in this state for the entire class, but today Hala deepened the lesson, pushing his meditating students to visualize their inward journey.

"Picture yourself in a dark hall. Search for your Flame. Look for the end of the hall and find the door. Behind that door is your special place. No one else but you can enter. You know what is behind the door. You can feel the heat. But can you touch it? Can you open the door?" Hala stopped and there was silence.

Rea was lost within her vision. She walked down a long tunnel with a light shining at the far end. There was a door with a glimmer of light beneath it. Her Flame was behind that door.

This was fun! It was almost too easy, but she was so ready. She ran toward her objective. But she made no progress. The light was there, she knew her Flame was behind the door, but her steps carried her no closer. Frustrated, she broke into a sprint, but still made no progress. The door remained out of reach, her Flame beyond her.

It occurred to Rea that she was approaching the door the wrong way. This was no jaunt in the forest, it was her future. She needed to approach her Flame with reverence. Rea concentrated on her pulse. The door was still there, just out of arms' reach. She felt her heart as a drumbeat, soft at first, then pounding, the rhythm thunderous. She was unafraid, and no longer eager. Her Flame would come to her on its own terms.

Now Rea understood the point of those first lessons. She needed to be one with her lifeblood. And in that moment, she took a step toward the door. This time, each step brought her closer. It was still a struggle, but she made slow progress. Her Flame was testing her resolve and commitment. Her Flame demanded effort. If it was to bond with Rea, her Flame needed reassurance that she was a suitable mate. Rea did not rush her approach. She would reach the door when she and her Flame were ready.

She reached the door. Rea placed her hand on the latch and pressed it. It did not budge. Another test. Rea relaxed again, took a deep breath.

In a strong, unwavering voice, she said "I come to you so you can come to me." This satisfied her Flame and the latch clicked. Rea opened the door and stepped through.

Where was this strange place? She blinked in the blaze of light and shielded her eyes until they adjusted to the glare. Squinting, she saw a round room with a single door in front of her. The door she had come through had vanished. Rea tried to identify the source of the light but could not. This was a gateway and she needed to pass through to find her Flame.

Rea tried the door, but it was locked.

She said, "I come to you so you can come to me," as she had at the first door. The latch remained locked. She tried again, to no avail. How could this be happening?

"After all this time, does this mean I'm not a Mage?" She felt something that was foreign to her: self-doubt. "Maybe I am just a failure!" Tears welled up in her eyes. She had not cried in years, believing it childish. Tuac was the emotional one. But the thought of failure was too great. All she wanted was to be a Mage.

In an uncharacteristic fit of rage, Rea slammed her hands on the door.

"I will not be defeated! Let me in, it is my birthright!" she shouted. The door did not respond. Exhausted, she sank to her knees and leaned against the door.

Through her despair, a voice spoke to her. It was Rea's Flame, asking to be heard.

"It is not your birthright, it is ours. I am yours and you are mine. But you have rejected me. You choose to be guided only by your intellect and reject your feelings. You consider empathy and compassion weaknesses that blind your decisions. You suppress your anger, believing rationality is all you need. You must embrace all that is you, all that is us, for I am not just the Flame, I am what completes you."

Rea now understood what it meant to become one with one's Art—a magician needed to look within herself and connect to her inner being. Self-awareness was not easy for most people, but for Rea this was especially difficult. She had convinced herself that every decision could be reduced to a simple choice of two alternatives, one right and one wrong. There were no shades of grey, no room for exception or compromise. Those things, borne out of misplaced emotions, interfered with rational outcomes. Tuac had followed his empathy and had been hurt so many times. Rea would never let that happen to her.

But now the walls and defenses Rea had built to protect herself were keeping her from the one thing that she had wanted most in life. She knew that if she was going to open the door she needed to open herself. Fear rose up in Rea. She steadied herself, prepared to face her worst demons.

She said, "It is our birthright."

Two doors opened: the one in front of her and the one inside of her. A cascade of emotions washed over her, the storm she had locked up for as long as she could remember. She did not cower, but embraced the wind, the rage, the chaos. The storm subsided and Rea's Flame shone before her, bright, shining, ready to join with her.

Rea opened her hands. "Come, let us be one." The Flame leapt onto Rea's palms. She felt the Flame warm her entire body. Her whole body surged with energy, with power. The room was gone. There was no further need for it. She and her Flame claimed each other.

Rea opened her eyes and discovered that many of her classmates had already left for the day. She sat drenched with sweat. From the suns' position, she knew that she must have been sitting here for several hours. Although she had missed her midday meal, she was not hungry. She had tapped a new source of energy and felt more alive than ever before. She tasted the salt of her tears.

Rea looked up and found Hala staring at her, his face glowing with pride. She wiped her eyes and returned the smile. Hala waved his hand, indicating that she was free to leave for the day. Rea picked up her school bag, then took a moment to study Hala. He was going to each New One, whispering in their ears and wiping perspiration from their brows.

When she returned to her quarters, she was surprised to find a new robe with a narrow crimson band on its lapel, a sign of acceptance and growth.

At the next lesson, a few of Rea's classmates wore new robes, but most did not.

Hala began, "Many of you have struggled and a few of you have joined with your Flame. The rest of you have farther to go and I will lead you there. This is not a race but a journey, and each of you must find your own road. And you will." Hala walked along the rows of New Ones, smiling at each of them. "The paradox of magic is that, while each of you must find your own path and will face different obstacles, the process of capturing one's Flame is similar for each New One. Each Mage must face their shortcomings and decide whether they are willing to accept the consequences of embracing their Art.

"Your Flame cannot be forced or bullied, but only welcomed. Those who accept their weaknesses and their frailty have let their Flame know that it will be nurtured and supported. By accepting weakness, one grows stronger.

"Our Terran ancestors had a word—'humanity.' To accept one's humanity, to embrace it, was to recognize that each of us is imperfect. This is what the Flame demands. We must embrace our own imperfection so that we can understand the areas in which we need to grow." Hala paused and his face turned grim.

"There is another aspect of this humanity. Remember that, as each of you has weaknesses, so do all other Mians. Worse, some people you will encounter blame others for their inadequacies, and act out of fear and insecurity.

"From time to time, magicians leave the confines of Basul to provide counsel to those in civil power. We also send magicians to various parts of Mia to catalog natural disasters, migratory patterns and other things that may foreshadow a coming threat to Mia. While we try to limit our involvement with the local populace, sometimes it is necessary. Some of the ungifted will fear you, as much for your inner strength as for your proficiency in your Art. We will train you to diffuse their fear. Many will ask you to use your gifts to settle their petty grievances. Power must not be used indiscriminately. This will test your patience and your dedication to the Arts.

"You are not the Prophet, you are not divine, you are only a person with a gift. Nabes did not understand this lesson, and his arrogance almost destroyed Mia."

Rea raised her hand. He nodded to her and she asked, "Why doesn't Basul take control of Mian society so magicians can use the Arts to benefit more people?"

Hala responded, "The Arts are a gift, New Ones. Although you may have only the best intentions, it is too easy to believe that magic solves all problems. Magicians are neither all-powerful nor omniscient. We cannot see all the consequences of our actions, so we must be deliberate when we use magic to avoid inadvertently hurting someone. If a Mage allows him or herself to be a tool, then there are few limits to the destruction they could cause.

"We will teach you about the beauty, the grace, and most of all, the destructive power of your Flame. You will learn how to use your Art to help as well as what lines must never be crossed. This is the tragic lesson of Nabes."

Rea contemplated Hala's statement. Much of her time at Basul she had focused on her power. Now, Hala asked Rea and her classmates to accept the responsibility of using magic wisely. She recalled those rare instances when she had seen Mages in her town. Whispers announcing their presence spread like a plague. People shuttered their shops and hid their children. Even though the mages kept to themselves, all knew they possessed powers that could kill. Fear of the mages permeated Stara.

Rea wondered how she would react when it was her wandering through a village. How difficult it would be when faced with such fear to hide her emotions, stay centered, and remain in control of her Art? Basul's mages chose isolation. Rea wondered if their choice risked avoiding conflict at the cost of indifference to the people of Mia. Hala's voice interrupted Rea's introspection.

"Those of you who have joined with your Flame, I have taught you all I can. You leave this class and take the next step of your journey, learning to control your Art. For those of you who still have work to do, I will stay and guide you. Fear not, I have never failed."

Rea wondered about the New Ones who had been unable to find their Flames. A part of her felt contempt that they had not accepted their burden. She had braved the journey, looked deep within and accepted herself. The others should do the same.

Another part of her demanded her empathy. Each person had their own struggle and she could not know theirs. As the contempt faded, she identified what had spawned it.

She was afraid. The expressions on the faces of the students remaining in this class nudged Rea to relive the fear of accepting her whole soul. Maybe this is what Hala meant by humanity, that seeing others' weakness forced Rea to recognize her own.

Hala waved his hand to indicate a table behind him, upon which there were beautiful pendants.

"I have a gift for those of you who have joined with your Flame. It's a gentle reminder to be kind to yourself and others. The amulet is a blood stone encased in pure silver. The back serves as a mirror. Remember, the Flame is part of you and encased by your weaknesses, just as the stone is encased in the weakest of metals. The mirror is a window so you can find yourself if you are ever lost."

With that, Hala led those students who had not yet joined with their Flame out of the room.

Those New Ones that stayed with Hala for more training would also learn to capture their Flame, even if the process took more time.

It was time for Rea to move on. Having accepted her Flame, she now needed to learn how to use it.

***

Rea's next assignment was the simple task of holding fire in her hand. She had to meditate, focus, and join with her Flame. She closed her eyes, visualized her Flame and willed it to spring forth. Over the course of three weeks Rea mastered this task. Rea turned to more demanding tasks, such as lighting kindling and enlarging a fire from embers to a raging blaze, then calming it again.

She was an adept student, mastering each new technique in hours or days, driven by her desire to control her Flame. She yearned for the ability to throw fire from her hand, to build towering walls of flame and to walk through infernos, all the hallmarks of great Fire Walkers. Rea believed she was becoming a powerful Mage. Her instructors, delighted with the speed of her progress, did not disabuse her of that notion.

An incident six months after her arrival at Basul taught her that she had much more to learn.

It happened on a day when all of the students were granted a holiday to celebrate the birthday of a revered Archmage. Rea decided to spend the day with Tia, who was training as a Water Sculptor. They left Basul early, walking toward Shi'Bo Coula. It was a glorious morning to be out, the wind stroked the grasses into ripples like water, and carried the scent of blooming orchards.

Rea heard a hursa scream. It was galloping flat out, heading directly for them. Then she saw its pursuer, a huge spotted animal with a serrated nose horn, fangs, and taloned feet. The hursa was faster, but was drenched in sweat and flagging, so the predator was gaining on it.

"It's a kiam!" she shouted at Tia. Rea looked for any kind of shelter, but they were in the long bowl of the valley, with nowhere to hide. She had never seen a kiam, but she had read about them in one of her father's books. The illustration had not done justice to the size, speed, or ferocity of the real animal.

The hursa stumbled, recovered, and ran on, but it had lost precious ground. As the kiam gathered itself to spring, Rea acted on instinct. She thrust out her hand and a small ball of fire leapt from her fingers. As it hurled toward the kiam, the roiling sphere expanded until it was large enough to engulf the predator. The kiam scrambled to a stop, flinging up clots of dirt and grass. Rea's fireball splashed to the ground in front of the animal, splattering flame across a wide area and igniting a grass fire.

The kiam roared, spun toward Rea and Tia, its orange eyes glowing with rage that made Rea's heart clench. Tia grabbed her arm and they stepped together, trembling. Rea had never seen anything like this animal's fury. And it was directed at them.

Rea guided the grass fire to encircle the kiam. The kiam paused and studied Rea for a long time. It shook itself, roared again, then turned and bounded through the flame away from them.

With the kiam gone, Rea sent her will out to suppress the fire, which was spreading, encouraged by the wind. She could not calm herself and focus. The flames rejected her efforts, feasting on the easy fuel. Rea panicked and ran to try to put out the fire. She swirled off her cloak to smother the flames, when a gush of water erupted from the ground. The wall of flames vanished, leaving wet ashes. Rea turned and saw Tia's grin. From that day on, they shared a special bond.

"You saw that didn't you?" asked Ki'lel.

"Of course I did, but it was two New One's testing themselves. We did that, too," Meaich said.

"I'm talking about the kiam. Why was it so close to Basul and hunting a hursa? The most dangerous predators in the realm avoid magic, and this area is saturated with it. Why was it here? We should report this to Ba'al. With the celebration, Basul's sentries might not have noticed disturbance. It was mere luck that we were outside the grounds and stumbled on Rea and Tia."

The two strode away and found Ba'al observing the festivities.

"Why am I not surprised that you two would be the first to come to me?" she said, a fierce edge to her voice. "If only my other advisors were as competent."

Ki'lel had never seen Ba'al's lack of decorum. Meiach had seen Ba'al chastise her advisors many times. He understood Ba'al's frustration. Basul's meritocracy usually made for good governance, but a recent spate of deaths and retirements had reduced the advisor candidates to mages without sufficient experience.

"Perhaps your advisors did not want to distress the others during the celebration," Meaich said. "We need to determine why a kiam ventured so close to Basul. Has anyone else reported incursions by dangerous predators?"

"Yes, we need to see if there is any historical precedent," Ba'al said. "But who should look into the matter? Meaich, since you suggested it, why don't you go down to the central library and see what you can find out."

"But Ba'al—"

"Enough. You're the perfect person to do this since you have no responsibilities now. Your student has been directed and you're not teaching the New Ones. Checking on the boy should not keep you from other work. You have wallowed too long in your moral conflict as a Mentor. While I have respected your decision, your handwringing interferes with your work. If the appearance of this kiam doesn't serve as a harbinger of a more serious event, I don't know what does. I need someone I can trust to be thorough and discreet. You are the perfect person for this task. Any questions?"

This stunned Meiach. In the same moment Ba'al had chastened him for his moral qualms and complimented his intellectual prowess. He heard Ki'lel chuckle.

"No, Archmage. I will start immediately." He turned, quirked an eyebrow at Ki'lel, and the two of them departed.

Six

Life is a maze of choices. Some choices look simple at the time, and may not appear to have a significant effect. If we continue to make poor choices over time, however, we will be lost. The key is to follow one's heart and to surround oneself with true friends. Inner strength will provide manna when we stray and true friends will lead us back to the golden path. Ultimately, each of us will make some poor choices. Those who learn from them, and do not repeat them, those who learn to trust and go forward on the right path, are the ones who succeed.

The Teachings of Prophet, Questions and Observations

Meiach spent the next two weeks in the central library, which included the inner library, with alcoves maintained by each of the Arts, and a seventh Alcove, which housed medical texts that had been maintained by the Healers. The inner library had early books on the Prophet, historical treatises, copies of course books that had been superseded by more modern texts, local literature, books on Mian religion, the complete papers of the Prophet, and some philosophical texts discussing the Prophet's teachings.

Any mage had broad access to the inner library and could request Art-specific materials. However, one section, the inner sanctum, was off limits to all but the Archmage or anyone acting under their direct authority. Given the urgency of the situation, she had granted Meiach permission to explore those restricted materials.

He started with the early records of magic. He studied the history of the Terran settlers, the growth of magic and interaction of magicians with local fauna. Meiach combed through titles that seemed relevant, but found little. He did find instances when local fauna had changed migratory patterns, but in each instance there was some cataclysmic event: a seismic event, flood, or fire. There were also stories about fauna avoiding magicians, even from the early days, before the Great Destruction. But no author reported a similar situation to the errant kiam.

Meiach decided he needed to go right to the source. He was going to have to *ask* the kiam why had it moved so close to Basul. To do that, Meiach needed the help of a Gaeist. Gaeists specialized in subtle interactions with flora and fauna—coaxing animals to herd, extracting fruit or other needed benefits from plants, determining the source of illnesses affecting both flora and fauna and suggesting a course for healing. Having a dialogue with a particular animal would challenge most Gaeists, but Meiach knew the current Acetos of the Gaeists, Chorra, could help.

Chorra jumped at the task when he asked her. It was an opportunity to use her magic instead of focusing on her tedious administrative duties.

Chorra had never spoken to any animal. Rather, her interactions involved shared imagery. As Chorra explained to Meiach, she could exchange basic emotions with animals. More adept Gaeists could sometimes also "feel" physical sensations to piece together events. But actually talking to a kiam—having a conversation about why the animal had done a particular thing —was a different matter.

They both ended up back in the central library looking for guidance, this time in the alcove maintained by the Gaeists. Most of the literature in the alcove addressed physiology and social patterns of animal life. They found little written about telepathic communication with animals. After several hours, Chorra found an old course book that had one chapter on inter-species communication.

"For as long as I can remember," Chorra said, "Gaeists have not taught students to seek dialog with a specific animal. These techniques must have been abandoned by the early Gaeists."

The chapter they found described how talking to the kiam required the mage to abandon the bias of thinking like a human. The approach surprised Meiach, but Chorra explained that Gaeists learned at an early age to abandon the belief of the primacy of humans in the biological order. The Gaeists' creed held that humans are one of many equally complex life forms on the planet, each with their own unique ways of expressing themselves. Young Gaeists first had to embrace a multitude of energies given off by fauna and flora, and then translate those impulses into feelings that could be understood by a Mian. This process was one of the greatest challenges for a new Gaeist.

As empaths, all Gaeists were able to do this on an emotional level. Chorra's text suggested that Gaeists had an intellectual bias that blocked inter-species communication. To accomplish what Meaich needed, Chorra had to not only embrace the kaim's emotional state but also reject the Mian construct of intellect and reason.

Chorra jumped into the task and started her mental centering exercises. She settled in her center, a plateau overlooking a valley. The two Mian suns shone down and she could feel their heat warming her body. Chorra saw the path that would lead her to the bottom of valley. With each step her senses became more acute. She sensed the flowers on the trail enjoying the same radiant light that she felt on her face, the trees stretching their limbs, all of the animals enjoying a moment of peace and balance. Joy surrounded her. When she reached the valley, its teeming life overwhelmed her senses.

This internal vision is where Chorra had found her Art. But she had never pressed on to cross the second border. She continued her walk. The valley melted away. She saw lights of different colors moving around her, some slow, some flitting about, and others speeding past her. These were the souls of the fauna. Souls! The fauna differed from humans only in form. They not only felt, but also reasoned and communicated.

She heard the various animals talking. Not words, but complex sequences of sensation and understanding, information about food, water, safety and something else. Danger. Chorra had found and stripped away the barrier. She was ready to talk to the kiam.

Meiach and Chorra left Basul, armed with Chorra's newfound skill. But now they had to find the kiam. The emanation of magic that normally kept kiams away from Basul now drove most of the local fauna away from the two magicians. They needed to suppress their magic until it was time for the dialog.

The two came to a field bounded by a brook on one side and Ba'al's fruit orchards on the other. Picking a spot in the middle of the field, they sat down and began to meditate. Focusing on her Art, Chorra visualized all the flora. Much as she had done in her centering exercises, she felt the blades of grass beneath her. She sensed the all the varied forms of life in the pond. Meiach sat beside Chorra doing his own centering meditation.

Chorra reached out and touched Meiach's hand, startling him. Sharing magic was a dangerous road, and the bond could result in one mage's Art being lost within the other's. But Chorra was a master of her chosen skill and Meiach was one of the strongest Fire Walkers. Casting doubt aside, Meiach embraced Chorra's magic and found himself transported into her psyche.

Most of the local animal life sensed Chorra's muted magic emanations and, as her magic blended with Meiach's, they did not consider him an interloper. After several hours, Chorra opened a dialog with a ktu. Ktus could fly, yet they preferred to travel by riding on other animals. Primarily vegetarians, eating berries and grasses, a ktu would ride until its transport rested. Then it would leave that animal, feed, and find a new companion. Ktus were indigenous to all parts of Mia. They had no migratory pattern and thrived in all of the Realms.

"Little one, do you understand me?" asked Chorra.

"How does foolish one speak to Kaa?" responded the Ktu. Chorra was both stunned and insulted.

"I can hear you and speak to you, Kaa, because I am blessed with understanding the languages of life.

Why do you call me foolish one?" Chorra inquired.

"All of you uprights are foolish. You neither fly nor rely on others, except poor hursas, to move. You spend too much energy and should let others do work for you. You are burdened, with no wings, and yet you cause your youths to travel great distances. I do not understand how there are so many of you uprights given your limits."

Chorra had to bite her tongue to keep from laughing. The ktu was right about the limits of Mians. *"Kaa, did you see the kiam--the horned, spotted creature, the other day?"*

"Kiiaam, you call it? No, I did not see a spotted one, but I only recently left from my home. It was once warm and I found enough food to survive. But now there is only the—" the ktu struggled to describe what had caused it to leave, *"—the cold. I came here on the back of a three hump."*

Because he and Chorra were joined in this work, Meiach could follow the conversation between her and the Ktu. He wondered what this cold might be since the ktu had difficulty describing it. Meiach did not think the animal was talking about seasonal weather.

What the ktu called a three-hump Mians called a jigt, a creature native to the Southern Realm. Related to a hursa, the jigt had short fur and fatty humps that held water. Their physical characteristics allowed them to withstand the barren lands and harsh climate of southern Mia. Jigts were not known to travel outside of their territory, making this all the more odd. Kiams were their natural predators and it was not hard to imagine that a kiam would follow a jigt and then pursue a hursa given the similarities between the two species. Was it this strange weather or something else that drove the jigts to leave the southern territories?

"Kaa. I appreciate your help. Is there anything I can do to return your kindness?"

The ktu shrugged his wings. *"You cannot carry me, so no. But thank you for your offer. It is somewhat surprising, as most carriers find my pressence annoying. I have never had a carrier offer to take me any place. May you find abundance as you travel."* With that, the ktu flew away.

Chorra released Meiach's hand and they came out of their

respective trances. They walked back to Basul. Ba'al was not going to like what they had learned. Meiach knew Ba'al would be forced to take action. There were worse things than a trip to the Southern Realms.

"This is alarming," Ba'al said. "We have kiam encroaching on Basul, which you say is not an isolated incident. Were you able to find any historical precedent for this?" The Archmage paced in front of her office window.

"Yes, we did." Meiach said. "Animal migrations have shifted in the past, usually prior to or in response to dangerous weather, floods, and so on. Prior to the Flood of 1232, animals from the Eastern Realm overwhelmed the Southern Realm. Sojur, who was Archmage at the time, said the Gaeists sensed the activity and issued an advance warning to evacuate the border towns."

"Do you think this is what we're dealing with here?" Ba'al asked.

"I'm not sure. The Southern Realm, unlike other realms, experiences seismic activity. However, we have not had a seismic event in over 400 Turns. None of our mages passing through there have reported temperature shifts, either."

"Since you know most about this, you should be the one to investigate. For safety's sake I want you to take at least one other Mage with you. And you and Ki'lel need to check in on— what was his name?"

"Tuac."

"Yes. You two can check on him on the way to the Southern Realm. Ki'lel's telepathy would be helpful in that part of Mia. Make sure you are properly outfitted. Select mounts from my personal herd and I'll alert the armory that you will also be dropping by."

Meiach considered whether he should request a third mage whose skills would be more useful in a dangerous situation. A Water Sculptor or an Air Rider could come in handy. However, he and Ki'lel had extricated themselves from difficulties in the past, and Ki'lel would be insulted if Meiach did not believe their paired skills would be enough. He looked forward to leaving Basul for the wide-open spaces of Mia but knew Ki'lel would not be pleased to be leaving Basul again so soon.

Ki'lel grumbled about these new orders. This was unfair. As part of his normal duties, he was away from Basul for the months leading up to the Journey. Since he'd become a scout, he had only spent one Journey within the warm confines of Basul, when he was laid up after a riding accident. Ki'lel thought it ironic that scouts missed the extensive Journey celebrations at Basul, the most lavish celebration of this cornerstone of their society. Instead, they spent the holiday in small towns and remotes villages. Indeed, even Journey festivals in the large municipalities could not compare to the feasting and splendor at Basul.

He barked at Meiach when he learned they would be going out on this expanded mission. But he knew he had no choice. He was the most travelled and experienced of the scouts and telepathy had its uses when the dangers they encountered involved Mians.

The two decided to make this a working vacation. Ki'lel looked forward to gaining access to the more arcane tools and devices tucked away in the Archmage's vaults. Ba'al's broad permission let them select as many items as they could carry. He would ensure that he and Meiach armed themselves well.

The two Mages' first stop was Basul's stables. There was a communal herd available to all mages, although each Art maintained its own tack built to accommodate the needs of those mages. The Air Riders kept no hursas as those mages rode the wind. Stone Movers had to stay in contact with the ground so they did not ride, either. Gaeists could call upon any hursa at any time, and their concern for the elegant animals' wellbeing meant they used wild ones whenever possible, releasing them after their service.

The Archmage's office had its own herd of hursas, and to their delight, she had offered these to Meiach and Ki'lel. Having a dedicated stable avoided the ministerial concerns of securing provisions for her entourage if she needed to travel on short notice. As a Stone Mover, Ba'al did not travel by hursa.

Ki'lel and Meiach brought Chorra with them to ask the hursas whether they wanted to assist the two mages in their journey. As this might be a dangerous mission, Meiach wanted mounts both brave and willing. It also gave Chorra an opportunity to use her new skill. As with the ktu, the hursas were surprised when she spoke to them. Chorra explained that they did not know what they might encounter, but they expected risks and challenges. The hursas accepted this and conferred among themselves.

Two magnificent hursas stepped forward. The first was Shining, a radiant white stallion and the second was Glory, a royal blue stallion.

"Two leg," Shining said to Chorra, *"We are honored that you have asked for our help. Two legs do not usually ask, they just mount us and expect us to be obedient. Neither Glory nor myself have ever allowed a two leg to mount us. Because you asked instead of assuming,*

we will join your herd as equals and allow you to ride us if you will have us on those terms."

After Chorra translated, Meiach smiled and extended a hand to Shining. The hursa breathed over his palm and then his face. They now shared a bond like none Meiach had ever known. Glory then approached Ki'lel and he, too, felt a special relationship.

They requisitioned appropriate food and traveling clothes, and then headed to the armory. When they entered, they saw rows of various weapons, grouped by Art. At the far end of the Armory was a door that led to the Archmage's private collection. Normally, Ki'lel and Meiach would have been satisfied with standard weapons. But this expedition was not normal. The Keeper of Arms, the magician responsible for the Archmage's armory, met them at the threshold. The Keeper had received confirmation of Ba'al's permission.

He opened the Armory door, revealing a smaller collection of weaponry that belonged to the Archmage's office. These were ornate with unfamiliar runes on them. The Keeper explained that normal weapons amplified their wielders' particular Art. But these weapons carried their own powerful magic, and when connected to a mage they unleashed deadly force.

Meiach browsed the collection, touching each item with reverence. Finally, he stopped in front of a walking staff that was two meters high and fashioned from a metal he did not recognize. The Keeper explained that it launched massive bolts of lightning. Ki'lel selected a serrated wand of gray metal that the Keeper said spewed fire. Both had markings on them that described their effects.

Before leaving, Ki'lel moved toward a double door of yellow oak in the back of the Archmage's armory.

"You may not go there," the Keeper said.

"We have Ba'al's authority to be outfitted as we see fit," Ki'lel said.

Unpersuaded, the Keeper stepped in front of the two and put his hand on an ominous looking wand.

"That is true, but you may not enter. That room requires more than the Archmage's approval. Entrance requires a formal edict from the Council that confirms we are in a Time of Crisis. All Keepers enforce the requirements for entry. Not even the Keeper or the Archmage may enter."

This stunned both Meiach and Ki'lel. There had only been three prior Times of Crisis: the conflict with Nabes, the passing of the Prophet, and the schism between Basul and the healers. Meiach wanted to know more, but the Keeper dismissed them.

A week out from Basul they reached Stara to check on Tuac. Meiach was still amazed that there were two potential mages in the same family, particularly as Rea's gift was so strong. In recent years, fewer and fewer New Ones had journeyed to Basul, and the number of mages was declining. He hoped the Acira family was a sign the trend was reversing.

Meiach expected that the two siblings would match the historical pattern of rare magical siblings in the records. The younger sibling was the more powerful and that boded well for Tuac's potential given the strength of his sister's gift. Sadly, there were also rare instances where the oldest grasped the elements of control of their Art while the younger sibling could not. Those younger children suffered a life where magic simmered within them but they could not achieve true proficiency. Many of them ended their lives rather than live with this chronic frustration and despair.

Meiach always had been curious as to why magicians so rarely had magical siblings. He used his status as a mentor to research the issue. Prior to the Great Destruction, magicians were more common and there were many families that had multiple members skilled in magic. In the early days of Basul, the trend continued and families with multiple gifted children were the norm and not the exception. Over time, this pattern faded and no one knew why. Meiach had felt the Flame burning in Rea so he had recognized the strength of her potential. He hoped that Tuac would be at least as proficient. The mage had a sinking feeling that Basul would need all the resources it could muster to respond to the source of the disturbance in the Southern Realm.

SEVEN

One of Mia's most fascinating inhabitants is the ackina. It has no feet and must rely on the tides to move. When it becomes beached, it sends out a smell that attracts carrion birds. Seeing the defenseless Ackina, a bird will fly down to its meal, only to be stung by the ackina's poisonous tongue. The ackina then attaches itself to the carcass to feed until a new tide comes in. Life goes on.

There is a lesson here: never underestimate your opponent, for those with true power may seem like the most helpless.

The Teachings of Prophet, Questions and Observations

Rea's departure had been harder on Tuac than he'd expected. He had long anticipated that Basul would come for Rea, and while he thought he had prepared for their separation, he was crushed when it happened. He considered Rea to be his best friend, though he suspected she did not feel that way about him. As they grew older, they had grown apart. Tuac clung to the hope that, in time, she would value and love him as much as he did her.

His parents' grief at Rea's departure made Tuac's situation worse. They loved Tuac and he loved them. Tuac aspired to be as loyal and just as Cisrena. Loree's smothering sometimes annoyed him but her love for him kept him warm and comforted. Since Rea's departure, they had focused on their loss to the point where Tuac wondered if they had forgotten they had another child. At every meal, they discussed how the house was not the same without Rea, and their unhappiness added to Tuac's. He struggled with his own feelings, and their obsession with Rea's absence made him wonder if he mattered at all. Worse, he had not manifested any magical tendencies despite wanting to be like his sister in every way. His failure had frustrated him.

After months of feeling listless, worthless and alone, Tuac decided he had to accept this new normal. He started by working on his physical appearance, as his grooming and dress had suffered while he was grieving. This morning when he studied his reflection in the mirror, Tuac was startled to see the how much he had changed. He knew he had put on height because his clothes no longer fit well and he could look down on his mother's head. Soon he would be taller than his father. The mirror reflected his broader shoulders and prominent muscles in his upper arms. His face looked thinner, and his whisker-speckled cheeks hinted at a beard to come.

Tuac wondered if anyone would consider him handsome. He combed his disheveled blond hair and daydreamed of finding a special love. He knew he was shy and awkward. Tuac's most passionate moments happened only in his fantasies.

The aromas of breakfast yanked him back to reality. As he looked at himself in the mirror, he knew that his life had changed dramatically a few weeks back and now was not the time for daydreaming. His memories returned to that day. He was in his room completing his school assignments, fiddling with a weather crystal that he had borrowed from his parents' store. Remnants of the Terrans, Mians used weather crystals to monitor storms and determine when to travel, plant, and harvest. An imminent storm turned it ash black. In fair weather, it was crystal blue. During heat waves and drought, it was pale yellow. Forgetting that he was playing with such a rare and valuable object, he accidentally lost his grip on the crystal. His mind flashed to his father's wrath.

"Bless the Prophet!" he gasped, snatching at it as it fell. As if his prayers had been answered, the crystal slowed and drifted down, landing without a sound on the floor.

At the time, Tuac was too frightened to think about the implications of what had happened. He returned the crystal to his father's workshop. Later, when he had calmed down, he considered what had happened and why. Something had changed in him.

Loree called Tuac to come down and do his morning chores, snapping him out of his deep thoughts. "I will be down in a bit, mother. I still need to clean up my room and get ready for school" Tuac responded.

He had a few moments before his mother would ask again. He selected a clean tunic and trousers, brushed his teeth, and gathered his books for school.

He reached into his pocket and pulled out a piece of glass. He cradled it in his palm, studying how the light played on its surface. It was heavy for such a small item. He set it in the middle of his desk and concentrated on moving it. Minutes passed. Sweat formed on his brow. It was hard to stay so focused. But he remembered the moment when the falling crystal had slowed just above the floor. He knew he had stopped its fall. Nothing happened. Frustrated, his foot tapped a staccato rhythm on the floor. What had he done with the crystal? He got up and paced his room, running his hands through his hair.

He refused to fail and glared at the glass. It moved, rolling a finger width to the left.

"Yes!" Tuac leapt, punching the air with one fist.

"Is everything alright up there?" his mother called again from the base of the stairs. Tuac took a deep breath and released it, erasing the glee from his face.

"Yes, mother, I'm coming." He trotted down the stairs, grinning at his success. He was a magician, too.

From then on, he would practice after school. Each day it became easier to move the glass. Within a few weeks, he could move it across his desk. Tuac longed to tell someone. If only he could show his sister. One morning over breakfast Tuac learned that his parents were planning to visit Rea.

That would be perfect! he thought. Showing Rea his new skill would be better than just telling her about it. He practiced harder, wanting to make his sister proud.

That day after school Tuac walked into the countryside. He looked for a creek bed, thinking to practice on the smooth stones of all sizes. He settled by a small stream and started to build a small dam of sticks and rocks. It was harder than he had expected, since the objects were bigger than his keepsake. He kept at it. Sweat dripped off the end of his nose. Piece by piece, the dam took shape.

"That's quite a feat, young man," a kind voice said behind him.

Tuac jumped and spun to see two mages watching him. They were the ones who had come for Rea.

"How long have you been doing that?" the first mage asked.

Tuac swallowed hard. "About a month. Am I in trouble?" He had not considered someone might find him practicing, especially not magicians.

"Not yet, no," the second mage said.

The first mage said, "Your focus is impressive, Tuac."

Tuac studied them. "Thank you, sir."

The first mage said, "My name is Meiach. I mentor your sister. She's going to be a fine mage. My associate, Ki'lel, and I were passing through Stara when we noticed you out here. It seems you'll be joining us at the University sooner rather than later."

Chills went down Tuac's spine. *I really am a mage! My parents will be so proud.*

"I can tell you're excited. Being a mage, in my humble opinion, is the finest profession in all of Mia. But it comes with responsibilities and duties. And here are the first two rules: you must not tell anyone what you were doing and you must stop practicing magic for now." Meiach's firm tone brooked no argument. Although they had said he was not in trouble, Tuac suspected he had been walking a fine line.

"Why? For how long?" His voice cracked and he cringed. He did not want to whine at these mages.

"There are a few reasons," Meiach. "First, magic is dangerous. You think you're playing with sticks and stones, but every time you use magic it sends a signal. Animals can sense magic and often fear it, so you run the risk of stampeding the local livestock. Second, you must be careful because there are those who would seek to harm you or take advantage of you if they knew you had magical ability and were not under the care of the University. Third, your ability is unchanneled and you could hurt yourself."

Tuac appreciated Meiach's candor. These were good reasons, things he had not known or considered when he started. He could see the downside of spooking livestock. Animals might trample fences or escape into the wild, which was unfair to their owners. He doubted that his small experiments could hurt him or anyone else, but it did seem possible that unsavory gamblers or thieves might try to exploit him.

"I understand. I'll stop practicing." The Journey was only nine months away. He could wait. "How is Rea? Can I tell her what I can do the next time I see her? My parents are planning to visit her soon."

Meiach smiled. "Yes, you can tell her. Rea has been assigned to the Art of Fire and this is the perfect time for your family to visit her. Our rules require families to stay outside the University grounds. But under the circumstances, I can arrange for you and your family to stay in the dormitories. Would you like that? You will get to see where you would live, eat, and study if you accept our invitation."

Tuac wanted to leap and shout, he was so excited. It seemed that the invitation was a formality and soon he would be joining his sister as a magician.

Meiach continued, "Would you mind escorting us to your parents? We can go talk to them now. Just remember, not a word about your experiments."

"This way!" Tuac set out at a brisk trot toward town. The two mages mounted their hursas and jogged after him.

When they arrived at the house, he hollered for his parents to come out and greet their visitors. When Loree and Cisrena stepped out of the shop, Tuac realized that his parents did not share his excitement. His father's brows knit with concern and his mother's hands clutched her apron. Neither of them smiled.

"Is Rea well?" his father asked? "Is she ill or injured?"

Meiach bowed to the Aciras and smiled. "Your daughter is a gifted pupil. She's settled in well and is making excellent progress. We are actually here about another matter." He tilted his head toward Tuac.

"My son?" Cisrena asked. "Is he in trouble?"

"Not at all," Meiach chuckled. "We believe that he, like his sister, has the gift and we will be inviting him to attend the University at the next Journey."

Tuac's parents looked at him. His mother's smile was not as wide as he'd hoped it would be and her eyes were sad. Tuac knew his father was masking his feelings under his habitual stoicism, though Tuac could still sense his disappointment. Two children, and neither of them would take up the family business or live nearby. The Aciras would never have grandchildren.

"I see," Cisrena said. "We are honored by your consideration." His formal voice made Tuac wince.

Can't they see how happy I am?

"Tuac tells us that you will visit Rea soon. We would like to invite all three of you to stay on the campus. You will get a better sense of where your gifted children will spend the next years of their lives."

"That is very kind of you," Loree said. Tuac heard the tension in her voice.

"We are on a mission to the Southern Realm, but hope to pass through Stara on our return. We can travel with you to Shi'Bo Coula and arrange your lodgings when we arrive."

"Thank you," Cisrena said, bowing to the mages. "Tuac will apply himself to his schoolwork until your return." He gave his son a stern look.

"Yes, I will. I'm almost finished with this term's lessons," Tuac said.

"Would you join us for dinner?" Loree asked.

"We still have several hours of travel left today," Ki'lel said, looking at Meiach.

"Nonsense, you need to eat. We have goat curry and red fruits are in season. You can eat and then be on your way."

The two mages conferred without words and Ki'lel said, "We would be delighted to join you, however we do not eat meat."

"No problem, I can grill vegetables and I have a pot of bean soup on the stove."

"I have a cask of stout that should be ready," Cisrena smiled.

After they finished the meal and Loree was clearing the table, Tuac implored the Mages to describe the wonders of magic.

"I'm no bard," Meiach said, "But I remember a story I heard the day I left for the University. Like Rea and you, I come from a small town—Ygath, in the Western Realm. It's known for its fur trading, so I had expected to join a tanners' or trappers' guild in one of the neighboring villages. But while I was working at our smithy, the shop owner realized I had an affinity for managing the forge fire. I later learned this was evidence of my magical skill. That caught the attention of the University.

"When my Journey approached, a scout named Tada visited my aunt to invite me to attend the University. She was overjoyed that her nephew had received such a great honor. The next morning, I set off.

"The first night I was feeling a bit homesick. To distract me, Tada told me the story of the Prophet and the chita. During the Great Destruction, the Prophet had to send spies to gain information about Nabes. In this particular instance, the danger was so great that the Prophet decided to undertake the mission himself.

"After he had learned what he had hoped to, the Prophet was captured by a group of raiders who preyed on those traveling the local highways. He was taken back to the raiders' camp. He learned that most of them were farmers forced to live a life of crime to provide for their families. Nabes had destroyed their village and demanded they swear allegiance to him. The raiders wanted no part of the battle with the Prophet, they wanted to be left alone.

"Had they realized who he was, they could have ransomed the Prophet. Instead, they put him to work on their meager farm. It was backbreaking labor, but the raiders were kind to him. The leader even invited the Prophet to join their forces.

"The Prophet could have used his magic to escape. However, doing so would reveal his location to Nabes, who would send forces to attack the encampment. Even if the Prophet defeated Nabes' soldiers, many lives would have been lost. The Prophet decided he would wait until he could escape without endangering the raiders.

"One night, while the Prophet was having dinner, a chita strolled into camp. With their powerful jaws and razor-sharp tusks, chitas are dangerous predators. The camp exploded in panic. People scrambled to escape the great cat.

"The Prophet reached out to the chita to learn why it was in the camp. He determined the chita was a new mother looking for one of her lost cubs. She intended no harm, but she would defend her cub.

"The Prophet extended his magical senses and searched for the cub. He found the little one trapped in a nearby cave by vines and mud. The Prophet freed the cub who soon bounded into camp, crying for its mother. The chita greeted her child, and together they left the camp. As she left, she nodded at The Prophet.

"The raiders realized he was a magician. They were grateful that he had not used his abilities on them, and that he had prevented the chita from harming anyone. They unshackled him and offered any help they could. Since the Prophet's magic was so subtle, he had not alerted Nabes. The Prophet returned home, his mission complete."

Tuac listened intently. At the end of the story, however, Tuac felt disappointed.

"What's wrong, Tuac?" Meiach asked.

"I understand that the Prophet was reluctant to harm anyone, but what if something had happened? Then, his mission would have been a failure. Worse, he could have been killed and then Nabes would have won! It seems to me that he was willing to sacrifice everything merely because he didn't want a few innocents hurt." Tuac said.

Tuac's parents gasped. He had just challenged the Prophet.

The question did not bother Meaich. "I've wondered that myself. I'll tell you what Tada said when I asked.

"She said, 'That is the wisdom of the Prophet.' I went to bed that night, no longer feeling homesick but quite perplexed by her answer. Later I learned that each of us, as Mages, must control our power and use it with caution and balance. I believe that The Prophet would have used magic if there had been no alternative. Sometimes, blood must be spilled. At the same time, the Prophet was willing to wait for an alternative to appear. One did, so he was able to escape the mercenaries without harm to himself or anyone else. The Prophet's wisdom was not in refraining from using magic but in weighing the consequences before he did."

Tuac nodded, although he was not convinced. Magic was power and power should be used for justice. If people are hurt in the process, that is an unfortunate consequence. And choosing not to fight also has consequences, since innocents are hurt when injustice prevails.

As Tuac mulled over the moral dilemma, he realized how tired he was and he asked if he could be excused. He was asleep the moment his head hit the pillow.

Tuac recognized this place, though he had never been here. He stood in a forest in front of a stone house. Several animals, including a beautiful chita, saw him coming. They were afraid of something, although it was not Tuac.

"Your place is inside, not with us," said the chita, startling Tuac. He stared at the elegant animal wondering how he could understand it. He stepped past the elegant creature and entered the house.

He found an inner courtyard with a fountain in a garden. Tuac saw a room to his left. Walking through that open doorway, he noticed an adjacent room with a welcoming fireplace and a table laden with his favorite foods. He longed to go into that room, eat, and lounge by the fire, never to leave the peaceful surroundings. Yet that felt wrong. He knew that place was not his destiny.

"You are right to fear that room," a voice said. Tuac jumped. He could not see the speaker. "Who are you? What am I doing here?" He turned to leave and the outside door slammed shut. The room had no windows.

"It is not time for you to leave. You have not found your gift. To find it, you must reject what you are told is the path. That way offers only a false promise, not the unity you seek." Frantic, Tuac yanked at the door. "Let me out!" he yelled.

There was no answer. As he fought with the latch, the room changed around him. The entry to the room with the fireplace vanished. Tuac stood in a room with seven doors, each bearing a strange symbol. He strode to one of the new doors, but it would not open. None of them would open. He was trapped.

He awoke curled into a ball, his clothes drenched in sweat and his face wet.

What was that place? Who spoke to me? He wanted to discuss it with Meiach. The next morning, however, the Mages were gone before he came downstairs. He could only count the weeks until they returned.

EIGHT

People often bemoan their troubles, yet strength comes from conflict. Consider the great oass tree. Every turn it suffers a variety of hard-ships: drought, storms, and infestations. Yet, the tree survives, growing stronger. Indeed, older oass trees develop almost impenetrable scar tissue that we use to construct our homes, and the tree's sap kills insects so we use to protect crops.

People are no different. All of us face challenges, some more than others. A true survivor turns difficulties into strengths, hardship into success.

The Teachings of Prophet, Questions and Observations

Ki'lel and Meiach left before dawn the next morning. They rode away from Stara, somber and determined. Neither knew what they would find in the Southern Realm, and both sensed that this mission might be their last together.

Ki'lel thought about their encounter with the younger Acira.

"You realize that some will not be happy with what you told the boy," he said.

"Why?" Meaich answered. "Ba'al told us to observe Tuac. We found that he's quite formidable, and reined him in before he could do damage. We've added to our ranks, and that's a reason to rejoice."

Ki'lel did not want to start their journey with an argument. But he believed that Meaich had been too forthcoming with the Aciras. While the stories of the Prophet's journeys were well known, Meiach's personal slant of using magic as a force of justice was not widely held.

"We should not give the ungifted a window into Basul's view of the use of magic," Ki'lel said. "You know that many would have answered that question differently, but you suggested there was a time for magic as a weapon. Others would have said the Prophet was exhibiting the restraint that all magicians should use, never intervening in the affairs of the ungifted. If anyone found out what you said, you could face grave consequences."

Meiach responded with an urgency that Ki'lel had never seen in his friend.

"There is something special about that boy. Given the clouds upon the horizon, we will need all of our resources: New Ones, weapons, insights. We cannot be hidebound by the rules and regulations of Basul. I gave that boy something to hold onto until he enters the University. I hope he won't conduct any more experiments before we return to Stara. I suspect he will be more careful. If you feel compelled to notify Ba'al of my actions, I will understand."

Ki'lel nodded and dropped the subject. That night, Meiach apologized to his old friend.

"I am sorry, Ki'lel. I'm not ignoring your concern or your Council. I am not sure that I want to admit this, but there is something terrible going on. I'm not a Gaeist, but I can feel Glory's unease as we ride closer to the Southern Realms. Shining is restless, too. Chorra bonded us to these hursa and they are scared. The farther we go, the more agitated they become. I don't know what frightens them, but I believe we will meet pure evil on this road."

Ki'lel was stunned. "Pure evil?" he said, stirring their dinner. He studied the hursas through the firelight. They snatched bites of their evening grain, then lifted their heads, ears pricked, to look out into the night, each in a different direction. The mages had rubbed the hursas down after unsaddling, yet new sweat shone on their necks and flanks.

Ki'lel said, "I agree with you." His admission startled him. He usually discounted Meaich's theatrics, but Ki'lel shared his friend's apprehension. "I wanted a boring vacation, not an encounter with evil. Thanks."

Meiach smiled, and passed his companion a slab of bread with cheese. Whatever they found, they would tackle it together.

Two weeks passed and each day Meiach's anxiety grew. He slept little and monitored the horizon constantly. The hursas obeyed them, but both mages felt the animal's reluctance, their desire to bolt northward.

They started practicing every night with their weapons. Ki'lel's staff increased his power such that he could move large trees and boulders. Meiach's weapon also boosted his innate Art, allowing him to launch massive fire balls in rapid succession. Ki'lel marveled that these weapons amplified their abilities so much.

Early in the third week, Ki'lel noticed a distinct change in their surroundings. They saw fewer animals and heard no birds.

The plants looked desiccated. Since the Great Destruction, the Southern Realm had had no Mian population, so the wildlife and native flora had flourished. This change alarmed him.

Ki'lel noticed that Meiach was also on edge. Alert to his surroundings, Ki'lel sensed the underlying wrong about this place. It felt menacing and hungry. As Meiach had said, this felt like pure evil.

Ki'lel shuddered. He was in pain and tried to protect himself from the assault. He blinked tears from his eyes. When Ki'lel caught Meiach studying him, Ki'lel nodded to his companion in recognition of what they shared. They rode on side by side until Meaich dismounted and untacked Glory. The hursa trembled and sweated, though the day was not hot and they were walking. Meiach felt animal's distress through their bond and could no longer ask her to stay with them. He released her and she bolted north, heading for home. Shining stayed with them, though Ki'lel did not ride her. He covered the hursa with a membrane of magical protection to insulate her from whatever was attacking them.

At the end of the third week, they arrived at their destination. They had just come through a pass in the Southern Mountains and there, in the center of the plain below, lay the ruins of Shalla—the site of the Great Destruction. On this battlefield the Prophet had defeated Nabes and his forces. They had suspected that this place was the source of the emanations, but they were not prepared for what they saw.

The plain stretched as far as the eye could see, perfectly flat except for the remains of a castle jutting skyward beside a lake. Around the ruins the ground had a sheen that was not natural, reminding Ki'lel of a glazed ceramic platter. He could not see any living thing—no tufts of grass, no low scrub, nothing. No birds floated on the placid lake water and no animals drank at its shore. He heard no insects. The shadows cast among the ruins appeared darker than they should be, a blackness his eyes could not penetrate, even with the two suns bright in the clear sky.

"I've been waiting for you," a harsh voice rasped beside them.

The mages spun to face a black figure. The figure's profile shimmered, the black edges fraying and reforming in the sunlight. Ki'lel could not find a face, or even eyes. It was a silhouette of emptiness, a void in the world.

"I have come to take my rightful place as ruler of this world. You will be my first two disciples."

Meiach raised his battle staff and a wall of flames flashed between the mages and the figure. Ki'lel could see the dark figure beyond the sheet of fire. It had not stepped back. It had not even flinched from the scorching heat. Ki'lel reinforced Meaich's fire with his own telepathic power, giving the wall even more form.

The figure stepped forward, tilting its head to study them.

Ki'lel felt another mind probe his own. Its touch was icy and lifeless, sapping his concentration in a way no other mind had ever done. Ki'lel altered his spell so that the energy that was directed at him fed into Ki'lel's protective wall, temporarily strengthening it.

"You have been trained well. But you are not prepared for what I can do," the figure said. The ground beneath their attacker burned, the poison spread under the wall of flame toward the magicians.

When it reached them, despair overwhelmed Ki'lel and he struggled to hold on to his magic. Meiach staggered, his fire wavered and diminished, and he could not maintain his defenses against this onslaught. Darkness stained his flames.

The figure waved a hand, Meiach and Ki'lel both wavered again and the fiery wall dissipated.

The mages stood stunned. Meiach collapsed and Ki'lel rushed to help him.

"I felt something in my mind and it tainted my flame," Meiach gasped. "I don't know how it did that."

Ki'lel helped Meiach stand and braced him. "Somehow it accessed my abilities as well," Ki'lel whispered. "How could it attack both of our Arts? No mage since the Great Destruction has been able to do that."

In unison, the two whispered, "Nabes."

"Yes, I am here," the dark figure rasped.

Ki'lel lifted his wand and aimed his amplified telepathic power at Nabes. The bolt bounced off of the figure and shattered the rocks behind it.

Meiach stamped his staff on the ground, igniting the stones and encircling Nabes.

"I can't hold this for long," Meiach said. "Get back to Basul and tell Ba'al everything."

"What about you?" Ki'lel said.

"I will hold him here. Run!"

Ki'lel vaulted onto Shining's back and Meaich slapped the hursa's haunch. She bolted, Ki'lel clinging to her mane, tears streaming from his eyes in the wind of their flight. He heard Meiach scream.

Meiach had given his life to ensure Ki'lel's escape. The mage wept not only for his friend, but for his world, for all those who would lose their lives now that Nabes had returned.

Ki'lel let the hursa run herself out, and slid from her back to walk beside her. They rested by a small stream that night, the hursa cropping sparse vegetation and Ki'lel huddled in his blanket, not daring to light a fire. He pressed north, trusting the hursa to set a pace she could maintain. They travelled so fast that he reached Stara in two weeks.

He decided to retrieve Tuac before the next Journey. Meiach had believed that this boy was powerful and Basul would need every possible weapon in their collective arsenal to defeat Nabes. Even untrained, Tuac showed promise. Ki'lel could not let that potential go untapped in this time of crisis.

An anger burned deep within Ki'lel. Nabes would be stopped, and Ki'lel would have his revenge.

The Watcher sensed Nabes' power surge as it consumed the life of the fire mage. The magicians' arrival marked an unfortunate turning point. Nabes had fed on Mian fear, and would have the energy to seek more. The Watcher knew that Nabes was still limited in its abilities, but that would soon change.

The Watcher had tried to save the two magicians, but could not. The Watcher was able to keep Nabes from reaching Ki'lel, by nudging the fire mage to slap the hursa, sending the second mage to safety.

Nabes turned to the Watcher.

"You!" Nabes screamed. "You have been with me all along. When my essence was but a flicker, you were there. You were powerless. But I am growing stronger. I will consume this world and then I will come for you."

The Watcher did not know fear but was surprised that Nabes sensed the Watcher's presence.

"Yes, I have watched you. I cannot terminate you, but I can guide the one who will. Your fate is sealed. It is only a matter of time. This time will be different."

"No!" Nabes bellowed. "I have learned from my battle with

the one called Prophet. He was weak. Your new champion will also have his flaws. Yes, this time will be different. This time I will win."

Nabes spoke bold words, but the Watcher sensed doubt. Though it could not resist Nabes' evil directly, that doubt was still a weapon the Watcher could wield to slow Nabes' conquest.

Mia's only hope was that the Mages, the Church, and The Emperor would unite under the Reunifier's banner, in time to stop Nabes. They would have to accept the true teachings of the Prophet. Many would die now that Nabes had fed on the mage's lifeforce. The Watcher hoped that the Reunifer could act quickly enough.

NINE

I leave this world, part stranger, part native. My heritage was both the solution and the problem. I have fought to protect this land. And after, I fought to insure evil never again threatens Mia's existence. So many choices debated and made.

Basul will be at the center of all, preserving life. May the leaders never forget their task.

From the Deathbed of the Prophet

Tuac's mind swirled from all that had happened in the last few days. When Ki'lel returned to Stara, Meiach was not with him. Tuac ran up to greet the magician, but Ki'lel brushed by him. The mage's eyes were haunted and his face looked drawn, his shoulders hunched with fatigue.

Ki'lel entered the Acira's home without knocking. Tuac tried to follow, but the mage slammed the door. Tuac tried to open it, but it was locked.

Tuac paced in the street in front of his home, muttering to himself. His mind raced.

Did I do something wrong? Am I still going to the University? He had followed the mage's instructions to the letter, but perhaps there was something else.

The door opened and Cisrena stepped out, arresting Tuac's spiral.

"You are leaving for the University tomorrow morning," his father said. "Go and gather your things."

"You're coming with me to visit Rea, right?"

"No, we won't be joining you. We need to stay."

"Why am I going before my Journey?"

Cisrena paused, and put a hand on Tuac's shoulder, giving it a gentle squeeze. "Mage Ki'lel says you are a special case. They know you belong at the University and want to start your training immediately."

Tuac swallowed hard. He had not expected this.

Cisrena pulled Tuac into a hug. His father held him for a long time. When he released Tuac, he turned away, wiping his eyes.

Tuac ran up the stairs to pack. This reversal of his expectations did not change his fear. Now he felt cheated and apprehensive. He would miss the Journey but he would start his training in a few weeks. His father's worry shook him, though. Tuac knew there was more to this sudden departure, but he had no idea what it could be.

Ki'lel left for the night as the Aciras could not accommodate his hursa. Loree made a simple dinner for the family. She told Tuac that she had wanted to make his favorites but she did not have the ingredients on hand. She could make him the honeyed

grain cakes he liked, but not the stew or the fruit tart. Tuac picked at his food until he saw his mother watching him, tears in her eyes. Not wanting to hurt her feelings, he ate with more enthusiasm, but excused himself right after the meal and went up to his room.

Their goodbyes in the early morning felt awkward. Without the anticipation and celebration of the Journey, none of them were prepared to say what they wanted to say. Tuac hoped he could return to visit his parents when he was a wandering mage, but he did not know if that was possible. This was it. He was leaving home forever.

Ki'lel waited for Tuac with a second hursa. He explained with gestures more than words how Tuac should mount and hold the reins. They left Stara without a word. Twice Tuac asked Ki'lel questions, hoping to start a conversation, but the mage answered with a grunt or a shake of his head.

"What happened to Meiach?" Tuac asked the first night.

Ki'lel looked up at him with eyes so full of pain that Tuac gasped, sorry he had said anything. Tuac realized the mage was grieving and did not ask any more questions. They travelled in near silence, Ki'lel only speaking when it was time to rest the hursas or set up camp.

Every morning Tuac woke to find Ki'lel crouched by the fire, his bedroll still tied to his saddle. The mage ate little, but provided simple porridge and dried fruit or bread and cheese for Tuac. They rode through all the daylight hours, taking breaks only to rest the hursas. Ki'lel pushed hard.

Ten days away from Stara, they stopped early to camp.

"We reach the University tomorrow."

Tuac tried once more. "Ki'lel, what happened?"

The mage ignored the question, poking the small fire. When both suns had set, he said, "Meiach's gone. Taken by a foe I never thought I would see. I am sorry you are being dragged into this. But Meiach—" Ki'lel's voice cracked "—believed in you." The mage said nothing more.

Tuac did not understand. What was he being dragged into? This made no sense to him. He was just a boy.

The next morning, the two entered the main gate of the University. A young mage greeted them and looked at Ki'lel for a long minute.

"Please follow me, Tuac Acira. I will show you to your room."

Tuac fetched his small satchel from the saddlebag and Ki'lel took the reins of the two hursas and walked away without a word.

The young mage led Tuac through a maze of halls to a dormitory. Tuac tried to engage his guide, but she spoke to him in monosyllables. Tuac stopped, his anger rising.

"Are all mages as welcoming as you are?" He kept his tone even.

"I do not know why you have arrived at this time of year. I was told to treat you like a New One. Here is your room," and she opened a door, gesturing Tuac inside.

The room held a bed, a desk, and a bureau. Light came in through a single narrow window. A stack of folded blankets and a bathing towel waited on the thin mattress. Tuac set his satchel on the desk and turned to thank his guide, but she had already left him. Would he be surrounded by grumpy people for his entire training period? Tuac's anxiety about starting his new life worsened as he considered that he might be friendless and alone here.

The bureau held white trousers and linen shirts that were approximately his size. There was a wash basin and pitcher of warm water on the bureau's top. A plain white robe hung on a

peg behind the door. He found sandals beside the bed. The desk held three candles, flint and steel to light them, pens, and paper. Everything was neat and in good condition, but strictly utilitarian. There was little color in the room and nothing ornamental. He put his few possessions away and stretched out on the bed, his heart heavier than he had expected. He washed his face and hands and changed into his new clothes.

He missed his parents, and worried that Rea had become as cold as Ki'lel and his guide had been. Would she welcome him when he saw her?

He was dozing off on the bed when someone knocked on the door. Tuac started, then scrambled to open the door. An older man in brown trousers and tunic stood in the hall.

"Good evening, New One," he said. "I am here to take you to the Central Hall. And then I will take you to dinner."

"Do I need to bring anything?" Tuac asked.

"No, but please wear your robe."

Tuac slipped the garment on over his linen uniform.

Tuac's guide led him through the labyrinth of corridors, galleries, and small courtyards, always turning toward the center of the huge campus. They reached a wide foyer with two grand doors made of a silvery metal Tuac had never seen. Each door had three panels with symbols embossed on them. Above the doors a half-circle of the same metal featured the University's coat of arms: Mia's two concentric suns, with six rays of sunlight extending from the inner one to the outer one.

Tuac's guide opened one door and led him into the largest chamber he had ever seen. It was wide and deep, with a vaulted ceiling that echoed with sounds of faint, distant conversation. Seven bright mosaics on the ceiling told the story of Mia and the University. Tuac's jaw dropped. He had never seen such intricate and colorful images. The first showed the creation, the second showed the arrival of the *Curiosity*, the third depicted the birth of the Prophet, the fourth showed the darkness and evil of Nabes' rise, a fifth showed the Great Destruction, the final battle between the armies of good and evil, the sixth featured the troops celebrating the Prophet's victory, and the last depicted the building of the University.

His guide said, "This is the Central Hall of Basul, as the University is known among its magicians. When the Prophet founded Basul, the magicians wanted to pay homage to their lineage. I have seen many versions of these images in churches and governmental buildings across Mia, but none can match the beauty and splendor of these."

Tuac loved the rich colors of the tiles and how the images jumped off the ceiling. As he studied the crest with the concentric suns, he wondered why he had dreamed that there were seven when there were only six Arts. He was about to ask about this, when another person joined them. She wore beige trousers and a matching shirt.

"This is one of Basul's many servants," Tuac's guide whispered in his ear. "Most have the potential for magic but could not capture their Art. Basul honors its obligations and the staff are given lifetime employment, room, and board in exchange for helping the administration of Basul. This one will take you to your next meeting."

"Please follow me," the guide said, gesturing back toward the main doors. They walked briskly along corridors and through courtyards to another beautiful room. When Tuac entered, he found six magicians waiting for him. They wore robes similar to Ki'lel's, though each had a different colored collar: red, gray, blue, clay, yellow, and green. The woman with the green collar spoke.

"Welcome, Tuac, to your testing. My name is Chorra. This

hall is where we greet new students, which we call New Ones. When they arrive from the Journey, they attend classes and meetings that help us determining their particular magical calling. We decided not to wait for your Journey, but to welcome you to Basul immediately. You will meet with each of us for evaluation.

"We will ask you to try tasks that will reveal your inborn gift and then you will join the school for that Art."

Chorra introduced the other five mages then said, "I will be the first to test you. You will meet with the Water Sculptor after that, and tomorrow with the others. Please come with me and we can start." She led him across the room and the others left them.

The tests did not make any sense to Tuac. The exercises started with physical challenges like push-ups and how high he could jump. He did poorly on the balance tests, but well on the tests for solving problems. Tuac sensed a certain urgency in the process. He was determined to join Rea at Basul, so he did his best to meet every demand though the process baffled him.

After Ki'lel delivered the hursas to the Archmage's stable, he went looking for Ba'al. As he rushed toward her office, he barked at those who blocked the corridors with slower errands or group conversations. He arrived at her chambers, where three other mages waited to speak to her and he ignored them, going to the door and pounding on it. The others grumbled, but he glared at them and they subsided.

When she opened the door, he barged past her, taking her by the elbow and pushing the door closed behind him. Touching any mage without permission was forbidden and dangerous. Before Ba'al could reprimand him, Ki'lel said,

"Meiach is dead. Nabes killed him."

"Start from the beginning," Ba'al said.

"We found a trail of blighted land. No animals, even the plants had died. We followed it to the Dark Castle. Nabes has risen. We fought, but he was impervious to our weapons, even the ones we had from your armory. Meiach sacrificed himself so I could escape and bring you word."

"Nabes? Are you certain?" Ba'al's face paled as she studied him.

"He named himself. We have never met such awful power, so much rage and hunger."

Ba'al asked him more questions, searching for a different explanation for Meiach's death. Ki'lel stumbled through his answers, describing how all life disappeared from the land as they approached the Dark Castle, the sudden appearance of that dreaded figure and the battle that followed.

"Nabes intends to conquer the entire continent," Ki'lel said, "He has already started his advance." Then his voice broke. He collapsed into a chair, lowered his head and wept.

After giving him some time to grieve, Ba'al dismissed Ki'lel. She was incredulous and shocked.

How could this have happened? The Prophet killed Nabes. The Archmage went into her private quarters and unlocked her desk. She withdrew an ancient glass tablet. The artifact had been handed down from Archmage to Archmage, but had not been used in recent memory. She was not even sure it worked any more, but she spoke the incantations and performed the hand gestures she had learned from the previous Archmage. This object and its peculiar qualities were secrets of her office.

Though different we are One. We follow The Prophet, ever waiting. I reach out to you, to convene a Council of the Three.

She did not know what would happen. She did not know whether the Emperor or the Prophet's Charge, the head of the Church, could activate their tablets, or if they would want to speak to her.

The tablet lit from within and after a long moment, then Emperor Hahook's image appeared above the sleek surface and he scowled at her. In another moment, the elderly face of Charge Gershawn, governor of the Church, materialized. Ba'al had met both of these men at her ascension ceremony. She and the Emperor were the same age, but the Charge was elderly and frail. She was saddened to see how feeble he had become in recent turns.

"Why have you called, Ba'al?" the Emperor said, his voice gruff. "You could have sent a messenger." Ba'al heard the whimpers in the background and took that as confirmation of the rumors about the Emperor's debauchery.

"Nabes has returned," Ba'al said. "He is already active in the Southern Realm."

The Charge gasped.

She related what she had heard from Ki'lel. She kept her tone level and calm. Then she waited.

They were silent.

Then the Emperor shouted, "Rumors and hearsay, Ba'al. You know as well as I do that stories of Nabes are a myth to maintain order! Your advisor is either suffering from mental distress or has some sort of agenda. Perhaps he and this Meiach fellow were lovers and had a falling out and now Ki'lel seeks to hide the fact that he harmed his paramour." The sounds in the background had ceased, responding to the ire in the Emperor's voice.

The Charge dabbed at his brow with a folded handkerchief. "We feared this time would come, Emperor. Both of you need to marshal your forces. Our survival depends on our unity. May Aced the Divine aid and guide us, and protect us all."

Emperor's eyes narrowed and he snorted. "I will summon my generals. But until we have more evidence than a mage's tale, do not mention Nabes." His face disappeared.

Ba'al and Charge Gershawn considered one another.

"Ba'al, I pray you are wrong. If this is true, the end of this age is upon us. I do not know if we will survive this time." Then he, too, vanished and the tablet went dark.

When the Prophet had created the triumvirate of governance, the Empire was charged with keeping civil order. The emperors used that role to amass power, wiping out the little fiefdoms that engaged in petty border disputes. All were brought under the banner of the Empire.

Hahook's father had defeated the last of the holdouts but it was Hahook who envisioned a world where the Emperor reigned supreme, unencumbered by the University or the Church. Hahook had realized that, to defeat Basul, the Empire would need to develop its own weapons that could counter the magicians. Hahook emptied the royal treasury funding research and exploring the ruins of Terran settlements. One of these parties discovered strange metal objects in a ruin buried since the Great Destruction. A member of the group lifted one of the treasures and looked inside the hollow tube. A blast erupted from the tube and his head vanished.

The Emperor's emissaries scoured the site and uncovered several similar objects, some contained in a crate marked with unknown words: *plasma rifles*. They presented the weapons to Hahook, who commanded his soldiers to search Mia for other Terran weapons. Over time, the Emperor assembled an arsenal containing a few hundred rifles. As the soldiers trained with the weapons, they learned that their magic was limited, so they were kept under lock and key.

TEN

Finding one's Art is a journey of love. Arrival is a unification of one's soul and one's power. Beware the temptations on the path, as they can only interfere, and one will not achieve one's true strength.

The Teachings of the Prophet, 1:2

Tuac returned to his room after another grueling day of interviews and tests. Tuac had hoped the screening would be quicker, but the only progress he saw was that the tests now focused on his magical ability. Unfortunately, Tuac's abilities had stalled. First, they asked him to describe symbols behind flash cards and he was right only a few times. When asked to move objects he could not, in spite of his earlier practice. He could generate sparks but not light candles. They asked him to swirl water in a huge bowl, but he only generated bubbles. He could not control or shape mud, or lift a sheet of paper with a breeze.

The Gaeist asked him to control a bird, but while he did feel its fear, he could not affect it.

"Are your accommodations adequate?" a voice asked from his doorway, startling him. A tall, slightly hunched gray-haired woman in magician's robes stood there. Her piercing eyes were the color of dark wood and they were framed by a face riddled with lines showing her advanced age. Her lapel displayed the colors of all the Arts, and was lined with a reddish brown. As Tuac took in his visitor, he noticed her weathered hands dotted with age spots. She gave him a warm smile. Tuac could feel power radiating from her

This is no ordinary magician, thought Tuac.

"My name is Ba'al. I hope your stay here has been pleasant."

Tuac was too astounded to answer. Outside of the testing, no one paid any attention to him. He even ate alone in the common dining room. Tuac was not sure what to say. The rooms, while sparse, were better than the housing throughout much of Mia and he was fed.

"They're fine, thank you," he said. "I feel a bit lonely, and to be honest, I am kind of bored. I go do my tests. I fail. I come back here. And I repeat that the next day."

"Tuac, I understand why you would feel isolated. But I cannot fault Ki'lel for his decision. We have not had a New One arrive off-term in a long time, and it will take some effort to assimilate you with the rest of us."

Tuac nodded. He had so many questions that he did not know where to begin.

"I am the head of what you know as the University. We use its original name, Basul. I am the Archmage, but I do not like that title. I see myself as a caretaker of all we have built. I like to meet each New One when they are going through the initial process of being directed to their Arts. You have shown considerable latent power and there is some concern for your, as well as others', safety." At that point, Ba'al winked. Apparently, Ki'lel had told Ba'al what Tuac had been doing in Stara.

"I do have another, more serious, reason for stopping by. Mia faces a grave danger. I will not go into details now, because I must first meet with the other leaders of Basul to inform them of the danger. After that, I will inform the entire student body and the rest of the Mages. I will tell you this: we need every Mage to fight this evil, and even one as young and raw as yourself will have a role.

"So, it is imperative that we get you directed as soon as possible. The difficulty for us—and for you—is that you have come to us between Journeys. We'll provide special classes so that you can catch up to our newest members. Your training will be quite intense. From what I know of you, I think you will be able to handle it, though. Any questions?"

Tuac asked, "What happened to Meiach?"

Ba'al stiffened. Then, in a low voice, she said, "Meiach is dead."

A lump formed in Tuac's throat. She confirmed what he had expected. He longed to say good-bye to the Mage. Tuac felt his eyes welling up, but he knew he should be brave. He gathered himself and nodded.

"Will there be a memorial service? I would like to attend, though I only met him twice. I will do everything that you ask of me and I will do my best to justify his faith in me."

Ba'al's eyes glittered with unshed tears. "I will send someone to bring you to the service." She turned and left him.

Tuac closed the door and got ready for bed. That night, his dream returned.

He was back at the house, but it had changed. There was the building, the forest, and the surrounding animal life. But unlike his previous dream, the trees and plants were withered. The forest was dying. He could feel something attacking the life force of Mia. This house resisted the onslaught. He walked inside and saw the alluring living room. He sensed another presence there.

"Who are you and why are you here?" asked Tuac.

"You ask the wrong questions. The issue is not who I am or why I am here, but why you are here." The voice came from everywhere and nowhere.

"I don't have time for riddles." Tuac tried to hide his fear.

"You are right. You do not have time. Nor does anyone else. Nabes has returned and can only be defeated by one who is strong in character, one who is willing to risk Reunification. I am not sure that you are that one, but, if you are not, then all is lost. There is no time to wait for another. Reunification must happen, or there will be no Mia left."

Tuac did not know what to make of this. He felt that he should believe this presence.

It continued, "There are many questions that I cannot answer. I can tell you that a terrible danger faces Mia—the danger that killed Meiach. He saw your potential, although he did not understand it. Even Ba'al can feel your raw power. You are the key, even if they fear the door that you will unlock.

"Here you will be faced with choices. Only the correct choice offers a path to survival. It will be fraught with danger, doubt, and loss, but you must persevere.

"It starts in the room with the fire. It offers power. But flames die. You must decide whether to embrace brute force or seek a different weapon."

"But I am just a boy," Tuac said.

"Do not underestimate yourself. Most who are called heroes or prophets were normal people who responded to challenges, sometimes insurmountable, to the best of their ability. The titles came later. I do not know whether you will be called hero or even villain. I do know

that Meiach was right about you and if you fail, there will be no one on this world to call you anything."

Tuac knew that the voice spoke the truth. He needed to make a choice. He'd promised to justify Meiach's belief in him. No matter what lay ahead, Tuac would keep his promise. He was not confident that he could succeed, but he would not surrender.

Tuac understood what the presence was saying about the room to his left. Despite the raging fire, there was no warmth emanating from the room. And while the food and furnishings tempted him, they were too inviting. He saw all his favorite foods, and a bed that looked more comfortable than any he had ever had. If he entered that room, he would never want to leave. It was surrender.

As soon as he saw the trap, the fire went out. The furniture disappeared, and the food crawled with maggots.

"Good, Tuac. You have made the right choice. You are about to embark on a journey that few have traveled since the Prophet created the Journey and Basul. Do not lose hope, do not lose sight of who you are and why you are doing this. Mia's salvation requires your stubborn determination.

"For you to succeed, you must fail. It will be painful and dangerous. Your failure will make you a target, for there are those that fear Reunification. But you must succeed. Reunification is the only solution."

Tuac felt the presence vanish. What did it mean, that he had to fail in order to succeed?

The building shifted, and he found himself back in the circular room with the seven doors. Each had a symbol on it. Six of these looked familiar but he could not place the last one. The inlay on the floor was similar to the etchings of the Mian suns in the Grand Hall. However, rather than six rays of sunlight, the two concentric circles were connected by seven rays. The colors were vibrant—yellow, silver, blood red, deep green, lush brown, rich blue, and the seventh was a rainbow

with all the colors. And here the suns were colored as well, the outer one black and the inner one white.

Tuac tried to open each of the doors with familiar symbols, but they were locked. As he walked toward the seventh door, Meiach appeared. He was translucent, and Tuac could not hear what he was saying. Meiach waved Tuac away from the doors and pointed to the floor. Loud pounding prevented Tuac from hearing Meaich's words.

He awoke, startled by the vehement knocking on his door.

"Wake up, Tuac. Your training begins today," a stern female voice called to him.

<hr>

The Watcher left, drained but satisfied. It had done all it could in the fight against Nabes. It was not much. The Watcher's resources were limited, and the boy was young and raw. Those traits would be both strengths and weaknesses. Tuac must find trustworthy allies to help him grow.

The Watcher decided to check on Nabes again. Nabes had gained strength and would be able to feed more. It was a perilous cycle—the more Nabes fed, the greater the despair, and the faster the contagion would spread.

The Watcher returned to the center of Fcha Province. Nabes' castle stood stark against the sky. The poor mages failed to recognize where they were. If they had, would they both still be alive?

Nabes had drained the life force from animals and plants nearby. Nabes was gaining allies. Mercenaries, sensing an opportunity for blood, gathered around the Dark Castle. Camp followers came with them, selling everything and anything in the hopes of a better life. Greed motivated some, and fear of death drove others. They would all suffer the same fate: if they were not raped or killed by the mercenaries, Nabes would take them.

The Watcher entered the Dark Castle. The mercenaries pursued their debauched pleasures inside. A few of the soldiers stayed out of the fray and tried to keep order. These were the sergeants of Nabes' growing army, promised power for keeping the mob in line. The Watcher could sense that several of Nabes' inner circle were mages. The leaders of Basul had not learned from the Great Destruction. Order was not enough to contain the lust for control. And magicians, like their ungifted brethren, were susceptible to promises that preyed on their cravings.

The Watcher entered the central tower. Nabes would make that the center of this new wave of terror. The Prophet had not eliminated the evil that had driven the Great Destruction. He had believed that light could erase darkness, and order could protect against chaos. It was not that simple.

To the Watcher's surprise, Nabes was not using a Mian puppet, but had taken corporeal form. A black knight sat in the center of the main hall, surrounded by minions. Tapestries on the walls depicted the battles leading to the Great Destruction, but from Nabes' perspective. The rise to power, the blood bath that led to the battle between the two most powerful mages that Mia had known, and the final meeting with the Prophet's forces and those of Nabes.

Nabes was holding court. "Enough, fool. Bring me a virgin for my next meal, or you will meet my wrath."

"But master, there are no virgins in the camps," the minister said, shifting from foot to foot.

"T'ca, you have until sundown. If you do not find me a virgin, I will dine on your entrails." With a flick of his hand, Nabes dismissed T'ca.

Nabes surveyed the room. Then he focused on the Watcher.

Although the Watcher wore no physical form, Nabes knew the Watcher was there.

"I was wondering when you would return. I felt you there, my jailer, the entire time I was imprisoned. You failed to see me regaining my strength. Who are you?"

The Watcher did not respond.

"Why do you hide? You have watched me all these years in silence. Are you not curious? You are immortal as I am, yet you have limited powers. Otherwise, I would not be here. You are no threat to me. Perhaps we can be allies."

Despite Nabes' confidence, the Watcher concluded that Nabes was wary. That boded well.

"My name is Haci, now known as the Watcher." It had been so long since it had used its given name. "Nabes, why have you returned? Why do you want to send this world into chaos?"

"Chaos is a judgmental word. And yes, I have returned just for that purpose. This world is weak. I am here to launch a new age. And when I am done here, I will conquer the other worlds."

The Watcher had anticipated Nabes' plan for Mia, but had not expected Nabes' vision to extend to other worlds. Nabes would need to recreate the technology of the *Curiosity*, the vessel that had brought both Haci and Nabes here. Mia's populace lacked the technical skills, but once Nabes controlled the planet, that would change.

Nabes had to be stopped.

The Watcher said, "You failed once. You will fail again. The New Prophet has arisen and he will succeed." The Watcher spoke as if there was no doubt this would happen. Victory over Nabes was just one possible conclusion, and probability did not favor it. The Watcher stated that conclusion because perception can shape reality and, if Nabes could be convinced that the New

Prophet was gaining strength, perhaps caution would slow Nabes's advance.

"Idiot! Do you think I am unprepared?" The dark knight stood and stormed toward the Watcher. "I have learned from my mistake. I spent millennia planning for the right moment. The functionaries who rule this world deplete its soul. None have the courage to stop me!"

The Watcher knew that Mia's promise had declined since the Great Destruction. The Church and Basul had warped the Prophet's words. Weakened, the Arts no longer protected the people. When the University ejected the Anthenes, it shattered the harmonious cooperation of mages. The gaps widened between good and evil, and justice and abuse. The current gulf provided fertile ground for Nabes' power to spread.

How could Reunification occur? In order to defeat Nabes, for Mia to survive, the society must reshape its foundations.

The Watcher needed to withdraw and prepare Tuac. Was there enough time? Soon the boy would be called into battle. The New Prophet must rise. Reunification must happen. There was no other solution.

"Goodbye, Nabes." The Watcher said.

Nabes waved a hand, dismissing the Watcher. "Go warn those who sent my first victim. I have awakened, and I am restless and hungry. I will not be defeated."

ELEVEN

"Protection," "security," "love," and "need." These are words that people use to justify conduct that cannot be justified. Beware of those who give no other explanation for their actions. While you may not like the reasons, you can trust one who tells you honestly why they have acted in a particular fashion.

The Teachings of Prophet
Questions and Observations

The first lessons started as private sessions with Ki'lel. He told Tuac multiple times a day to meditate.

"Close your eyes and listen to the sound of your breath," Ki'lel said. "Center yourself in a place of calm. Feel your heart's beat."

Meditation was not something that came easily to Tuac. He was drawn to the house but he feared it. And when he tried to picture other places—fields, mountains, lakes—they felt forced. His mind would wander and his concentration would lapse. Finally, his mind's eye settled on nothingness. A dark, empty space. He felt safe there, though there were no boundaries. It held all the potential of the void the moment before creation began. The first time he found himself there, he was startled by the change and ended his meditation. Ki'lel soothed Tuac's anxiety and explained that the change reflected his growth, and that Tuac was starting to become one with his Art. Gradually, Tuac embraced this place that was no place. Ki'lel sensed that Tuac had taken yet another transformative step.

"Good work, now breathe longer, stronger. Feel your heart as it beats with more power. Tell me what you see now," Ki'lel said.

As Tuac measured his breath, looking through his inner eye, the nothingness gave way to images, and he was staring at his favorite hursa from home standing by a pond. He reached out to the hursa but nothing happened. He wanted to go towards it, but Tuac could not move. He wanted it to come to him, but it did not respond. He raised his hand, and the lead rope came to him. Instantly, the hursa was next to Tuac and he felt the warmth of its body as if it were really there. But then everything changed—the hursa panicked, waves shook the water, the wind gusted, and the ground beneath him moved. Tuac clutched the lead but it snapped and he returned to the nothingness. Tuac opened his eyes and told Ki'lel what he had seen.

"You saw the hursa and then it was pulled to you. And then chaos ensued and it ran, correct?" Ki'lel asked. Tuac nodded.

"I need to consult with the trainers of New Ones," Ki'lel said. "These images are allegorical and I need to understand their significance." Tuac remained in his quarters, reading chapters from the enormous *History of Basul* that Ki'lel had assigned, and practicing the meditation exercise.

Ki'lel did not return the next day, so Tuac continued his practice. The vision was similar but reached its conclusion sooner. Over that day, Tuac slipped into the nothingness many times, always transitioning to a pond where he would find the hursa. Each time, the elements fought with him and the vision returned him to his starting point. He was exhausted that night but felt a strange sense of satisfaction.

That morning, Ki'lel came and told Tuac that he was a Telepath. The key part of the vision was his ability to summon the hursa's lead rope. That subtle use of magic revealed Tuac's true Art. It was settled: Tuac would join Ki'lel's school and learn to harness his skill as a telepath.

Once they knew his Direction, Tuac underwent an accelerated training, working alone with his teachers. Ki'lel continued to teach him, and Tuac's lessons focused on skills such as telekinesis, mental probes and blocks, and receptivity to other minds. This specialized approach differed from the broader educational background new magicians usually received in their first year, during which they learned about each of the six Arts and the commonalities they share. Some classes were with novices of a particular Art, but many classes included students from all of Basul.

Tuac learned that every Mian could tap their center if they learned how to meditate. What separated magicians from the ungifted was their ability to step through that center. Ki'lel explained that one's center formed an internal barrier, beyond which lay magic. Those without an Art could not scale or break through this barrier. A mage could breach it, releasing a wave of raw power. The mage's task was to control that wave with their Art without being swept away.

What normal acolytes had weeks or months to learn was compressed into mere days for Tuac. Hour after hour, Tuac read in the main library, studying concentration, focus, and meditation techniques.

Much to Ki'lel's surprise, Tuac found his center quickly. He was reading *The Basics of Meditation—Finding One's Center*, a first term assignment for all Acolytes. The theories were straightforward. First, one finds a quiet place away from distractions. Tuac used one of the many study areas in the main library. Second, one closes one's eyes and breathes slowly and deeply. When one is calm, a small flash of light will appear. Most people discount that flash as a trick of the eye. But those with magic see the light for what it is—the entrance to their inner powers. They must embrace the light. It is the door beyond which their power lies.

After reading the text, Tuac decided to start his exercises. The first two times, he saw the light but could not control or widen it. The third time, however, he could.

He felt a change. His skin tingled, and he smelled the flowers in Basul's gardens though he was deep inside the building. He could sense the dew in the air around him, feel the fire and taste the stew being made in the kitchens. He could even hear the thoughts of those in the library. It was scary, yet exhilarating.

The intensity increased until it overloaded his senses and he lost his center. His eyes snapped open and he panted. He felt drained, not only of his strength but also as if something had been torn away from him. Tuac stopped practicing until he could speak to Ki'lel.

Tuac had expected Ki'lel to be excited by this advancement, but Ki'lel's reaction was measured.

"I am pleased you had such a breakthrough, but we must be careful. There are rules for a reason and your accelerated training does not change that. Unlocking your powers without appropriate supervision puts you at risk because you have not developed techniques for channeling the flow of power. The sensory overload you felt is like being downriver when a dam breaks. Given your progress, you are ready for more advanced training."

The next day, a different teacher took over Tuac's education. He learned to hold his center and expand it in a controlled manner. Tuac mastered this in less than a month. He was catching up with the most recent class of Acolytes and would be able to join his fellow students when the next class arrived at Basul.

Tuac started specific exercises to strengthen his true Art. Each morning he rose before dawn and met with his master for practice. Initially this went well, but in the second week his progress halted. He could use telekinesis to move small objects, but he could not do more. After several frustrating days, Ba'al visited Tuac.

"Tell me what you feel, child," she said.

"It's a wall. I see it, try to pass it, climb it, or go around it, but I cannot. I can't break through it, either. I return to my center as I've been taught. The wind swirls and the water rages, and I can settle them. But the hursa seems afraid of me. Yet, when I move the lead rope she comes to me. I clutch the lead to embrace my Art and try to do more advanced telepathy. If I try to connect with the minds of others, I find that their thoughts are jumbled and my mental voice is garbled. If I try to move things, they vibrate as if I've angered them, then they calm down and refuse to move. I've tried and tried, but nothing works."

Ba'al considered Tuac's statement. "We have pushed you so hard. I believe you need a break from the intense training. Take the next few days off and we will take this up when you are rested."

He appreciated the reprieve, but did not believe it was the solution. Tuac took a long bath and a much-needed nap in his room. The few days stretched into two weeks without work, lectures, and assignments.

He explored Basul and the surrounding countryside. One day, he found his sister. Rea was on her way to one of her classes when she and Tuac ran into each other.

"Tuac, what are you doing here? No one told me that you came to visit. We don't get visitors until the new Acolytes are admitted to Bas—I mean the University."

Tuac was not surprised by Rea's reaction. At home, they had only talked about her going to the University. Even now she missed the fact that Tuac wore Acolyte's robes. Tuac knew she considered him to be the little brother who needed to be protected and nothing more. He remembered how often she underestimated him. Tuac longed for her approval and her respect.

"You mean *Basul?*" Tuac grinned, waiting for her to put the clues together.

Rea looked at her brother from head to toe and then she beamed at him. She clutched Tuac, who was smaller than her, and swung him around. Her hug squeezed the breath out of him. This was a rare moment when he felt the depth of their bond.

"You're a mage! Hurrah, the two Aciras, together again. Have you started your training? What is your True Art? I'm a Fire Walker. Oh, we have so much to talk about." Tuac's feelings of inadequacy vanished and all that mattered was that he was with his sister. All was right in the world.

The two spent the entire day together discussing their training. After Rea had updated her brother, their discussion turned to Tuac's admission. He told her about meeting Meiach, Ki'lel, and Ba'al. Rea was stunned by what her brother had experienced, especially because she had seen no perceptible change in her teachers. The two concluded that the menace facing Mia must be grave indeed if the mages were afraid to alert the new students. Rea also found it odd that none of her teachers had mentioned that her brother had arrived at Basul.

They shared much, but Tuac withheld both his dreams of the strange Watcher and the abrupt, unexplained halt in his progress. He knew that Rea would be needed in this coming battle. He was concerned that he might distract her from her role if she worried about him. As it was getting dark, the two parted. They promised to see each other again soon. Their destinies would prevent this.

Over the next few days, Tuac and Rea tried to see each other, but Rea could not miss any more of her classes. Tuac used his free time to pursue other interests, especially reading in the various libraries of Basul. Tuac enjoyed reading about the history of Basul, the Prophet, the Great Destruction and magic. The librarian helped him select books as he finished each one.

One evening when he returned to his room after dinner he discovered a volume waiting for him on his desk. It was *The Journal of Samuel R. Orris.*

The Librarian must have left this for me, he thought. Most manuscripts were bound in stiff paper, but this one was covered with animal hide. The image on the front showed a strange white hursa with wings. Inside, instead of printed words, he found handwritten notes, sketches, and blurred passages. On the first page he read:

Curiosity, 4022 SY.

Today we pulled into orbit around our destination. The planet's atmosphere approximates Earth's prior to the Change, about 20% oxygen with the remainder largely nitrogen. There are several land masses surrounded by saline oceans. We have begun scanning and found abundant fresh water. We are optimistic. We have no choice but to be so.

Tuac did not know all the words, but he knew this was the actual journal kept by one of the *Curiosity's* crew.

Outstanding! He held the words of one of the original Terran settlers written as they landed on Mia. He heard the call to dinner. Tuac's training happened in isolation, but he joined his fellow students at mealtimes. This was one of his few pleasures, and he never missed it. Orris would have to wait until another day. He tucked the Journal into his book bag and left it on his desk. He was hungry and dinner was ready.

"It is no use, Ba'al. We have tried everything we can. He is not a true mage. He cannot find his Art," Eis said, relaying the decision of the committee chosen by Ba'al to guide Tuac. Eis, the Acetos of the Fire Walkers, demanded that the issue of Tuac's advancement come to a close. For over an hour they had debated the boy's fate. Eis favored dismissal from Basul, as the mages did not have time to worry about "dims", those who could not manifest their magical potential. Ki'lel, offended by Eis's stance, and carrying on Meiach's fight for more compassion in the Direction process, argued that they should give Tuac more time. But his defense of the boy was half-hearted. Ki'lel sensed a strange quality in Rea's brother, but he could not put his finger on it. He wondered if part of the problem was that Tuac had not entered Basul in the conventional fashion so his Direction process was atypical. Ki'lel also believed that these were trying times, and every magical resource needed to be maximized.

Ba'al let the discussion play out. Ki'lel felt that she shared his viewpoint. Tuac was not a Telepath as they had originally thought, and he should be given another chance.

"We do not test twice, but this is an exceptional situation. Ki'lel, work with Tuac's vision and try to find our mistake. Misdirection does happen, though it is rare. If he does not find his Art, he will be offered a position among the staff as we have done with others."

Tuac and Ki'lel worked through his repeating vision in fine detail. What color was the hursa? Could Tuac hear the thoughts of the beast or feel its emotions? If Tuac was a Gaeist, the presence of the hursa would be the key. Yet Tuac's lack of connection with the animal suggested that was not his Art, either.

The pond! Tuac described it in such vivid detail. If Ki'lel had had experience in detecting a Direction, he would have focused on the boy's connection to the water sooner. Biased by his own magic, Ki'lel had assumed that Tuac had levitated the twigs, when he had used water to manipulate them.

Ki'lel reported this to Ba'al, and Tuac began the rudimentary lessons in controlling water. He responded well to the new training. He could shape streams, move small amounts of liquid, stop the flow of moving water, and use water to move small objects. Unfortunately, after a few weeks, Tuac reached another wall.

Eis called for a vote of the Direction Committee. It was five to three in favor of terminating Tuac's apprenticeship. Only Chorra had voted with Ki'lel and Ba'al. Ki'lel wanted Ba'al to veto the Direction Committee, but knew that was unlikely. Issuing that kind of executive order put the Archmage above all other mages. She would not risk fracturing the unity of Basul. Ba'al nodded.

"This matter is closed."

Ki'lel felt disgusted that Ba'al did not use her authority. She was the Archmage and could exercise her prerogative, yet she did not. Mia needed assertive leaders who would use their office to protect the populace from Nabes, even if that meant overruling the Council and consolidating their authority. Ba'al believed in the boy and Ki'lel felt Ba'al should act upon that belief. Ki'lel left, irritated that he had to follow the instructions of a weak leader.

Ba'al flinched when Ki'lel walked out, his shoulders stiff with anger.

"Ki'lel will talk to the boy," she said, "and let us hope he makes the right decision." She kept her own doubts about their ruling to herself.

Eis said, "Can we trust Ki'lel to handle this? He does not agree with our determination, and is still troubled by Meiach's death—"

Ba'al cut him off. "Enough Eis." There had always been tension between them, ever since Ba'al had been chosen as Archmage over her hawkish rival. "Ki'lel knows the Prophet's wisdom and will not circumvent our decision. He will be kinder in delivering the verdict than you would be. The rules about Direction are clear, but Ki'lel is permitted to find a compassionate outcome for Tuac's future. I may implement the Council's decision as I see fit. Unless you want to call a vote of no confidence, there is nothing more to say."

The members of the committee looked away or muttered among themselves. They could call for such a vote, but just as the Archmage seldom overruled a Council vote, a Council member rarely exercised this right. The ability to do so was enough to maintain the balance of power.

"I will talk to Ki'lel." Ba'al gave them a moment, but there were no objections. Then she, too, left the room in disgust.

Despite Tuac's enthusiasm and persistence, his success with water sculpting was the same as telepathy. After learning the basics, he could advance no further. His teachers had not offered him any new lessons, so he sat in his room and read, anxious and frustrated.

When will I meet with Ki'lel and Ba'al to discuss my next steps? he wondered. A knock on his door startled him. He jumped to open it and found Ki'lel in the hall, looking troubled.

"Tuac, young one. Come walk with me. We have serious things to discuss." Ki'lel gestured for Tuac to accompany him.

"As you know, one of our most important tasks is to Direct New Ones. Proper Direction is critical to the safety of both the New One and, more importantly, Mia. Occasionally, there is a mis-direction, where a New One is Directed to an Art that is not their True Art. We try to minimize those instances but, when they happen, the New One repeats the process to find their correct place. Sometimes, however, despite our best efforts, a New One cannot become one with an Art.

Basul has a place for those Mians too. We call them "Prophet's helpers," because these are the individuals that staff the libraries, stables, kitchens, offices, and infirmaries. You have interacted with some of them, they guided you when you arrived. Basul needs people who understand the Arts and the demands of the work to assist the mages. The Prophet's helpers fill that role."

Tuac had heard derogatory terms for the Prophet's helpers. The students he met in the dining hall mocked and teased them.

Ki'lel continued. "Most often, Prophet's helpers are those with an affinity for the Arts but little more. These individuals are gifted, but in a minor way. Those willing to serve Basul receive more than they could ever hope for in more routine jobs.

"In some instances, people with significant gifts cannot develop a connection to their Art. Recognizing that their lives have been disrupted, the Prophet determined that we owed an obligation to them. They, too, are offered positions as Prophet's helpers but in more complex and challenging positions as assistants to mages. These special individuals are critical to Basul's administration. Individuals like you.

"Tuac, we would like to offer you such a position and, because I am fond of you, I would like you to assist me. It is not formal training in the Arts, but it has its rewards. Given the threat we face, I need a smart, capable, and magically attuned assistant to do all that I must.

Tuac's stomach tensed as a wave of nausea swept over him. He put all the pieces together. The Council had determined that he was not a true mage. Tuac's first thought was to plead for another chance, but he realized that there would be no more opportunities. Basul was telling him that he would never master an Art. Rage flooded through him.

"How dare you and your Council!" he yelled at Ki'lel. "You pulled me early from my family, with promises of becoming a mage. You deprived me of my Journey. All for your precious *Basul*.

"Let's be honest. I can either be exiled to fend for myself, or stay here with the likes of you, pitied and denigrated as a malformed mage." Tuac headed back to his room. Then he spun and shouted, "Tell the Archmage that I reject her *gracious* offer. I would rather try to make it on my own than spend my life supporting the arrogant mages of Basul. Since I am not welcome here, I will leave tomorrow morning."

He knew he had hurt Ki'lel but he did not care. He also did not care if Ba'al had his interests at heart. All that mattered was that his dreams, so new and welcome, had been shattered.

As Tuac stormed down the hall, Ba'al and Eis stepped out of the shadows.

"We had hoped he would make this decision voluntarily," Eis said.

"Ba'al, stop this process." Ki'lel said. "Right now, we cannot follow outdated rules. And who knows, if he stays in Basul, maybe he will find his Art. Maybe he is not responding because we have pushed him so hard and so fast."

Ba'al studied her trusted advisor. But she could not question the Prophet or the Council. In chaos, she thought to herself, there must be strength and order. Even if it is not always the best decision, certainty and steadiness offered their own rewards. No, now was not the time to rethink the Direction process and Basul's treatment of those who were unable to master an Art. If they survived whatever it was that was draining the lifeblood from Mia, then perhaps there could be changes.

"I'm sorry, Ki'lel. While I do not share Eis's prejudices, I am bound by the decision of the Council and the Prophet's teachings. We invited Tuac to be a helper. The Council has no obligation to explain its decisions or what happens if a New One rejects our offer. In fact, I probably let you say too much to the boy. He made his choice."

She turned to Eis, who was smirking. Ba'al said, "Make sure

the boy leaves only with his own possessions. Keep him away from Rea. She has promise and should not be distracted."

As they started to leave, Ki'lel said, "Please, Ba'al. Give me one more chance to change his mind. Perhaps after he has time to consider our offer he will come around."

Ba'al sighed. She understood why Ki'lel was fighting so hard. But if she acceded to Ki'lel's plea, then she jeopardized the Council's confidence in her. If she stood firm, he would think her heartless. She saw an answer that might strike a balance.

"Okay, Ki'lel. You have one day. If he does not change his mind by then, then we will all have to live with his decision." Ba'al had ruled, and there would be no more discussion.

Ki'lel left to find Tuac. Eis was about to follow Ki'lel out but Ba'al stopped him.

"Come here Eis. *Now.*" Ba'al pointed to her side. Although Ba'al's command had the desired effect of wiping Eis' smile from his face, Ba'al was no fool. She knew that, without her intervention, Eis would carry out the Council's directive in a ruthless way. Because she owed much to Ki'lel, Meiach, and the boy, she reined in Eis.

She continued, "I have seen how much you relish this outcome. I will not permit you to make a mockery of this poor boy's fate. Although I follow the old ways, I do not do so blindly. In this case, I see no choice. Test me, and not even the Council will be able to protect you. *Do I make myself clear?*"

This time, it was more than just a command. The stone floor beneath Eis shifted, then softened around his feet. Eis' face blanched. He nodded and left the room. Ba'al smoothed his footprints away. She sighed.

"Prophet, I hope I have made the right decision."

Tuac went back to his room and packed his belongings, which did not take long. He debated whether to keep Orris' *Journal,* and decided that he would. It was stealing, but Basul owed him. They would probably never miss the book. Although his mage's garb was so comfortable, he left the white garments in the dresser. Tuac considered wearing his gray tunic. In a moment of rage, he unleashed his magic at it. Blinding light washed over the garment. At first, he thought he had destroyed it, but he could not even do that simple task. Rather, the tunic now sported a kaleidoscope of color no dyer could create. The mages were right about him. As a bright badge of his failure, Tuac put on the tunic. A voice outside his door startled him. Tuac opened it to find Ki'lel.

"Where did you get that?" the mage asked.

Tuac did not feel he owed Ki'lel an explanation. Tuac glared at him, considering his next words. On one level, his anger towards Basul and its bureaucracy felt limitless. On the other hand, Ki'lel had been a good guide and seemed to want only the best for him. But Tuac's anger ruled the day. He knew his words were harsh.

"Are you going to ask me again to be your glorified servant?"

"I was given a day to try to convince you to stay. I can see this is a fool's errand. I'm sorry. I hope you understand that. But your decision is made so I will not press you further." Ki'lel forced a smile.

Tuac sensed unexpected urgency in Ki'lel's voice. The mage's demeanor made Tuac realize he had not thought this through. Self-doubt flooded him.

What happens to me now? Where will I go? How will I make a living without having done the Journey? His rage fought the self-doubt. *I need to get away from here.*

"I've made up my mind. The University has no place for me. My road and my Journey lead elsewhere. With each passing day, I knew this was a mistake. Ba'al has just made the decision easier for me. I must leave."

"At least stay for breakfast and supplies. Eis has been commanded to make sure you have enough to take care of yourself. He should have been here already."

"No. I'm leaving now." replied Tuac.

Knowing the conversation was over, Ki'lel then held out his hand. He offered five iron coins called cobles. Tuac looked at Ki'lel's hand and then his face. Tears rolled down the mage's cheeks.

"I cannot offer you much, but what I have is yours. Please, this is not from Basul, it is from me."

Ki'lel's gift touched Tuac. Five cobles would not buy much, but the gesture had real value. For a moment, Tuac's rage eased. He nodded, took the coins and gave the mage a meek smile. Then he picked up his satchel and walked past Ki'lel.

TWELVE

Power is a sharp blade. It can cut or protect. Whether it is used for good or evil is up to the wielder. Basul must be the light in the dark, the protector of this planet and all its people. I can only hope it wields its blade carefully.

**The Teachings of Prophet
Questions and Observations**

Tuac hurried along the corridors toward the front courtyard and the main gates of Basul. No one else wandered the halls at this early hour. He arrived at the courtyard and stopped. The gates were open but unattended. The magicians of Basul wanted him to leave. There would be no pat on the back, no sendoff. He was on his own. Head held high, he strode toward the gates.

Despite his bravado, Tuac could feel his heart beating faster. He kept walking. He believed in himself even if the magicians did not. As he approached the gate, his anxiety increased and his steps slowed. The hair on the back of his neck rose. He dragged his feet.

Tuac hesitated. Doubt swamped his confidence.

This is crazy! I should go back. Being Ki'lel's assistant would not be so bad and I will starve on my own. Maybe if I stay, I can earn a chance to try another Direction. Maybe I can learn how to get past my walls.

His mind raced from anxiety, to self-doubt, to guilt for abandoning those who had done so much for him.

I'm being rash. What will Rea think? What would my parents think?

He pressed forward, one painful step at a time. A headache built behind his eyes and he blinked in the morning light. Finally, he reached the gate's threshold. His temples throbbed and he felt queasy.

He started to turn back.

Yes! You're making the right decision now. This is merely a detour. This is not failure.

For Tuac, the thought of failure brought a wave of anger. He had grown up in a home where his parents set a high bar, which Rea always managed to reach.

Something stirred behind his anger and anxiety. His failure now felt like a slap in the face. He felt a wave of cold wash over him. Abruptly, his mind cleared. The headache vanished and, in its place, he felt calm and resolve.

This may be the wrong decision, but I will only know if I try. I can only go forward, not back.

With newfound purpose, Tuac walked over the threshold.

As soon as he stepped beyond Basul's gates he felt a weight lift from his shoulders. He felt relieved leaving the University— he would not call it Basul now that it had expelled him. He did not know what the future would bring, but it would be a future of his own making. His pace quickened. The farther he moved from the University, the more confident he felt.

Eis watched from a window as Tuac passed through the gates. How was that possible? He was dumbfounded. The boundaries of Basul pulsed with strong magic, a fusion of power from each of the Acetos. It kept out the unwanted and kept in those Basul wanted to watch. Yet the boy had walked out.

How had he done that? Eis wondered. Even if the boy was strong enough to resist the magic directing him to turn back, he should never have been able to resist the boundary spell. The boy should have died on the threshold. Eis hurried to report this to Ba'al.

He found her pacing in her chambers. Ki'lel had arrived before him, and Ba'al's agitation told Eis that she had heard the news.

"How did the boy get out?" she asked. "There is no way he could defeat that spell and he was not given leave to exit. Those wards have been in place since the Split. *No one* enters or leaves without our permission!"

"I cannot explain it," said Ki'lel. "He even resisted my efforts to bend his will. Perhaps we were wrong about this one. Maybe he is a Telepath."

"First Nabes, and now this! We cannot let him fall into Nabes' hands. If Tuac has any magical ability, it will be exploited. We know the risk of an untrained magician and this is why we have the rules we do. Such a one is bound to service at Basul, where they can be watched and controlled."

Eis said nothing. There were no good answers here. He had

disagreed with Ki'lel's handling of the boy, but he had been overruled. Ba'al and the Council preferred to follow the old ways. They were weak.

"Enough then." Ba'al said. "Eis, take care of this personally. I will not tolerate any more mistakes. This is what you had wanted to do in the first place, so I know you will not be squeamish. Do not be reckless." She dismissed them.

Outside, Ki'lel and Eis went separate ways. Eis smiled, relishing his assignment.

It was well past second sunrise before Tuac stopped for a break. His adrenaline rush had faded leaving him drained, hungry, and thirsty. In his haste to show Ba'al and the others that they were wrong about him, he had never considered that he should have stayed long enough for breakfast. With only the money that Ki'lel had given him, Tuac did not have many options.

He got up and started toward Shi'Bo Coula. It was the closest city to the University. New Ones were told to stay away, as its citizens distrusted magicians. But Tuac had no other choice. He needed food and shelter so he could plan what he would do next.

Tuac figured that it would take all day to reach the city. He decided to leave the main road and travel through the scrub lands to avoid meeting anyone. After several hours, Tuac found a tree and sat down in the shade. His stomach growled and his mouth was dry. As soon as he settled, exhaustion washed over him. It was not just the emotional drama of his expulsion. There was some deeper cause. Every fiber of his body felt like he had been under siege.

Tuac decided to set up a makeshift camp and take a short

nap. He found some berries that lessened his hunger and soon fell asleep.

He was back in the house. Once again, the living room had a roaring fire and all of his favorite foods. He looked at the room and wondered if he had made the right choice. Was surrender so bad?

"Tuac, do not succumb," the voice said. "You have chosen the right road. Believe in yourself and do not trust the leaders of Basul. Now your true Journey begins. It will be rewarding and perilous. It will be both the beginning and the end. Many will try to stop you. In the end, you will need to trust in others even when you feel alone."

Tuac shouted, "I know I made the right decision!" But that was a lie. He wondered if he had done the right thing, but at this point he could not go back. "Unless you have something useful to say, leave me alone. Let me find my own way."

"You have suffered boy, and this is only the beginning. Your Journey will take you down a road once walked by the Prophet. Your Journey will prove that the Prophet's teachings are correct and yet they are also misunderstood. You are the bringer of life and of death, of light and of dark, of all things and of nothing. You will be attacked by those whom you will defend. You will need to face your greatest fear. If you survive, you will reach your true potential. If you do not succeed, if you are not strong enough, every living thing on Mia will vanish and all the lives among the stars you see at night will be endangered."

"Your final challenge will involve reliving the Prophet's choice: whether to embrace or to reject the source of all power. The Prophet chose power, hoping to have both power and peace. But his choice allowed Nabes to return. If you reject power, Mia's development will regress, but Mians will survive.

These words shook Tuac. The mages' urgency had indicated there was a threat to Mia, but he presumed they would deal with it. But now the voice said he was the key to Mia's survival. How could that be when he was not capable of capturing his Art? The voice's words suggested that he did not need to be a mage and was destined for other, greater things.

As if reading the boy's mind, the voice continued, "You should not underestimate yourself. I have little time. You must carry the banner of justice against the coming evil, and you must do so even while others say that you bring destruction. You must not give in to fear, to loss, to loneliness. Weather the storm. Your true strength must resonate if you are to withstand Nabes.

"You will need allies. Some will seem sympathetic when they are not. Choose wisely. Some will call you a heretic and destroyer, but your true family will support you.

"Spare me your riddles," Tuac said. "I need food, I need direction. If you are not going to help me, then be gone."

Tuac expected to feel the voice departing, but this time it did not leave.

"You are right. You deserve guidance. But I can only give you limited information. I am not permitted to intervene. However, I will answer three questions— use them carefully. I cannot see the future, but I can tell you of the past and the present."

Tuac stood motionless. Three questions. His first question was easy.

"Why was I brought to the University?"

"This is why." The house faded. Tuac stood on a dim, empty plain. Above him there was nothing: no stars, no suns, no moons. It was cold. Lifeless. Hopeless.

"A terrible danger faces Mia. That danger is called Nabes. Evil incarnate. The bringer of chaos, the taker of life. Only you can defeat Nabes. Ba'al and the others do not know how to do this. The Prophet's teachings have blinded them. If they understood the nature of Nabes and the Prophet's true vision, you would be leading that charge. You will have to convince them to abandon their misguided ways and see you for what you are. It will take a unified Mia to defeat all the evil Nabes will marshal."

These words baffled Tuac. He had learned in school the stories of the Great Destruction and how the Prophet had defeated his arch enemy, Nabes. How could this Nabes now be alive? And how was Tuac supposed to save Mia? He was just a boy.

"Second question: how can I defeat the most powerful evil known to Mia?"

"That question I cannot entirely answer. I can only see the past and the present. What I can say is that you will be able to do things not seen since the battle between Nabes and the Prophet. Ba'al and the rest of the Council made a mistake. You must show them they are wrong, that the Prophet was wrong, and that by following the Prophet's errors they have allowed Nabes to grow powerful. There will never be another chance to stop Nabes. What is your last question?"

"What am I to do with myself?"

The house reformed around them.

"You must unlock the power of the suns. To do this, you must travel far to the west and find the seventh Art. Seek those who have kept the Prophet's true vision alive.

"I must leave," the voice said. "One last thing—I have not introduced myself. My name is Haci, although you can call me The Watcher.

Tuac sensed the Watcher was gone.

Tuac woke sweaty and trembling. What had the Watcher meant about finding the seventh Art? The University recognized only six Arts: fire, water, air, ground, Gaeists and telepaths.

Now there are six Arts, but there used to be seven. Should I find those who practiced the Art of healing? That school had been disbanded Turns ago as the mages deemed healing was not true magic.

Wait, Tuac thought, *maybe they have treated others the way they treated me.* As he considered the possibility that he was not alone, he wondered if the healers had managed to survive outside of the University. Stara always had a healer. No one knew where the healer had come from, they just arrived. Every town had a healer. When he reached Shi'Bo Coula, he would ask the local healer where he should go in the west.

Now that Tuac had a plan he stopped feeling sorry for himself. He opened his satchel and something slender fell out. It was Ki'lel's wand. Ki'lel must be one of his allies. Tuac slid the wand back into his satchel. He folded his brightly colored tunic and stowed it, then slipped on a gray tunic.

Tuac trudged along, considering the Watcher's words. He had not asked to be drawn into this battle. He could just walk away and let the mages fight for Mia. Wasn't that what mages were supposed to do? But he had never heard of mages helping Mia's people. They did not intercede in border disputes, famines, or other disasters. He remembered the story of the Prophet and the chita, and how the Prophet had refused to use magic in that situation.

Why should this be any different? This made Tuac furious. Mages were too concerned about the consequences and not concerned enough about people's suffering. But this situation with Nabes was not his fight.

As much as he tried, Tuac could not convince himself to reject the Watcher's words. He worried about what would happen to his family. If he was truly the key, he must not be as indifferent as the mages had always been. But something else tugged at him. He latched onto the Watcher's words for another reason.

Who are the mages to tell me I have no value? How dare they choose my sister and not me? I'll show them all. I'll realize my poten-tial. I'll be a weapon of change, and they will regret belittling me.

As he walked, his neck began to tingle. Tuac had experienced a similar sensation when one of his childhood pranks was about to be discovered. He had learned that this was the basic warning system of a mage. Honed, it could distinguish between a magical danger or a natural one, though Tuac had not learned that skill yet. But he knew there was a threat.

Tuac stopped. It was silent.

The sensation alerted him again and he turned around. Something materialized out of thin air. At first, it was just a ripple in space. Then he saw a flaming figure. Tuac panicked. The fiery being shot bolt of fire at his head. Tuac ducked. The flames missed him but they singed his hair.

The wand! He dropped to the ground and rummaged through his satchel. Another blast of fire blew past him.

He found the wand. Acting on instinct, Tuac visualized water extinguishing fire. The wand pulsed. Tuac felt a strange vibration. He knew he had a chance. He concentrated on water using the techniques the mages had taught him. Tuac focused on dousing the attacker. He heard a crash of thunder. It started to rain. The wind howled. Tuac had created an isolated storm. He felt the power raging within him.

Tuac glanced at the creature and saw that his defense was working. The water was not enough to kill the beast, but it interfered with its attacks. The storm's wind pushed it back and the rain lashed at it. Between the two elements it could not launch fire balls. Tuac saw his chance, and bolted for the main road. He ran until his legs and chest burned. Exhausted and covered in mud, Tuac collapsed.

He did not see the fiery figure pursuing him. The rain diminished to drizzle and the wind died. He felt drained. By the time he had caught his breath, Tuac hitched a ride with a group of merchants.

He had survived. But someone was after him. There was only one logical conclusion. Nabes was bent on killing him even if Tuac did not believe that he posed a real threat. Nabes must have more faith in Tuac's abilities than he, or the University, did. He wanted to scream to Mother Mia that she was being unfair, but he knew that would accomplish nothing. This was not about fairness, this was about reality. He had no choice. Tuac needed to learn to fight back.

Thirteen

Sometimes we are forced to sacrifice a few for the greater good. While we can justify the goal, it is nonetheless a difficult decision to make. Unfortunately, with the passage of time, sacrifice is often forgotten. Loss and victory are all that remains.

The Teachings of the Prophet, 3:2

Shi'Bo Coula was a sleepy city. Because of its proximity to the University, few willingly settled here. The city had been a bustling trade hub when the University was founded. However, with each Journey, the population of Shi'bo Coula gradually declined—the young left and were not replaced as the only new blood passing through were the acolytes who came to the University. New Ones making their Journey in other trades feared the magic and saw no benefit to being so close to the University.

Shi'Bo Coula's leaders created incentives that they hoped would attract new settlers. The Guilds offered stipends and the city gave generous tax benefits. Money and new opportunities overcame fear and the population stabilized.

While it was much smaller than Stara, the Shi'Bo Coula supported a full complement of sanctioned guilds: alchemists, tanners, blacksmiths, and other skilled trades. Unofficial guilds governed thieves, prostitutes, and drug dealers. Every town suffered from those who prefer to earn their coin outside the confines of the law, but the criminal guilds ensured that their members followed strict rules. Prostitutes took steps to avoid pregnancies and transmitting diseases, thieves were only permitted to steal from the wealthy and travelers, and narcotics dealers were forbidden to sell dangerous drugs. All of them forbade murder. With these limits on crime, Shi'bo Coula was safe for most of its citizens.

Tuac needed a place to stay and finding one would be challenging as he had so little money. Because he had not done his Journey and needed only short term work, he could not approach an official guild. Tuac looked for an inn or livery where he could work for his room and board. Most New Ones bartered for room and board until they joined a guild. He would concoct a tale to explain why he was in the city.

Walking down the main road, Tuac saw the Wandering Eye, a well-kept inn with a freshly-painted sign that suggested prosperity. He entered, pleased by the small, clean lounge with local citizens drinking mead and eating spicy stew. To his left patrons drank at a bar tended by a girl about his age.

"Is the manager here?" Tuac asked. The girl looked at him and Tuac froze. She was his height with light brown hair in neat braids. She wore loose clothes and an apron stained with food. He could see the muscles in her forearms flex as she carried multiple tankards to customers. He could not help but note the supple curves of her body. He was lost in her hazel eyes.

"Who asks?" she said, her demeanor polite but firm.

"My name is—Ton'ku. I am a New One in search of a profession. I was wondering whether I could trade work for a few days' room and board while I visit the local guildhalls." The girl studied him.

"Before I bother the master of this inn, I have a few questions. First, why Shi'bo Coula? Few seek their calling in the shadow of the University. Second, how long have you been on your Journey? The last celebration was some time ago. Third, what skills do you have?

"I come from a small fishing village to the south. Because we only have a few children, guilds do not come recruiting there. We have to leave home prior to the Journey and find a town where we can join the process. I could not find any towns in the south willing to include me. This made my Journey difficult and unsuccessful. I came north and found that most places were preoccupied with their own children. A guildsman in the last village suggested that I come here because Shi'bo Coula needed apprentices. It seemed like a good fit.

"I have a strong back, a keen eye and am fairly good in the kitchen. I will do my best with any task the manager gives me. I realize that may not be much, but this is my only option." His voice held an urgent edge.

Without a word, the clerk left. She returned moments later with a portly woman with flushed cheeks. Her apron matched the girl's, perhaps with more gravy and less ale. Tuac gave her his most winning smile. The girl nodded toward him, whispered to the woman, then left to take a pitcher of ale into the lounge.

"My name is Guale, and I am master of the Wandering Eye.

My daughter says that you are a New One and you are looking for room and board."

"Yes, mistress."

"Well, you seem like a stout enough lad. You can stay here as long as you follow a few simple rules: You awaken before the guests. You eat after the guests. You sleep after I have closed for the evening and you have cleaned up. You will do what I say, when I say it. If you prove your worth, I may consider paying you." Guale studied Tuac's face. Her brows lowered. "The most important rule is that, apart from normal work activities, you stay away from my daughter unless I have given you my permission to be with her."

"Yes, mistress. Thank you," Tuac said. Guale gave him a curt nod and strode away. The girl returned.

"You've passed my mother's test. She rarely lets New Ones stay here. Ever since my father died, she trusts no one. She must see something in you.

"You look tired and hungry. My mother has said that you can eat and rest today, 'for tomorrow you work!'" She gave a good imitation of her mother's voice. "I'm Merle, by the way, first and only daughter of the Mistress of The Wandering Eye." Merle offered him a curtsy and waved her hand as though they were being introduced at a formal function. They laughed, and Tuac felt at home for the first time in months.

Merle gestured that Tuac should follow her as she led him along a dark corridor behind the kitchen. In the back, the Inn opened into a small courtyard lined with rooms. With another sweeping gesture, Merle opened a door.

"You stay here. Normally, you would stay in the common quarters above the stable. However, you are younger than the other workers and my mother thought you should stay in the main quarters in our extra room. You don't have a lot of bags—do you have a change of clothes?"

"Yes," Tuac responded.

"Good. I will draw you a bath and have your clothes washed. You stink," she smiled.

Tuac winced at her candor, but felt oddly at ease.

Merle continued, "We will eat as soon as you're clean and presentable." With that, Merle turned and walked out.

Tuac almost fell asleep in the bath, but his hunger kept him awake. The food was simple—a stew with root vegetables, homemade bread and apple cider. After eating, Tuac retired to his quarters and fell asleep before the second sun set.

The next few days were calm. Tuac adapted to the demanding schedule of the Wandering Eye and performed his chores with vigor. Guale promoted him to waiter and, though he was not paid, she permitted him to keep a portion of the tips. The coins were Imperial currency. The smallest denomination was an iron coble. Ten cobles made a copper shut, and fifteen shuts made a silver copp. Once he saw a patron pay with a gold garrett, worth twenty copps. Through travelers staying at the inn, Tuac learned the value of other currencies made of exotic metals, such as a green metal called ambritz, a white metal called plat, and a black metal called ember. A meal and mead cost three cobles, so he could earn a few cobles a day in tips. In a good week, he earned a shut.

As a waiter, Tuac could eavesdrop on the Inn's patrons and keep up with the news. It was not good. Strange things were happening in the south. People had been found with their bodies split and their entrails missing. Emissaries of the Empire and the Church, and mages from all over Mia, passed through Shi'bo Coula on their way to the University. Rumors suggested they were attending a conclave to consider new procedures for invigorating the Journey. Tuac knew better. They were forming a war Council to stop Nabes.

Tuac's comfortable situation did not divert him from his goal of finding a healer. He needed to explore Shi'Bo Coula. His chance came when traffic for the war Council lessened and Guale gave Tuac and Merle a much-deserved day off. Guale suggested that Merle give him a formal tour of the city. He was delighted to have her as a guide, and by asking the right questions, Tuac directed Merle to the alchemist's quarter. Before long, Tuac found what he was looking for.

"What's that?" Tuac asked, pointing to a shop called The Splint.

"That's Amafi's shop. She's the town healer. To hear some people tell it, she can practically raise the dead. Want to go in?" Without waiting for an answer, Merle walked into The Splint.

Inside, Tuac found a nightmarish world. Glass jars of all sizes and shapes contained dead animals, animal parts, and what he thought were human organs. Herbs hung in bunches from the rafters, smaller jars held colored powders, and several wooden boxes in one corner were piled high with bones, some of them enormous. Candles burned in every nook and cranny. Toward the back of the shop, he saw a dusty desk. Behind it was a doorway draped with a tattered sheet. Merle, fearless as usual, roamed through the shop picking up objects to examine and reading labels.

"Excuse me, *miss*," a stern woman's voice said, "Please do not touch my stores. Do you need anything or are you here just to play." A towering woman swept aside the sheet and stepped into the cramped front room. Despite her worn features and blunt tone, Tuac sensed her warmth and saw laugh lines beside her eyes.

"Hey, Amafi," Merle said, "I'm not here for anything. My

friend Ton'ku wanted to come in and look around. I hope we haven't disturbed you." With a smile that could melt butter, Merle diffused the tension in the room. She was a charmer, that one.

"Merle, you're always welcome here. I heard the noise and thought that it might be someone else. Not a lot of visitors these days, eh?" Amafi smiled at Tuac and her eyes followed him around the room. "May I offer you two something to drink? You look parched." Without waiting for an answer, Amafi left.

Tuac looked at Merle and marveled. She was no older than him, but had the poise of an adult.

Maybe if I had been given the same attention my parents gave to Rea, and the same opportunities, I would be like Merle. I wish I had the confidence she has. Amafi's return brought him back to the moment.

"Here's a pot of tea, and I made cookies yesterday." The herbal aroma filled the shop and, though Tuac had not been very thirsty, he salivated. Merle's grin suggested that she had had the same reaction. The two stepped up to the counter.

Amafi handed each of them a cup of tea and offered the plate of cookies. Tuac devoured two cookies and drained the first cup of tea, then extended his hand for another of the crunchy treats. He smiled at Amafi in appreciation. Merle sipped her tea while wandering around the shop. As Amafi refilled his cup, Tuac thought to broach the subject he had come to discuss. Before he could say anything, she cleared her throat, and when she had his attention, shook her head slightly. Merle ogled jars holding some kind of sparkly gel.

Amafi said, "Do not worry about Merle, Ton'ku—if that is your name. She is honest, loyal and easily distracted by the things in my shop. You have come here for something."

Amafi's directness startled Tuac. He glanced again to make

sure Merle was out of earshot. She had settled into a chair and appeared to be napping.

"What did you do to her, Amafi?" Tuac considered reaching for his wand.

"Look, boy. I would never harm Merle. She is as close to me as a daughter. She has gifts and her time will come. I put her to sleep so we could talk. She will wake in an hour feeling rested. That will give us enough time to become acquainted. Now, *why did you come here.*" Amafi's tone was firm.

"My name is Tuac." Amafi nodded, recognizing his honesty. He continued, "A terrible danger threatens Mia. One named the Watcher called it Nabes. I came to you because the Watcher told me to find the Seventh Art. I figured that might mean a healer. I need your help."

Amafi studied the boy. She nodded.

"Tell me more," she said.

Tuac could not tell whether Amafi believed him or not. Over the next hour, Tuac told the healer as much as he could remember. How he had been picked by the mages to come to the University, and how Meiach had died. Tuac described his failure to find his true Art despite multiple attempts, and how he had been attacked by Nabes after he had left the University. Tuac answered Amafi's questions about his meditation and his dreams.

The only details Tuac omitted were that he had Ki'lel's wand and *The Journal of Sam Orris*. The former was Tuac's edge and he did not trust Amafi completely. He considered the book to be compensation for what the mages had done to him. Amafi listened but her expression revealed nothing.

"Your story is troubling, Tuac. I'm not sure what to do. I will have to seek counsel. In the meantime, go back to the Wandering Eye and wait for me."

Tuac wanted more but realized that Amafi's assistance must happen on her terms. He would have to be patient, which was not easy for him.

Merle shifted in her chair. Amafi chuckled.

"You two have kept me in stitches. Now, it's time for me to get back to work. Off with you." Amafi kissed Merle on the cheek, patted Tuac on the head and ushered them out of the Splint. The touch comforted Tuac.

"I love going to Amafi's," Merle said. "After Guale, she is the closest thing I have to family. My mother died giving birth to me. The mid-wife called Amafi, but it was too late. I think she feels guilty that she couldn't do more. I don't blame her, though. Mother Mia had other plans for my mother."

This surprised Tuac, as Merle had called Guale her mother.

Seeing his confusion, Merle said, "My father did the best he could. He was stern and fair, but not a warm man. When I was three, he met Guale and she moved in with us. I don't know if they ever married. When I was five, my father died in a horrible accident. Guale raised me as her own. I wonder what it would have been like to grow up with my birth mother, but Amafi and Guale have been wonderful to me. Amafi checks on me and she's even taught me a little about healing. Guale has scant respect for most people, but she does respect Amafi.

Merle was unlike any person Tuac had ever met. Tuac had known many people who complained about their lives. Here was someone dealt a cruel hand by Mother Mia, yet Merle embraced the good and did not let the bad drag her down. In spite of her losses, she was not bitter. After their afternoon together, he felt closer to her.

With each passing day, Tuac found it harder to use his alias with Merle. The dishonesty bothered him, and he felt anxious about his situation. He had to await Amafi's help, and once he left Shi'bo Coula he would no longer have to lie to Merle.

There was one benefit to the delay: he could spend more time with Merle. To Tuac's surprise, Guale said nothing about him and Merle spending their free time together. Tuac resolved to make each moment count. They explored the city. Nothing intimidated Merle and Tuac basked in her courage. He enjoyed Merle's attention but it also made him uneasy. Some days she paid no attention to him and he worried that he had done something wrong. Other days, she did not leave him alone. She enjoyed making him squirm.

As they spent precious hours together, Tuac learned that Merle had not given any thought to her Journey and hoped she could stay in Shi'Bo Coula. The city's unique population problem meant that New Ones were not asked to leave. While some did, others remained. Merle loved the Wandering Eye and was devoted to Guale.

Tuac was infatuated with Merle's light. He was drawn to her warmth and part of him wanted to stay, but he dared not risk Merle's safety. Nabes was looking for him and Tuac was no closer to the lost Art. He could not take the chance that she might be hurt if he remained. He also worried how she would react if he told her about his alias and background.

Tuac's torture ended about two weeks after their visit with Amafi. It had started off as a normal day. Tuac stoked the fires and set the tables for breakfast. Merle made fresh juice, sausages, and eggs, and the aroma of fresh bread permeated the inn. Tuac watched Merle as he did his morning chores. She peered at him from behind the bar.

Tuac scrubbed tables as the morning regulars straggled into The Wandering Eye. Amafi entered and took a seat near the door. The room fell silent when she appeared. The healer seldom left The Splint and when she did, it was usually an emergency call. The patrons of the inn whispered to each other, wondering who was sick or if this was a social call.

"To what do I owe this pleasure?" Guale said as she came to Amafi's table. Amafi cocked an eyebrow and Guale became serious. Tuac moved to clean a table closer to their conversation.

"It's been a long time, my friend," Amafi said, "I have never asked you for anything, but today, I must. I am getting old, and I need to teach a New One to carry on for me here. The other day, Merle—blessed Merle—brought a young man to my shop. Although he is raw, I sense that he might be a perfect apprentice. I would like to take your waiter and teach him to become a healer. I am prepared to offer the customary compensation." Amafi put a sack of coins on the table.

At last, Tuac thought.

Amafi's offer stunned Guale.

Why did Amafi want that boy? She thought. She had no real claim on Ton'ku. Guale and Merle glanced at each other, and she recognized disappointment in Merle's eyes. For years, Guale and Amafi had shared wine and planned for Merle to learn healing arts. Somehow, Ton'ku had displaced Merle.

Guale sensed there was more to Merle's disappointment. Then it hit her: Merle had grown close to Ton'ku. Guale had been afraid of what impact the boy would have on her daughter, but also saw the goodness in his heart. As she had come to know the boy over the last few weeks, Guale wondered whether the two could have a future together in Shi'bo Coula.

Amafi's request inflicted two injuries on Merle—depriving her of her true path and stealing her new-found best friend.

How could Amafi ask such a thing? Guale studied the healer and saw pain in Amafi's eyes. She understood the difficulties of the situation.

Could Amafi take both of the children?

Guale knew she would have to force the issue because Amafi would never ask. Guale had hoped that she would be spared the anguish every parent felt when the Journey arrived. Guale knew she had no choice.

"You've not paid me enough. My daughter is quite fond of Ton'ku and I'm not going to be stuck with her moping around miserable after he leaves. If you take Ton'ku, you must take my daughter too. And that means you must pay me more." Guale spoke loud enough for everyone in The Wandering Eye to hear. She smiled at her old friend.

Amafi's eyes glinted with tears. She said, "You leave me little choice. This town needs another healer. If I must take Merle in order to train Ton'ku, then that is what I will do. Of course, we must ask Merle." She winked at Guale.

Tuac gaped. *How can Amafi put Merle in danger this way?* he wondered. *She knows Nabes is after me.*

Merle ran to Guale and clutched her arm.

"You gave me a home when I needed it, but it's time for me to make my Journey. This is what we had all hoped for. I want to go with Ton'ku and Amafi and learn healing."

Guale hugged the girl. "I've never been prouder of you. I remember when your mother died, how quiet you were. But you've grown into a fine young woman with a good head for business and an even bigger heart. You will be a fine healer.

Merle looked at Guale with adoring eyes and an impish grin. "And I'll be with family."

Guale, blinking back tears, rapped the table.

"Look, *healer*. That boy may be worth one sack of coins, by my daughter is worth far more than that. You'll have to do better."

Amafi smiled, stood, and extended her hand to Guale. "Why don't you and I go to The Splint and iron out the economics. That will give the two New Ones time to pack. We'll be leaving tomorrow morning."

Arm in arm the two left the Wandering Eye.

"Isn't this exciting?" Merle hugged Tuac.

Tuac's head spun. None of it had followed his plan. He had wanted it to be quick and simple. Now, Merle was coming with them. Realizing that Merle was waiting for an answer, Tuac smiled and returned her hug.

"I certainly didn't expect this," Tuac said. Merle's embrace made Tuac's body burn. He breathed in the scent of her hair. This was getting awkward. He gently broke the hug. Thankfully, she seemed not to notice the blush on his ears.

That evening, after they closed the bar, they packed their belongings. Tuac enjoyed Merle's excitement about their coming Journey, but inside he was anxious. He would not be able to protect Merle. For Prophet's sake, he did not know how he would survive and now his wonderful friend was also at risk. Tuac vowed to keep her safe. She was his family now.

Tuac realized Merle deserved to know she had been calling him by an alias. When he had chosen the name, he did so to protect himself and those who might befriend him. He did not know how she would respond, but it was time to tell her the truth.

The opportunity came when the two finished their packing

and they went to the kitchen to get a late snack. As Merle set out bread and cheese, Tuac said,

"I have something to tell you."

Merle smiled and passed him a slice of bread. "And what would that be?"

"Merle—" When he looked into her eyes, Tuac panicked. Merle was pure. Her love of life had no limits. She saw the good in people. She was a source of light, empathy and hope. And now she was in danger because of what he had done. After a long pause, he found the courage to continue.

"I've lied to you. About myself, about everything."

"Ton'ku, there's nothing that you could do or say that would offend me. Whatever you think you've done, I'm sure it's not as serious as you believe it is. Tell me about this great *lie*." Laughing, she took another bite of the bread.

"Well, first, my name is actually Tuac." He let the statement sink in. Merle's eyebrows went up and she stopped chewing. "Secondly, I didn't come from a small village, and I'm not in search of a guild. I came from a large town called Stara and two mages selected me before my Journey. I started at the University, but when I couldn't find my magic, they expelled me."

"They picked you outside of the Journey? Tell me more."

Initially, Tuac was hesitant. Merle listened and asked sympathetic questions until Tuac's reservations disappeared. So Tuac shared his story with a second person, but this time he did not omit any details.

Tuac was exhausted when he was done. Merle said nothing when he concluded his tale. She ate her snack bite by bite and Tuac did not press her. She put away the bread and cheese then sat down with him again.

"Let me get this straight. The mages chose your sister, then because of some cosmic disturbance, they came back for you because you showed potential. You get there and you can't master an Art, so the mages kick you out. On the way here, a fire creature attacks you and you defeat it with your wand. You come here, lie to me, and trick me into introducing you to Amafi. The two of you concoct this little scheme so she can take you west to the healers. And now I'm going with you, putting my own life at risk. Did I get everything?"

Tuac didn't know how to respond to Merle's biting sarcasm.

"Well, all but the last part. I hoped Amafi would take me to, well, wherever it is that she's taking me. I never suggested a scheme and I didn't want to involve you. I'm sorry."

Merle threw her arms around Tuac and gave him a strong hug. It was wonderful.

"I accept your apology."

Merle rose and headed for the door. As she left the kitchen, she said over her shoulder, "If you *ever* lie to me again, you will wish the fire creature had succeeded."

Tuac winced. He didn't intend to test Merle's forgiveness ever again.

Guale let the two sleep in. It was their last day at The Wandering Eye. Amafi came to collect her apprentices shortly after they got up, bathed, and had breakfast. Guale gave her only child a long hug. Tuac saw Guale struggle to hide her feelings. Merle wept, but her eyes were bright with excitement and she smiled through her tears.

Guale turned to Tuac. "Boy, you had better be worth all of this. If you ever need anything, send a messenger for me." With that, she went back into the inn.

Amafi, Merle and Tuac took the road out of town, not stopping by The Splint. When Tuac realized their direction, he looked at the healer.

"Amafi, aren't we going back to your shop?"

"No. The shop is closed for now. We're heading to the western coast. There is a small fishing village in Pri'an. We are going to a place nearby called Liat."

Merle and Tuac exchanged startled looks. Neither of them had ever heard of it.

"Liat?" they said in unison.

Amafi smiled at her young apprentices. "Did you think the mages were the only ones with a university?"

LIAT

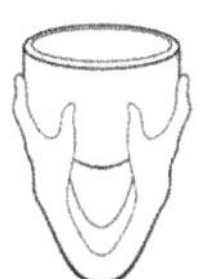

FOURTEEN

We descended from the hills to find ourselves in a valley so beautiful it defied words. After years of being outcasts, we had found a home for those expelled from Basul. We were delivered from the hands of Death into the warm, embracing arms of Mia herself.

From the Journal of an Unknown Anthene

The journey to Liat took a month. Every morning before dawn, Amafi would brew a potent herbal tea that warmed the bones of the travelers. Most of the days, they had salted meat and bread for breakfast. After dousing the morning campfire, the three would ride until the noon hour, when they would give their hursas time to rest and graze. The three travelers ate fruit in companionable silence. Every night, just before sunset, they made camp. Amafi had an uncanny ability to find spots not far from the main road, yet secluded. In the evenings, Merle and

Amafi traded stories of this friend or that relative, including Merle's father. Sometimes, Tuac joined the conversations, but usually he was content to listen and watch the hursas. He felt their calm and took strength from it.

Tuac and Merle grew closer during the journey. In a few days, Tuac found himself unable to get her off of his mind. Merle's smile struck him to his core and her eyes looked into his soul. It was an odd paradox. He felt uncomfortably disarmed whenever she was around him and he could hide nothing from her. And yet, though he felt so exposed in her presence, he did not want to flee, he wanted to be in her arms. He felt an inner heat and light when he was around her, and he craved it. Tuac struggled to identify this unique sensation. He thought it might be love.

This kind of love was unfamiliar to him, and it made him uneasy. He was close to Rea but she was his big sister. Larger than life and equally domineering, she was more his protector than his confidant. He knew his sister cared for him and he felt safe around her, but he was not sure whether her affection was due to her fondness for him or her devotion to their parents. Tuac knew his parents loved him, but their love seemed to be measured. He felt inadequate in part because he did not feel that they understood or accepted him. They offered answers or pressed him toward solutions to his problems even when, at times, what he wanted was for them to simply listen. He also felt that he was never as loved as his sister. They celebrated Rea's accomplishments. Tuac's were expected and so not praised. When he sought attention for his successes, they accused him of jealousy. Ultimately, Tuac pushed down his feelings of inadequacy and built walls to protect himself. He resolved to work harder than anyone else and those walls gave him the focus and strength to do so. Yet, the walls also prevented him from embracing this new kind of love that Merle offered.

Tuac's relationship with Merle was the first time anyone had cared about him simply for who he was. Tuac realized that he wanted to let her inside his defenses and needed to figure out how to take down the walls that had served him so well.

Her affection energized him and he hungered for it. He surrendered. Within a few days, she knew everything about him and many things that no one else knew. Talking about his emotions was difficult, but when he was with Merle his words flowed freely. Merle gave him what his family never had.

Five days out, when Tuac was gathering firewood, he stepped around a huge tree and bumped into Merle. They both fell and after an awkward moment, they burst out laughing. Tuac could hardly contain himself. Touching her shocked him, sending tremors from his head to his toes. The inner fire rose to his skin. He looked into her eyes and his world stopped. Nothing else mattered except this moment. She smiled and Tuac's heart raced. The pounding was delirious and frightening. He did not know what to do. And he wanted to do *something*.

Sensing his awkward innocence, Merle kissed him. He had never felt a kiss like this before. Soft and sweet. Eager and playful. Just enough to excite but not overwhelm him. And then it was over. If Tuac could have lived in one moment forever, it would have been that one. She let her breath linger on him then pulled away. She stroked his face, rose, and dusted herself off. Her eyes twinkled as she looked him, melting his reservations.

"The fire at camp won't get started that way." Merle grabbed some of the wood he had collected and left, laughing. In that instant, he knew he was hers forever.

He did not rush back to camp. He had so much to think about.

What do I say to her when I get there? What will she say to me? His mind raced, driven by both elation and uncertainty. He had never kissed a girl. *Did I do it right?* He questioned every interaction he had had with her. *Am I too passive? Am I good enough for her?* Doubts skittered through his thoughts. *Is she just playing with me?* At the edge of camp he saw Merle. She didn't look at him. *I didn't kiss her the right way.* His heart clenched.

Merle tilted her head and smiled at him. *There's her light.* A sentry for him in the dark. He knew she was willing to be his anchor. It was now or never. He took a deep breath. He wanted to be beside her, to smell her essence and to touch her hand. She gave him hope and light.

He walked into camp, masking his feelings so Amafi would not know what had changed between the two. Merle said nothing. They all ate in silence. Merle glanced at him now and then through the flames of the campfire but nothing else happened. As they put the fire out and laid out their bedrolls, Tuac thought he had kept their secret from Amafi.

Then the woman whispered into his ear, "Enjoy these special moments, for you never know how long they will last." She did not look back at him as she went off to her own sleeping place. Tuac stood blinking in the dark.

The following days came with fine weather and no mishaps. Merle and Tuac spent long intervals in the forest searching for firewood. The two of them could not keep their hands off each other. Tuac thought the first time they made love was the best day of his life. Merle was patient with him, knowing he had not been with anyone before. She showed him what she liked and coaxed him to tell her what he enjoyed. It was glorious. There were awkward moments, too. After their first time, Tuac worried that Merle might become pregnant. She laughed, reminding him that Amafi had taught her what herbs to take to prevent unwanted consequences.

Amafi never said a word, only smiling warmly after their forays into the forest. Those smiles told them everything they needed to know.

As they drew closer to Liat, Amafi talked to them about what to expect once they arrived at the Healer's school. Amafi avoided any discussion about the relationship between the magicians and the healers. Once, Tuac asked a question that touched on this, and she deflected it.

"We will discuss that later." She changed the subject, describing the medicinal effects of the plants she had collected in the forest.

At noon on the twenty-fifth day they crested the Barrier Mountains. Amafi halted on the narrow summit and they took in the view. Tuac marveled at the beauty of the valley below them. Flowers of every color imaginable covered the lush green hills with a plush carpet of radiant blue, blood red, glowing orange, and bright yellow. Beyond the valley they saw the mirrored surface of Luan, the Sea of Glass. Tuac had heard stories that the Luan was so pure, one could see to the floor of the ocean even when sailing far from shore.

"That is our destination," she said. At first Tuac thought Amafi was pointing to a small village at the mouth of the river where it flowed into the Sea of Glass. Tuac realized she was pointing to a gathering of buildings bisected by the river about two or three miles inland.

"The fishing village was here in the estuary when we founded Liat. It serves as the perfect place for shipping our salves and medicinal cures, without drawing attention to our Anthene community. Many of the villagers are healers and some just want to support us."

Compared to the University, Liat was simple and compact. A lattice of roads connected several clusters of buildings. Between them were open areas that looked like parks. Bridges over the river joined the sides of the town. Tuac felt drawn to this place.

As they rode down the steep incline, Tuac noticed the air was clear. He saw no smoke from kitchen or work fires. In fact, he did not see a single chimney.

What powers this town?

He also noticed that no fences kept the farm and draft animals from roaming across the valley and slopes. Flocks of sea birds floated in the calm waters of the harbor. There was harmony between Mians and animal life. The parks featured colorful gardens, and he saw small gatherings of people meditating. Here the people lived as guests of Mother Mia.

"You expected something different, didn't you?" asked Amafi.

"I have never seen another town like it. It is so beautiful and clean. Where are the fires? How do they cook? How does the blacksmith do their work?"

"The Healer's Council planned it this way." Amafi stopped her hursa and dismounted. It was too early to make camp, but Amafi gestured them down. She released her mount to graze and settled on the lush grass, motioning them to join her. "It's time that you learned the truth about the Healers, Liat, and its relationship with Basul," she said.

Tuac cringed when Amafi mentioned the University. It was still too raw for him.

Amafi continued, "It's a complicated story. I wanted you to see Liat in all its splendor before we discussed the troubled relationship between the Healers and the *other* magicians. You must decide for yourselves whether or not you wish to join Liat."

Tuac noticed her emphasis on *other*.

"Tuac, as I'm sure you learned at Basul, about one hundred turns after the University's founding, there was a schism between the Healers and the Mages of the other Arts. Basul's historians describe this in a benign way, like 'The Council decided not to study the healing arts' or 'The Council considered Healing to be a minor offshoot of the *True Arts*'."

The venom in Amafi's voice startled Tuac. Amafi was one of the sweetest persons he had ever encountered, and she seldom showed disdain for anyone. Hearing hate in her tone disturbed him even though he had no love for the mages of the University. Tuac could only imagine what pain Amafi and her colleagues must have suffered. Her face was cold and her eyes stern. He noticed that Amafi's tone also startled Merle.

"The truth is very different. We had survived Nabes, but the Council's anticipation of the next terrible enemy blinded them. They obsessed over battle magic, and rejected the Art that could heal the injured of war. They argued that Anthenes wasted resources, but what they meant was that there was no identifiable military use for our Art. Air, water, fire and stone magic had obvious military applications. Telepaths could control the minds of enemy forces or hurl objects. Gaeists could stampede livestock, infuse courage into the mounts of cavalry, and cause grasslands and forests to rise up against an army. But, they argued, Anthenes wasted resources because Anthenes did not practice battle magic. Even recognizing that our skills could heal those injured in armed conflict, the magicians felt our gift could be replaced by commonplace healers.

But we Anthenes do not just care for the health of Mians. Liat studies the interaction of nature and man, and we use our art to heal and live in peace with Mia. We are linked with the very soul of Mia. What Basul refused to accept was that our skills were similar to those of the Gaeists, but we focus on Mians' bond with the energy and flow of our planet. From that bond comes the energy we use to heal and do so much more."

The magicians rejected us, driven by their fear, ignorance and arrogance. In what amounted to a coup, the leaders of the Arts, except for the Gaiests, decided that the Art of healing Mians' bodies was unworthy. The magicians even denied us our true name, Anthenes."

Amafi gave Merle and Tuac time to take this in.

"The Council ordered the Anthene Art to be disbanded and gave each of them a choice—they could stay as servants or be banished from the Prophet's house of learning. The Council calls that event the Split, hiding the malevolence behind their decision. We refuse to let them disguise their actions and we call it the Betrayal.

The Gaeists encouraged the Healers to leave. The members of the nature Art felt a strong affinity with the Anthenes and believed that the healing Arts should remain equal with the other Arts. The Gaeists felt that over time, they could persuade the Council to reconsider their decision. If the Anthenes left, tempers would calm, and give the Gaeists room to negotiate.

"The morning after the ruling, every Anthene left along with a few senior Gaiests. The Mages were shocked. They had not believed the Anthenes would leave the safety of the University. After the Betrayal, The Council surrounded the University with wards so that no one can enter or leave without their permission." Amafi paused, her eyes locked on Tuac's. "One of the things that intrigues me about you is that you were able to pierce those wards."

Tuac blinked, remembering the strange sensation he'd experienced when he had approached the gates to leave. *Was that the result of these wards?*

"Had the Anthenes known what they would face," Amafi

continued, "they might have remained. They wandered for months, suffering huge losses from storms and wild animals which the Gaeists had usually prevented. The nature mages with them could not protect everyone. After three seasons, we reached this place, the Valley of Redemption. It is said that when the refugees came over the mountains and saw this lush valley, their tears of joy joined the river flowing through the town.

"For years, the only contact between the Mages and Anthenes were clandestine communications with the Gaeists in Basul. We wanted no other communication from the University.

"We settled in and built Liat Center. "Liat" means "wisdom". The Center serves all those, gifted and otherwise, who seek inner calm, the peace of the soul, of life, and of light. We turn no one away. The Anthenes believed it disrespected the Prophet's name to build another university available only to the gifted. We also did not want to antagonize the Council. We cannot defend ourselves against that kind of power and hoped deference would spare us.

"We grew and thrived. The Acetos of Nature Arts continued to stay in contact, often sending young magicians to the Center. We experienced cooperation between the Arts not found in Basul, and we developed practices unburdened by the agenda of war. For instance, we found plants with powerful medicinal applications. When we shared our discovery with the Gaeists, they realized that these plants store energy from the suns. We saw how animals cluster around these plants for warmth in winter, and that gave us the idea to harness the energy to power the city. The Anthenes and their magical brethren also developed sustainable farming techniques that made Liat a center for agriculture and the cultivation of medicinal herbs. We use the port to ship our products though we mask their point of origin.

"About fifty Turns after Liat's founding, the Council uncovered the contact between Liat and the Gaeists. By that time, war was a memory and the rulers of the University had recognized their foolishness, if not their arrogance. They *permitted* the Anthenes to rejoin the University, but they did not acknowledge what they had done to us. We did not trust them. We refused to abandon what we had built here.

"The Council reluctantly accepted our refusal. To mask their shame, they deflected all interest from students about Liat. They agreed to protect us. We now have wards similar to those around the University. But Liat's wards keep out only those with ill intentions. Those who come here bearing greed, hate, or longing for power see nothing but the flowers. Those seeking safety, healing, justice, or tranquility see Liat's true magnificence.

"The magicians also agreed to find acolytes for Liat. As they conduct their interviews during the Journey, they also test for the markers of Anthenes. A New One with potential gets directed to a local healer who guides them here. We trade resources and information with Basul. It is a more symbiotic relationship. The truth about the Betrayal and our existence faded, forgotten by all, other than a few senior Mages. Those Mages, I am told, agreed to pass along our history from generation to generation so the Council does not make the same mistake again. We do not forget and teach the true story to each generation.

As the Prophet said, only by understanding and remembering the past are we truly able to understand the lessons of our forefathers."

Amafi stopped. Merle reached out and grasped the woman's callused hand. Tuac felt his anger at the University rise again.

How could the University have tossed these people out like rubbish? he thought. *Mother Mia, I am so grateful these are the people who will help me.*

The three sat in silence for some time. At length, Tuac stood and looked out over the Valley of Redemption. Merle joined him and took his hand. Amafi rose and put her arms around the two. They remounted their hursas in silence and started down the steep trail.

They rode toward the main gate of Liat. As they drew closer, Tuac realized that the town and Liat were larger than he had guessed from their first view of the valley. Huge walls, as tall as three men, enclosed the Center. Massive white wooden doors marked the entrance. Each door featured the symbols of three of the magical arts. A copper arch over the doors carried a symbol Tuac had never seen: two hands holding a cup. It felt so right to have all seven symbols together this way, with the missing Art restored.

"The Nature Magicians gave us these beautiful doors. We were the ones to name them Gaeists, after a term we learned in stories from the *Curiosity*. That is also the source of our name."

"Where did they cut down the enormous trees to build this?" Merle asked.

"They did not cut it. The Gaeists searched the forest until they found a tree that was willing to give itself to protect Liat. The Anthenes believe that no life should be taken without permission. The doors are impenetrable because of the love and sacrifice of those trees. The hands in our symbol represent our custody of Mia's energy held in the cup. That symbol has been erased from Basul and most of Mia, but here it shines".

Tuac studied the symbol array, appreciating its unity but also wondering why the Anthenes would include the other Arts.

"I would have thought, given the Betrayal, that the founders of Liat would not have honored the other magicians."

After a long silence, Amafi said, "That question goes to the heart of Liat's foundation. When the Anthenes found this valley, they knew they had been blessed by The Prophet. Some Anthenes thought this sign of good fortune meant that their Art should be favored above all others. Others opposed that proposition. They felt that none of the Arts were superior to the others: they were parts of a greater whole. We needed to rise above the Betrayal, not sink into it.

"The founders reached a compromise. If we truly wanted a center of wisdom, we needed to embrace that greater whole. Yet, Anthenes would still be favored in Liat. Hence the arch—we celebrate that although we are one of a collective, we are the focal point here."

FIFTEEN

Structure is vital to our society. Without it, there is nothing but chaos and anarchy. But structure is only as good as the hearts and souls of the leaders who govern.

Introduction to the Journal of the First Anthene Headmaster

Rea's lessons progressed rapidly, which prevented her from dwelling on Tuac's departure. She had been elated when she ran into him here and felt a sense of loss now that he was gone. She was not sure what had happened. Her instructor had only told her that Tuac could not join with his Art so he was asked to leave.

When Rea did have some time to herself, she thought about her brother. She was not surprised by what had happened. She believed that Tuac was too rash and emotional to achieve the necessary inner peace and balance to become a magician. Back in Stara, Rea had often wanted to shake her little brother and tell him to grow up. It frustrated her that he had clung to the misguided belief that all Mians were basically good. She, on the other hand, knew that some people were inherently better, like magicians. Basul was no place for juvenile sentimentality. She was sure that Tuac's inability to embrace the moral supremacy of the gifted contributed to his failure.

Rea loved her brother despite his naivete, and perhaps because of it. There was nothing she would not do for him, and she was now concerned. Because their parents were elderly and often busy with the store, Rea had always kept an eye on Tuac, making sure he was safe. She had allowed others to pick on him, hoping he would grow tougher. But she never let it go too far. Several boys had almost injured Tuac before Rea stepped in. She made sure Tuac never knew about her help, as she wanted him to fend for himself. But she doubted that he had developed true self-sufficiency.

Now that she grappled with what had happened to Tuac, she realized she had never considered who would protect him after she left on her Journey. She knew Tuac was vulnerable to predators. He would give someone the shirt off his back and had done so more than once, almost dying from a horrible cold after one instance. That was her little brother, goofy but kind-hearted.

Who will take care of him?

Rea wished Tuac was more like her. Emotions created weakness, and so were tools to be manipulated. She reserved her affection for her parents and her brother. She distrusted the idea of friendship. She had let down her walls in the past, only to be rewarded with disloyalty or dishonesty. Once, she had befriended the baker's son. For weeks, they did everything together. But he mistook friendship for something more. On the longest night of the year, the boy convinced Rea to come to the hilltop so they could watch the stars. When they arrived, he made his true intentions known. He only wanted one thing. After beating him to a pulp, she stole his clothes and made him walk back to town naked. Rea doubted that he would ever disrespect another girl, and it pleased her to have taught him a lesson.

Would Tuac ever be able to see the true nature of people? she wondered.

Rea buried herself in her studies to avoid thinking about her brother. The intellectual environment suited Rea. Here, everyone was equal and the best mages were rewarded. No politics. No ulterior motives. No need to trust anyone but oneself.

Rea was a quick study and a natural. She rose to the head of her class. She was enrolled in an advanced class for Fire Walkers and excelled there, too. Soon, one of the teachers picked her to be an intern allowing her access to more books, more study time, and more magic.

She vowed that she would be the best member of the Fire Arts. She would make a name for herself. And when she did, she would have enough power to protect Tuac. Rea knew she was supposed to live a solitary life, but her sibling needed her.

Ba'al and Ki'lel walked together across the campus after a Council meeting.

"Rea is powerful," Ba'al said. "We have to manage her carefully after the debacle with her brother. What is the status of Tuac? We must make sure he does not fall into Nabes' hands. The boy is undisciplined and, if he has any magical ability, Nabes will be able to exploit it."

"My sources tell me that he is with the Anthenes," Ki'lel

said. "They want to consult the ancient texts and make sure they understand and apply the Prophet's directive appropriately in Tuac's case. They have never had to deal with this kind of situation, since we find their acolytes for them. They feel we failed to find his true Art and that he should be allowed to stay with them. In fact, they hope he can learn to be a healer. You know how the Anthenes are."

Ba'al glanced at him, startled by his choice of words. Others might accuse Ki'lel of suggesting the healers were magicians. She knew he did not believe that, but his language was a bit too casual even for her.

"They are planning to keep Tuac contained in the meantime," Ki'lel said. "Chorra speaks to the Anthenes often. The Anthenes trust her, since she is the Acetos of the Gaeists. I think we should wait to see what develops in Liat. I also think it best that Eis not get a second chance to deal with Tuac. He only knows one way to solve problems and I believe we should explore other options."

"Be careful. I give you considerable leeway because I know your true heart and I trust you. But there are limits. I will discuss the issue with Argent myself. It is time I take matters into my own hands." Rebuke colored her tone.

Ki'lel nodded to her. "Understood, and I apologize if you believe I have failed you. You know I'm loyal to you and I will do what I need to do. I just worry that Eis savors certain aspects of his job too much."

They reached Ba'al's office and she walked inside, sending Ki'lel away with a small gesture of dismissal. She did not disagree with Ki'lel's perception, but Eis served a purpose. He was willing to do what was necessary. She believed there was only one way to deal with one like Tuac. The Anthenes would test him, and they would reach the same conclusion. It was only a matter of time.

But time was not on Basul's side.

Merle and Tuac joined other students in a compact, comfortable dormitory. They had a few weeks to acclimate and were able to use the time to see each other, often at night. There were no rules to forbid it, but they did have to avoid being out after curfew. The dormitories gave each student a room of their own, with common eating areas and bathrooms. That allowed Merle and Tuac private time, which they used both for searching conversations and lovemaking. Their bond deepened.

When he was not with Merle, Tuac wandered the halls of Liat. He felt at ease with his fellow students, each of whom had come to Liat seeking acceptance and hoping to contribute. Tuac was driven by a larger mission, though if he had been given the choice, he would have stayed in Liat's community.

Once his formal education began, Tuac realized that Liat was nothing like the University. The University's teaching regime was regimented, and every stage was a step one passed or failed. The process reflected the magicians' black-and-white view of the world.

Tuac learned from his teachers at Liat that magic was far more nuanced. All magic was driven by the same thing, a Mian's connection to planet. One's success as a magician depended on training one's mind to direct that energy. Each mind was different, so the lessons took into account the individuality of the students. The key was meditation.

The University also used meditation, but primarily during the selection process. The magicians saw no value in communing with one's Art after one had joined with it. The Art was the user's to command, and meditation was only a tool to identify their Art. Anthenes, in contrast, considered magic to be a partnership that grew with mutual respect between the user and Mia. Meditation was the door to joining one's Art, but also the way one cultivated symbiotic growth.

The differences between the University's and Liat's understanding of magic were more than theoretical. Liat's techniques for teaching were also different. At the University, teachers gave the lessons and students repeated them, learning by rote and repetition without deeper appreciation and gratitude. All Tuac had done in his University classes was repeat exercises. When he learned one spell, he started on the next.

Here at Liat, the training was holistic and grounded in love. Tuac's first class was called Understanding Magic and was taught by Headmaster Argent, who was unassuming and approachable, welcoming questions and delighting in dialogue. A short, portly fellow, he had a soft voice which belied his status in Liat. In his class, the students read revered texts about the nature of magic.

"I welcome you all to Liat," he said on their first day. "You have come here, some by intrigue and others by long arduous voyages—" he nodded at Tuac, "—to learn Mia's most noble, powerful, and humble Art, that of healing the Mian body. While we are called 'healers,' that phrase minimizes the true nature of our Art. If you study and work hard, you will be able to see into the hearts of other Mians. You will be able to see what ails them, both physically and mentally. And you will be able to assist them in remedying their ailments. You will have the power of life and death, happiness and sorrow. Do not underestimate the power of the Anthene."

This description of Liat's Art surprised Tuac, who had never thought that healers did anything other than tending bruises, broken bones, and fevers. Yet now Tuac recalled instances when the local healer in Stara had sought out those in trouble, and had soothed them emotionally as well as healed them physically. Healers attended funerals in the village and spoke to the bereaved, comforting them. Tuac remembered feeling relieved after such a conversation at the memorial for a school friend.

"Today, we start your trek by learning the foundation of magic," the Headmaster said. "Magic is not just about power. Magic is about responsibility. One can only master one's Art when one understands the balance between the two."

Tuac considered this. The University's magicians called those with ability "gifted". The word reflected their belief in their inherent superiority. For Anthenes, though, magic was a call to duty, an act of service to Mia and her people. Tuac preferred this approach. He did not want to be feared, he wanted to be serve others. He did not want to use his power to dominate, but rather to help. Liat's approach to magic comforted him. He belonged here.

The Headmaster's lessons on the fundamentals of magic captivated Tuac more than any class at the University had done. Tuac learned that each Mian had the ability to perform magic, but only some Mians had the innate ability to harness it.

The Headmaster said, "Have you ever been to a carnival and wondered how the performers were able to perform a difficult trick? Or have you ever had a friend or sibling who could finish your sentences? These are acts of those with magical ability. They can do small things that bring us joy or relief, even if they are not as powerful as Anthenes or magicians." Tuac thought of a local blacksmith who could repair pots and pans by reshaping the metal in ways Tuac had not thought possible. Now he understood that the blacksmith was using the Stone Mover magic and had never realized it.

Next, the Headmaster explained why some people were more powerful than others. Anthenes had spent generations studying this issue and determined that magical abilities tended to be stronger in certain families and in certain regions of Mia. Over time, since the Prophet had instituted the Journey, magical gifts had become less powerful and rarer.

The University and Liat responded differently to this trend. The University refused to expand its search to include new territories and families, while Liat accepted everyone. As a result, the University's ranks had thinned while the Anthenes sustained their numbers. Tuac remembered Ki'lel and Meaich welcoming his gift because previous Journeys had yielded few potential magicians.

After a few sessions devoted to magical history and philosophy, the lessons turned to practical applications of magic. Tuac applied himself with fervor, though these lessons were tiring and frustrating. After a few weeks, he settled into a daily routine. He started the day at breakfast with his dorm mates, then they had rigorous physical education where he learned different stances and movements to calm his mind. Then they ate the afternoon meal, and attended a discussion session where students talked about their backgrounds and experiences in magic. Their afternoon class emphasized aspects of healing, followed by two hours reading books ranging from the *Prophet's Teachings* to one called *The 7 Arts: What We All Share*. His day finished with a small meal and a little time to relax. He enjoyed schooling, even if he felt awkward and graceless during his physical exercises. His only misgiving was that he had little private time with Merle.

One evening, after a long study session, he was walking back to the dorm when he accidentally bumped into someone.

"Excuse me sir," Tuac blurted, "I'm sorry, I was distracted." Tuac blurted out. Then he recognized the Headmaster.

"You're Tuac, correct?" the man said. "Amafi told me about you. How do you like your studies here?"

"It is beautiful and peaceful. I feel very much at home here, sir."

"Please, call me Argent." He studied Tuac, who felt a gentle probe from the Headmaster's magic. Tuac resisted, not out of anger but out of fear. He did not want anyone to know how fragile he felt.

"Interesting," Argent said, tilting his head. His probing stopped.

"Tuac, you pose a bit of challenge for Liat. Our balance with Basul is tenuous. There are some among us who want a more formal alliance and feel that we should forgive and forget. Others do not believe that the Council has accepted that their forebears' arrogance caused the Betrayal. I see both sides, which is why I was elected to lead Liat. I try to avoid situations that complicate our relationship with the University.

"Your arrival means we must take up this argument again. They are some who are angry that you are here and demand that we return you to them. We can surrender you in exchange for stronger ties, or we can honor our commitment to being a safe harbor and risk their ire. It is a difficult choice. What do you think I should do?"

Tuac gaped. It had never occurred to him that the University would want him back. It made no sense—they had given him a choice, he had taken it, yet now they wanted Liat to return him. Given all that Liat stood for, why would they even consider this request?

I need to be careful here, Tuac thought.

"Argent, I can't answer your question. I have no idea why the University wants me back. They made it clear that I did not meet their expectations. To them, I am a boy with no apparent gift.

"As for your choice, am I not entitled to make my own decisions? Isn't that what the Anthenes did when they left the University? I was told that I have a greater purpose, and to fulfill it I needed to come here. I don't understand my role, but I owe it to my family to protect them and I swore to avenge Meiach's death." Tuac kept his voice measured and his tone respectful, though he was angry.

"Again, interesting." Argent started walking, gesturing for Tuac to join him. Argent led him away from Liat's center, heading toward a low hill north of the school.

Tuac saw two guards standing on either side of a door into the hill. When they were still some distance away, Tuac stopped. The two guards were magicians—one a Fire Walker and other an Air Rider.

Argent stopped when he did. "I've decided to trust my instincts and offer you sanctuary. I am also going to share with you our most important secret, one that only a few here at Liat know.

"Our ties to the University are closer than many Anthenes realize. As you know, there were discussions of the Anthenes rejoining the University. The Council's invitation was not altruistic. They also had concerns that we would be vulnerable to attack from those seeking our most treasured treatises, writings that concern the heart of magic. It troubled the University's Acetos that we were not only going to preserve the past but also continue our studies of Mia's relationship to her people. They worried that our studies might fall into the wrong hands.

"We chose to maintain our independence, but there was a cost. We agreed to keep certain historical texts and magical tomes in a secure location, the Alcove under this hill. Of course, we would share our research with the leaders of the other Arts. In turn, Basul provided the wards that protect Liat and two seasoned magicians always guard the Alcove. The Arts rotate their posts among themselves. The Alcove's wards are so strong and intricate that only the Acetos and the Headmaster know how to unlock them. The guards live in the Alcove so the Anthenes rarely see them.

Argent paused at the base of the hill. "Tuac, I sense a mystery about you, and I suspect that we can shed some light on it by consulting some of the ancient texts in the Alcove.

At the entrance, Argent nodded to the two guards and they nodded back. As Tuac tried to pass, one guard, an Air Rider, intercepted him. She rose a few inches and glided into his path. Tuac felt his neck tingle and knew that the guard was weaving protective spells. She was creating a wall of wind, and coiling another wind into a fist to strike at him. Tuac balked. He wanted to bolt.

Argent caught the boy's startled expression. The Headmaster put a hand on Tuac's shoulder. Tuac could feel reassurance flow into him.

"He's with me," Argent said to the guard. The Air Rider raised her eyebrows but said nothing. She also did not move.

"I understand the rules," Argent's voice held an edge of command. "He is with me and though you are tasked to guard the Alcove, ultimately, I am in charge. You serve here at the discretion of the Anthenes, and me. If you need me to contact Ba'al to clarify this, I will. I am entitled to bring guests with me."

After a long moment, the Air Rider relented and Tuac felt her winds dissipate. She glided back to her position. Tuac almost admired her beauty and grace. Almost.

Argent strode through the door with Tuac beside him. They entered a circular room with seven doors. Three to the left, three to the right and a larger, more ornate door in front of them.

"We must be quick here," Argent said in a low voice. "I was bluffing. Ba'al would neither let you in here nor bow to my claim of authority over the Alcove. It is a complicated relationship and I have blurred some of the lines. No one other than the Head of the University or a master of one of the Seven Arts is permitted in here without approvals from all of the Council and me. Bringing you inside might create trouble for me and Liat. But desperate times call for desperate measures, and there is something about you that I cannot explain. It's best that we accomplish what we came to do and get out before the guards check with the Council." Argent opened the ornate door and beckoned Tuac to follow.

The hallway descended steeply. Handrails lined the passage and lights guided their way. The incline led to a circular stairwell. They went down three rotations, and the stair ended in another circular room. The shallow dome of its ceiling was ten feet high. Tuac marveled at the magical ability it must have taken to hollow out the room.

"The Stone Movers created the Alcove and all of the rooms are subterranean," Argent said, his voice reverent.

In the subtle pattern of the ceiling Tuac saw the seven symbols of the Arts. It pleased him to see the symbols in their rightful grouping. In Liat, all magic was welcome.

This room had only one door. Argent placed his hand on the latch, said a few words under his breath, and Tuac saw a shimmer of force. Sensation washed over Tuac, making his skin tingle. His vision sharpened and he could hear his heartbeat.

Argent noticed Tuac's reaction.

"This is the second time I've seen you respond to magic. While skilled magicians can feel the stirring of Mia's currents, you should not be this sensitive to more sophisticated spells. The one I just used is powerful but subtle. Only the Masters and Acetos would be able to sense it. My instincts are proving right."

Tuac shrugged, unsure if he should answer. Argent stepped through the door and Tuac followed him. He was not prepared for what he would find.

Sixteen

Magicians have lost their way. They believe that to protect, they must control. To control, they obfuscate. True protection can only come with honesty, information, learning, sharing and benevolence. The Chamber will serve as a monument to the Prophet's teachings. It will be ready when the time comes, though shrouded in secrecy until then.

The Journal of Armac, the First Headmaster of Liat at the time of the Treaty Ending the Betrayal

The room of his dreams was real! Tuac trembled. These were the seven doors that would not open for him. He now recognized all of the symbols, including the last one. *How could I have envisioned this room? Argent said it is unknown to all but a select few.*

As he surveyed the space, he was struck by the detail and accuracy of his dream. Each of the symbols were the same size.

The doors were identical. Even their spacing was consistent with how he had seen it in his dreams.

I have been in this room!

As Tuac took in the rest of the room he noticed one difference. In his dream, there was no carpet. He stared at the decorative rug. It bothered him. It was not supposed to be there.

"I always thought it was odd that in the middle of this cavern, there would be creature comfort like this carpet," said the Argent. "Rumor has it that the floor is decorated with a carving of the two suns of Mia, with six rays of sunlight stretching out, the symbol of the University. The magicians wanted to make everyone know that this room was their domain. Over time, the carvings wore down. The official story is that the Council covered the floor, believing it disrespectful to leave the University's coat of arms in a tattered state. Another theory, one that I believe, is they wanted to cover it since it was a reminder of the Betrayal. I don't know what actually lies underneath."

"I have been here before," Tuac whispered.

"What? You've been here before? That's impossible, Tuac."

"I can't explain it either, Argent, but I have seen this room in my dreams. I saw the carving—it was not the symbol of the University. Instead of the six rays of sunshine, there were seven. All were inlaid with rich colors—the ones associated with each of the magical Arts and a rainbow for the seventh ray. And the suns in my dream were not the usual dull yellow. One blazed white and one gleamed as black as a starless sky. I saw each of the seven doors, but at the time I did not recognize the Anthene door.

"It makes no sense. How could I have seen this when I have never been here? And you said this room was a secret."

Argent rubbed his face, which had gone pale, with his hands.

He moved toward one corner of the carpet and tried to lift it. "Come here and help me. Let's see what this hides."

Tuac was scared. Together the two rolled the corner of the carpet back. They revealed the carving, first one circle, then the second, and finally the seven rays from Mia's two suns. They were faded, with only traces of color caught in the deepest grooves. Argent stared, nodded, then abruptly rolled the carpet back.

"Do not talk about your dream!" Argent hissed. "If anyone who knows about the Chamber finds out about it, you would be in danger. Come with me." Argent strode to the Anthene door and opened it. Argent spoke a complex phrase, and warm, magical light bloomed in a small room with worn furniture, chairs with faded cushions and a table whose surface was smoothed by generations of hands. Argent pulled down a book titled *Understanding the Refuge* and gave it to Tuac. The first page of the book featured an etching of the Chamber.

Argent said, "The Chamber was intended it to be a safe haven to study and find true enlightenment. Each Art has its own room and may place there whatever tomes it sees fit. But the rooms are small, forcing each Art to select only their most important texts. *Understanding the Refuge* is the Anthene's most sacred text."

Tuac took the book reverently. As soon as he touched it, he felt a tingle and a flash of vertigo. He shook his head to clear it.

Where is Argent? Tuac spun, realizing he was alone there. Panic rose in his chest. The furniture had changed. He saw bright cushions and crisp wooden surfaces that looked new. He backed out of the room into the center of the Chamber.

The carpet was gone, and the carvings' bright color matched his dreams, vibrant and alive. There was a delicate balance, almost a dance, between the two suns. Tuac froze when he noticed seven other figures in the room with him.

No, I am not here in this time or place. This is another vision.

A figure dressed in the brown robes of the Stone Movers spoke.

"Armac, as Headmaster, you have a duty to all magicians. This monument you are building to the Prophet can only lead to trouble if others come here and find out the truth."

Armac, clothed in white with a rainbow sash, said, "Sheel, do not presume to lecture me. Let's be very clear here. It was the Council who expelled the Anthenes. It was Basul's Betrayal. You cannot come to Liat and challenge all we have built. We remain committed to the Prophet's Teachings. The Prophet made it clear that if we do not plan for the future by remembering the sins of the past, we will be ill-prepared when danger appears.

"The Council long ago decided it was best to diffuse power and to remain aloof. However, the Council's refusal to use magic for the good of all created a vacuum filled by an Emperor who seeks only power and a Church that perverts the Prophet's words in order to scare Mians into submission. The acrimony between the branches of Mia's government invites evil. If that happens, Mians will need this room.

"If Nabes returns, Reunification must happen and the Chamber will be needed to identify the Reunifer. The Council accepted our terms for co-existence. So, Sheel, will you abide by the Treaty or not?"

Sheel looked to the others, each cloaked in the colors of their Arts. One after another, they nodded, and Sheel relented.

Armac moved to the white sun and held out his hands. Sheel took Armac's hand, and one by one the other Masters joined the circle. The room began to hum with magical energy.

The seven chanted in unison: "Prophet, lead us, guide us, and empower the Reunifer to us to save us from Nabes." There was a sharp snap and the etching glowed. As the glow faded, the seven dropped hands and started to file out, Armac leading them.

Sheel stayed at the back with the Fire Walker.

"Sheel, you don't actually believe this?" the Fire Walker said. "If a Reunifer comes into their magic, Mia will be destroyed."

Sheel looked at the Fire Walker and the overlapping discs of the two suns. With a single harsh word, he cracked the white sun from top to bottom. The spell cast moments before was broken. Only Sheel and the Fire Walker knew this, as the crack was barely noticeable.

"What have you done, Sheel?"

"Consider it a test for the Reunifier. They must start in this room, and repair the spell before they can be considered fit to rule. I have spoken to the others on the Council and we all agree. We will control the Journey and make it as difficult as possible for the Reunifer to reach Liat. I do not believe all of this mythology. We do not need the Reunifier to protect Mia, and I have just insured that the Reunifier can only ascend under the control of the Council."

With a wave of dizziness, Tuac's mind snapped back to the present. Argent stood there, beckoning Tuac to follow. Tuac struggled to process what he had seen and was grateful that Argent had not noticed anything. Tuac considered whether or not to tell Argent what had happened, but decided not to. Tuac needed time, and he was not sure how much he should trust Argent given that the Council was pressuring the Headmaster.

He heard Argent say something about keeping *Understanding the Refuge* and then Tuac looked at the book.

"Argent, I appreciate your willingness to protect me and to

allow me to study this sacred text. But if anyone caught me with it, they might ask questions neither of us want to answer."

Argent nodded. "You are wise beyond your years. There are plenty of other books and much to learn in the meantime." He took the book from Tuac and reshelved it. They left the Chamber, and walked out of the Alcove, heading back to the school grounds.

Later, when Tuac spoke to Merle, she shook her head. She trusted her beloved, but it was hard for her not to be skeptical about what he told her.

She said, "You think you went back in time to when this Alcove was created? You saw the Magicians and the Headmaster cooperating to create a secret room that awaits the Unifier?"

Tuac reached for her hand to calm her. "Reunifer, not unifier," he said. "I don't understand why or how, but somehow I was meant to see what really happened in that room. It doesn't match the story Argent knows. The Council sabotaged the spell.

"The Watcher said I needed to come here to unlock the power of Mia's suns. I don't know what he meant, but I know that the Chamber holds the key to defeating Nabes."

Merle's brows knit with worry, which unsettled Tuac. Since they had first met, Merle had been the brave one. He had never seen Merle rattled like this.

"So now what?" she asked.

Tuac looked out the window of the dormitory. The valley of Liat lay tranquil as Mia's first sun rose. It had been a long night and he was tired. He wanted to run and hide, but he knew he had to stay. Too many people were now involved in his fate—

Argent had risked his status with Ba'al. The Anthenes had protected him and risked the Council's ire. And of course there was Merle.

"Come to bed." Tuac said. "I don't know what the future holds. What I do know is that I need to feel you next to me. It's the only time I feel whole."

Merle smiled and stroked his cheek. "That makes two of us."

Argent returned to his room. His quarters were modest, in keeping with Anthene tradition. Unlike their brethren the Magicians, being Headmaster of the Anthene Art was about sacrifice, not about authority or power. To Anthenes, less was more—resources should go to the common good, riches to feed the poor, magic to serve all of Mia. Magicians were guided by their arrogance and thirst for power. They also felt entitled to luxuriate in the fruits of their endeavors.

Argent was troubled by what he had witnessed. He knew taking the boy to their most sacred place was risky. But given what he had heard, he suspected that the texts in the Alcove would help him understand this boy. It wasn't just Tuac's prior vision of the Chamber that troubled him. The fact that Tuac felt at ease at the Alcove was equally perplexing. Although Argent had unlocked the wards, Tuac should still have experienced uncomfortable side effects. Yet the boy had entered the Alcove and the Chamber without exhibiting any nausea or shortness of breath. Argent had prepared a curative spell to ameliorate Tuac's symptoms, but the spell was not necessary.

This made no sense. It was like Tuac belonged there. It took Argent years and many painful failures to enter that revered spot without feeling the wrath of the wards, and somehow this boy, not even of age, had walked in without any resistance.

Argent went to his bureau. He had always liked this piece of furniture. It was supposed to be one of the original pieces made in Liat. The bureau was three cubits high and about as wide. It could hold more than any Anthene Headmaster would own, but everyone who had occupied this room had valued its age and grace.

He opened the top drawer and pulled out a frame of polished metal that held a pane of silvered glass. When Ba'al had contacted Argent a few days after Tuac arrived in Liat, Argent learned that this device could be used by anyone with magic, even an Anthene. All of his prior contacts with Basul had happened in person. But that night, while Argent prepared for bed, an image of Ba'al had appeared in his chamber. Ba'al had explained that Nabes had emerged and asserted that the boy was a threat to Mia's existence. When Argent asked her why, she gave no explanation. In fact, Ba'al had been inconsistent on the matter—first asserting the Council's domain over magic and then describing Tuac as having minimal aptitude at best. It did not take long for Argent to figure out Ba'al was being evasive and not giving him all the facts.

Argent had not been sure what to make of Ba'al's communication. He had met with Amafi shortly after she arrived. She explained that Tuac sought her out after his interaction with the being called the Watcher. While curious, it did not suggest anything nefarious. Yet, Ba'al was very worried about Tuac and Argent felt that Ba'al's urgency was sincere.

In order to avoid escalating the situation, Argent had promised to keep Ba'al abreast of how the boy was doing. Since then, he had had regular conversations with Ba'al and informed her that Liat was testing Tuac to confirm the Anthenes' suspicion that he could become proficient in the healing Arts. He had not repeated Amafi's story, figuring Ba'al would only seize on it as a reason to want Tuac back. Ba'al pressed Argent each time they talked, growing more and more insistent that Tuac be returned to Basul.

This communication was likely to be different. As much as Argent wanted to keep the peace with Basul, he could neither reveal to Ba'al what had just happened nor could he hand the boy over. It was clear that the Council had already made up its mind about Tuac. As the Anthenes had suffered much from the Council's dogmatic approach, the Council's evaluation of the boy made Argent uneasy. He sensed that Tuac was special, but could not yet determine whether the boy was an ally or a potential agent of Nabes. The Anthene Headmaster was not going to condemn an innocent without clear evidence. He sighed and started the incantation that Ba'al had taught him for using the tablet:

"Prophet, bring me to my brethren. I open myself. Ba'al, come to me." The tablet emitted a shimmering light that enlarged and formed the spectral image of Ba'al.

"Ah, there you are. I was wondering when I would get my next report. What news do you have for me today, Argent? Have you finally realized you are wasting your time with Tuac?" Ba'al said.

"Quite the contrary, Ba'al. I have met the boy. He is resourceful and I believe he has potential. He is entitled to sanctuary here and we will help him realize his power. Given what you said about Nabes' rising, we will need every Anthene."

"I've suffered this situation long enough. We want him back, Argent. Now. You know the rules of the Treaty. Basul governs the Direction. The Council will determine whether Tuac is an Anthene."

Argent studied Ba'al's translucent face. She was stern, resolute, and hiding something. He suspected that Ba'al wanted this boy for more than testing. After a long silence, Argent responded.

"I am afraid, Ba'al, your knowledge of the Treaty is not quite complete. The document grants Basul only the right to control the Direction for one of age. In this case, Tuac has not yet undertaken his Journey. So, his choices are outside of your jurisdiction, and we have offered him safe quarter until he makes his decision. That will not be for several months, plenty of time for him to learn to become an Anthene. And per the Treaty, once a Mian has passed the test to become an Anthene you are prohibited from making any claim on them. This was part of the Treaty's purpose, granting Anthenes permission to teach those who came here seeking a safe haven. Will you threaten the foundation of our rapprochement?"

Argent's interpretation of the Treaty was precise, but the Anthenes had little power if Basul wanted to push the issue. Argent saw Ba'al scowl and was grateful that he was addressing her specter.

"I have no wish to revisit the Treaty's terms. But understand there is a limit to my patience. And I will hold you responsible if Tuac jeopardizes Mia's security." Ba'al waved her hand and ended the communication.

Argent knew he could not resist Ba'al indefinitely. He would have little time to unravel the mystery of Tuac's abilities.

"Damn him!" Ba'al snarled. Mi, the Acetos of Telepathy, stepped backwards. Eis's eyes gleamed with irritation.

"The Anthenes have always been intractable," Eis said. "Ba'al, let me take a group of magicians to extract the boy. We will keep casualties to a minimum."

"As much as I am tempted, Eis, no. Now is not the time to start another rupture with the Anthenes. I am not happy about Argent's power play, but he is correct about the Treaty. Of course the Headmaster would know that document down to its finest details. We should have intercepted Tuac before he got to Liat. Now we will have to take other measures.

"Mi, please contact our representative in the Emperor's court. The Emperor believes that brute force works better than negotiation. Perhaps we can use this to our advantage and have the Emperor's troops bring the boy back before Nabes gets to him. The Emperor's troops will need our guidance to get past Liat's wards. In the meantime, Eis, focus on the acolytes. We will need every mage if we are to withstand what is coming."

She dismissed Eis and Mi. Ba'al poured herself a glass of wine and stared into her fireplace. Despite its warmth, Ba'al felt chilled to the bone. Things were spinning out of control and Argent was playing a very dangerous game. Ba'al hoped it would not endanger Mia.

Esa, the commander of Emperor Hahook's military, watched the University's ambassador leave the throne room. To Esa's surprise, the ambassador had conveyed a request that the Emperor's forces arrest arrest a boy in distant Liat. For some reason, the University did not want to engage the Anthenes. Ba'al wanted the Emperor to do the magicians' dirty work.

"Emperor, this is our moment," Esa said. "The mages have asked us to fix their petty problem. We can use a greater show of force than they expect and, if we eliminate the boy, they will be in our debt. They will also learn the power of our new resources."

Emperor Hahook cut her off. "Stop!" he hissed. "Do not discuss the armory. Even in my inner sanctum I cannot evade the prying eyes and ears of the *mages* and the *Anthenes*".

Esa was no fool. Hahook had often ranted about kissing the feet of Ba'al and the indignity of pleading for healers from Liat. The Emperor chaffed at the rules, the rationing of magic, and the Journey, all of which constrained the growth and power of the Empire.

Esa shared the Emperor's conviction that the mages did not do enough for Mia. But her vision of a world order included the University and Liat, though they would be under the Empire's control. The Emperor's tone caused Esa to wonder if there would even be a place for magicians in Hahook's domain.

"Esa, I am talking to you!" Hahook barked.

Esa snapped to attention. Her moral quandary would have to wait. She needed to focus on her Emperor or the results could be fatal.

"I am sorry, Emperor. We can march on Liat by the next moon. Ba'al has given us an excuse to deploy our troops and when she learns what we can do, it will be too late. Ba'al will have no choice but to swear fealty to you. It will dismantle the triumvirate and the Empire can assume its rightful role as the supreme protector of Mia."

Esa's quick response pleased The Emperor. "Do it. Make this a total victory. No survivors."

The Emperor dismissed Esa and turned toward his chambers. As he opened his bedroom door, Esa heard the cries of multiple young voices. The Emperor called them his toys. Esa smelled sweat and blood, and knew that Hakook would need new distractions soon. Esa fought nausea as she left the room. Perhaps this Emperor was not the right steward for Mia.

SEVENTEEN

We divide people into bad or good, yet we are each capable of being either. Often, we do one in the name of the other. At some point, each of us faces a choice that will define us. Whether we stand for morality, humanity, and order, or whether we try to undermine those things. The truly evil are not only those who undermine justice, but also those who remain silent when evil is done.

Journal of Armac, the First Anthene of Liat, from his speech celebrating the opening of Liat

Tuac had met with Argent several times since their visit to the Chamber. First, it was to give Tuac books to study and later to check on his progress. During their most recent conversation, Argent had explained that Ba'al had demanded several times that Tuac return to the University. He said that the Anthenes had given Tuac the right to stay with them in Liat. But Argent had told Tuac that he must unlock his power so that he could officially join Liat. As Tuac had failed to find his true Art at the University, Argent did not understand Ba'al's request. Tuac realized Ba'al would only stop harassing him when he came into his Anthene magic. Then he could focus on his role in the battle against Nabes.

Tuac believed that the path to his Anthene magic lay in the Chamber. In meditation he returned there, seeking answers. Closing his eyes, he approached the hill and walked to the Alcove doors. There were no guards, so he continued to the Chamber. There, Tuac studied the etchings on the floor and the doors. First, he went to the Anthene door, thinking he had found his true nature. But it did not open. Then he would try a different door. None of the doors would open. His panic rose and shattered his concentration.

Tuac wondered if he was not focusing the right way. He read everything he could on meditation. Though his research did not help him unlock his magical ability, in Liat's texts Tuac found writings on balance and connection. The idea of being in tune with all of Mia resonated with him.

He added Yiao, a moving meditation, to his morning routine, hoping to dissolve the wall between his physical and spiritual state. At first, he practiced the movements in private because he felt awkward. Soon his confidence overshadowed his fear of clumsiness, and he joined the communal session.

Every morning, he woke at firstrise and walked to the garden where Anthenes of all ages gathered to practice Yiao. He found comfort in the shared spiritual exercise. It fed a hunger that he had not known he had. A group of people with particular spiritual clarity rotated their leadership of the class.

Tuac especially liked Maeva. She was tall and muscular, yet lithe and feminine. Her deep red hair glistened. Even in the dark of the early morning, her spirit shone over them. Maeva's words wrapped Tuac in warmth. Though the practice was well attended, Tuac felt that she spoke to him in particular.

"Breathe. Feel the air fill your lungs, and then exhale. Imagine your heart beating. Not just blood, but energy and magic. Feel the strength. Feel the balance. Feel your soul. See your light. See your dark.

"What makes each of us whole is not that we are either light or dark, good or evil. We are all both. Do not fear the unknown, do not run from hate, do not give in to sadness or despair, do not blame death. All of these things make us who we are. They define our character. They shape our decisions. And ultimately, they all serve to guide us through life.

"We cannot fight evil if we do not learn that good, too, can be used to do harm. We cannot serve good if we do not learn that evil can result from good intentions. We cannot know love until we learn that we cannot force our will on those we care about simply because we believe we know what is best for them.

"We are peaceful warriors. We protect the weak and heal the injured. Remember that we do these things out of duty, not for reward or acclaim. We seek to balance the scales, knowing we will err and when we do, we will try again." Maeva finished her session. Everyone and everything in the garden, even the wind and the animals, were silent.

Tuac picked up his cloak, wiping the sweat from his brow.

"Tuac, can you please come here?" Maeva said. Surprised, Tuac walked to her. She radiated power and majesty. Her smile was as bright as Mia's suns and her eyes the cobalt blue of the ocean.

"Well, young man. You and I will be spending some time together." She smiled.

Tuac blinked and cocked an eyebrow.

"I gather that Argent has not spoken to you yet. I will be your new instructor. We will try to resolve this block you're suffering from. I must warn you that I'm a demanding teacher, and I intend to push you physically and mentally. Are you up to the task, my cub?"

Tuac tensed. "Cub?"

"As in brea cub. Breas are majestic beasts that rule the forest. From a distance they seem cuddly, which is why their likeness is a common soft toy for children. In reality, you should not approach either a cub or the adult. You remind me of a brea cub. You are innocent, but power flows from you. If you are not careful, your darkness will consume that power. My role is to help you understand your power and harness it, to control the dark and feed your light."

Tuac shook his head. "I don't understand. How can controlling my darkness feed my light? Good is supposed to fight evil, and evil cannot be a building block of good. That makes no sense!" He blurted this out before recalling the words of her lesson that morning. Tuac shrank back, expecting a rebuke which did not come.

Maeva studied him with kind eyes. "You are ready for your first lesson. Today we will consider the true nature of magic, good and evil. Walk with me." Maeva turned and strode away, her forest green robe rippling as she crossed the lawn. The animals did not move when she approached, because they felt no fear of her. She was one with them.

Tuac had to rush to match her long stride.

"It took you long enough to catch me. What did you learn while you were running?"

Tuac struggled to catch his breath at this pace. He did not know how to answer her question.

"I learned that you are very fast!"

Maeva stifled a laugh. "Anything else?"

Tuac, catching a second wind, settled into his own long stride. He thought of what else he had observed.

"You are one with this place. I don't know why or how, though."

"Good!" Maeva said. She spun around. Tuac stumbled but stopped without colliding with her. "Excellent work. I *am* one with this place. Did you notice how you became more aligned with this place when you matched my stride? Does that make sense to you, my cub?"

Tuac looked at her and did not know what to make of the question. He could tell her no, but that might be the wrong answer. He could say yes, but that would not be honest. He opted for truthfulness over success.

"No, it doesn't. I know you're an Anthene and not a Gaeist, so I am baffled. The only thing I feel is your connection to everything and everyone. When I am around you, even in the back row of the morning sessions, I feel your warmth, your passion, your light." He blushed. He was not attracted to Maeva in a physical sense. His true love was Merle. But, in this moment, he was drawn to Maeva's mind and spirit.

Maeva tilted her head, studying him. He knew Anthenes could not read minds, but they could feel souls. Tuac could not hide from her regard, and he did not want to.

"Hmmm," she said. Then she turned and walked on. Tuac jogged to catch up and strode beside her.

In twenty minutes, they were no longer in Liat. Tuac saw a path through the lush grass that led to an outcropping. As they got nearer, he saw ruins of a building, stone walls roofed by the sky.

When they arrived, Maeva said, "These were here when we founded Liat. We do not know much, but we do know that this culture was anchored in law and justice. We have found records of their people—births, deaths, marriages, crimes and sentences. We think this was one of their temples. They worshipped the gods in the stars and believed in a greater divine path. Their society ended during the Great Destruction. Our destination lies over there," Maeva pointed beyond the ruins to a mound. Seven pillars rose skyward from its top.

As they got closer, Tuac saw that they were engraved with the symbols of the Arts, the six he knew from the University and one for the Anthenes.

"That," Maeva said, "is a shrine built for the Prophet when Liat was founded. There, among these monuments to each of the Arts, we will find your light."

Rea had not slept the night before and nervous excitement kept her from eating breakfast. She felt neither tired nor hungry, energized by anticipation. Today she was taking her final exam. If she succeeded, she would be recognized as a Mage.

The previous months had been a whirlwind for her. She had never doubted herself when she entered Basul, but the speed of her progress had surprised her. Her bravado had gotten her into trouble a few times. She was still on detention for an incident when she had molded her fire into an arrow and it had gotten away from her, incinerating the lab. The teachers were furious but restrained their punishment. Rea had thought she would be expelled but instead she found herself sentenced to a month of cleaning duties at the lab, shoveling the dung from the stables, and kitchen duty. Hard work, but manageable.

Now she stood before the double doors of the Fire Walkers' Council room. Looking at the bright flame symbol emblazoned on the wood, she shivered with excitement. She took a breath, straightened her robes and stood tall. Hala, her first teacher, startled her when he appeared at her shoulder.

"Rea, are you ready?" His deep voice had a stern, formal quality she had never heard before.

"Yes, sir," Rea said. Hala strode past her and opened the doors, ushering her in. The room was full of faculty, mages, and her fellow students. Rea put her hand on the amulet that Hala had given her and followed him in. Hala positioned her opposite himself in the center of the chamber.

He addressed the audience. "Today we are here for the final examination of Rea Acira. Let us begin." Turning to her, he said, "Rea, what is the secret of the Art of Flame?"

Rea collected herself.

"Master," she began, "there is no secret to the Art of the Flame, though one must understand its truth. Perfection of the Art can only be achieved when the user understands their own imperfection." Rea had given this concept a great deal of thought. The Flame was powerful, capable of being shaped to the user's will, and had no limits other than those imposed by the user. Rea grasped the core truth that a Mage must look inward and know their own shortcomings in order to prevent these from tainting their fire. That was why she could not control that fiery arrow—she had been overeager and undisciplined. Her failure had been as painfully embarrassing as it was pointed. As she considered this truth of her Art, she wondered if it applied to all Arts.

Rea met Hala's steady regard. Where she had been arrogant,

now she looked at him with profound respect for the Acetos and his power. She framed her answer to demonstrate that she had grown since their first meeting.

"Explain," he said.

"There is no perfect Flame. Our flames shape themselves to fit our souls, and our flames are unique to each of us. Our moods, and therefore our flames, vary in any given moment." She paused to check his response but his face was impassive. Anxiety stirred in her heart but she steeled herself and spoke the lesson she had found most difficult.

"Our Flame is an outward projection of who *we* are at that moment in time. Sometimes, it burns hot if we are passionate. Other times, it simmers, reflecting a contemplative, deliberate approach. We can shape it as we shape ourselves and our thoughts. So, to master the Art, one must accept and embrace one's own imperfection, knowing that the Flame reflects our imperfection. In my case, I am arrogant, rigid, and quick to react. But I am also unyielding in my insistence on justice. My Flame reflects my passion, but also my haste and inflexibility." Rea waited for a reaction.

Hala nodded. Rea wanted to whoop in triumph. This public admission of her faults had frightened her. The remaining questions would be less daunting. She glanced at the audience. Ba'al and the heads of the other Arts sat in the front row. It was quite the crowd.

If only Tuac were here, she thought.

Hala said, "Rea, why do you want to be a Fire Walker?"

"Master, I do not *want* to be a Fire Walker. I do not *want* to be a Water Sculptor, an Air Bender, a Gaeist or any other practitioner of the six Arts. Each Art picks its student and each student must accept their Art. I *am* one with the Flame. It is not by choice, by luck, or by blessing. It is who I am."

It was hard for Rea to say this. She needed to be in control of her decisions, but she was no more in control of the nature of her magic than the color of her eyes. Being a Fire Walker was built into her core. When she had first come to this conclusion, she had resented the idea that, except for this inborn trait, she was no better than anyone else. Being a Fire Walker was no different than having curly hair. There was no choice, and no ability to alter the end result.

Hala waited for her to say more. Rea shifted her weight, her palms sweating. She blinked and exhaled. Then she had an epiphany.

"I am a Fire Walker because I accept that my role is to harness my Art as everyone must harness their talents. I am no different than the farmer, though my crops are flames. I am no more talented than the blacksmith, though I use my will and my fire to shape metal instead of needing a hammer or anvil. The Flame is not a weapon. It can be used to injure people, but also to warm and protect them. The Flame is neither good nor evil, just as I am neither. I am one with the Flame because the Art teaches all of us that we must use the power of magic to protect Mother Mia. I am not here because I *want* to be part of the Art of the Flame, nor am I here today so you can anoint me. I am here because I am Fire Walker and have to come to affirm that I accept who I am, all that it means, and all that I must do."

Hala smiled. Rea basked in his warmth and took a deep breath. She saw him turn his head to look at Ba'al. Ba'al nodded. At once, all of the Acetos stood up and bowed. Rea released her tension in a long sigh of pride and accomplishment. She felt, for perhaps the first time in her life, complete. She was crying tears of joy and relief after all of the years of trying to live up to her parents' expectations. She could be herself now. She was one with the Flame.

There was a small celebration with ale, bread and cheese. Each of the Acetos came up to Rea to congratulate her, as did many in her Art. They presented her with her ceremonial robe with its red collar.

"Breathe" Maeva said. "Feel Mother Mia's energy flow through your body. Visualize your lungs filling and your heart beating. In every way you are connected to Mia. Feel her lifeforce coursing through your skin, your blood, your bones. Take in Mia's scent—the flowers, the air, the lingering smell of the animals that were in this field when we started this exercise. Hear her talking to you—the rustle of the trees tells you that she is at peace, the chirping of the birds is her singing the joy of all that is good in the world, the sound of the air coming and going invites your soul on a journey across the expanse. This is how you find your Art. This is how you become one with your true self. Magic is merely the harnessing of Mia's presence in you, and once harnessed, you will be able to help those in need."

Tuac did his best to find his center. He calmed his mind and envisioned himself in the Alcove. He knew that was where he should go. He could feel the energy coursing through his body. He knew that the Anthene door was ready to open. But there was something holding him back. He could not explain the obstacle and he could not get past it. He could only get so close. His mind would wander to the other doors. Yet he knew the answer lay behind the Anthene door.

Today, he refused to accept failure and resolved to cross that gap. He deepened in his meditation. Sweat beaded on his forehead. Every muscle tensed. He refused to retreat. He pushed hard and something within him shattered.

The Chamber was gone. He was floating over Liat, and he could see for miles. The view below him followed the path of his life, touching on those places and people in the present moment. First, he soared over Stara, glimpsing his parents. Then he was whisked away to a room where Rea, surrounded by many magicians, received a robe with a red collar. Then he was over Liat, where he saw himself meditating among the seven columns.

He had no anchor. He felt the emotions of those he loved, starting with Merle. He felt the air, the intricate, busy lives of the wild creatures, the depth of Mia's ocean, and even the flame burning so bright within Rea. It was breathtaking. Then he realized he was not alone.

"This is your true Art, the Watcher said. *This is the answer. You must accept it, for in the absence of structure true power exists. You must be all things to fight nothing."*

The Watcher's words settled him, and he relaxed into the vast experience. As he accepted his Art, he was drawn off to a place he had never been. He felt like water swirling down a drain, drawn off in a specific direction. He tried to resist, but had no skills to control this wild flight.

He sped across Mia toward a curtain of darkness along the horizon. As he drew closer, he noticed dying grass and trees, their leaves dry and drained of life. The fetid aroma of decay smacked him so hard that he felt sick. Everything was rotting, not just the physical forms of plants and animals, but their life force itself had disintegrated. Despair flooded Tuac, accompanied by enormous grief. He felt evil saturating the landscape below him. All life, everything good, was being strangled. He gagged, grappling with terror and revulsion.

What would cause this? Desperate, he struggled against the current that pulled him closer to the darkness. Tuac panicked. He could not clutch anything to hold himself still, he could not steer or slow his progress. He traveled faster, the features of the land beneath him blurring as he sped over them.

He swept past the dark curtain and Mia lost its form. The scenery vanished and he hung in empty, lightless space. This was not the black of night. This was the black of a void. Tuac fought harder to turn back, but he had no purchase on this emptiness. He knew where this would lead him: Nabes.

This realization sped his flight into the abyss. Tuac saw something shift in the black, a different texture within the darkness. He saw lines and angles, then the towers and walls of a castle. As he came closer, his flight slowed and the force drawing him in abated.

The pull released his astral form as he stumbled on the dusty ground in front of the castle's gate. Tuac's mind tried to sort the shades of black. He could see a path and stepped onto it. As he did, he felt malevolence creeping up his feet to his ankles.

I am not strong enough to defeat Nabes.

The malevolence spread, feeding on his anxiety. It reached his knees. Terror gripped him. Just as he thought he would die, he heard

"Breathe." The Watcher's voice broke Nabes' hold on Tuac. He seized that presence and steadied himself, returning to his core. Mia flowed through his body and he could fight. He called the flames of the suns, and his body ignited. He shone with bright, white light and the black shriveled away from him.

Tuac felt a momentary rush of triumph. He could now sense his ethereal body surrounded by the nothingness of Nabes. But now he had a protective barrier: Mia. She protected him.

Tuac had no choice but to continue this journey. His feet slipped on the path and he almost fell into the dark. He steadied himself and concentrated, drawing more on Mia's lifeforce. He gestured and flung a beam of light, pushing back the blackness with each step. He approached the castle's foundation. The structure's stone and wood cried out in pain and he longed to heal it. He touched the gate and for a brief moment castle's pain eased.

"You are not ready yet," the Watcher whispered. Tuac did not want to stop, as every fiber of his being felt that he needed to heal the pain caused by the blackness. But Tuac was forced to admit the Watcher was correct. He took his hand off the gate.

With his will, Tuac pushed the gate open. In the courtyard, countless desiccated bodies lay strewn in postures of anguish. The anguish of their deaths showed on their faces.

Rage flared in Tuac. Even if he was unprepared, he would not leave Nabes's victims this way. He clenched his fist, feeling his heart race. The castle shook and dim light appeared. It could not dissolve the black entirely, but the building took on more shape, more presence. The bodies turned to dust and sank into the ground. Mia had taken in the dead. They were at rest.

In the dim light, Tuac saw the inside of the castle. Intricate ornaments made with love and skill adorned the fortifications. Delicate arches framed the inner doorways. He saw faint glints of colored glass in the elegant windows.

How could this have happened in a place of such beauty?

"Now you see the grandeur of Shalla," a rich, charismatic voice spoke in Tuac's mind, its tone suffused with arrogance.

A knight in armor appeared in front of Tuac. The black metal plates drank the dim light.

"Nabes. Your reputation precedes you." Tuac braced himself against the urge to flee.

"I smell your fear, boy. Do you think you are up to the task? I brought you here so you could see that defeating me is impossible."

Stunned, Tuac sought his center again and steadied his breath.

The dark figure chuckled. "You cannot harness Aced against me. Basul rejected you. Those at Liat will do the same. Your foolish reliance on Mia will not help you.

"Know that I am not your only enemy. Surrender, boy. Seal the fate of Mia. It needs to be cleansed." Nabes waved his hand and the black oozed up from where the bodies had lain.

"Do not give in to him," the Watcher said. *"His power is your fear. Your power is in realizing the truth. That is what he is trying to prevent. You need to understand the true nature of Aced."*

Sensing the intrusion, Nabes screamed, "Watcher, you cannot interfere! Begone!"

Tuac felt his guide leave him.

I am alone here, Tuac thought. *I have always been alone. My family only cared for Rea but neither they or she cared about me. I had no friends, no loves, no one. I never belonged. Even at school, I never fit in. I am a no one. I am a failure. Maybe Nabes is right.*

I can't fight the evil that Nabes has spread. How could one person stop it? I can barely use magic and I am supposed to fight nothingness?

Tuac gave in to his despair and started walking toward Nabes. He was done fighting. He wanted to rest. Let someone else stand in the way of the dark. This was not his battle. He had never volunteered for this burden. He was done.

"Good, my boy," said Nabes. "You have finally realized the futility of fighting me." Nabes moved to embrace the boy.

And then, in his heart, Tuac saw Merle's smile. Her eyes shone with love and courage, brightening his soul as they had done so many times. She healed his hurt. Her smile cleansed him of his insecurities. Something bloomed within Tuac when he realized he was loved. His fear did not dissipate, but now it fed his anger. He had something to fight for. He stopped walking and growled,

"*No.* You may win, Nabes, but not today. I will do everything in my power to stop you." Nabes lunged for Tuac, who evaded him. The black knight's form flickered.

Weird. That's not a physical body. I did something that shook his control. Nabes' confusion allowed Tuac to escape.

Abruptly, he was back in Liat with Maeva. He opened his eyes. Maeva crouched beside him, staring at him.

"What happened?" she asked, a tremor in her voice. "You were going through the exercises, I saw you go deeper into your center, and then you were *gone.* Your soul left your body. I could sense you fighting but I could not reach you. And now you're back." She laid a hand on his arm.

Tuac clutched her hand, tears streaming down his face. He did not know what had happened or why. But Nabes was coming for him. And, if he could believe what Nabes had said, Tuac had other enemies, too. He did not know whom he could trust, other than Merle, and his sister, and perhaps Maeva.

As he thought of Rea, guilt welled up. Even if it was Nabes' doing, Tuac had given into his childish fears that she would abandon him. Yet he knew she was his ally and she had always looked out for him, even when he annoyed her. Whenever he was hurt, she had cared for him. She had protected him from bullies, and even from their parents when their tempers had gotten the best of them.

And he was not alone. He had never been alone. Even if he had not fit in with the popular kids in Stara, he did have his friends. There were plenty of summer nights he'd gotten into mischief and played wonderful ball games with them. And now he had Merle. She had saved him.

Nabes had sown fear, discontent and loneliness in Tuac's

heart to weaken him. Tuac needed to remember his guide's message now if he was going to withstand Nabes' attacks. He could not control who was coming for him, he could only control his response. He could not prevent an attack on his memories or fears, but he could remember who he was and that he was loved. He might not succeed, but he was not going down without a fight. And he knew there were others who would fight with him.

Tuac closed his eyes and steadied his ragged breathing. He had learned that Nabes feared him, though Tuac did not know why. He could and would make a difference.

The Watcher believes in me. Nabes should be scared.

Nabes had said unsettling things. Now Tuac considered who else might be his enemy. He needed to be on guard because he did not know where or when these other enemies might strike. When he regained his composure, Tuac released Maeva's hand.

"I breached my inner barrier and found myself soaring." Tuac said. "I floated across Mia. I could look down and see all the places I've travelled through, and see those I love. Then I started exploring and lost myself in the moment."

Maeva asked, "I felt you fighting. What was that?"

Tuac was not ready to tell her everything.

"I was wrestling with inner demons. And I won." Tuac met Maeva's kind eyes. Maeva regarded him for a while, and then nodded.

"Let's get back to work then."

Tuac was relieved that Maeva had not pressed him to explain further. Her willingness to trust him suggested that he could trust her.

Nabes raged. *How could this boy escape me? Tuac is too young to resist the Dark. Without Aced supporting him, he cannot be strong enough.*

Nabes realized that Tuac posed a definite threat. Nabes needed to spread its disease faster. Tuac may have won the day, but Nabes would not be defeated again. Not by ACED, not by the Watcher, and certainly not by a mere boy.

Eighteen

We have failed. We tried to create a utopian society, but we repeated the mistakes of our forefathers. We thought magic would make a difference, allow for a better society for all. All that we did was substitute one power and evil for another. Humanity never learns. The only way that humanity can achieve an enlightened age is for us to realize that we cannot mandate perfection. Instead, we must love and appreciate the imperfection in all of us.

The Journal of Samuel R. Orris
Circa Turn 980

That night, in his room, Tuac told Merle about his breakthrough, the soaring journey, and his confrontation with Nabes.

"You saved me, my love," he said.

"As you saved me," she said, resting her head on chest. He knew that Merle was his soulmate and she would always be there to protect him. This love would strengthen him for the coming battle.

Over the following days, Tuac intensified his training. He had no more problems connecting with his Anthene Art. He practiced Yiao to calm himself, pictured the Alcove, then the Chamber and the doors. But rather than try any doorknob, he spread his arms to embrace his magic. In moments, he was soaring over Mia. This was no mere vision. He was seeing the entire planet, even places he had never been to physically. He felt the webs of plant and animal life, the flow of water and the patterns of the winds. He returned from these flights filled with gratitude and wonder.

After each session, he related his experience to Maeva. The first time that he told her what he had seen, she dismissed his experience as a vivid meditative state. But he had described in detail all the people doing Yiao in the park, and when they walked back from the ruins Tuac pointed each person out to her. Maeva never questioned him again.

Tuac waited for Maeva to start specific instruction in the Anthene skills, but those lessons never came. Instead, Maeva focused on his Yiao training. She drove him to move faster, with more precision, and to hold each pose much longer. Although he wasn't using his magic, Tuac appreciated the physical challenge of his sessions. He was fond of Maeva and enjoyed his time with her. Tuac grew to trust her completely.

After one grueling session, Tuac stopped to catch his breath and asked,

"Who is Aced?"

"Where did you hear that name?" He heard surprise in her voice.

"I heard the name from Nabes."

"You spoke to Nabes?"

"Remember when you asked me if I was fighting that first day I went traveling across Mia? I didn't tell you everything that happened to me. I'm sorry. I didn't know who to trust, and we had just met." They settled on the grass and Tuac related his experience in the dying lands and the horrifying castle, and his struggle with Nabes. He felt relieved to share this with her.

"Your love of Merle saved you," she said.

"Yes. And the guidance of the Watcher, who called me back to myself so I could fight."

"You are stronger than you know, my cub." She took out their midday meal. "Now I will tell you our creation story and you will understand where magic comes from.

"Aced was Mia's mate. Together, the two gods created all that there is. The Church has tried to erase both of them and promote only the Prophet's teachings. Yet some of us remember, although we do not pray to Aced any more than we worship Mia.

"In their lessons on the history of Mia, Anthenes learn the story of Mia and Aced's love. Unfortunately for you, my cub, I've been too busy with your training to cover this. Now is a good time to rectify that. Let's take a break, shall we?" Maeva created a small fire and put water on for tea.

"In the beginning," Maeva began, "there was only Aced and Mia. They loved one another and were always together. Aced longed to prove his limitless affection for Mia, so he created the stars and planets. The two traveled, visiting the new worlds. On each planet, Aced's breath created air and clouds. Mia's touch brought forth plants and animals from the ground and waters. In this way, they created the universe. The two created countless vibrant worlds but they were the only sentient beings."

Maeva sipped her tea and smiled. "Mia confided in her beloved that she was lonely. The gods discussed ways they could create a higher life form but struggled to find the right spark to ignite intelligence. After one failed attempt, Mia said, 'I would give anything to be with you forever, but I would give even more to share you with others.'

"Mia and Aced continued their experiments. Each world was more wonderful than the last, but without the special flame of sentience. Then the two came here. When they arrived, this planet was barren rock. There were no hursas, birds, fish or even cubs." Maeva smiled again at Tuac.

"After they had created many kinds of life here, they felt this world was the jewel of the universe. Mia was content, but Aced was inspired to do more. His winds swirled faster and faster. Mia sensed that Aced was planning something and panicked. Great energy flowed out of Aced. Mia screamed at her lover to stop. But he did not, and the wind blew harder.

"Aced said to Mia, 'Trust me, my love. I am giving you what you desire most.'

"Lightning bloomed from Aced's whirlwind and surrounded the planet. When it came to ground, we sprang to life. Aced had found a way to imbue their creations with sentience. We were few, unique to this world, a new beginning.

"Elated, Mia moved to embrace Aced but his form wavered, pale and colorless, fraying into the grasses and breeze. 'My love, what have you done!' She gathered him up, but his lifeblood was failing. He had given her the ultimate gift but it had cost him his life.

"Aced said, 'I knew you longed for companions, so I wanted this for you. In every one of these children, part of me exists. Even when I am gone, you will always have me with you. Now you can tend to them as your flock.' Aced's essence wavered.

"Mia wept as her companion faded. 'I said I wanted to share you with others, not rule over a flock!' How could she heal him?

She was stronger than Aced. An answer came to her. Mia swirled herself into the wind. She merged with Aced in the bright currents of air, giving him strength. 'We will watch over the flock you have created' she whispered. Together they vanished into the life of this planet."

"Where did they go?" Tuac asked.

"Their fused essence lives in all of us. We call it magic. We honor their sacrifice. We call our planet Mia, so that we never forget her. We always remember that death is part of life, and that magic flows from love."

Tuac reached out, hoping to sense the two gods. They had given everything for the creation of life. But Tuac felt unsettled.

Why do we remember Mia but Aced lives only in tales shared among the gifted? Why had Nabes mentioned Aced? I need to understand what Nabes was worried about.

Esa's forces camped at the base of the long slope near Liat. The Emperor's army had reached the top of the valley and encountered Liat's protection. As they had planned, Basul's emissary unlocked the wards, allowing the troops to march on Liat. Esa commanded ten legions of the Emperor's best knights armed with Terran weapons, more than enough to end the Anthene problem. The Anthenes would come investigate the army's arrival, and Esa would strike without mercy.

Would Ba'al seek vengeance or would she be more concerned about Nabes? Esa wondered.

Despite the risk, she could see no other way. Even before Nabes's return, the University had failed in its duty to the people. The magicians sat in their chambers, researching magic but never aiding the populace, not in famine or sickness, flood or fire, or in times of local strife. They refused to participate in the life of Mia. Their self-isolation had allowed Nabes to return.

The Church was worse. The magicians had power but they refused to use it. But the Church, while demanding tithes and obedience, offered only fiery sermons on the Prophet's teachings. They controlled the people through guilt and fear.

Esa believed that the Empire's duty lay in protecting Mians from chaos. She shared the Emperor's view that the triumvirate would lead to Mia's destruction. Mia needed order and justice administered by a single central authority. With power divided between the Church, the Empire, and the mages, Esa felt that there was little accountability. The return of Nabes was proof that there needed to be a change.

Esa was driven by her desire for a strong hand to rule Mia, unfettered by the concerns of the feckless magicians and the cowering followers of the Prophet. She ingratiated herself to her commanders and rose within the imperial ranks. Hahook promoted her to be his second in command giving her command of the plasma rifle initiative, assigned to secure and harness the alien technology.

Esa used her position to devise the strategy to consolidate the Empire's power and liberate Mia. Today was the culmination of that plan. Once they incinerated Liat, the University would have to acknowledge the supremacy of the Empire. The mages would need the Empire's might in order to defeat Nabes. Hahook's actions also allowed the Emperor to displace the Charge and bring the Church under direct imperial control, giving Hahook another tool for controlling the people.

Hahook would rule Mia, but his immorality would be his downfall. Esa, by then a military hero, would offer a brighter path, one with morality as its foundation and the loyalty of the

Empire's forces as its strength. Esa's commitment to the just use of power would be welcomed with open arms.

Esa surveyed Liat in the valley below, rehearsing her plans for the assault. Her troops would be ready for the Empire's ascension and the golden age of Mia. Her coronation would follow.

Tuac returned to his room, considering Maeva's story. Merle was not in, so Tuac took advantage of his time alone to read more from the *Journal of Sam Orris.*

Curiosity, 4032 SY

We have been here for approximately 10 star years, and we have little show for it. We had tried to land in an isolated region in the southern hemisphere to establish a base camp. Unfortunately, we were caught in an energy field that our sensors had not detected. It fried most of our equipment.

The landing was hard, and we suffered casualties. After we had erected shelters, we sent an exploratory group to study the local populace. We kept our contact to a minimum following the standards for interstellar interference. We used our remaining computers to interpret their language. We call them Mians, after the name of their primary deity.

We were surprised to discover that Mian DNA significantly overlaps our own, and we share key physiological traits. Perhaps the cosmic theory about a single wellspring of life is true.

The Mians have an intricate mythos explaining life, the seasons, and other natural phenomena. They live in isolated communities supported by basic agriculture and their social organization is feudal.

Our initial interactions went well. However, half a star-year after we settled, tribal leaders launched an attack against us. Their challenge invoked the names of their gods. We had perimeter defenses and a cache of plasma rifles, so we thwarted their attack, though we did lose nineteen people. Our successful defense curtailed their aggression, but we also terminated all contact with them.

Two years after landing, a pandemic swept through the Mian population. Initially, they did not seek our help but with death tolls rising fast, the leaders of the closest village contacted us. We determined that the disease was a variant of measles. Their DNA's similarities put them at risk, and its differences meant the disease was more fatal. We tried to help the afflicted, but the Mians viewed us as godlike warriors. They feared we would take revenge for their prior attack and rejected our medical assistance. Many of our crew contracted the virus, so our resources were stretched thin. Had more of our equipment survived the landing, we would have been able to develop treatments and vaccines to save everyone.

At this point, we leave the Mians alone and they keep their distance from us. Our meager equipment keeps us safe but restricts our choices. This is not the beginning I had envisioned when I joined this expedition. I will keep a record of our experiences and I hope my report reaches Earth. One day they will arrive here and find our children.

A shout outside his door startled Tuac. He opened the door and saw Maeva, disheveled and breathless.

"You need to leave! The Emperor has come to take you. Basul

is behind this, as Hahook's forces should not have been able to get through Liat's wards otherwise. Argent will delay them, but that only buys you a few minutes. Your time at Liat is over. You will have to walk your path earlier than I would have hoped."

Maeva shoved Tuac's few possessions into a rucksack she had brought with her.

Tuac froze. As fast as his mind raced, he could not process what Maeva had said. It made no sense.

"I've given you what I can. This pack has a bedroll, some dried meat and cheese, water, a change of clothes and a few other things you might find helpful. Now hurry!" She shoved the bag into his arms.

Tuac snatched up Orris' *Journal* and tucked it into the pack.

"Wait! What about Merle?!"

Maeva put her hand on Tuac's shoulder. "We can search for her, but we have little time. I have no idea what the Emperor is planning, and I fear he is up to no good. This intrusion does not appear to be just about you. But you are too important to risk."

Tuac trusted Maeva, but he would protect Merle. He closed his eyes and started to breathe, centering himself. He traced his connection to Merle. For a moment he felt her panic. The connection was tenuous because he was still learning his Art. His connection faltered under the weight of so many things he wanted, he needed, to say. Desperate, he sent an urgent command to *run* and then the thread snapped.

Maeva pulled his arm. "It's now or never, cub."

They bolted, racing through Liat toward their training site. Chaos swirled through the school and ground. He heard teachers ordering the acolytes to lead students to the building's center. He saw other instructors locking rooms and running with armloads of books and scrolls. He bumped into one Anthene, who dropped several bottles, most of which shattered. The woman swore. Tuac apologized, and helped her retrieve what was left of her precious cargo. The instructor ran into the building.

"I knew Basul could not be trusted," Maeva hissed.

He stopped. "Maybe I should give myself up?"

"Absolutely not! The Empire's forces are too large for this to be only about returning you to Basul. There is evil in their hearts. The Empire and Basul are working together here. The only way those troops could be camped outside of Liat is with the assistance of Ba'al. I fear for what purpose." Maeva led him into the stables.

"Wait, how do you know all this?" Tuac resisted her tug.

Out of breath and exasperated, Maeva paused. "We don't have time for this!" She flung a bridle at Tuac. "Work and I'll talk."

Tuac picked up a saddle and selected a hursa. As they tacked up the animal, Maeva explained.

"Anthenes do more than heal. With proper training, we can see into the body and soul. More powerful Anthenes, like Argent, can expand their vision in a way similar to your floating. They can also communicate over long distances, sharing feelings or emotions."

How was I able to reach out to Merle without proper training? Tuac wondered.

"Argent looked into the soul of the enemy. He cannot tell what they want, but it is not good. He alerted all the teachers to prepare for the worst."

Nausea struck Tuac, worse than any he had ever felt. He doubled over in pain, falling to his knees. In the aisle, Maeva gasped and crumpled, too.

Tuac felt scores of Anthenes die, including Argent. Rage roared through him. He staggered up, ready to join the battle.

He did not know what he was going to do, but he wanted revenge. He needed to make them pay.

Maeva grabbed his shoulder. "Stop! You are not strong enough. You would die, too. I understand you want to fight, but now is not the time." She secured his pack on her hursa. Then she bridled another animal. "I had not planned to go with you, but Liat is gone. Let's ride."

Tuac glared at Maeva. His mind raced. He wanted blood. He could feel the Empire's forces. He knew where they were.

It would be so easy to end them.

"Center yourself, cub. Breathe. You will make a difference, but you must do it the right way."

Tuac collected himself. "Fine," Tuac snapped. He mounted his hursa and did not wait to see Maeva's reaction. Now he could feel her soul. She was afraid. Not of the Empire or the mages, but of him.

Esa had not expected the battle to end in mere minutes. Argent had approached the Empire's forces, probably to parlay. But she had her orders. She issued the command and her troops opened fire on the Headmaster and his entourage. Esa directed her forces into Liat and they slaughtered anything that moved. They met no resistance.

Esa had just ordered a search for the boy's body when a telepathic wave struck them. She writhed on the ground, gasping in agony. She wanted to give up, to stop the pain. Some dark hunger was feeding on her body and soul, and she it would kill her. She was not ready to die. Mia's people needed her. She anchored herself in her core belief that she was a warrior protecting the oppressed. She fought back.

The pain ceased. Esa staggered up, surveying the battlefield. Many of her troops had died. Some had ripped their eyes out. Esa recognized the few that survived. They were her most loyal soldiers. And they were weeping.

Our attack unleashed something horrible, Esa thought to herself. She had never felt anything like it. *What have I done?*

Esa had known that the destruction of Liat would change Mia, but now she feared it would be changed in a way she had not envisioned. She no longer plotted her ascendency. Instead, she wondered if she would survive.

Ba'al gasped. She felt the fabric of magic tear, a detonation followed by the release of a new, powerful force. Something had destroyed the Anthenes. That was the only explanation. And with that violent act, Nabes had gained immeasurable strength.

How could this have happened? Ba'al had not sanctioned any actions against Liat and Basul would never attack the Anthenes. *Did Hahook attack them? We gave Esa the keys to unlock Liat's wards. What have we done? We only wanted the boy.*

Ba'al shuddered and sank to the floor, her legs too weak to hold her. She had been complicit in the destruction of the Anthenes. As she grappled with her guilt and horror, she wondered what the Emperor might do next.

What did he use against Liat? Will he be at Basul's gates soon?

Rea wiped vomit from her mouth. Rage, greed, delight, hunger, hate and contempt roiled in her heart. These were not her emotions, they flooded into her from elsewhere. Burning among them she sensed a bright spark of love, protection, and hope. It was faint and fighting to survive against the tide of darkness and despair. The spark fought, but it was alone and confused. It wavered, unsure of itself and its power.

Rea recognized Tuac's light. She did not understand why she felt him, or what he was going through, but she knew her little brother was in danger and needed her. Yet all she could do was believe in him.

Nabes felt so alive. The massacre of the Anthenes infused him with delicious terror and anguish, and the attackers' arrogance and hatred fed him well. His power bloomed. Aced could not stop him now. The petty Mians had sealed their fate by attacking one another.

The Watcher saw the carnage caused by the Emperor's forces followed by Nabes' feeding frenzy. Time was running out.

Nineteen

What is the secret to following one's true path? We know what we must do, yet we make excuses for not choosing the right action. We rationalize our actions in terms of the benevolent use of power.

I had a choice. I knew what I needed to do. I convinced myself to take a different road. A choice based not in altruism but in fear. Fear of the unknown. Fear of struggle. Fear of change. I justified my actions as being for the good of all, but I had just surrendered to the intoxication of Power.

The Teachings of the Prophet 9:8

When Tuac opened his eyes, Maeva stood over him. He felt dizzy and sick. She tugged him to his feet.

"We need to change our plans" she said.

Tuac grabbed his bag off the hursa and followed her out of the stable. He struggled to make sense of what had happened.

Bodies lay everywhere. He glimpsed men in uniforms moving through the school grounds, pointing strange metal tubes at anything that moved. If a person shifted, the men aimed the tubes at them. Tuac saw a bolt like lightning, then heard a hissing boom. The light disintegrated whatever, or whomever, it struck. The lucky ones disappeared, but Tuac found many who had died slowly, bleeding out from gaping torso wounds or missing limbs.

"Stay with me, Cub. Don't let them see you."

Tuac joined Maeva and they ran, staying low behind the hedges and walls. He forced himself to stare at her back instead of the carnage. They crept toward the center of Liat.

Why aren't we trying to get out of Liat? he wondered. *We need to get away from the school.* But Maeva moved with purpose and he trusted her.

They slipped into a small building and stopped at a plain door.

"What's in there?" Tuac asked. Maeva touched the door with reverent hands.

"This door was to be opened only if there was a threat to Mia's existence. Few know it exists. We were told it leads to salvation. As a member of Liat's inner circle, I learned the rituals that open this door. I never thought I would be the one to do it.

"To pass through this door, you must embrace everything you have been taught. You must face your truth. With truth comes understanding, even if it also brings forth guilt. This is your moment, Cub. Are you ready?"

Am I? Tuac flinched, dread stirring in his belly. *What if I am not strong or virtuous enough to enter? What if I disappoint Maeva, Rea and Merle?* Tuac knew he was not pure or pious, but flawed and imperfect.

"Make your decision. If you are unsure, you will not survive. Are you ready for me to start the invocation?"

Tuac accepted his truth. He felt an eruption of anger and embarrassment at his failures, and remorse about his actions. Rather than suppress his feelings, he embraced them.

Yes, I am flawed. Yes, I could and should have done better, but each time I learn. My shortcomings motivate and strengthen me. I am prepared for what may come.

Tuac said, "We are only perfect when born. We make mistakes, but they do not define us. What makes us who we are is how we respond. I see my truth."

The door opened. Maeva stepped back, her eyes wide.

"How could you know the words that open this door?" Outside they heard a distant shout. Not waiting for Tuac's answer, she pushed him through the door and closed it.

Sunshine filled the room from skylights. In the center of the room Tuac saw a standing mirror set in an ornate frame glazed in blood red. Unlike a regular mirror, the glass shimmered. Around the frame, Tuac read

We are many. But we must be one. With true acceptance comes redemption. With redemption comes reunification. With reunification, good can overcome evil in the final battle.

"What is this?" He scanned the room and saw that the door had vanished. There was no other way out. "Now what?"

Maeva looked at him with a blank stare and then put her pack down. Tuac did the same. Tuac examined the room. It resembled the Chamber. The etching on the floor showed the same two concentric circles and rays connecting them. They had not been worn over time but the connecting rays displayed none of the color he had seen in his dream. He could see the circles had the same balance of light and dark. He ran his hand over the circles and felt a break similar to the one he had seen in his vision.

He saw the outlines of seven doors etched into the walls. They had circles where knobs would be if they had been actual doors. Each door also had an etched symbol of one of the seven Arts. Tuac studied the mirror. His reflection looked more mature. The Yiao practice had honed him and put muscle on his shoulders. He needed a shave. Tuac was no longer a boy and it shocked him.

"I'm sorry, Tuac" Maeva said. "You should have had the opportunity to enjoy your childhood. But that is not your path."

Tuac nodded. He was a survivor. He would move forward and grieve the past when he could. But at this point, too many people were counting on him and he needed to figure out why. And there was the matter of avenging those that the Emperor murdered.

The mirror's surface shimmered.

It reacted to my anger, Tuac thought. He looked beyond his own image and saw that the mirror did not reflect the room they stood in, but instead showed him standing in the underground Chamber. *How could that be?*

He stepped over to examine the intricate doors carved into the stone walls. The detail conveyed the texture of wood.

These must be the way out, but how do we open them? Once again, I am brought to this place to open my door.

Tuac suspected that the mirror was the key. It was a masterpiece. The seamless wood frame had been molded by Gaeists. The gleaming red finish reminded him of glazed pottery. *Fire Walkers did that.* Tuac reached for the glass, but a force pushed his hand back. *Telepaths made that ward.* He tried again, this time moving his hand slowly, and penetrated the protection spell.

When he touched the mirror's surface, it was cold and rippled. *Water Sculptors and Air Riders made this.* The inscription on the frame was made with delicate clay letters. *Stone Movers wrote that.*

Members of each magical Art worked together to create this mirror. Tuac marveled at the effort and cooperation that had gone into making it. Tuac heard a soft voice say *"That which was sundered must be repaired."*

He looked at Maeva and she was staring elsewhere. He realized the presence was speaking only to him. It had a warm and inviting quality to it, and he knew this was neither the Watcher nor Nabes.

It continued, *"See your true self."*

The mirror! The Anthenes gave this object a soul, Tuac thought. He read the inscription again. *When I accepted myself, this room opened for me. The mirror tells me to go deeper. It will show me which is my true door.*

Tuac shifted the mirror so that it faced the etched doors. First, he aligned it to the Anthene door. The reflection of the engraved door changed, and it looked like the Anthene door in the Chamber. He stood sideways so he could watch himself in the mirror as he reached for the door on the wall. Nothing happened.

How could this be? I'm an Anthene.

As he adjusted the mirror, it reflected the Fire Walkers Door. His image changed. He wore a robe with a red collar. He touched his chest, and his reflected hand settled on the robe.

"How did you do that?" Maeva said.

"I don't know. The mirror spoke to me. It said I needed to see my true self. I thought the mirror might let me see my Art."

"The mirror shows my true self. In this view, I am a Fire Walker." Tuac said. He turned to the etched door and reached for the knob shown in the mirror, but there was no knob on this side of the mirror.

This is not the right door. Or maybe I haven't accepted that I'm a Fire Walker like Rea. He noted that Maeva was in the reflection, yet her appearance was unchanged. *Was this mirror's message meant for me?*

Tuac moved the mirror to the Stone Movers door. In the reflection, his robe changed to match that Art. Yet there was still no knob on the etched door, no way to open it. The same thing happened for all of the other doors.

Tuac sighed through gritted teeth. This room and the mirror embodied his magical impasse. The mirror showed his potential, but its guidance did not help him solve his riddle. *How could this be?"*

"We're missing something, Cub."

They leaned against a wall and slumped to the floor. Above them, the sky darkened with approaching evening, and the room was getting dark. They had not heard any detonations nor felt any of the nausea triggered by deaths since they entered into the room. The attack on Liat had run its course.

Tuac stared at the floor. The concentric circles. The balance of black and white. The break.

That which was sundered must be made whole, Tuac thought, his eyes following the dark line of the fissure. *The reflections are not different views of me but show me that I can be many things at once. If I accept that I can be all the Arts, maybe I can repair the etching.* Tuac stood.

"What are you doing? We're stuck in here—you need to conserve energy until we figure this out."

Tuac did not acknowledge Maeva. He was in a trance. He was not sure he would survive, but he had to try this. Tuac knelt beside the etching on the floor.

"Accept the light and the dark," the mirror said.

Tuac laid a hand on the white ring and felt warmth deep within himself. He placed his other hand on the dark ring and felt the chill of despair. He wanted to reject the black, but then he saw its purpose. The black filled in the cracks where the light was not present. There was balance between the two. They defined each other. Despair defined hope, evil defined good, hate defined love.

Tuac hovered his hands over the crack. He felt pain and distress. The light longed to be whole. He closed his eyes. He felt his skin warm, becoming a fever. He centered himself in meditation and floated above the room. His skin glowed brighter and brighter until it seemed that the room held Mia's sun.

He concentrated on the etching and directed his heat into the stone. It softened, then flowed and he pushed it to fill the fissure. Tuac tried to connect the severed ends of the circle, but they were blocked by a force as the original spell worked against him. He focused on the scarred ends, pleading with the force to accept a reconnection. He felt a slight shift as individual grains of stone wove themselves into the new configuration. With the circle complete, he cooled the air above the stone, soothing the molten material and setting it into place. He imbued the circles with the love of all living Mians, human, animal, and plant. The soul of the etching flared to life again.

And then it was done. Tuac slumped and Maeva caught him. Tuac's eyelids fluttered. Maeva steadied him and offered him water.

"Slowly, Cub. I don't know what you did. I can feel a balance between the light and the dark that was never there before. The Anthene Door here has opened. We have a way out."

Tuac sipped water and found his voice. "I am the Reunifier."

Then he passed out.

***

The Watcher sensed the dark surge of Nabes' power and the fierce, wild light of Tuac's self-acceptance. Nabes had reached full strength, and Mia's leaders were not prepared for what was to come. If only ACED had not been unleashed on this world. No one anticipated how it would change Mia, how magic would run rampant, and Nabes would rise. ACED was not the creator of life, as the Mians believed. ACED was destruction and Nabes was its instrument.

The one they called Prophet had tried to save Mian society from its own collapse. He had battled the evil and won. He had known what he had to do, but in a moment of weakness he failed to finish the task. He had hoped that social constructs could regulate magic and prevent the evil of Nabes from returning. Later in life, the Prophet had realized his mistake, but he could not repair the damage.

In the generations that followed, those charged with protecting Mia had made the situation worse by revising history. They had deified the Prophet and centered their religion on some of his teachings. The Church had called those who knew the truth of the Prophet's failure heretics. Those in power distorted the Prophet's writings and those words lost much of their guiding power. Now Nabes had arisen again.

The Watcher could not intervene, but it could plant suggestions. One of these was the creation of the Chambers, designed to unlock the Reunifier's magic. The Watcher had also helped the boy with the invocation to enter into the room, but knowing the words and believing in them were different things.

Now that Tuac had accepted his true path, the Watcher believed that Nabes could be defeated.

Tuac was strong enough to accept his magic, but was he strong enough to withstand the cost of Reunification?

"Are you alright? What happened? After you fainted, all of the doors appeared. Including the door we entered by." Maeva asked when Tuac stirred.

He nodded, drank a bit of water, and his clarity returned.

"I accepted who I am, and that brought the magic in the Chambers back into balance.

"What is the Reunifer? You mentioned that before you passed out." she asked.

"I'm not sure, but I think it means that I'm able to access all of the Arts. The concept came to me right before I fainted."

They stood, gathered their packs, and walked to the door through which they had entered.

"Are you ready?" Tuac asked.

"Yes. We need to get our hursas and flee."

Tuac opened the door. He was expecting to step into the hallway of the school building. But they were staring at the hallway in the Alcove.

"I've heard of things like this from the days of the *Curiosity*" Maeva said. "They had magic that could create portals, allowing them to travel long distances in the blink of an eye. Somehow the two Chambers are connected."

Tuac extended a hand through the doorway. It felt safe. He stepped through. Maeva followed him and closed the door. Tuac checked his belongings. Ki'lel's wand had fallen out of his pack. He retraced his steps but it was gone.

It must be in the other Chamber connected to the school, he thought.

"What are you looking for?" Maeva asked him. Tuac explained that his wand had fallen out in all the confusion and was now lost. The Emperor had taken another precious thing from Tuac.

"It was just an object. The memories it carried are still with me."

The hallway leading to the main door was empty. The guards were gone. They opened the outside door and discovered why—the guards lay scattered through the grove.

As they made their way back to Liat, they searched for survivors. Tuac held hope that Merle might have survived the massacre. All that remained were bodies, or pieces of them.

"What weapon could make wounds like this?" Maeva said, tears streaking her face.

"Why would they have done this? If I had surrendered, they would still be alive."

"This is not only about you, Tuac. Your presence here was an excuse for the Emperor to wipe out Liat. We don't know why he did this. The University must have helped the troops get past our wards. We don't know why they did that, either."

They continued their search. They found the bodies of the attackers. Anguish warped their faces.

"What killed them?" Tuac asked.

"Liat's death took them. It must have been the wave of force we felt. The evil that sprang from the massacre of the Anthenes slaughtered these attackers."

Closer to the stables, they found Trada, one of Argent's trusted advisors. He was alive, but badly injured.

"Trada!" Maeva said, "how did you survive?"

"I'm too bitter to die yet, my friend." He grimaced as he spoke. Maeva examined his injuries.

"You have internal damage and several broken bones," Maeva said.

She rolled up her sleeves to begin the difficult work of healing. But Trada placed a weak hand on her arm.

"Don't waste your magic on me. You need to get away from here," Trada wheezed.

"If I don't do this, you'll die."

"I will die either way."

Tuac laid a hand on Maeva's shoulder. "Let me help."

"Joining your power to another's is dangerous. I would need to draw on your power, but if I do that, you could be harmed."

"I need to do this," Tuac said. "We can save him." Maeva held his gaze for a long moment, then nodded.

"We do this together," and she grasped his hand.

He felt her accept his energy, and concentrated on that flow. He sensed her surprise, and then her unease.

I'm overwhelming her. I need to moderate my energy. He imagined his magic as a river, and placed a dam to contain it. Then he opened the floodgates just enough to let her tap his power. She could take what she needed without drowning. He felt Maeva respond, adapting to what he had done. Tuac knew their bond revealed his soul to her. He was showing his light and his darkness, and the balance between them. Their tether strengthened and he saw her soul and its brilliant light. With their connection stabilized, Maeva began her work.

Tuac observed how she used his energy to scan Trada's body. First, she eased him into a deep sleep so he felt no pain. Next, she focused on repairing the most crucial organs first, steadying the man's heart, his brain, and his lungs. He felt her relax once Trada's pulse strengthened. Tuac felt her weariness and knew she intended to stop now that her patient was out of danger.

I have more energy, let's continue, Tuac said to her through their bond. He released more of his flow, directing some of it to support Maeva, and the rest into Trada.

Thank you, Cub. Let's mend those bones. Tuac watched as she rebuilt Trada's shattered knee and shoulder blades, smoothing his broken ribs and the hairline crack in his jaw. Then she tended his bruised abdominal organs, and eased the many lacerations. She eased him out of the deep sleep toward wakefulness and then withdrew.

Maeva released the flow from Tuac and he was alone in his own head again.

Trada stirred, then opened his eyes. "Maeva, you should not have spent so much on me."

"How do you feel?" she asked.

"Better than I have in years. How could you do that?" He sat up, his brows knit in concern.

"Tuac and I worked together, a desperate measure in an emergency."

Tuac and Maeva walked Trada to his quarters. Not wanting to be separated, they all rested in his quiet rooms.

That night, the three of them performed the rites for the dead.

"What has happened here is an evil not witnessed on this planet since the Great Destruction," Maeva said.

Rage simmered in Tuac. "He took everything from me: Merle, Liat. He will pay."

"I know you want revenge, Cub, but evil cannot be countered with evil. Only love and the pursuit of justice can defeat evil. This is just our first battle and I am not suggesting you should not fight back. I am urging you to plot our resistance based on protecting Mia, not punishing those who did this. Merle would not want you lost in the abyss."

At the mention of Merle's name, Tuac turned to Maeva. She blanched at the anguish in his eyes.

<hr>

The next morning, Tuac awoke and heard Trada and Maeva talking.

"Trada was about to tell me what had happened," Maeva said. "I asked him to wait until you were awake. Trada, if you're up to it?"

Trada washed down a bite of bread with some water and began.

"It happened quickly. As you know, Argent had warned us that the Emperor's troops were massed outside of the valley entrance to Liat. He'd hoped to diffuse the situation and went to parley. I had planned to go with him, but he sent me to the Alcove to marshal the guards. We had thought their magic could protect us. I ran toward the hill but saw the Emperor's troops firing on the guards. I've never seen weapons like the ones they used. I ran back to warn the others."

He paused, swallowed hard, and sipped his water. Tears streaked his face. "Those weapons butchered us. Everything those beams touched disintegrated. There were explosions. I was hit by the force of a blast and flying debris. I felt Argent fall, and then I felt nothing. The Emperor's troops must have thought I was dead. When I woke, I heard them wandering the school grounds looking for survivors. I heard the screams. I could do nothing."

Maeva put her arm around him. "Were there any other survivors?"

"I think so. Argent had ordered several teachers to take acolytes and evacuate as many texts as possible. I don't know if they made it."

Hope rose in Tuac. "Where did they go?" Tuac asked.

"Basul. Argent knew that magicians bypassed the wards, but he did not believe Ba'al would move against us this way. Argent suspected that the Emperor would not risk a full assault on Basul. Ba'al could offer us sanctuary."

Tuac closed his eyes and focused on Merle.

Where are you? He felt no tremor along the thread that connected them, but the thread was still there. *Maybe she is too far away.*

They left Trada's rooms to search for survivors. They found none but they did find what was left of Argent. They buried him and made a monument of nearby rocks to the last Headmaster of Liat. All that remained of the Anthenes were the three of them and those who fled. The three agreed that Trada should head to the University. If any Anthenes survived, he was the logical person to lead what was left of their Art.

After Trada left, Tuac and Maeva returned to the room in the school that connected to the Chamber of Reunification to look for Ki'lel's wand. Even though Tuac believed he could access different types of magic, he thought it could be a useful weapon and he associated it with his memories of Meiach. The slender object had rolled across the floor and lay flush against one wall. Tuac picked it up and tucked it into his pack.

"Is this the last thing you want to take, Cub? If so, we need to leave."

"Where are we going?"

"We can't go to your home. They'll be watching there. And even if the University is safe for Anthenes, I don't think it is safe for you. We only have one choice. We must go to the eye of the storm." Maeva paused to adjust her pack. "We will go to Tush-man. There we can seek out the Prophet's ancient texts. Maybe we will find something in them that will help. We will be in the Emperor's city, and I hope he'll never think to look for you there."

They left Liat. The Valley of Redemption had become the Vale of Tears.

TWENTY

I had always pictured a different life for me. One of peace, not war. Of life, not death. But Mia had other plans for me.

I look at the faces of those around me. They see me as more than I am. I was just unwilling to remain silent, but now they view me as a leader. They inspire me to be my best self, but I am not sure they understand I am just like them. Flawed and imperfect.

The Teachings of the Prophet, 9:4

Esa fidgeted as the Emperor paced back and forth, ranting because Ba'al had summoned him to the University.

"How dare she!" His shrill voice rang in the throne room.

His petulance is childish, she thought. The summons had not surprised her. Esa had hoped the elimination of the Anthenes would stay secret long enough for the Emperor to control the narrative. That changed when the wave of anguish and despair had crushed half of her troops. Esa knew the magicians would have felt it, too. They would investigate and discover what the Empire had done. Esa was relieved that Ba'al wanted to talk before retaliating.

While marching back to Tushman, Esa developed several plans for engaging the University. She believed the Empire could navigate this crisis, but had faced an unexpected problem upon her return. Emperor Hahook had become unhinged.

The Emperor had never been benevolent, but now he was unrestrained, paranoid, and delusional. Once she had respected his tactical mind.

He used to say it was better to tax slightly less than the people can afford than to demand more than they have. Grumbling was easier to put down than sedition. Now he has no moderation at all.

When she had returned to Tushman from Liat, Esa had learned that Hahook had ended the Journey. Now he conscripted all fit young Mians, male and female. Any of them who would have gone to the University now lived in the barracks of the imperial army. None of these children joined the trades or the Church. Hahook had also proclaimed that sermons critical of the Empire were treasonous and he had put the Church under imperial censorship.

Ba'al must know he is seizing power.

Esa suspected that Ba'al could handle the challenge. She was willing to engage with the Empire, but on her terms and in a setting of her choice. Hahook responded to Ba'al's summons by ordering Esa to prepare her plasma troops for another battle. Esa urged the Emperor to be cautious, but he wanted to display the Empire's new power. Esa chose not to push the issue.

"She underestimates you, my liege." Esa said. She considered how long it would take to train the new conscripts and integrate them with her surviving troops. "I will assemble and equip our soldiers. We will be ready to march in two weeks."

"Those mages are no match for our plasma magic."

"We must deploy our weapons strategically, my liege, striking when the University is most vulnerable."

"Go and prepare my forces," he barked, "I will decide when we will strike."

She saluted and left. Esa felt his glare on her back as she strode from the room.

Esa trained the new recruits and assembled her battalion. She worried Ba'al would lose patience with the Emperor's delay and level Tushman. To her relief, Hahook finally agreed to the meeting date, but only after Ba'al agreed that Hahook could bring an entourage. Her messages discussing the details revealed her ire. If this were not a battle for the heart and soul of Mia, Esa would have enjoyed the brinksmanship between the Empire and the University. Perhaps she needed to rethink her allies.

As the date approached, Hahook assembled his forces. One morning he met Esa, and her commanders at dawn outside the city gates, and the imperial army started their march to the University. It should have taken two weeks but the Emperor ordered Esa to take a slower pace to draw things out. This did give her time to continue training her soldiers, but it also increased her unease with Hahook. She wanted this mission to be over. The Emperor rambled constantly. At times, Esa swore he was conversing with someone, though she could not see with whom.

They set up camp in a flat field in front of the gates when they arrived at the University. The agreed plans called for Hahook to meet with Ba'al upon arrival, but Esa knew he was making a statement. He ordered Esa to deploy the Emperor's forces as if preparing for a full siege of the University. But Esa knew this was also for show. Any direct attack on the magicians was foolish. Even with the plasma weapons, attacking the University would result in mass casualties for both sides.

As they fortified their positions, Esa expressed her concerns. The Emperor dismissed her reservations, revealing that he had a cadre of magicians sworn to him and his cause. This surprised Esa, and she wondered whether any magician would openly challenge Ba'al. Yet magicians on the Emperor's side could shift the balance of power.

Ba'al did not send an emissary to their camp. Esa gave Ba'al credit for her strategic insight, as Ba'al's patience unsettled the Emperor. He grew more agitated by the hour. By evening, he had worn a track in his tent's carpet with his pacing. He commanded Esa to send a messenger inviting Ba'al to attend a banquet in her honor at the Emperor's camp. Ba'al sent the messenger back with a response.

Esa read the message aloud: "Your entourage is larger than we expected, and is unwelcome. I will see you in my chambers tomorrow at first light." *The Emperor has overplayed his hand*, she thought. "My liege, we have our answer."

Hahook flung a goblet across his tent, the dregs of the wine splattering dark on the canvas.

"Begone! We will allow her to think she is in control, but tomorrow she will learn who wields the power in this land."

Esa left. She heard Hahook ranting to his unseen companion far into the night.

At first sunrise, Esa walked to the University's gates with her deranged ruler. She was not sure whether either of them would return.

A mage greeted them at the gate. The magician looked at Esa and started to hold up a hand to stop her. Then she paused and lowered her hand. *I am permitted access.* Esa thought. *Another move in the game by Ba'al.*

A second mage came up to the two and led them through the wards and onto the University grounds. They entered the largest building, and approached double doors adorned with the six symbols of the Arts.

Their guide spoke a word and the doors opened. They entered a vast octagonal chamber. Its ceiling was four stories above the tiled floor. There were seven floor-to-ceiling windows in frosted glass. Six of them featured faint colors representing the six Arts. Ba'al stood in front of the seventh, which was clear. Ba'al glared at the Emperor.

"What in the Prophet's name were you thinking?" Her voice boomed in the huge space. Esa held her composure, but she saw the Emperor flinch.

"You fool!" Ba'al took three strides forward. "Nabes has risen and you chose this moment to upset the triumvirate? Mia must unite against this evil. Why slaughter the Anthenes? They were defenseless!" The Archmage's voice rang against the walls. Hahook took a step back, forcing Esa to step aside. Esa hoped Ba'al directed her wrath at Hahook and not at his military commander.

I followed orders, she thought.

The Emperor rallied. "I see you disagree with my actions. I realize the Anthenes had a long and important history for all of us, but they were weak. I cannot afford to have you distracted by protecting them.

"I do not underestimate the power of Nabes. He devastated Mian society before, and only our combined forces won our survival. I destroyed Liat for Mia's sake. Their altruism weakened us. Nabes' disease must be eliminated with fire and fury, it cannot be healed.

"Now the Empire and Basul must ally to control and safe-guard Mian society in the coming battle. By the way, we solved your problem with that renegade boy."

Hahook's bravado impressed Esa. By omitting the Church, he signaled to Ba'al that the three branches of power were now two. Magicians disdained the Church. Hahook's offer to govern with the University offered a compromise. His remark about the boy was masterful. Esa knew Ba'al considered that a touchy subject.

Ba'al's glare did not change. "Your attempts to consolidate power are neither appropriate nor appreciated. The triumvirate was created so that Mians may present a united front should Nabes return. You have weakened us. For everyone's sake, let us hope we can overcome this. The boy was a minor irritant compared to what we face.

"My emissaries returned from Liat to report the carnage caused by your weapons. Whatever power you used, do not think you can use it against Basul and survive."

"I would never turn against my ally," Hahook said.

Ba'al waved her hand and a wide table rose from the stone floor. An assistant unrolled a detailed map of Mia. The southern quarter, centered on Shalla, was black. Ba'al looked at the Emperor.

"This is now a war Council. Let us discuss how we're going to respond to Nabes. The Charge will be here tomorrow."

Esa relaxed. They had survived the day.

Rea had been listening outside the great room. She had been summoned earlier, but instructed to wait outside with other magicians. Her brazen eavesdropping shocked them. This did not surprise her.

They're all older than me, and used to obeying Ba'al, she thought.

The invitation to this meeting testified to her recent successes. She had potential, power, aptitude, and confidence. She had attracted the attention of the upper echelons of Basul, who included her in briefings. She knew that Nabes had risen and Liat had been destroyed.

Everyone had felt the massacre. But she had sensed more than the others. She had told no one that within the wave of anguish she sensed Tuac's survival.

Tuac was attacked by the Emperor? And Ba'al was involved? They do not know Tuac lives.

They will learn that Tuac survived. He will need support when that happens. Rea decided that the best way for her to help her brother was to gain enough respect and standing to intercede on his behalf. Ba'al's confidence in Rea would bring her authority and access.

Rea vowed that once Tuac was safe, she would hold everyone who had attacked him accountable. She needed to bide her time. She might use the Emperor as kindling for her blaze.

Tuac and Maeva avoided people as much as possible on their journey to Tushman. They trusted no one. They discussed the implications of what had happened at Liat. Coming out of his trance in the mirror room, Tuac had called himself the "Reunifer". They needed to understand what that meant and what it might mean for his role in the coming battle against Nabes.

One night, Tuac tried to start a campfire with his flint and steel. He could generate the sparks, they settled on his tinder, but they died when he blew on them.

"My Cub," Maeva said, putting a hand on his shoulder. "Every task deserves the same level of attention. Whether it is a complex spell to heal the soul, or starting dinner, you must focus."

Tuac knew he had been rushing. He closed his eyes and slipped into meditation. He focused on the sparks and how a smooth breath would coax them to spread into the fuel, and how the warm fire would bloom when they did. He opened his eyes, struck the rocks, and sparks flew. Tuac exhaled a plume of flame from his lips. It flowed into his tinder and caught. He was so startled he coughed and looked at Maeva.

"How did you do that?" she asked.

"I don't know. I've never done that before." Tuac recalled that the Chamber of Reunification had shown him different views of himself in front of each door.

I healed the breach with all types of magic. Maybe I can master any Art? Maybe there is only one true Art? Tuac knew from his limited time at the University that no single person could control more than one Art. *Was that because it wasn't possible or because it is forbidden? Is this what Reunification means?*

He reached for the flame and started playing with it. Tuac laughed as he made it jump between his hands. He spun it into bright skeins and balls, tossing them high and catching them when they fell. Tuac made the campfire roar and then subside. With each maneuver, he felt the fire speaking to him, and its delight became his.

Maeva laughed, clapping her hands each time he willed the flame to do a new trick. They relished the moment, a brief reprieve from their burden of grief.

"You are truly special, Cub. We need to explore your gifts

with all the other elements. But right now, let's get dinner started."

Tuac obliged by settling the fire into bright embers ready to heat their soup. Their mood during dinner was lighter than it had been for days.

Before going to sleep that night, Tuac settled into a meditative state. He searched for Merle's bright strand but could not find her. He did not know if this was because she had been lost at Liat or because they were now some distance from Liat. Perhaps the intensity of his feelings for her interfered. He was terrified she might be gone forever. Instead, he reached out to Maeva. He tapped on her mental shield to see if she would let him in. She responded, and he was enfolded in her warm embrace.

I'm glad you finally figured that out, she said through this new bond.

From then on, they were connected.

They used the trip to hone his ability to wield all the Arts. On a small scale, his new skills helped them barter for resources from fellow travelers and villagers. When their supplies ran low, Tuac played the role of a tinker. He would fiddle with a broken pan or rake, deploying magic to fix the item. He masked his use of the Arts, the small deployments of fire to mold things, telekinesis to reposition broken parts, and stone moving skills to mend broken pots.

His experiments usually succeeded, but both of them knew he needed to strengthen his command of the elements. Each day he focused on understanding and mastering one Art. Using the same techniques that Maeva had taught him in Liat, he explored and exercised proficiency in each magical area. Maeva began each practice session the same way.

"Focus, Cub. Out of darkness comes light, confusion leads to clarity, chaos turns to order. Learn to see that which pushes you away as well as that which draws you in. Balance is the key." On one day he called forth fire and formed it into a staff that he could wield. The next day, he created a telepathic shield. As they traveled, he rotated through each Art several times.

His strength and precision increased. During one session, Tuac shaped clay into a sword. He swung it like a metal weapon and lost himself in an imaginary battle. The sword crumbled.

Maeva saw what had happened.

"Whatever Art you use, you must never lose yourself in the moment. If you do that when you are in battle, it could cost you or someone else their life. But this was a good start."

Maeva's ability to know what he was thinking or feeling sometimes annoyed him. It was a downside of their bond. But she was right, he had lost focus. He vowed to do better. He helped Maeva erase their campsite and prepared their packs.

Later that morning, Maeva pointed to a mountain range now visible on the horizon. "There," Maeva said, "That is Mia's Wall. Beyond the mountain range is a frozen tundra. It is said that when Aced and Mia first created this planet, it was frozen. Together, they pushed away the ice and formed a wall to keep it out. The Mians built Tushman at the base of the mountains to be closer to Mia's touch."

By midday, traffic on the road had increased. There were pilgrims, merchants, and some seeking refuge in the city. Tuac and Maeva crested a ridge and Tushman appeared in the valley below. Huge stone walls anchored in the mountain range surrounded the city. Where the wall joined the cliffs, Tuac saw an ornate building carved into the living stone. They could see the towers of an enormous palace rising above the great wall.

It's magnificent, Tuac thought.

Closer to the city, Tuac realized the fortress walls were ten paces thick and taller than any tree. They were built of massive stone blocks stacked and fitted so precisely that he could barely see the seams. They would be impenetrable.

Stone Movers built this.

There was only one entrance into the city. They headed to this wide gate and Tuac marveled at the massive doors. The milling crowd of other travelers slowed as they made their way through the narrow opening. Tuac noticed the faces of some were distraught and exhausted. Fear haunted their eyes.

They're running from something, he thought. Tuac and Maeva stepped out of the flow so he could study the great structure. An elderly woman with kind eyes and a wide smile stopped next to Tuac.

"They open with something called a pulley system. Steam turns a great wheel, and it pulls cables to open the gates, and unrolls the cables to close them. Unless the pulley opens them, those gates will not budge." She nodded in awe of the craftsmanship. "It is a testament to the power of the Mian mind. Hundreds could push at the gate but it would not move. Yet one guard, activating the pulleys with one hand, can open the gates. They are open all day and closed each night. Tushman welcomes all. Except that the Emperor feels obliged to tax those seeking refuge from the south."

"Why just the south?" Maeva asked.

"So many of them arrive every day," the woman said. "This started a few months ago, and there are more of them every week."

The crowd in front of them shifted forward, step by step. The three of them eased back into the traffic. They followed the older woman. Tuac noticed guards standing in alcoves built inside the walls. They were checking each person seeking entrance to the great city.

They may welcome all, but they are still cautious, Tuac thought.

Maeva sensed his concern. She pulled his hood over his head. He slouched into his clothes. Maeva answered the guard's questions, explaining that she and her son were here to visit the cathedral. He waved them through into the busy thoroughfare. Their elderly companion had vanished into the crowd on her own business.

Maeva said, "The city is built in concentric half circles. This one is the business zone since it was closest to the gate. The next circle contains workshops and places for travelers to stay. The three interior arcs are residential. The closer you are to the inner city, the more expensive the neighborhood. The City Center contains government buildings, the University's embassy, soldier's quarters, and the Emperor's Palace."

"You have been here before?"

"Yes, years ago."

"Other than hiding from the Emperor, why are we here?"

"We are going there," Maeva pointed toward the building carved into the mountain and anchoring one end of the wall. "That is the Cathedral of the Prophet. Unlike the city, it has no gates. The Church is always open for prayer. I hope we can find information about your ability to use all forms of the Art."

Tuac bounced on the balls of his feet, restless among the foot traffic that slowed their pace to a walk. The crowd thinned as they got further from the gates, and they joined the flow of pilgrims heading toward the Cathedral. Maeva strode along and Tuac stayed behind her, no longer slouching though he kept his hood up. He could sense through their bond that she was watching to make sure no one was following them.

Soon they stood in the Cathedral's courtyard. Two huge columns formed from natural outcroppings of the mountain framed the entrance. Up close, Tuac could see engravings on them. These told the story of Mia and the Prophet. The first pane at the bottom of the left column showed the *Curiosity* landing and the Terran explorers meeting with the Mian ancestors. The panel above it featured a map of Mia with boundaries and family crests of the early warlords. The final panel at the top showed a huge castle with the rays of Mia's suns radiating behind it.

The top panel of the right column showed the same castle broken, its towers collapsed. Sinuous lines of flame curled around its base.

The Great Destruction, Tuac thought.

The panel below showed a man in simple robes. He held a staff in his right hand and cradled a book in his left elbow, the most common depiction of the Prophet. He stood before the partially constructed fortress wall of Tushman. The last pane was split into three triangles. One contained the six symbols of the magical Arts, one contained a book that was the Church's signet and the last featured the Emperor's crest of a flying lizard breathing fire. Tuac felt Maeva next him.

"Shalla," she whispered.

He sensed her melancholy and reached for her hand.

"Shalla was a beautiful fortress, then it was the site of the Great Destruction. That is where Nabes was defeated. Led by a lad about your age, the Prophet. He was a gifted magician who convinced the warlords opposing Nabes to band together under Cedric, the first Emperor. That is his war crest depicted on the column. He rallied his allies under the symbol of a Terran beast called a dragon. He took this creature as his standard after reading many Terran books and learning that the dragon was the most frightful, powerful beast to inhabit the Terran world. It was immune to magic's touch, and Cedric believed that he and his forces would be blessed by Aced with similar protection. It was said the Prophet was able to call those dragons across time and space to fight for Cedric."

"Some of the stories are a bit exaggerated," interrupted a middle-aged woman dressed in a grey robe. She had come over to stand beside Maeva and Tuac. "The dragons who fought in the war were not real. They were the creations of the practitioners of fire, water, stone and air who shaped their magic into an echo of these great beasts. According to the Church's chronicles of the Fight for Enlightenment—what you call the Great Destruction—the beasts were unstoppable."

"I had not understood that from the histories that I read," Maeva said. "My name is Maeva and this is my son Ton'ku."

"My name is Frea, and I am with the Order of the Prophet. May I be of assistance?"

Tuac studied Frea. He did not want to use magic to read her, both because he was new to the Art and because he thought that it would be a violation of Frea's privacy. Even without magic, Tuac sensed her warmth and compassion. He could also sense that she *believed* in the Prophet.

"I am a docent of the Great Cathedral. I give historical tours of the building and grounds. Would you like to see something specific?"

"We're interested in the history of the Prophet and the Great —the Fight for Enlightenment," Tuac said.

"We are from the West," Maeva said. "A healer's college that also teaches the ways of the Prophet. We have been asked to compare a few points in our scholarly works with the texts in the Church's library to ensure that ours are consistent with the true history of the Prophet. Our records are remote from here, and we do not want that distance to create inaccuracy. Given that I was wrong about the dragons, we have work to do."

"Of course!" Frea said, rubbing her hands in delight. "Our

library is Mia's largest and is open to all. I'm gratified that I can help you confirm the glory of the Prophet's teachings! Follow me, and I will show you to the main reading room." Frea led them across the courtyard and through the main entrance. Tuac noted the imperial soldiers stationed on either side.

That's odd. Why would the Emperor be guarding the Cathedral? Tuac wondered.

When they were out of earshot of the gate, Frea said, "The guards have been here for a few days now. We have been told there is some unrest, and the Charge requested assistance protecting the followers of the Prophet. The soldiers look intimidating but they have been polite and haven't bothered anyone."

Inside, the full majesty and enormity of the Cathedral stunned Tuac. Frea led them into a huge rotunda hollowed out of the mountain. The walls and ceiling were smooth, and Tuac could sense the residual magic that had created this space. On the floor he saw a picture similar to the one on the column, showing the Prophet looking over the valley of Tushman. He had a staff in one hand and a book in the other, but in this depiction the walls of the city rose complete, and beyond them, the great Cathedral and the Emperor's palace.

People crossed the echoing space. Those in beige robes strode with purpose on Church business. Pilgrims in street clothes stopped and gawked at the enormity of the room and its ornamentation. They headed for the door opposite the entrance.

"There, to the left, are the quarters for all of the members of the Order," Frea gestured with the practiced ease of a tour guide. "That wing also holds private meeting rooms, a kitchen and store houses. Ahead of us, where the pilgrims are going, is the main chapel. We are going to the right, which leads to the library.

"Do we have time to look at the chapel?" Tuac asked.

Frea beamed. "Of course. We have services there, twice daily, and followers of the Prophet may enter at any time to find peace. The doors are never locked."

Tuac walked up to the chapel's entrance and peered inside. This space was by far the largest enclosed room Tuac had ever seen. Though he was not religious, the grandeur of the chapel inspired him. Patches of color dotted the floor and lower walls as light streamed through huge stained-glass windows. They glowed even though they were within a mountain.

Magicians must have had a hand in this too, Tuac thought.

The stained glass featured various scenes from the Prophet's life: him as a child, him meeting with Cedric, him leading the forces against Nabes, and the battle at the Great Destruction. In all of the images, he appeared brighter and larger than those around him.

Ranks of pews built from beautiful brown wood occupied much of the floor, and at the front stood an ornate podium. In spite of the steady stream of pilgrims they had seen, the chapel seemed empty, its size dwarfing the crowd of the faithful.

"Fewer and fewer come to services." Sadness shadowed Frea's voice. "There was a time before I arrived when the chapel was full even with ten services a day. Now, it's rare to have more than a few hundred true followers at a service and many times there are only a handful. There is even talk about cutting services to once a day. Quite disheartening, given all The Prophet teaches."

Frea steered them toward the library entrance. She opened the door and led them down a long corridor. Unlike the Rotunda, the hallway's walls were not smooth, but retained chisel marks. The craftsmanship had incorporated the natural protrusions and craters of the original stone. The builders of the Cathedral felt no need to be grandiose for those seeking knowledge, only for those seeking enlightenment from homilies.

Perhaps the Church would have more followers if it offered truth instead of grandiosity, Tuac thought.

The deeper they went into the mountain, the cooler the air became. Their steps disturbed a thin layer of dust on the floor.

Not many people come this way. Are there fewer pilgrims seeking knowledge or does the Church discourage research?

"Sorry about all the dirt," Frea said. "As with the apathy toward The Prophet's teachings, the desire to study his words and those of Order have diminished. But here we are!"

They had reached an unassuming door, plain and well-made. There were no locks or guards.

No need to protect the truth if no one wants to know it, Tuac thought.

Frea opened the door and gestured them into the vast library. Tuac felt like he had been whisked through another portal. The hallway had been narrow, but the library was cavernous. It stretched farther than Tuac could see, with row upon row of shelves holding books and scrolls. The ceiling was higher than the central rotunda, and showed the rich textures of the natural rock. The cool air stirred with a faint breeze.

"This cavern was here when the Cathedral was built, and we expanded a narrow fissure to create the hallway. Rumor has it that the Prophet hid in this cave at one point. There are some that believe he wrote his Teachings here."

"Over there is where you can request the books." Frea indicated a small desk manned by a member of the Order. Beside it Tuac saw a set of drawers with small labels, and the clerk had two drawers on the desk. He was sorting cards and tucking them into the drawers.

Frea said, "Each card represents an item in the library's

collection. You can look through the cards to find a particular author or topic, then bring the card to the desk and we'll fetch it for you. We also have private alcoves, available only to members of the Order and certain members from the University and the Empire. The environment in this cavern preserves paper for hundreds of years, safe from moisture and insects."

Frea pointed to a series of tables with chairs and enclosed oil lamps. "That is where you may read the books. If you need to go somewhere, just leave whatever you're studying on a table with a card that indicates that you're working with it. The librarians will not disturb your book if you return within a reasonable amount of time. After a few days, though, the books will be reshelved.

"If you think that you are going to be here for several days, we can arrange accommodations for you close by. Rooms for pilgrims are located down the hall. The quarters are very basic, with only a bed, a reading desk, and a small chest for your belongings. You also have access to a common washroom. We can offer food but we ask that you eat in your rooms and wash your hands thoroughly before handling any library materials."

Tuac and Maeva had not discussed where they were going to stay and with the Empire looking for them, hiding in the depths of the Cathedral seemed like a good idea. He let Maeva know through their bond that lodging here felt safe.

"We would love to stay here," Maeva said. "We have much to accomplish and little time. Can you please show us to our rooms and let us know the cost?"

"We have no set cost for the rooms, asking only that you consider a donation to the Order when you leave. Meals are an Imperial copper per person per week. You'll be eating what the members of the Order eat, so it is simple fare."

Tuac and Maeva had withdrawn her savings from the

reserves at Liat before they left. It was not much, but it would support them for some time if they were frugal.

"We are blessed by the Order's kindness. The Prophet be praised," Maeva said and bowed. Tuac followed her lead. Frea led them to their rooms and left them. The two decided that a meal, shower, and a night of rest in a bed would give them a better start the next day.

"So, the boy escaped Liat?" Ba'al said. Given what she had heard about the scope of the massacre, she was impressed that Tuac had survived and eluded her agents for so long. "Ki'lel, he is your responsibility. Assemble your team, find him, and deal with him. We need to get to him before Nabes does. Work quickly. We need you and your team focused on Nabes and our response to the Emperor's trespass as soon as possible." Ba'al paced around the war table. The Gaeists had imbued the table with their magic to track the progress of the dead zone advancing from the south.

Ki'lel said, "I have a plan. It needs to be done carefully so it doesn't attract attention from the Emperor or the Charge. I will take care of it.

Twenty-One

I stared into the eyes of evil. I fought for those who could not defend themselves and confronted despots who cared only for power. I did these things in the pursuit of justice, even if I have no claim of moral authority, no power to see into the future nor ability to change the past. I chose to fight back because I could not continue to look the other way.

The Secret Teachings of the Prophet

Tuac and Maeva developed a routine. They rose, ate breakfast, went to the library and researched the Great Destruction and the reconstruction of Mian society afterwards. They found a table deep in the library's cavern where they would not be disturbed. They hoped to find the secret of Tuac's role and power as the Reunifier by studying the early use of magic in Mian history.

Frea hovered, her supervision friendly but constant. Her official duties gave her discretion, and their questions intrigued her, so she was eager to assist. Every time they found a useful reference, she would get almost as excited about what they would learn as they did.

The stories of the Great Destruction, whether fictional or historical, bore marked similarities. All accounts discussed Nabes' rise to power, the appearance of the Prophet to counter Nabes' spread, the Great Destruction, and the creation of the triumvirate, the three branches of Mia's government.

Tuac had learned about Nabes when he was in school. He had been taught that Nabes was a descendent of the Terrans who had assembled an army to control Mia. His campaign had begun by stamping out villages and enslaving those that survived. Soon, he had assembled a formidable group of magicians and soldiers. Most Mians had seen Nabes as another petty warlord and were unwilling to put their lives at risk for strangers. Nabes had taken advantage of the situation, extending his reach. Before long, the entire southern region of Mia had fallen under his shadow.

Neither Tuac's schooling nor the texts he was now reading shed much light on the Prophet's origin. Tuac had been taught that the Prophet had simply appeared, with no description of where he was from or his ancestry. He had championed justice and the need to ally against Nabes. The texts Tuac and Maeva now explored provided more background about the Prophet than either of them had ever learned. One account described the Prophet's approach to a local chief.

The Prophet had said, "There are only two sides, the evil of Nabes and the good of those who willing to resist. Refusing to take a side is the same as supporting Nabes. Indifference is not acceptable." That warlord was Cedric, who became the first Emperor of Mia. Though the Prophet gained Cedric as an ally, many rejected the Prophet's pleas. Whether gifted or not, most chose to avoid the conflict, believing they could continue their lives as before, regardless of who won.

All chronicles described the Prophet as a powerful mage. However, Tuac could find no stories of the Prophet using magic. Oddly, the story of Prophet and the chita was not in the library. Tuac suspected that the Church was selective in preserving records of the Prophet.

Why? We know he was able to use magic. If I am the Reunifier, was he the Divider? Tuac wondered.

Tuac learned details omitted from his schooling, even at the University. To his surprise, the Prophet was not initially successful against Nabes. In fact, the Prophet lost ground and the situation was grim. Cedric and his followers lost confidence. Just when they considered negotiating a peace with Nabes, the Prophet found a spark of hope that changed everything.

That spark was a charismatic magician named Luina. She protected a small town from marauders intent on selling the town's children into slavery. Each time the slavers approached, she burned them where they stood, letting one survive to warn others. Her reputation grew and the attacks stopped. The tale of her defense reached the Prophet and he sought to recruit her. She did not agree with the Prophet's emphasis on diplomacy, but she shared his passion for a more just world and agreed to help him.

As they worked together, their relationship deepened and they became lovers. Luina's fire was exactly what Cedric's followers needed to regain their conviction. Her strategic leadership allowed the Prophet to continue his diplomatic efforts. The two scoured Mia for mages and others who fought injustice or Nabes' forces. Often they assisted, winning new allies. They assembled an army of more than a hundred gifted Mians and thousands of non-gifted warriors. After the Prophet had assembled many different magicians, they had discovered that individuals displayed affinities for particular types of magic. Some specialized in fire, others in water, stone, air, the natural world, and mental connection. Tuac noted that no chronicler mentioned healing.

Luina had grasped the strategic possibilities of focusing one's discipline in a specific Art. She formed a group of magicians also skilled in manipulating fire. She directed those with other specialties to band together and develop their particular magical Art. The magicians pushed each other to invent novel and deadly uses of their magic. The Fire Walkers formed dragons, Air Riders mastered tornados, and Water Sculptors called intense storms out of thin air. Stone Movers, Gaeists and Telepaths shaped their respective Arts to help Cedric's army defeat Nabes' troops.

One battle at a time, this strategy turned the tide of the war. Nabes' magical forces were quick to copy the techniques deployed by the Prophet's mages, but the Prophet had more resources and mages motivated by their just cause. When Nabes replicated one weapon, the Prophet countered with another. The collaborative approach used by the Prophet's followers allowed rapid response and innovation, giving them a tactical advantage. Nabes' forces were limited by its imagination, as it tolerated no disagreement among its lieutenants. Both sides suffered heavy casualties, but the Prophet gained ground, liberating villages and towns and driving Nabes' forces back into the south toward Shalla.

Tuac found a detailed recounting of the final battle between Nabes and the Prophet's forces.

"Look at this," he said, setting the heavy book next to Maeva. "This is the Church's copy of the record written by the First Emperor's scribe."

. . .

The Prophet's forces encircled Nabes and his minions, and many thought this would be the final engagement and Nabes' defeat. Cedric and the Prophet believed that peace was still possible, so they called a cease fire. Both sides collected their dead, and healers attended to Cedric's troops. Luina, Cedric, and the Prophet met with the foremost practitioners of the six Arts to discuss the final steps to end the conflict.

The war Council debated for hours. Some wanted to erase Nabes and all of his followers from Mia, punishing them for the horrors they had committed. Others argued that lasting peace could only grow from reconciliation.

Luina wanted vengeance, but her beloved had a higher calling. The two agreed to let the leaders of Mia reach a peaceful resolution and did not try to influence the outcome. During the debate divisions grew. Some focused on degrees of complicity among their opponents, arguing that indifference should not be punished as harshly as active conspiracy. Others focused on the individual's ability to influence the outcome, arguing that the enhanced should be held to a higher standard than the conscripted, given the former's deliberate intent and their power to inflict more harm.

The Prophet, tired of the back and forth, left the Council in disgust. Luina stayed, hoping to guide the debaters to a resolution. Cedric slipped out of the tent, concerned about the Prophet.

Nabes considered Cedric's ceasefire to be a moment of vulnerability. He created a huge black dragon and sent it to attack Cedric's camp. Cedric's forces panicked and scattered. Cedric and the Prophet heard the commotion and ran to see what was happening. They ordered their forces to fall back out of range of the beast's fiery blasts. The Prophet rallied his magicians, and soon dragons made of other elements attacked the black monster with their breaths of fire, ice, and air. They could not stop it.

The black beast swooped over the camp toward the war Council's tent. It exhaled a black plume that melted the tent. Luina and the rest of the war Council had been inside. Screams echoed over the battlefield. The Prophet sensed Luina's death and sprinted for the tent. Only the iron anchor stakes remained among the smoking ashes.

Nabes' forces attacked during the pandemonium. The Prophet wavered, stunned by grief. Cedric pulled him away from the battle and sounded a retreat. Their troops would regroup.

The Prophet had taught that the discrete use of magic was the solution to the war, and he condemned magic's unbridled use. He was committed to defeating Nabes, but believed Mia's future must not be anchored in blood or vengeance. In that moment, though, he lost himself. He wanted to end Nabes. Cedric saw the change and readied his troops for a final assault, though he worried that the Prophet might destroy every living thing on Mia.

A new dragon rose above the Prophet. It gleamed in the evening sun, its white body equal to the black dragon's. The white dragon howled, summoning its nemesis to battle high above Shalla. The two beasts tore at the other with their massive claws and jaws. With each wound, the dragons poisoned one another. Nabes could not heal his beast's wounds, but the wounds on the Prophet's dragon closed, and it lost neither blood nor strength. The white dragon reared back and released a glittering plume of colors over the black dragon. The black beast faltered, its wings and body disintegrating. The white dragon snapped off the black drag-on's head. Nabes' beast vanished.

Cedric's troops rallied. There were no more debates. The final battle of Shalla had begun. While Cedric's army eliminated Nabes' forces, the Prophet strode toward Shalla to confront Nabes. His robed form radiated rage and he passed through the carnage untouched. Some of Nabes' forces tried to surrender but Cedric's soldiers gutted them. The Prophet passed through the gates of Shalla. With a gesture, he slammed them shut.

Despite years of investigation, I have not uncovered what happened at that final confrontation. There were no witnesses and the Prophet refused to discuss it. We know only that the battle was brief.

When the Prophet returned, all he said was, "It is over and now we must rebuild."

Tuac closed the book. Keeping his voice low, he said, "Did you notice how the Church erased Anthenes? This author only mentions six Arts. Other than the Prophet's own writings, this appears to be the last story about the Prophet. We've found no records of a Reunifier, nor any reference to the meeting I witnessed in the Alcove." He felt drained.

"Let's get some food and rest, Cub. Tomorrow, we start again." She closed her book, put the card on it to indicate she was still using it and Tuac did the same. Several feet away Frea nodded at them.

A loud crash echoed through the cavern, making Tuac and Maeva jump.

"What was *that?*" Frea gasped.

In the dim recesses of the cavern, they heard more crashing and the thump of heavy things falling. Something was destroying the stacks. The sounds grew louder and closer.

"Frea, you hide over there—" Maeva pointed to a space behind one of the bookshelves. "Cub, stand near me—be prepared."

Frea darted into the niche and crouched low. Tuac moved in front of Maeva. This would be his battle.

A pair of bookshelves parted, each falling to one side. An eight-legged beast as tall as a hursa scuttled through the gap on taloned feet. It had six eyestalks and chitinous plates protected its body.

Maeva shoved Tuac to the ground, just as the beast spit at them. The glob swished over his head and splashed on the desk behind them. The wood dissolved under clinging ooze.

Another bookcase fell. The beast lifted its segmented tail and struck at Tuac with the pincered end. He leapt away. The tail snipped off a table leg.

"That's an uruh!" Maeva said.

Tuac had never known such creatures existed. Frea's reaction told him that this intrusion wasn't a library problem. The beast was there for Maeva and Tuac.

He calmed his breath. Tuac had not practiced Gaeist magic, so he reached out telepathically to the thing. He did not want to harm the beast if he could avoid it.

The attacker's mind felt primitive. Tuac sensed hunger and rage, but he also detected another mind controlling the beast. He reached toward that mind and it retreated. The uruh's rage increased, fed by its fear of the other mind. There could be no peaceful solution. Tuac would have to kill it.

The pincer lashed at Tuac again, missing his head by inches. He threw up a telepathic shield and it deflected the next strike. The uruh stepped back, startled by the magical defense. He tried to break the connection between the uruh and its controller but Tuac was not strong enough. The other mind felt different than Nabes' intense evil. A mage must be doing this.

The uruh lunged and Tuac reinforced his shield. Sweat ran

down his face and his hand shook with effort. The creature pressed forward. He was out of time.

Tuac doubted he could penetrate the uruh's armor by throwing something. The close quarters meant that stone moving would be too dangerous, and he did not want to release fire or water into the library.

He had an idea. Tuac visualized a bubble of air around the uruh. Then he summoned the air out of that bubble to suffocate the beast. To his surprise, frost formed on the armor and the eyestalks.

I'm freezing it! I need to keep it enclosed long enough to kill it.

The uruh lashed out at the bubble's surface. Tuac reinforced it with a swirl of wind but knew the air was not enough to hold the animal.

Do not give up, The Watcher said. *This is your destiny. Reunification will be an end, but it will also be a beginning that Mia deserves. You have been lied to for too long. Others with your gift have come and gone with the ability to correct the errors of the past but the mages suppressed them. Now Nabes is here. If you do not embrace Reunification, all is lost. Do not give up.*

Then the Watcher was gone. Tuac was alone again. Then, at last, he understood.

That's what Reunification means: It isn't just that I can use all the Arts. I can bring the Arts together. The plume of the Prophet's dragon held the colors of every Art.

Can I use my other Arts to make a stronger barrier? He had never heard of one mage using multiple Arts at the same time, but he needed to try.

Tuac visualized the room with the doors. Storm winds poured into the room through the open Air Rider door. Since he had used telepathy earlier, he focused on that door. If he could open it, he could create a stronger cage. He grasped the handle but could not lift the latch. He feared the implications of what he was trying to do.

Tuac reached for the Telepath's door again. He poured all of his remaining energy into turning that latch. Just as his strength wavered, it shifted. His confidence flared. He visualized the latch lifting. It clicked and the door swung open. Two streams of magic flowed around him. It felt glorious! He wanted to open all the doors.

Maeva screamed. "Cub! The uruh is escaping!"

Tuac's mind snapped back into the library. He unleashed both Arts. First, he reinforced the wall of the sphere with telekinesis, then he sucked the air out of it. The uruh struck at the walls but could not pierce them. It thrashed, swinging its tail and rearing back to slam into the invisible barrier. Its eyes could not move, stuck to its face with ice. One by one, its legs failed, curling up under its body. Finally, it collapsed, curled into a ball as ice crystals gleamed along its chiton. It was dead.

"That was amazing!" Maeva hugged him hard. Tuac collapsed in her arms. He was exhausted.

"We need get out of here." They surveyed the ruins of the room. "Where's Frea?" Tuac staggered toward the fallen shelving. Together, they lifted the heavy bookcases. Frea lay crushed beneath them.

"Let's go," he hissed through clenched teeth. "We're fighting a war on two fronts. A mage controlled that uruh, not Nabes. The University had a hand in Liat's destruction and now it seems they want us dead. We need to know why."

Maeva's eyes widened at this news, but she nodded. Tuac strode toward the exit and she followed.

"What happened? Did it work?" Ki'lel said.

Chorra wiped the sweat out of her eyes

All of Ba'al's inner circle knew Basul intended to end Tuac. At her direction, Ki'lel had tracked Tuac and his traveling companion to Tushman. They believed that his companion was the last Anthene.

He was not sure why they had gone there, but it presented an opportunity. He met with Chorra and she had agreed to summon an uruh living nearby. While they would not normally attack Tushman's population, uruh had been known to breach the inner walls of the city near the Cathedral.

Ki'lel watched over Chorra as he had communed with the uruh. At this distance, only the most skilled Gaeist could have joined with the creature. Chorra had convulsed several times and Ki'lel sensed she was fighting. Then Chorra collapsed and her eyes opened, ending the connection with the uruh.

"I'm not sure what happened. I had the uruh under my control as we had planned. It cornered them in the Cathedral's library, but the boy fought back and killed the uruh. He must have had help, but I did not feel another mage."

"Uruhs are one of Mia's deadliest predators. How did they kill it? Who is his ally? Ba'al will be furious."

"I can only tell you what I saw through the eyes of the uruh. The last Anthene and Tuac were with a third person when the uruh attacked. A telepath entered the animal's mind and discovered me there. Then the boy encased the uruh in an air bubble. His skills with air rival those of our advanced students. The beast was strong and almost escaped, but the walls around it hardened with psychic energy. That telepath helped him, and they are strong. Together, they contained the uruh long enough for Tuac to freeze it to death. I'm impressed with their strategy."

Ki'lel studied Chorra. Even without his telepathy he could

tell she was telling the truth. The third person must have been a renegade telepath.

"What happened to the third person?"

"I don't know. I lost track of them when the uruh died."

"Speak of this to no one." Ki'lel said. "We must not reveal that Tuac has mastered his Art. Nor do we want to suggest he has an ally who is violating Ba'al's edicts."

He did not look forward to bringing Ba'al this news.

Esa stood silently by as the Emperor ranted at Charge Gershawn. Esa's spies had uncovered the destruction in the library and the Charge's subterfuge in not reporting it to Hahook earlier. It was the perfect opportunity to advance the Empire's sole governance of Mia.

"Gershawn," Hahook snarled as he paced the throne room, "I am furious that you kept this from me. You're lucky I have not taken your head! The magicians violated our control of Tushman. Worse, the boy was in your grasp and you let him escape. Ba'al wants him for some reason and your failure cost us leverage. For all I know, you were coordinating with Basul to hide all of this from me." He stopped in front of the stooped, elderly Charge and glared. The old man recoiled.

Esa knew much of this bluster was theater. Hahook and Esa had discussed their response. Hahook would use this situation to consolidate power. They would deal with Nabes in due time, but the Emperor wanted the Church under his control now. That would allow him to control the masses and turn them against the magicians. Ba'al would have to beg him to protect Basul. Esa watched the Charge tremble, and counted Mia's blessings that the Emperor's tantrum was not directed at her.

"Please, Emperor, forgive me," Charge Gershawn wheezed, his voice creaky. "I did not know that Ba'al had not informed you of the incursion. I would never have kept the incident from you. My loyalty is to the Empire, first and foremost." The Charge bowed as low as his fragile bones allowed.

Now the Emperor will strike, Esa thought.

"I should close the Church, but I am magnanimous. My forgiveness comes at a cost, however. As of today, I am now the Charge. You will continue your daily oversight of the Church under my supervision, and from now on, I am the word of the Church."

Gershawn blanched. The man staggered and seemed about to speak. Then he swallowed hard and bowed. Esa almost felt sorry for him. This was a terrible blow after a lifetime of service to the Prophet.

Hahook paced as he outlined his new official duties. "I will be responsible for the weekly benedictions. All of Mia will look to me for protection. You will give me immediate access to all of the Church's ceremonial troops and to its texts. We are fortunate that so few know that you keep the true teachings of the Prophet in your vault. Those two were trespassers were looking for something. Henceforth, access to that collection is restricted to me or my staff."

"Yes, your Majesty, I will do whatever you ask. I am your humble servant and I embrace your wisdom." Gershawn groveled. The Emperor raised an eyebrow.

The old man cleared his throat and said, "Pardon me. Yes, my Charge". The Emperor smirked and dismissed the man with a wave. Gershawn fled.

"Well done, my liege," Esa said. Esa realized as she said this that her remark might seem brazen. She hastened to add, "You have dismantled the triumvirate and now Basul must accept you as their equal partner."

The Emperor turned to Esa with a wicked grin. "Partner? I will not share power with Basul. The magicians are untrustworthy, withholding their secrets and blabbering on about the second coming of Nabes. I wonder if they are responsible for whatever is going on. Maybe some experiment went wrong, or there's a rogue mage. They need to be eradicated like the Anthenes." Hahook stepped over to a side table and poured himself a goblet of wine, draining it in one draft. He poured himself another, and gestured widely with the glass as he paced, ranting about the devious nature of mages.

Esa felt that the Emperor was losing his grip on reality. She had read her agents' reports and Ba'al was not behind the contagion. Esa was accustomed to the Emperor's mood swings and debauchery, but now she feared what she saw. While she believed only the Empire could impose order on Mia, she had never anticipated outright war with the magicians. Yet the Emperor was poised to attack, motivated by his own wild conspiracy theories.

Hahook stopped in front of her. "It is time for the Empire to assume its rightful role as the *one and only* protector of Mia. We need to expand our army. I want you to enact a conscription. Absorb the Church's forces. Press your agents to find more plasma rifles.

"Yes, sir," Esa saluted.

"And find me someone who has been to the vault. I want to know what The Church has been hiding. And get me that mirror so I can talk to Ba'al. She needs to understand that she has transgressed against the Empire."

The Emperor stared off into space. As Esa studied his face, her gut clenched. The Emperor's eyes had gone entirely black.

Nabes had received another surge of power when the Emperor took over the Church. Next, Nabes and Hahook would attack the magicians, spreading hate for the University among the people. Hahook had been easy to infect, filled as he was with self-interest and depravity. Every night, Nabes entered the Emperor's dreams, twisting the Emperor's memories to convince him that Basul had assassinated his mother and father in order to seize control of the Empire. Nabes fed the Emperor's ego with images of adulation as Mian's celebrated his consolidation of control. Hahook longed to be a savior and a hero, so it was simple to hone his wrath and prejudice.

The former Charge also fed Nabes. Evil was born of many traits, including hate, anger, and prejudice. But Nabes' favorite fuel came from those who sacrificed their principles for the sake of power.

Rea continued to advance within the Fire Walkers. She was a trusted advisor in the war Council. Mia faced a two-front war. Nabes had risen, and his black poison was spreading throughout the south. Many towns and villages had been lost, and refugees fled north. Some came to Tushman, only to be met with taxes, harsh restrictions on refugees, and prejudice. Those that could pay the highest fees were spared the most punitive regulations. The Emperor argued that his first duty was to the current citizens of Tushman. He claimed that the new revenue would provide resources for the refugees, but reports said people slept in the streets and begged for food.

Ba'al's war Council considered whether they should invite

the refugees to Basul. The institution was not noted for its charity, and historically the Council refused to involve itself with mundane concerns like the health and safety of the general populace. Now Basul must focus on defeating Nabes.

Rea fumed at Basul's refusal to assist Mia's people. Basul had a duty to use its power to protect Mia from Nabes. She believed that should include opening the gates of Basul to those ravaged by the war. She was the most junior member of the Council and should have kept silent, but she lost her temper.

"How can we be so uncaring?" All eyes turned to her.

"What did you say?" Ba'al asked.

Rea studied Ba'al, who gave no indication whether she agreed with Rea or intended to punish her disobedience.

"I said we cannot be so uncaring. I understand that Basul is dedicated to the study of the Arts. I understand that we have limited resources. I understand that we must focus on Nabes. But we are better than the sum of those things. We are Mians. We are blessed by Aced with our magical Arts, and we would be turning our back on the Prophet's teachings if we did not help those in need. We have room. We have the ability. We should take in and protect as many refugees as we can. We should set an example for the feckless Emperor who would rather let all those outside his gates perish. We need to stop turning away the refugees who come here for safety."

The war Council was silent.

Ba'al raised a stern eyebrow at Rea.

"Let's get Basul ready for our guests," she said. "Now, on to our other preparations."

Rea thought, *I have won the battle, but at what cost?*

During the meeting, the Acetos created teams for their respective Arts. One team focused on Basul's defenses, another on training the other magicians for battle, a third team researched how Nabes was defeated before, another team enlarged Basul's infirmary, and one small team addressed the refugee situation. Rea did not receive a team assignment. She knew she was being punished.

Ba'al dismissed the war Council. As Rea gathered her notes, Ba'al said, "Rea, you stay."

This is going to be unpleasant. Rea sat down again.

"You are arrogant and impertinent. You know that, yes?"

Rea considered her answer. It might determine her future as a magician. She decided to stand her ground. She was who she was, and would not apologize for speaking out. If there were consequences to her devotion to justice, she would accept them.

"I am committed to the true meaning of my place at Basul. I will not stay silent when others turn their backs on our calling. We have power. But to use power only to maintain it, is to misuse it. We have an obligation to use our power for the greater good and not merely the good of Basul."

Ba'al studied her for a long time. Then she nodded once and Rea caught a twinkle in her eyes.

"I agree with your beliefs, but *we* have a problem with your approach."

Rea expelled the breath she had held.

"You are arrogant and impertinent. Good intentions will not convince everyone. At times you need diplomacy. Just because you are right does not mean you will carry the day. Forcing the issue on a colleague can create an enemy when you need an ally."

Rea thought about this. *Why do I need to restrain myself when the right answer is staring everyone in the face! But Ba'al has a point about strategy. I spoke out of turn and that gives justification to those who disagree with me. And it gives Ba'al an excuse to dismiss my ideas.*

"I understand," Rea said.

"Doing the right thing is harder than understanding what is right. You must assess your audience and guide them to the correct conclusion. They may not want to get there, whether their disagreement is driven by fear, or hate, or uncertainty. To be a warrior, you only need to battle. To be a leader, you have to convince others to go to battle with you, often when they do not want to."

"Is this why I was not assigned a team? I am not a leader? I'm sorry, Ba'al. I understand that I overstepped. I will be more strategic about expressing my opinion, but please do not exclude me from this mission. I want to help."

Ba'al smiled. "No, you have shown that you can lead. And I did not assign you to any other team because I want you as my assistant. You do need to temper yourself in front of others. I find your candor refreshing after dealing with the Council, and I did agree with your position. I want you to understand that the rest of the Council are either afraid of their shadows or too self-absorbed to participate in a solution."

"We need to discuss our plans for dealing with that uncaring autocrat in Tushman. He just threatened Basul and I believe we are headed toward another conflict. And we need to have a difficult conversation about your brother."

Rea left the meeting disturbed by what Ba'al had said about Tuac.

Why did Ba'al trust the Emperor to retrieve Tuac? She should have known he would–use the opportunity to his own advantage. Though none of us knew that he had those weapons, Ba'al put the Anthenes at risk. Now they are all gone.

Rea's faith in Ba'al was shaken by her bad judgement. But Rea knew their real enemy was Nabes.

The news that Tuac was alive and an Air Rider surprised her. Ba'al had explained that his renegade magic was a distraction from the coming war. Tuac needed to be convinced to return to Basul. Rea was now torn between her love for Tuac and her allegiances to Basul.

How could her awkward, naïve, annoying brother really be a risk?

Ba'al had explained that Nabes would target him as a resource. That could not be permitted. Rea could not believe that Tuac would ally himself with evil. He had a steadfast belief in the greater good, in true love, and he had a strong moral code.

If more people were like Tuac, perhaps we wouldn't be in this situation.

Rea had hoped that Tuac would find a small village and be swept off his feet by a local girl. He had talked about finding his soul mate. His romantic longings made her want to gag, but right now, that was what she wanted for him.

Rea viewed this as an opportunity to help Tuac. He had magical skills. If he could be convinced to return, they could confirm his chosen Art and start his training. They needed every mage for the coming war. Ba'al had quizzed Rea for information that could help them find her brother, but there was not much Rea could offer other than stories showing his character. She was back in her room when she remembered that she had not told Ba'al that Tuac was terrified of heights.

Maybe Ba'al could use that information to rule out certain places to look for Tuac, making the search more efficient. Rea headed back to Ba'al's chambers.

As Rea was about to knock on the massive doors to Ba'al's quarters, she heard voices.

"I'm sorry about the damage to the library," Ba'al said. "We have tried to be circumspect, but things got out of hand. I appreciate you not calling the Emperor's attention to our little incursion, and I do apologize that we had to use magic in the Cathedral without first consulting you."

Rea was confused.

Why was Ba'al talking to the Charge? What had happened at the library? Then she heard the Charge's answer.

"Ba'al we have too much to do dealing with that lunatic Hahook. We can't devote resources to some ancient rules that *Basul* has about testing magical proficiency. Do not treat me like a fool. I know much more than you give me credit for. You failed in your effort to eliminate this reject. It should have never come to this. You should have taken care of him as you always do.

Ba'al interjected, "You may know our secrets, but do not discuss this aloud."

"Do not lecture me. You let an untrained magician loose in a time of crisis. That is unacceptable. I will instruct our private security forces to watch for him. But I strongly recommend that you clean up your mess before I have to. We cannot allow Nabes to find this boy."

Rea stumbled back, bumping into a floral display, which rattled. She bolted down the hall and ducked into an alcove. Just as she stepped into the shadow, she heard Ba'al open her door. Rea's heart was beating so hard she was sure that Ba'al could hear it. After a long minute, Ba'al closed the door.

Rea's world crashed down around her. Until the meeting with the Council, she had believed that Basul's decisions were above reproach. But this situation demonstrated that many mages had questionable ethics, and that Basul would enforce immoral policies against those who did not fit its rules.

Her little brother had angered a lot of powerful people and was now a defenseless target.

He's just a boy with no real power. My little brat of a brother! Why does Ba'al consider him a risk?

She rushed back to her chambers. Rea knew she had to play their game, and she hated it.

She would be the best assistant Ba'al had ever had, and hope that Ba'al would confide in her. Even if she didn't, Rea would find out what was really going on. Then she could use that information to save her little brother.

That night, Rea could not sleep. In the small hours of the morning she heard a commotion outside. She dressed and crept out to investigate. From the shadows, she saw Ba'al striding up to the gates.

"Let them in. We are welcoming refugees."

A stooped old man accompanied by ten other people walked inside. Their caravan consisted of carts piled high with books and scroll cases.

A crowd of magicians and staff had gathered at the gate. Rea joined them and moved closer to hear Ba'al's conversation with the stranger.

"You're all that is left?" Ba'al said. Rea could hear both sadness and urgency in her voice.

"We don't know. We fled early in the attack."

"I cannot ever compensate for the injuries the Anthenes have suffered, but I can offer all of you a home at Basul."

Rea's stomach dropped as the last of the Anthenes walked past her. They were exhausted, filthy, and footsore. No one rode in the overburdened carts with their cherished cargo. Most had blank faces, stunned by their experiences. Until this moment, the descriptions of the Emperor's attack on the Anthenes had been sterile and remote for Rea. Now she saw the cold reality of war. She stepped behind a shrub and vomited.

A young Anthene woman rushed from the line, and held

Rea's hair away from her face. When Rea had finished, the stranger handed Rea a small bottle.

"Here, drink this. It will calm your stomach."

Rea took a sip and in moments her gut settled. Her faced flushed with embarrassment. Then she looked into the eyes of the disheveled figure who had aided her. The young woman's expression was kind but haunted.

She is so caring. After all she's suffered, she helps someone from the institution that was complicit in that attack. Rea's embarrassment and sorrow deepened.

"I'm sorry." For the first time in her life, Rea was at a loss for words.

"For what? You didn't attack us," the Anthene said. Her smile lit her dusty face and filled Rea with warmth.

If I had experienced what she has, I would not be as charitable.

Rea did not know what to do. She was not an affectionate person, but she put her arm around the girl's thin shoulders and squeezed.

"My name is Rea. If there is anything you need while you're in Basul, please seek me out."

The Anthene stiffened, then settled into the hug and returned it with more energy than Rea expected. The woman pulled back, and rejoined the rest of the survivors.

"Wait, what is your name?"

The young Anthene smiled again. "My name is Merle. Your brother is my beloved." Then she turned to help an elderly woman who stumbled with fatigue. The Anthenes disappeared into the corridor leading to the guest quarters.

Rea watched them go, her mind whirling. *I guess my brother did find his soulmate.*

Twenty-Two

I worry about my legacy. Will I be loved or reviled? Am I a hero or a villain? Will I have inspired Mians to do good or to allow evil? I am leaving my writings for those who come after me. I hope these words provide guidance and will not be used to enslave those who read them.

The Secret Teachings of the Prophet

Tuac and Maeva walked to their rooms. Tuac wanted to run, but Maeva reminded him that they must not attract attention. Tuac knew that she was right. Ba'al's spies had found them. Whoever controlled the uruh would have felt it die. Soon the University would attack them again. Tuac would defend them, but he had no desire to kill.

They arrived at their rooms without being noticed. Once inside, Maeva used her magic to change her appearance. She altered her hair from deep red to smoky grey, which made her look much older.

She's still beautiful, Tuac thought.

Maeva taught him how to alter his own appearance. It felt strange to turn his Anthene Art on himself, but after two attempts he managed to go from blonde to black hair, and his eyes changed from blue to hazel. They gathered their meager belongings and headed out of the Cathedral. On the way, they found an unattended storeroom and looked for provisions. Unfortunately, the inventory was furniture and clothing, not food and bedding. They selected two robes. Maeva put on a priest's rob and Tuac wore an acolyte's. They headed to the gates as priest and student.

As they passed through Tushman, Tuac felt anxiety among the guards.

They are looking for us, Tuac shared with Maeva. She nodded.

Several times guards and soldiers looked their way, but the disguises worked. No one stopped or questioned them so they left the city without incident. They walked along the main road across the valley. At the top of the ridge that overlooked Tushman, they camped for the night. Tuac told Maeva what he had discovered in his battle with the uruh.

"Cub, I believe what you're telling me," Maeva said, "but we were in one of sections of the Church built from a natural cave. Perhaps it sat over an uruh hive, and that creature breached a wall and panicked. You are new to your magic and maybe you felt its fear? I don't understand why the University would sanction an attack against us."

"I understand your reluctance to see Ba'al as the villain. But I know I felt magic controlling the uruh. Its master targeted us. It was not a random natural event, but a calculated assault. The only question is why."

Tuac wondered if the University was finishing what it started —ending the Anthenes. He dismissed that possibility for two reasons. First, Argent had explained to him that the University and the Anthenes had reached an accord. Tuac was sure that some magicians still considered Anthene magic to be inferior, but genocide was another matter. Second, neither Maeva nor Tuac had seen any evidence that Basul's magicians actively participated in the slaughter of the Anthenes. There was no question that Ba'al had helped Hahook's forces approach Liat without triggering its protections. But the injuries and deaths Tuac witnessed were caused by the soldier's strange weapons. There were no other signs of magic.

I know enough from my brief encounters with Ba'al to believe that even though the University had conspired with Hahook, her intent was to not erase the Anthenes. Argent told me she wanted me, so she must have thought to use the Emperor to accomplish her goals. So then why did the uruh attack us if not to kill Maeva? Tuac reviewed what he'd felt in the animal's mind, searching for clues.

No, it wasn't after us. *The uruh was after* me.

He was the target. He was sure of it.

They let me leave and now they want me dead. I don't understand. He recalled his exit from the University and then it struck him. *All that self-doubt came from telepathic suggestion. Why didn't I think of that before? Someone wanted me to give up in despair. And the attack after I left the University—that was not Nabes. I was never meant to leave, and now Ba'al wants to eliminate me because I did.*

None of this makes sense. Why would they do this now, when we face Mia's deadliest enemy in Nabes?

Tuac shared his conclusion with Maeva, hoping she could find some flaw in his reasoning. She listened and asked probing questions. She accompanied him through his memory of the gate experience and felt his anxiety. Viewing it this way, he realized how peculiar that situation had been. He chuckled when he remembered his worry about what Rea would think if he left.

Rea had never wanted me to go to the University. She had dismissed my magical aptitude and my recruitment surprised her.

"Yes, I'm convinced now that the magicians are involved," Maeva said. "I've heard rumors that the University isn't transparent about the students it finds for Liat. They sent us only the strongest of Anthenes, and we suspected that there should have been others who gift was less pronounced but still worthy of training. Why should they be so rare compared to those with gifts in the six elements? What had happened to them? Perhaps the University did not want them to leave, either. And since the University does not yet know about your magical ability, Ba'al must be focusing on you because you were *able* to leave."

Tuac considered Maeva's points. *The Watcher did tell me that there had been others. Is all of this connected?*

"I think you're onto something," Tuac said. "They want to keep a secret, an important one. We need to know what they're hiding."

"That's a problem for tomorrow, Cub. Let's get some rest." They unrolled their blankets and settled for the night. As he lay there looking at the night sky, Tuac realized just how much of a friend he had in Maeva. She owed him nothing, but she was his ally, his mentor and his teacher. He was not sure what might be coming, but he knew that Maeva would be there every step of the way and he was grateful that she was in his life.

Tuac and Maeva walked for a day on the main road. They had decided that they needed a place to regroup. They passed several inns but pressed on, hoping to get as far as possible from Tushman before taking lodgings. As second sun was setting, they found a quaint inn and went inside. There were few guests in the main tap room so Maeva and Tuac sat down at a table. The barmaid came over and asked what they wanted.

"A meal and some mead, please," said Maeva holding out a few coins. The barmaid looked them over, took the coins and disappeared. Soon she returned with two mugs, some smoked meat, cheese, and fresh bread. It was uncomplicated and satisfying—the kind of meal that Tuac would have shared with Rea when he was a child.

Tuac felt a pang of loss, missing his family, and his father in particular. Tuac recalled Cisrena's booming laughter, and Tuac had no doubt that he had only survived this long because of his father's teachings.

"Honor, integrity, duty," father said to me every night at bedtime. "When you leave this world, the only thing that remains is who you were." His mind wandered to his mother, and he longed to see her smile, which could command a room. She was a force of nature and not to be trifled with. When it came to family, she was as protective as a kiam is of its litter. He and Rea were blessed to have been raised by such amazing people. He hoped he could live up to their standards.

"You had a moment there, Cub. Everything okay?" Maeva asked. Tuac knew Maeva was being polite, since their connection allowed her to sense his pain.

"I was thinking about my family, what they mean to me, and how alone I feel without them. I am—" he stared at his mead— "scared." Maeva listened in kind silence.

"Ba'al is trying to kill me. I'm supposed to be the 'Reunifer' and am expected to stop Nabes. But I'm just a kid. Rea was the one who was destined to be the powerful mage. So why me?" His eyes stung. Tuac took a long swallow of mead, embarrassed by his outburst.

Maeva laid a hand on one of Tuac's, and he felt her warmth spread through him.

"The Anthenes tell a story of the first student to come to Liat. Her name was Frice. She was an awkward girl, easily overlooked in any group. She liked games but was not athletic. She was the definition of ordinary.

"Leading up to her Journey, she had been rejected by everyone. The University had not invited her to learn, believing she had no magical ability. The Emperor thought she lacked the attributes to make a good soldier. The Church did not think she had the necessary presence to lead a flock. Even the local officials of her village did not think she was smart enough to be a civil servant.

"Her family had focused all of their attention and resources on Frice's older brothers. They secured entrance for them into guilds that would allow them to become valuable members of the community. Her family loved her, but she was not deemed important for its survival. Her brothers expected to take care of her. But Frice wanted to do more, to be more. She wanted to be special.

"And Frice was indeed special. She had an unquenchable desire to help others. She would befriend the old widow living alone, and the single mother with children who could not handle them by herself. Frice would watch over children of families too poor to hire help. Frice became someone in their lives who gave them love, comfort and empathy. When a disaster hit, Frice was always the first on the scene, organizing help, support, and even donations to get affected families back on their feet. When a wedding happened, Frice would coordinate the party and assist the lovers in setting up their new home. The villagers appreciated all that she did, but these were not skills on which to build a career." Maeva paused to take a bite of bread and meat.

Tuac knew that he and Frice would have been friends. After all he had been through, a person who worked hard to make the world a better place was the sort Tuac would feel drawn to, someone he would emulate.

"One day, Frice heard about a place that trained healers—a new place, beyond the forest, founded to teach healing skills. They welcomed everyone. Frice left her village to find Liat. She wandered from town to town along the path, helping people along the way. Her heart felt full when she arrived in our valley.

"She strode to the main gate, where two male Anthenes stood guard. She asked to speak to someone about being a healer. They two scowled at that term, the Betrayal still fresh in their minds. They turned Frice away.

"Dejected, she left. An Anthene who was returning to Liat saw what had happened and approached Frice.

"'Child, why are you so quick to give up? What do those two boys know of your true worth? Come with me.'

"The Anthene continued toward the gate, motioning for Frice to join her. Frice wavered. She had lived her life being told she had no value. What if she was not meant to be a healer? The woman paused to wait for her. Frice remembered why she had come to Liat, and she followed the Anthene.

"As they approached the gates, the guards saw that Frice now accompanied an Anthene. This time, Frice held her head high and walked through the gate as if she belonged. The guards nodded.

"The Headmaster tested Frice, but she did not display any magical skill. Some Anthenes suggested that the school had insufficient resources to devote to a person with no noticeable proficiency. But her love for others radiated through everything she did and touched. Outside villagers had heard about Liat, and there was a daily procession of the hurt, the maimed, and the hungry. Each day, Frice would do all she could to help. She would fetch warm blankets or water, care for the children, make and serve food for all.

"Her presence was not commanding, it was soothing. It was rumored that if she walked through a garden, the flowers would open and flourish. Her detractors dwindled. The Anthenes decided that Frice had an unnamed magical ability worth cultivating.

"They admitted her to Liat, where she excelled at her classes even as she helped her fellow students with their own studies. She advanced within the order of Anthenes, and later led the University for five turns, the longest tenure of any Headmaster. She is the reason we never turn anyone away, as we have learned that there is no fixed path for magicians to find their gift. They just need time."

Maeva blinked back tears. Tuac sensed her sadness, realizing that she might be one of the last Anthenes who would tell Frice's story.

"Frice was more than a Headmaster. She created Liat's mission of caring and empathy. In contrast to the mages, Frice insisted that Anthenes could only serve Mia by leaving Liat to help others. She developed a group of Anthenes who traveled wherever tragedy struck, such as a flood or an epidemic. She led not merely with her magical prowess and strategic thinking, but also through her insatiable desire to help others. She inspired all of us to do the same.

"When Frice passed, the leadership of the Anthenes planned a quiet ceremony. But when others learned that Frice had died, multitudes came to show their appreciation for all she had done. To accommodate the mourners, the Anthenes built a huge funeral pyre in Liat's main courtyard. The visitors included the children and grandchildren of all whom Frice had touched. They all called her 'Aunt Frice'. She had embodied compassion.

"We were required to tell her story to every incoming student at Liat so they understood that making a difference is not about fitting into others' expectations but rather being true to oneself, and that compassion for others may be the greatest magic of all. Helping one person creates ripples that spread, resulting in a torrent of good. We must never underestimate the power or importance of love and empathy. They are unstoppable."

Tuac thought about that ripple effect. *Do I really have the power to make things better?*

"Cub, I do not understand what is happening or why. We know there are several evil forces at work. Nabes stands on one front. The Emperor on another. And Ba'al on yet another, doing who knows what, or why. Mia's survival is at stake, and you have been thrown into the middle of this battle.

"I don't know why you were chosen as the Reunifer. What I do know is that you have a good heart. You know right from wrong, and you are willing to call out those who do not. You are willing to fight against evil, doing so even though you doubt your ability to make a difference. What defines you is your own voice, not what others think of you. And like it or not, your voice is important right now.

"Don't question whether you can make a difference. You can, and already have. I am here because of you and, if not for you, I would have been slaughtered with my family at Liat.

"As we continue down this road, we will face more challenges and impossible choices. The real question, Cub, is whether you will continue to be true to yourself and speak from your heart, or whether you will let your self-doubt confuse you.

I am here to guide you as best as I can. I believe in you. And I am grateful to be your teacher."

They finished their meal in silence. Tuac considered the lesson of Frice while Maeva sat with her grief. Tuac took strength from Maeva's words. Love and compassion were powerful. It was just a question of voice.

In a few weeks of hard work, Rea became one of Ba'al's most trusted confidants. Rea was one of the strongest Fire Walkers to appear in recent history. She outpaced the normal progression for students. Soon, she was third in line to become Acetos of the Fire Walkers.

Ba'al valued Rea for more than her skill and candor. Ba'al valued Rea because she shared the Archmage's conviction that Mia faced an existential threat. Most of the members of the Council were ill-prepared for their dire circumstances. They underestimated Nabes and believed the Emperor was just a petty warlord. Rea suspected that some members of the Council secretly agreed with the Emperor's genocide of the Anthenes.

Only Ki'lel and Rea joined Ba'al at her daily briefs about Nabes' onslaught. The updates were bleak. Nabes now had mercenaries under his command. With each village lost, the land, livestock, and wildlife around it died, reduced to a black ooze.

Rea marveled at Ba'al's composure in the Council meetings. She exuded confidence while giving updates and outlining the day's tasks, all of which she had discussed with Rea the night before. Students learned battle magic and searched Basul's records for information about how the Prophet defeated Nabes at the Great Destruction.

In private, Ba'al was very different. She expressed her despair and frustration, and Rea would sit with her for long hours in silence. While Rea still had misgivings about Ba'al's judgement, Rea also knew that Ba'al was the best leader for this moment. Rea struggled to provide emotional support, but she had little choice. She felt the irony of the situation, allying with the magician trying to kill her brother, whom she loved above all others. And to her distress, Rea found that she genuinely liked Ba'al.

The Archmage did not share any explanation about why she wanted Tuac dead. Rea was, after all, his sibling, and it would create a painful conflict of interest. Rea used her time with Ba'al to learn about the relationship among the Church, the Empire, and Basul. One day when they were sitting by the fire, Rea asked why Basul coordinated with the Emperor and the Charge.

"Only a few know the secret of our cooperation, much less why," Ba'al said. "The Prophet was the architect of the triumvirate. He knew that Mians needed to avoid the power vacuum that had allowed Nabes to rise. He also knew the dangers of tyranny. So he divided power between these three branches of governance to keep each in check.

"The triumvirate controls most aspects of Mian life, especially the Journey. Although you were taught the Prophet devised the Journey to destroy regional prejudices, that isn't the main reason. The Journey, based on his teachings, was devised after he died. It was designed to manage the free will of the population. You have been taught that the Journey celebrates a person's coming-of-age and diffuses territorial allegiances. But at its core, it steers young Mians into professions where their skills will not endanger Mia.

This startled Rea. *What? I was always taught that we controlled our own destiny. I would never have turned down an invitation to*

Basul, but it did not occur to me that I could not if I had wanted to, or that New Ones were being manipulated.

"Advance teams, with representatives from Basul, the Church and the Empire, canvass every part of the civilized world and report back on the children eligible for the next Journey. The teams research parental lineage, investigate magical acuity, and assess leadership skills. Basul invited those with magical power to ensure they would get properly trained, the Empire invited those showing tactical prowess and the Church gathered those with charisma. The invitations from the Empire and the Church are as selective as those of Basul. Those not found worthy to work in one of the three branches of Mian governance are allowed to choose a guild or other trade. They usually join guilds where their parents had apprenticed as the New Ones usually had learned some skills as children, blacksmiths raising the next generation of blacksmiths, and so on.

"By skimming the cream from the top, the Journey ensures Mia's survival. The Empire remains the sole military might, as the towns are stripped of anyone who might cause trouble or who might think about orchestrating independent forces. Strategic minds are either co-opted or broken. The Church remains the sole voice, and interpreter, of the Prophet's teachings. There can be no heretics or alternative religions if all the charismatics are spreading the same vision. And if all follow the same teachings, we are united by a common culture. And Basul remains the sole domain of magicians. We ensure that anyone with magical affinity is taught by us and under our supervision. Renegade magicians cannot harm Mia if all the gifted are under the control of the Archmage."

Rea realized that Ba'al's last statement was the key to Tuac's present status, but she did not push for more information. Now she had a direction for her investigations when she had more time to pursue them.

Although Rea had not been able to help her brother directly, Rea could do one thing for Tuac—protect Merle. Rea found Merle settled in at Basul's infirmary. The Anthenes had assumed command there, preparing Basul for an influx of refugees and war casualties. They set up triage facilities, prepared medicines, rolled bandages, and boiled surgical tools. They trained those who had managed Basul's routine health care to deal with traumatic injuries. Merle had a natural talent for instruction and organization and led this process.

Rea checked in on Merle several times during the week. The two shared stories about Tuac. Rea related tales of their shenanigans growing up, and Merle told how they had fallen in love. Rea was comforted that Tuac had found Merle, as she was the kind of woman Tuac deserved. Merle was intelligent, courageous, and strong, yet had a softness to her as well. She had all the makings of a fearless partner, motivated to protect those she loved.

Rea did not tell Merle that Basul was hunting Tuac. When Merle asked if Rea had heard anything, or when she mourned Tuac's absence, Rea comforted Merle, saying that Tuac was alive and the two of them would find him. Rea was not sure if she convinced Merle. Rea was not sure she convinced herself.

Nabes had reveled in the power released by Liat's destruction. It was not only the delicious pain of those killed by the Emperor, it was also the elimination of a powerful restriction on Nabes' appetite: the Anthenes' love, empathy, and kindness.

The new strength restored Nabes' memory. Nabes remembered the war with the Prophet. The two most powerful beings on Mia had locked in an epic battle for control, while their collective minions had fought amongst themselves. Nabes had feasted on the death and despair. But the Prophet's ability to unify the protectors of Mia had weakened Nabes. Nabes had tipped the balance of the conflict by feeding its Dark Dragon with poisonous power, until the Prophet had countered it. But in that final battle, the Prophet had taken advantage of Nabes' weaknesses.

Nabes was not sure how that had happened. One moment there was a feverish battle, the dark against the Prophet's light. The Prophet had withstood Nabes' evil and gained strength even as Nabes' power withered. Then Nabes' physical vessel was destroyed. Nabes still existed. Fortunately, the Prophet had not taken the final step to end Nabes, and Nabes, though wounded, was not erased.

Nabes was not alone. There was also the Watcher. Nabes did not know who or what the Watcher was but knew that the Watcher was an enemy.

Over the centuries, Nabes stayed alive by consuming the small deaths of insects and rodents. Growth was slow but constant, as was Nabes' hunger for power and the control of Mia. Occasionally, wanderers had stumbled into Shalla. Nabes would touch them and gain more power. But Nabes' hunger had never been satiated and it drained its victims quickly.

Nabes recalled the day everything changed. The day T'ca stumbled on Shalla. Nabes knew this one was different— stronger, with skills that could support Nabes' ascendency. Nabes took from T'ca only the energy needed to give Nabes control over the sniveling fool. Nabes' contagion would ulti- mately consume T'ca, and already strained T'ca's body. Now hunched, bald, and pale, T'ca was not the same sturdy warrior that had sold his soul to Nabes in return for the promise of being Nabes' second in command.

T'ca was good at his job and provided enough sustenance for Nabes. With T'ca's assistance, Nabes' strength grew. Evil spread. Then came the gift of Liat. Nabes gorged on the annihilation of those weak, spineless fools. That feast was enhanced when Nabes discovered the insane, self-absorbed fool who had ordered the Anthene massacre. He, too, was ravenous for power, and so easy to manipulate. Nabes found a new puppet in the Emperor, and discarded T'ca's spent husk. Nabes knew Hahook presented the key to conquering Mia. The best part was that Hahook came with an army that would feed Nabes further.

Something interrupted Nabes' plotting. It was that annoying boy.

Nabes' mind reached out to find Tuac. Nabes sensed that the boy had found a weapon that could thwart its plans: hope. Nabes needed to subdue Mia before this irritation became a real threat.

Nabes studied the boy, looking for some sort of weakness. It did not take much digging. The boy stewed in self-doubt, the opposite of hope. All Nabes needed to do was feed that darkness inside him.

TWENTY-THREE

My time here is done. I am ready to join my grandfather. I have so missed him. His character was my strength and his integrity my shield. He blamed himself for Nabes' rise to power, for unleashing that evil. I tried to comfort him, to remind him it was unintentional, that no one could have predicted it. But he never forgave himself. We will be reunited and I can tell grandfather that I completed his mission and was able to do so because of him.

When I see him again, will he agree with my decision? My grandfather believed evil will always exist, so his solution to Nabes was drastic and final. I rejected my grandfather's last words. I chose a different route. Instead, I believed that the good of the Mians will restrain Nabes from rising again. My grandfather and I will watch over Mia, and I can only hope my decision was the right one.

The last entry in the Secret Teachings of the Prophet

Tuac felt refreshed for the first time in weeks. After they finished the meal, Maeva told the innkeeper that she and Tuac were pilgrims returning home and asked if there was any lodging. They were in luck and there was a private room for a reasonable price. Tuac slept well that night.

He awoke feeling inspired. Some of this was his love for Merle. Even if he could not connect with her, he believed she was alive and he needed to protect her. He was also driven by his duty to the Anthenes. He needed to avenge their deaths and repay their kindness to all of Mia. He was fed up with the threats to himself and Maeva. He was done running.

After much discussion, Maeva and Tuac decided to travel to the University. They needed to understand why Ba'al wanted Tuac dead. Only then could he address Ba'al's concerns and earn her trust. Only then would he be able to work with the magicians to defeat Nabes. Perhaps part of Tuac's destiny was to bring unity in the way the Prophet had done. So, after breakfast, they procured two hursas and set out for the University.

Their trip would take about three weeks and they made steady progress, using their travel time to continue Tuac's training. He hoped he would not have to deploy his new magic against the experienced Arts of the mages, but it was a possibility and he needed to be prepared. He focused on using magic as a weapon, throwing fire balls and ice javelins. But Tuac recognized that he would be one against many. Simple magical weapons could not carry the day. He explored merging his magical Arts. Before long, he could use telepathy to launch projectiles, combine water and air magic to create storms, and fire and stone-moving magic to make sheets of molten lava.

Maeva pressed Tuac to work on his physical stamina. Their mornings started with Yiao and Maeva often made him jog alongside his hursa while doing magical exercises. This daily training sharpened and defined his muscles just as the meditation sharpened his mind and magical skills. He was in spiritual and physical balance, each supporting the other.

They had time to share stories. Tuac talked about his family —missing his father and mother, wondering about Rea and her studies, and of course he missed Merle.

Maeva opened up as well. She told him how she had come to Liat. As a child, she had always wanted to be a teacher, but her plans changed when her mother and father were taken in a plague. There was no one in the village who could care for her and the village elders told her she would need to leave before her Journey. They sent a message to the healer in a neighboring village to come and collect her. Maeva did not want to leave the place where she had been raised and where her parents were laid to rest.

Everything changed when she met the healer. They spoke for a while, and there was an instant bond. Maeva agreed to go with him. Their first day on the road, the healer explained that they were not going to his village, but rather to Liat, a place where she would realize her potential. When the Headmaster evaluated her, she learned that she not only had a natural calling for Anthene magic, but she was also talented in helping others find their core. She had grown into a teacher after all.

The training and discussions distracted Tuac but the closer they got to the University, the more anxious he felt. His magic was becoming violent, destructive, and even chaotic.

"What's bothering you, Cub?" Maeva asked over breakfast.

"I'm distracted. I want to make them pay for what they did to Liat. All of them—Ba'al, the Emperor, and Nabes."

"Revenge isn't the key to victory. Evil cannot be defeated if revenge drives your magic. After all, vengeance is one manifestation of evil. Only good can defeat evil, only light can defeat the dark."

"But if that is the case, shouldn't we just give up? How do I fight evil if I have no tools to defend us? The vengeance fuels me."

Maeva looked at Tuac and smiled. He felt her warm embrace through their connection. Her love cleansed him of his despair and rage. As he studied her, he saw fatigue in her eyes and strands of gray hair. This was hard on her, too.

"Do not confuse giving into evil with resisting it. There are times when force is necessary to defeat evil. But it is the motive that defines you. Evil is driven by the relentless hunger for power over others while justice is driven by longing for the greater good. Evil sacrifices others, while justice requires self-sacrifice.

"Defending justice from evil requires a measured use of force —enough to accomplish the goal, but not be punitive. The goal of justice, and that deliberate use of force, is equity for all.

"Those who let darkness stain their quest for justice do not measure their force with love and empathy. You are not that person, Cub."

Tuac considered this. "Those are ideals and we are not living in a perfect world. How can I just dismiss my rage at what has been done?"

Maeva smiled again and another wave of psychic support suffused Tuac. "Of course you're angry. We've all lost so much. If you ignore your grief, you will become numb and unable to appreciate all that is good in the world. None of us are all light or dark, all evil or good. We are in flux, a mix of choices, that when balanced make us who we are.

"Acknowledge your anger and grief, but do not act on them.

If you are to deliver justice, you must control those darker feelings and not let them control you."

Tuac felt ashamed. Maeva was right again. He forced himself to acknowledge that things could have gone far worse for him. He could have stayed at the University, where he would never have realized his power or had an opportunity to combat Nabes. He could have ignored his dreams and the Watcher's guidance. He could have gone to a different village or have stayed at a different inn and never met Merle. He could have chosen to stay at Merle's home and never have gone to Liat, where he was fortunate enough to find Maeva. Each decision had inserted a thread into the tapestry of his life. He was meant to be in this moment, at this place, on this day. And it was with this level of awareness and acceptance that they made their way to the University.

No, to Basul, where I belong.

Rea should have been happier today. She was about to be anointed as the Acetos of the Fire Walkers, the youngest head of an Art in recorded history. Hala had died unexpectedly, opening the position. There were two Fire Walkers more senior than Rea, Jaru and Eis. Jaru, the first in line for succession, was in ill health and declined the role. Eis had a dark streak in him, and his failures with Tuac strained his relationship with Ba'al. The Council believed that Rea would make a stronger candidate. They lobbied Eis to step aside.

Rea deserved the honor. She was smart, hard-working, and dedicated. Since her arrival, Rea had devoted herself to her studies and responsibilities. She had no close friends, as she worked every waking hour and was did not concern herself with gossip or the troubles of her colleagues. Whether it was physical illness or personal conflict, Rea had no time or patience for it. She was not rude, she was simply uninterested. She focused on the task at hand—harnessing magic for the coming battle. Rea excelled at magical innovation and problem-solving. She saw solutions others missed and, with every success, her reputation grew.

Rea secured her role when Ba'al had directed her to research war magic. Basul had included military studies in the general curriculum but during Mia's long period of peace, most lessons involved strategy rather than deployment. Rea devoured everything she could find. She discovered books explaining how to create the great beasts of Terran lore, the most powerful of which were dragons. When she reported this to Ba'al, Ba'al told her stories of the Prophet's use of dragons in the Great Destruction. Ba'al thought those formulae had been lost ages ago.

Rea recreated some of the designs and guided a select squad of Fire Walkers in shaping their magic into weapons. The results were magnificent and terrifying: crafted in pure fire, they rose into the air on the heat they generated and were capable of spraying flame at any target. Rea also shared the relevant texts and the results of her experiments with the other Arts. Soon, the Stone Movers could form lumbering lizards and mud giants, and the Water Sculptors and Air Riders worked in tandem to form ice dragons. Ba'al called the group her "Dragon Squad" and Rea was their leader.

But in this moment before her confirmation as Acetos, all Rea could think about was her little brother. There were so many things she needed to tell him. He needed to know that she loved him and that she was sorry for all the times she had not been available for him. He needed to know she would shield him from Basul's misguided actions. In her new role she could protect him from Ba'al's judgment. But Rea needed to find him first.

Her time with Merle gave Rea hope that she would have a chance. Merle was an anchor keeping Rea from losing herself in her drive to excel. When this was all over, after Tuac had returned and his safety was assured, Rea would thank Merle for all she had done.

Rea heard a rustle of robes behind her and knew it was Ba'al. It was time.

"Are you ready to become the First Keeper of the Fire?" Ba'al said, her voice resonating in the Fire Walker's meeting hall.

Rea stood before the entire school of Fire Walkers, all of the other military leaders and the members of the Dragon Squad. Normally, ascension to Acetos was a private ritual, with only a small group from the Art and the Archmage in attendance. Today, Ba'al wanted to make a statement.

Rea's mind went blank.

Ba'al whispered, "Well?" with a wry smile.

Rea caught herself and mumbled, "Sorry," under her breath. She focused on the audience.

"Yes, I am ready. I will shepherd all who have joined with their Fire. I will guard them and their Flames. With my every breath and my own fire I will preserve and protect our Art. I will stand for the strength, form, and purpose of the Fire." This was the oath Rea had memorized. Then she added, "I will lead the Fire Walkers in our righteous battle against Nabes! Basul will prevail and Mia will be protected!"

The crowd erupted and Rea basked in their enthusiasm. Ba'al raised her eyebrow. Rea knew that she would get an earful later, but Rea was starting to exercise her authority. She would need it to guard her family.

Tuac and Maeva approached the boundaries of The University. They had discussed Tuac's options several times and always came to the same conclusion. Tuac needed to confront Ba'al and persuade her to see his merit. He was exceptional, having come into his magic outside of Basul's training and their narrow categories. Perhaps he could help others to view magic through a different lens. Unfortunately, his uniqueness might be the reason for Ba'al's animosity. He threatened her order.

Maeva and Tuac also believed that he needed Basul as much as Basul needed him. He needed guidance in channeling his raw power. Maeva could only help him so much with his focus. His magic was beyond her, and Maeva worried that Tuac could lose himself without further education.

Tuac assured Maeva of his strength. He grasped her lessons and anchored his resolve in justice. But on the day before they reached Basul, Tuac discovered how much more he had to learn when they were attacked by twenty rogues.

The leader of the group sauntered up to them, waving his sword, with two of his henchmen flanking him. One was a scarred, lumbering brute and the other was whip-thin and sinister.

"Keep your hands where I can see them," the brigand barked. "I'll make this easy on you. Give me all your provisions, and I'll let you leave unharmed. Resist me, and I'll let these two have at it. I am sure you, lady, will not like that, but I promised my boys a reward if they have to fight."

Tuac knew that the thieves would not let them go. Through the bond, he assured Maeva that he would protect her.

First, he waved his hand and snapped the necks of the three

ruffians like they were dry twigs. The rest of the criminals roared their defiance and charged before those bodies hit the ground. Five archers stayed back attacking with arrows from behind boulders.

Foolish. They dare to attack me? Tuac raged.

A volley of arrows arced toward Tuac. He blew at them. The arrows tumbled off course, striking three of the charging mercenaries. The remaining ruffians scrambled to a stop. They looked confused. The archers ran.

You should have fled like your comrades. Tuac strode toward the remaining thieves.

With another wave of his hand, five of them burst into flame, screaming and slapping themselves. A chasm opened beneath three others, who disappeared into it, shrieking. The remaining four bolted back under the trees. Tuac raised his hand to render his final justice.

"Stop!" Maeva screamed, breaking Tuac out of his blood rage.

The four surviving rogues charged at them from the left, running in a tight pack. Before Maeva could stop him, Tuac snapped his fingers and melted them.

"You see!" he screamed at Maeva. "This is what happens when we show pity. People take advantage of us and think we're weak. Basul does not respect weakness!"

Through their bond, Tuac felt Maeva's horror and sorrow. She rushed to Tuac.

"Hush, Cub," she soothed him with her voice as she would a dangerous animal. "We are fine. You protected me. This is all new to you. This is why we need Basul." She hugged him hard.

Tuac stiffened at her embrace. He felt her Anthene magic probing him and allowed it to happen. She was trying to determine what was wrong with him. He wanted to know, too. Both of them sensed an outside force fueling his rage.

Nabes.

Tuac isolated the alien energy and ejected it. He relaxed into Maeva's warmth. He looked at his surroundings and saw the death he caused. He could have resolved matters without taking any lives. But he had given in to to his anger. His stomach clenched and he gaged at what he had done.

"I'm sorry, Maeva. I don't know what to do. I want to be a simple man, to be with Merle, and study with you. But every step I take, someone attacks me or those I love. This has to stop. I'm not strong enough to continue this fight."

"You have experienced things that no one should suffer. I can promise you two things: it will get worse, and I will be with you every step of the way." She eyed him. "Consider your self-doubt. Is that truly you, or is something making it worse?"

Maeva was right. Even now, after controlling is rage, Nabes still tainted him. *I will not let Nabes win.*

Now, as they looked toward Basul, he thought about Maeva calling him Cub. It was an apt description. Breas could comfort and protect, but they could also destroy.

The pieces were all falling together. Nabes had infected the Emperor and through him, both removed the Anthenes as a threat and taken control the Church. All of those hapless worshipers would now be fed hate and prejudice, their rising anxiety and fear adding to Nabes' strength.

Nabes' only obstacle was that Tuac was not yet turned. The thieves had provided Nabes with the perfect opportunity. Nabes had thought that Tuac would give in to his inner rage and thirst for revenge. Nabes had not predicted Tuac's strength of character. But there would be other chances for Nabes to win over the boy.

TWENTY-FOUR

What is the best way to protect Mia? Do we leave people to make their own choices, hoping that our society will respect and value all life? Or do we anoint a few to protect the many? In the first case, we may aspire to achieve balance, but if we fail, destruction and chaos follow. In the second case, we must rely on the character and integrity of the anointed. If they lack those qualities, the cost of protection will be servitude.

An early writing from the First Archmage of Basul

"Here we are," Tuac said. They stood before the gates of Basul at midday, as Mia's suns were at their apex. *It's been a long road. What happens now?* he thought.

"Yes, here we are, Cub." Maeva put her hand on his shoulder. "Are you ready? You have nothing to prove. You have no regrets. All you have to do is explain what has happened and hopefully they will listen. If not, we thank them and we will leave. But we will not fight."

He nodded. It was time to confront Ba'al. Tuac had considerable power, but she was stronger. He hoped Ba'al would listen to reason. He was no threat to Basul's order. But if he failed to win Ba'al over, Nabes would win. He only wanted to help, not to fight.

Unless I need to fight to protect the ones I love, he thought.

With each step, he felt waves of energy washing over him like water over a stone. The waves pushed against him, but they were not strong enough. He looked at Maeva and could feel through their connection that she was struggling.

"We're feeling Basul's wards," Maeva said. "They were set years ago to protect the magicians from raiding parties. Ba'al must have reactivated them and now only those that Ba'al allows can pass through. I can sense that they have no effect on you. It must be another aspect of your unique magic. I'm sure the ease with which you dispel their effects causes Ba'al much consternation right now." She staggered and fell, the wards overwhelming her.

Tuac knelt by her side and took her hand. He focused, surrounding his teacher with his magic and love. The effect was immediate and Maeva stood.

"Thank you, Cub. I'll need to stay close to you or I won't be able to pass."

They walked hand in hand.

"I felt similar sensations when I left Basul," Tuac said. "I never really gave it much thought, but now I can feel the web protecting Basul. I can see its construction and feel it resist me. And I can shove it aside."

They walked on. Nothing was going to stop him.

As they got closer, the effects of the wards felt stronger and more complicated. Some wards flooded them with fear, urging them to turn back. Others triggered the ground or the plant life to attack them. Each time, Tuac willed the wards off. With each step, he gained more confidence in his abilities and purpose.

Did she activate these because of Nabes or because she believes I am a threat? Did she even consider that I might come back? Tuac wondered. They passed through the final wards and reached the closed outward gates. "Basul isn't being very hospitable. They know we're here. I would have expected Ba'al to come welcome us, given all she has done to find us."

Maeva stifled a laugh. "Good. You're keeping your sense of humor. It will help you remain grounded. They are trying to figure out how we made it to the gate."

"What should we do?"

No longer affected by the wards, Maeva dropped Tuac's hand. She rummaged in her backpack for the last of their bread and cheese and handed some to Tuac.

"I'm hungry. If they're going to make us wait, we should have some lunch."

Tuac appreciated Maeva's light-hearted approach. He needed to confront the magicians with confidence, not fear. He dropped his backpack and sat down to eat. Ki'lel's wand rolled out of his bag. He studied it.

I do not need you anymore.

He tucked the wand back into his bag. He hoped he could return it to Ki'lel.

Ba'al was having lunch in her quarters when she heard the alarms that indicated Basul's the outer wards had been breached.

Who would have the power to do that? It can't be the Emperor, my spies would have warned me. Ba'al thought, jumping up from the table. *Has Nabes launched an attack?*

More alarms sounded, and she heard running and shouting outside her chambers. Her mind raced.

Could some mage be helping our enemies, rooting out my spies and defeating our wards the way I helped with the wards at Liat?

She tried to dismiss the idea that any magician would side with the Emperor, but it nagged at her. Basul's spies in Tushman had reported the Emperor's coup over the Church but had gone quiet since then. The triumvirate was broken.

Perhaps some of my brethren felt it would be safer to side with the Emperor.

Ba'al rushed to the window in her chambers to see what was happening at the gate. She used an eye piece that magnified distant things. What Ba'al saw surprised her.

No army. Just a young man and older woman. She focused the lenses and recognized the young man. *Tuac!*

He had left, innocent, rudderless, and uncertain. Now he had returned, walking through their strongest wards. The woman with him must be the Anthene, Maeva. Ba'al's mages overseeing the Anthenes had told Ba'al of the whispered references among the survivors of the Emperor's slaughter to the woman who was the "spirit and soul of Liat". She was said to be one of the most powerful and learned of the Anthenes.

Seeing Maeva now, Ba'al thought she indeed looked impressive. *She must have negated our protections. Under different circumstances, we could have been friends. Why did she have to protect that boy?*

Ba'al felt a pang of guilt. She had not wanted to harm the boy but, even before the threat of Nabes had arisen, Ba'al needed to protect the order of Basul.

No. Not even the most powerful Anthene could get past our wards. It must be Tuac!

Ba'al's thoughts raced. On a superficial level, the risk that Tuac had innate magical ability posed a threat even if he could not reach his Art. Even without schooling, Tuac's nominal power could be manipulated by those with evil intent. This is why Basul tried to keep anyone with magical ability, no matter how insignificant, under its watchful eyes.

Nabes' emergence presented an even bigger problem. The magicians could not allow Tuac to fall into Nabes' hands, as Nabes was capable of unlocking what was otherwise unavailable to the boy. That magic could be used against Basul.

But Ba'al knew there was another, more dangerous threat: nascent, unbridled power able to access all the Arts. While some failed Basul's screening because they had no potential, there were the rare individuals who showed significant potential but were not bound to a single Art. They were called unified magicians, and they could wield several of the magical Arts. Ba'al believed that these powerful magicians had stoked the struggle between good and evil that led to the Great Destruction. Mia had been fortunate that forces of good, led by the Prophet, had defeated Nabes' forces. The founders of Basul knew they could ill afford another civil war.

Tuac must be a unified mage! He's come into his power, and he is the one who is defeating our wards. This explained what had happened at Tushman: Tuac had combined the Arts to defend himself. Now he had returned to Basul.

"Ba'al, the wards have been tripped!" Ki'lel said as he burst through her doors. "We're under attack. Should I alert Rea and her Dragon Squad?" He was winded and must have come to her before seeing who had arrived at their gates.

She had to act. But she wondered, *Is Tuac here as friend or foe?*

"Ba'al, we need to do something!"

Ba'al's instincts told her to marshal Basul's forces and obliterate Tuac. It could be costly, but everything she had learned from the chronicles of her predecessors dictated that Tuac must be eliminated. Yet they now faced an Emperor bent on domination, and Nabes had risen again. Could a unified practitioner be a powerful ally? How would Rea respond?

Maybe there is a different answer here, she thought.

"Tell Rea to summon her Dragon Squad, then she is to report here. Her brother has returned and you will need to watch her."

Rea was in her chambers when she heard the alarms and the commotion. Someone was attacking Basul.

Who would be foolish enough to attack us?

She could have sought out Ba'al, but Rea knew what to do and did not wait for orders. She left her chambers. She passed one of her lieutenants who was also racing towards the disturbance.

"I will go assess the threat. Muster the Dragon Squad in the courtyard behind the gates," she shouted.

What weapons would the enemy have? Could Basul counter their force? Rea had prepared her Dragon Squad for both magical and non-magical aggression. She was about to be tested, but she knew her elite fighting group would be ready. Rea would make the attackers pay for their arrogance.

Rea found a spot a fair distance behind the gates and soon her Squad had assembled. They were close enough to respond in seconds, but far enough back to be hidden from the opposing forces. Rea beamed with pride. Her Squad included the best and brightest of Basul. Each of them shared Rea's belief that the magically empowered needed to protect the ungifted and that the masses could not be trusted to care for themselves or Mia. All of the Dragon Squad believed that only the magicians had the necessary skills and that they were above corruption. Rea led them, ensuring that good would prevail.

"It is time, Dragon Squad! We are ready. Prepare your weapons and wait for my command. For Mia!" Rea barked and her Dragon Squad yelled back their confirmation.

Ki'lel ran up to Rea. "Ba'al needs you. Pass command to your second to lead Dragon Squad while you are at the front gates, then come with me."

What does Ba'al want? Ba'al said I needed to lead the Dragon Squad into battle. Something is off.

Rea ran with Ki'lel, and they joined Ba'al as she strode toward the gates. Then she saw who had triggered the alarms.

Tuac! How did he make it through Basul's defenses? Rea saw Ba'al and Ki'lel exchange a look. *She doesn't just want me here. She is testing my loyalty.*

It was all happening so fast. She did not know why Tuac was here. But she knew Ba'al was concerned that he had returned.

Will the Dragon Squad's first battle be against my little brother? Rea knew that in a matter of minutes she might have to pick a side. For the first time in her life she did not know what to do.

"They don't look happy to see us," Tuac said. He reached out with his telepathic skill to assess the auras of those behind Basul's gates. They were confused and afraid.

He narrowed his search and found Ba'al. To his surprise, she was not just afraid, she was afraid of *him*.

Why would she fear me?

Then Tuac detected another strong personality. He felt a familiar righteous arrogance. A protector, ready to fight the enemies of Basul. But also there to defend against evil. This was an honorable person, willing to lay life and limb in defense of justice.

Rea!

He sensed her inner conflict, forced to choose between Basul and family.

Tuac kept searching, trying to determine the motives of those around Ba'al. He felt a new aura on the periphery of magic. It burned bright, full of compassion and warmth. He drew closer, trying to determine if this was an ally. Tuac connected with the source and there was a moment of resistance. The being was protecting itself from intrusion. But suddenly, they recognized him and pulled him into their aura's light, and flooded with love, relief and elation.

Merle is here! I found her! Tuac felt whole for the first time since the massacre at Liat.

He lingered in the moment and then composed himself. He sensed that Merle was safe with magicians. But he had to act. He must ensure no further harm would come to her.

Tuac stepped up to the gates. It was time.

Merle and her team had rushed to the center gates in response to the alarms. They were under attack and Anthene magic would be needed to help the wounded.

Her focus changed the moment she felt a particular awareness sweep the area. She resisted at first, then she felt a familiar connection and embraced it.

Tuac! You're here!

Since the magicians had not yet opened the gate, she did not know if they realized their visitor was Tuac. But she recognized his aura. He was still the innocent boy that had been afraid to touch her the first time they'd made love. But the massacre at Liat had changed him. She sensed grief, anger, and confusion. She yearned to embrace him.

"You are not alone," she repeated under her breath.

As she wove through the crowd of onlookers close to the gates, Merle felt something else she had never sensed in Tuac: a desire for vengeance.

Does he think that the only way to show his value is by taking revenge on those who did not believe in him? I can feel something more driving him.

Around her, Basul readied its defenses. She needed to do something or Tuac would be hurt. She sprinted forward. It was pandemonium, so no one tried to stop her. She skidded to a stop behind Ba'al, Rea, and another mage. She tried to probe Ba'al, but the Archmage was too powerful. Merle saw Rea and reached out to her, but was blocked. The other mage was a telepath. When he deflected her probe, Merle realized that he was poised to stop Rea if she helped Tuac.

She did the only thing she could and threw herself into Ba'al. Merle's desperate act caught everyone off guard. Ba'al stumbled sideways and turned to Merle. Ki'lel stepped in front of Ba'al to catch her, and Rea reached for Merle. The magicians around them summoned their powers to defend their leaders.

Merle was now the threat.

I don't care. I must save him. Merle met and held Ba'al's fierce gaze. The Archmage muttered something and the ground beneath Merle melted. Then a headache so intense that her eyes watered made her waver and she knew it was the telepath's attack. She hunched in pain.

"Please, help," she said to Rea. Merle collapsed.

Through tearing eyes Merle saw Rea step between Merle and the telepath, hands starting to blaze.

Rea shouted, "To me! We must save this girl!" Merle sensed conflict in the hearts of some of the Dragon Squad but also their loyalty to their leader. In moments, protectors surrounded Merle and Rea. A shimmering wall enclosed them, the ground firmed, and the psychic assault diminished. As the pain lessened, she could see Dragon Squad deployed to defend Rea. The situation was now a dangerous standoff.

This is out of control, Merle thought. If Rea attacked Ba'al, there was no telling what would happen.

"Everyone, stop!" she screamed. Her cry cut through the crowd like a knife. Rea's fire subsided and the attacks on Merle stopped. *The magicians have realized I'm not a threat.* She took a steadying breath.

Then she realized she was wrong. Her plea had not resolved the conflict. Everyone had turned to face the real threat.

Maeva heard Tuac's scream "No!" He leapt to defend his beloved. Through their bond, they both felt Merle's pain. A telepath was attacking her. Tuac's rage dissolved his restraint. Maeva knew he would try to rescue Merle.

What happened next frightened Maeva. Tuac waved his hand and blew the gates of Basul to pieces. That should not be possible. But anger, love, and his need to protect Merle fueled Tuac's magic. With another wave of his hand, a shimmering, translucent wall manifested around Merle and another woman clad in Fire Walker's robes. A few Water Sculptors hurled ice javelins at them, but the projectiles disintegrated when they hit Tuac's wall.

He's using his telepathy the way he did against the uruh, she thought.

Maeva realized the woman with Merle must be Rea. Tuac's sister stood, hands blazing, between Merle and Ba'al. Rea had chosen Merle's side in this conflict.

Maeva scrambled to join Tuac where he stood in the ruins of the entry.

"Ba'al," Tuac screamed. "You aided the Emperor's massacre of Liat. You sent assassins after me. This ends now! Basul must stop harming those it should be protecting."

Tears flowed down Tuac's face. He had hit his breaking point and all his insecurities, grief, and rage erupted. Maeva knew she must intervene or Tuac's magic would destroy them all.

"Cub, this is not you," she kept her voice calm. "You've protected Merle and now they know how powerful you are. Stand down. Remember what we practiced! Don't give into your rage."

Tuac met her gaze. His eyes were solid black. He cut off their bond.

He continued his assault. He raised his hand and squeezed. She saw Ba'al gasp for breath. The telepath and others in Ba'al's guard writhed in pain. Tuac spared only Rea and Merle.

He means to end Basul. Maeva studied her protégé. *He is infected. Nabes is using Tuac's anger and self-doubt to fuel this attack. If we can't intervene, all was lost.*

Maeva needed to counter Tuac's insecurities. She reached out for Rea. With every fiber in her being, Maeva emoted *save him.*

Rea knew she had to intervene. She ordered the Dragon Squad to protect Merle, then headed toward her brother. He had begun to glow. She raised her hands, showing him that she meant no harm.

She had seen other magicians glow, but nothing like what Tuac was doing now. He blazed white, but his eyes were not the hazel eyes she knew. They were entirely black.

Undeterred, Rea kept walking. Tuac was still her little brother and she loved him. She knew that she had not said that often enough. That had been a mistake. She had not known how much he had needed her. But now it was clear and she would not fail him. She needed him, too. Rea stopped a few steps from him.

"Tuac, stop. Ba'al is not your enemy: Nabes is." Rea hoped that invoking their mutual enemy she could redirect Tuac's wrath. "Join us. *Join me.* Help me rid Mia of this evil force. Please, Tuac."

Tuac's dark gaze locked on her. He laughed. Rea had never heard him laugh like that before. It was loveless, sick with hate.

This is not my little brother.

"Join you?" he hissed. "Why would I ever go back to being just your little brother? You were never there for me. You had your own friends, and I was a nuisance. But now that I'm more powerful than you, you want me to join you? Do you realize what I can do? Why should I join you when I can't even trust you?"

Tuac stepped toward her. The ground rumbled.

Fire and earth magic! How can he use different Arts? she wondered.

They were now close enough to touch. She wanted to dispute his blistering accusations, but he was right. There were too many instances where she had been unkind to him.

"Tuac, you're right. I'm sorry." This was a confession she needed to make, and he needed to hear. "You deserved better from me. I have always loved you more than anyone else, but I rarely showed you how I felt. I thought emotions made me weak. I figured that you would just know I cared. And until now, I did not realize my mistake.

"Seeing you here, I understand that love and empathy strengthen us. Please forgive me. Give me a chance to prove myself to you. I promise I will never fail you again. You will never be alone. Merle is back there, and she will stand at your other side. Together, we can and will protect Mia and all who live here. We will all die unless we do this together."

Rea reached for him. At first, Tuac recoiled. He shoved her back but she held on. He hit harder. She knew he could kill her, and she sensed his turmoil.

She would not fail him again. Rea pulled him closer even as he struggled.

"I'm so tired," he sobbed, "I can't do this by myself."

"And you won't have to," Rea whispered and kissed him on his forehead. She stroked the tears from his cheeks.

The black in his eyes faded, and the familiar hazel returned. His expression softened and the glow subsided. Her brother stood before her, clutching her hands.

All of a sudden, someone tackled Tuac, pulling him away from Rea. Her magic flared to defend him, but the woman with Tuac grabbed her arm.

"Wait, Rea."

Rea saw that Merle embraced him and he clung to her. Rea blinked away tears.

When was the last time I cried? This reunion lit a different kind of fire within Rea, and she realized that warmth of familial connection that she had suppressed for too long.

She stiffened up and barked to her Dragon Squad, who had arrived with Merle.

"Protect these three with your lives," she ordered. The Dragon Squad split, one team circling Rea and Maeva, and the other Merle and Tuac.

Rea looked back at Ba'al. If Rea's gaze could carry her Fire, she would have incinerated Ba'al.

Tuac's hold on Merle eased and he looked up. They were surrounded by magicians, but these were under Rea's command. They were here to protect him.

He stared at Basul's obliterated gates and at Ba'al's forces. He could feel their uncertainty. They wanted to defend Ba'al but they now knew that he was a formidable foe. Magical energy hummed through the crowd, but no one moved.

Tuac needed to take the next step. He opted for peace.

"Ba'al, I am with my family. I have the strength of their conviction and I intend to protect them. You have a choice. You can either join me against Nabes, or you'll see I'm more than you expected. I am the Reunifer. I am here to protect Mia.

"While most mages do not understand what that means, I know that you do. Will you ally with me or will you oppose me? If you choose the latter, the resulting destruction will be on your head."

Ba'al and Ki'lel exchanged glances. The magicians in the rubble of the gates circled their leader. Tuac suspected they were poised to attack. Rea and her Dragon Squad were also on alert. Merle clutched his hand.

Maeva stepped between the two camps.

"Stop. You're all acting like petulant children. Sometimes

force is necessary, but *not* today. Cub, focus! Don't let others dictate your actions." Maeva then turned to Ba'al. "Archmage, you know better. I've heard about you for years, how you have the empathy that many magicians do not. You've lost yourself."

Rebuked, Tuac released the tension in his body.

"How dare you!" Ba'al shouted. "I have devoted my life to Basul and Mia. You do not know the burden I was forced to accept and the decisions I was forced to make. All take a toll." Ba'al gestured and her magicians called forth their magic.

The ground rumbled and lightning lit the sky. The Dragon Squad responded in kind, raising their magical beasts. The cacophony from the wind, thunder, and lightning was so loud that people covered their ears.

Tuac remained calm. He realized Maeva was right. Force would not bring about change, only cooperation could do that. Destruction was not the answer, even if outrage was justified. He needed to show Basul there was a different way.

With a wave of his hands, the remnants of the gates of Basul levitated and swirled. As the debris turned, the gates reformed. Tuac could not rebuild every part of the structure as some scraps were too small. He reached out to the trees surrounding Basul and asked for volunteers. As in the construction of Liat, the oldest trees answered his call and surrendered to his will. He transported the trunks of the tallest trees and they arrived trimmed and ready to be installed. But he was not done. The ground began to rumble, and seven balls made of metals and minerals rose from small fissures. Tuac heated them to white hot. A gust of telepathic force blew the fluid material so that it splattered across the gates ornamenting them with gems and bright highlights. When they were complete, Tuac hung the restored gates on Basul's walls. He gasped and staggered, leaning on Merle. The effort had taken a lot out of him.

Tuac had demonstrated to the magicians that he was not their enemy. He had also shown his command of several Arts simultaneously. He had included relief panels featuring the symbols for each of the six schools of Art. A seventh plate reinstated the Anthene symbol in the center of the gates, its white symbol representing the need for healing. Tuac hoped the finished gates would appeal to most of the mages, though he suspected that there were some who would never accept the inclusion of the Anthenes.

Tuac wanted Ba'al to see his power and understand he could have directed his magic at Basul. Instead, he had chosen to mend what he had broken. He also aimed to heal Basul's heart by restoring the Anthenes to their rightful place among the other Arts. They must all work together if they were to defeat Nabes.

As word spread through the crowd of combative mages of what Tuac had done, Ba'al's forces stood down. The wind subsided. The Dragon Squad's creatures faded.

Rea rushed to Tuac, amazed by his work. Tuac reopened his bond with Maeva, and felt her love pour into him.

Well done, Cub. I am so proud of you. You have done what I once thought to be impossible. Welcome home, Cub.

Tuac's show of strength was impressive, and Ba'al was not sure that all of the might of Basul would have been able to defeat Tuac. She had no doubt that the two siblings and Rea's Dragon Squad could destroy the rest of the magicians. Ba'al had believed that a magician capable of using multiple Arts was the greatest threat to Mian society. But this had been explained as a risk of wild magic.

Instead of war, the boy had chosen peace with a compelling

message. Tuac demonstrated his remarkable maturity and superb control, so Basul's concerns had been misplaced. To Ba'al's relief, Tuac offered hope. She stepped forward to examine the gleaming gates.

"Well met, Tuac. You have shown thoughtfulness and respect for magic. I'm not sure what I can teach you, but I will tell you everything I know about the Reunifer."

Nabes had witnessed it all, thinking it did not matter if Tuac won or lost. The carnage from the conflict would have weakened the magicians to the point where they would not be a threat. Tuac might even have died or become one of Nabes' allies.

Nabes had not anticipated that the boy's reason and passion would supersede his anger, and that he would unite the magicians. This alarmed Nabes, as the exile of the Anthenes from Basul had broken the wards that contained Nabes's power and allowed it to gather strength again.

The boy presented a formidable challenge, and Nabes resolved not to underestimate him again. Nabes felt a sense of urgency. Nabes had been defeated when all Mians had united under the Prophet. This time would be different—even if the mages were now united, Nabes had the military force of the Empire.

Nabes was not done with the mages. There were others in their ranks vulnerable to exploitation.

SHALLA

Twenty-Five

We gather under Cedric's banner to defeat Nabes. The goal is simple. But we cannot lose sight of the means to victory. How much force should we use? We want to minimize loss of life, but what should we do with his followers?

I believe that we will defeat this evil, but I am unsure whether we will answer these questions the right way. If not, we will be doomed to repeat history.

Chronicles of the First Archmage

Although Ba'al was ready to ally with Tuac, she faced opposition in the ranks of Basul. Tuac's attack outraged some magicians. Others were worried about his power. Both groups argued that Ba'al should take action against the unified magician.

Rea's conduct created a bigger conundrum. She had been

insubordinate, and perhaps even traitorous. Several demanded her removal as the leader of the Dragon Squad and her resignation as Acetos of the Fire Walkers. But either action by Ba'al risked alienating those loyal to Rea, in particular the members of the Dragon Squad.

In a perfect world, time would cure the open wounds. But time was in short supply. Ba'al knew Mia could not afford a civil war among the magicians. She opted to create space between Tuac and the rest of the magicians in the hope that cooler heads would prevail.

Ba'al housed Tuac and his party in quarters reserved for honored guests, which were in a separate building. Tuac, who was exhausted after the confrontation at the gates, appreciated the opportunity to recover. Merle and Maeva joined him, and Rea also moved in with six hand-picked lieutenants from each of the Arts as guards.

Unfortunately for Ba'al, the separation did not ease the tensions, in part because Rea's decision to stay with her brother was another act of defiance. Ba'al decided to act. She called a meeting of all the Acetos except Rea to resolve the issue. Ki'lel also attended. The majority of the Acetos and Ki'lel wanted retribution. Only Chorra defended Rea, arguing that she had saved Basul. Ba'al shared Chorra's sentiment that Rea had made the right decision to protect a valuable asset in the fight against Nabes, even if her decision was colored by familial loyalty.

Ba'al summoned Rea to defend herself. Her position was simple but fell on deaf ears—she had sworn a duty of fealty to the Fire and she honored that oath. Basul's enemies were the Emperor and Nabes. Tuac did not pose a threat. She remained in the room as Basul's leaders decided her future.

Ba'al understood that grievances needed to be aired or they would fester. Unfortunately, the opposing sides refused to yield.

We were in an untenable situation, she thought, *and only Rea had found the middle ground and served the greater purpose. I need to reach the middle ground, too.*

"Enough," Ba'al raised her voice to silence the argument. "I appointed Rea as the leader of the Dragon Squad and she has proven herself. Her decision to protect Tuac was the right choice for Basul and for Mia. I do not demand blind obedience as proof of loyalty."

Turning now to Rea, she continued.

"Rea, you walked a fine line and used your authority to stop the bloodshed. For that you should be commended. But I will not tolerate mutiny. You came close to acting against your brethren, which is forbidden. You have lost the right to lead the Fire Walkers. You are removed as Acetos. You will still lead the Dragon Squad. That is my judgment.

"We have a war to prepare for, so this meeting is dismissed." Ba'al looked at Chorra, who nodded in agreement. The other Acetos filed out and Ba'al heard some grumbling.

That's not surprising. I hope that's as bad as it will get. We have to get past this.

Rea remained with her head resting in her hands.

"You *did* do the right thing," Ba'al said. "However, you stood against the institution of Basul. Even if I agree with you, people in power do not like to be challenged. My goal is to defer this disruption while we defend Mia from Nabes. But if we survive, we will have to contend with the damage you did. Know this—I will do all I can to protect you and Tuac, but I suspect you will need to make some very difficult decisions for which I can offer no safe quarter. Stay strong, Rea."

Ba'al hugged Rea. Ba'al felt she needed to say goodbye.

Two days later, Ba'al went to talk to Tuac. She needed to explain to him why he was considered so dangerous to the fabric of Mia. This would not be an easy conversation. Much of what she needed to say had been secret oral history passed down from Archmage to Archmage.

Basul is not the bastion of justice and protection it claims to to be, she thought as she walked into Tuac's quarters.

Ba'al studied the members of the Dragon Squad standing guard. They regarded her with distrust, though they did not stop her. She reached the door to the antechamber. Before she could knock, she heard Tuac.

"Come in Ba'al."

She opened the door and peered in, wondering how Tuac had known she was there.

"One of the guards alerted me telepathically that you were coming." Tuac said.

Ba'al entered. Merle stood behind Tuac and her love for him warmed the room. Maeva was also there, looking resolved. Ba'al knew Maeva would do anything for Tuac. Ba'al was envious of Tuac's devoted family. She doubted that any of her Acetos or even Ki'lel would brave threats to protect her.

"Why are you here?" Tuac's tone was calm and courteous.

"I promised to share with you my knowledge of the Reunifier." Tuac's eyebrows went up. *He never really expected me to explain,* Ba'al thought. *Good. Maybe I can earn his trust despite all that has happened. We will need it.*

"You did," he said. Maeva and Merle pulled a table over and set up five chairs. Ba'al had hoped to have this conversation in private.

"I have no secrets. If people are going to risk their lives for me, they deserve to know the truth. Please, make yourself comfortable."

Ba'al sat, and the others found their places.

Rea entered and said, "Sorry I'm late for this conversation. Dealing with a few Dragon Squad issues."

Ba'al acknowledged Rea. *Tuac called her telepathically. He certainly has all the attributes of the unified magician.* Ba'al had never imagined telling this story to so many.

"As you all know, Basul was founded after the Great Destruction, after the Prophet defeated Nabes at Shalla. The Prophet had called a great convention of magicians and military leaders. There they had decided to manage Mian society with a shared power structure. The Journey was designed to implement that management.

"The founders of Mia's governance had a deeper concern than management. They wanted control to prevent another threat from rising. The Church weeded out any potential heretics. The Empire identified and contained potential revolutionaries. And Basul ensured there would be no rogue magicians. I have shared much of this with Rea, but I did not tell her that the Prophet and Basul had a secret objective.

"Prior to the Great Destruction, there were some magicians who could use all of the Arts. The Prophet and Nabes were both so-called unified mages. Their rise to power as leaders of the forces of good and evil, demonstrated that this ability should be avoided. A magician able to wield multiple Arts could usher in a golden age or bring about Nabes' return. Magic itself is neutral, but power, which is tied to an individual, is not. The Prophet believed it was critical that no one magician ever have that kind of power again. Basul's oversight would dilute magical power by allowing magicians to practice only one Art and the Journey would be used to bring all magicians under Basul's control. At first, once in a generation a person able to wield unified magic would appear, but under Basul's management this tendency faded. We have not seen a unified mage in centuries but we could not forget the threat that they posed.

"Tuac, you are one of the rare magicians who can practice multiple Arts. When we could not direct you, we thought that your power was minor. We offered you a position on Basul's staff as we have done in prior instances. This was intended to keep you from coming into your aberrant magic. When you rejected us and left, walking right out through Basul's warded gates, we grew concerned that you had greater abilities. That was why we attacked you.

"Our efforts were not based on arrogance, but rather fear. Fear that you would learn a form of magic practiced by magicians prior to the Great Destruction. The Prophet designed the separation of the Arts as a way to prevent anyone from wielding such tremendous power. He thought that by channeling the gifted into specific Arts, the trait tying each mage to one Art would become dominant. And over time the ability to control multiple Arts would diminish to a level that did not threaten Mia and would eventually disappear.

"The Prophet's plan was largely successful. Unified magicians became rare. All but the Archmages forgot about them, though we stayed vigilant. We called them 'Reunifers' since they were tangling together what we had taken apart. Once every few generations, a student exhibits the abilities that you have— magic not confined within the Prophet's artificial boundaries. According to my research, most were diverted but there were a few instances when Basul had to use lethal efforts. There has not been a documented Reunifer for hundreds of turns.

"The Archmages' records reflect the dilemma posed by our obligation to control Reunifiers. At best, we deprived our brethren of the beauty of their magic. At worst, we sacrificed them for the greater good. But our rules are clear.

"The wards you felt at the gates when you left were a safe-guard established by the last Archmage who had to deal with a Reunifer. They were designed to keep unified mages within Basul to avoid loss of life. They were intended to affect any magician with latent unified magical ability who tries to leave Basul. You were the first to activate them. I'm awestruck that you had the power to evade their effects.

"When you left Basul and were granted asylum by the Anthenes, I directed our magicians to defeat Liat's wards so the Emperor could secure you. I had tried to get Argent to hand you over and, when he resisted, I grew frustrated. I knew the Emper-or's agents were capable of extracting you, and I even autho-rized him to use force. I believed I was obligated to counter the threat you posed. I never questioned that obligation. I never questioned the means. But I never imagined the Emperor was capable of genocide. There are no words to justify what I have done and I can only say I am sorry."

Ba'al could not meet Tuac's eyes. She sat in silence.

"Do I understand this correctly that you and the other Arch-mages claim the authority to decide who should live or die? What is your intent now that I have enough power to defend myself?"

The hair on Ba'al's neck rose. She felt Tuac's magic stirring. His hands began to glow.

He wants retribution, Ba'al thought. *I can't blame him. If I die now, I deserve it for all that I have done to him in the name of Basul.* "Tuac, words escape me. There is no satisfactory answer to your questions. I did what I did in the belief I was protecting Mia from a greater threat. The intent was sincere, but without consideration of the cost. I see the errors of my blind conviction and will accept whatever punishment you deem appropriate."

Ba'al felt Tuac's magic recede. The glow of his hands faded.

I reached him, she thought.

"I respect you for confiding in me. Basul's edicts were immoral, but the threat posed by Nabes prevents us from revisiting these rules. We must keep our attention on our survival. It's time to develop our strategy for stopping our common enemy."

He's wise beyond his years. If I survive, I will make sure these injustices never happen again. Ba'al resolved to be an instrument of change. It was not enough to apologize; she needed to act. She would stand by his side and use all of her efforts to protect him and his family.

"I know you are familiar with the Alcove at Liat, but did you know about the Chamber that was connected to it? That is where I learned that I was the Reunifier. Or, I should say, a reunifier."

"Rea related to me what happened to you at Liat. I can only offer some guesses, based upon what I have read," she answered.

"As I noted, the truth of Basul's selection process and purpose was more widely known earlier in Basul's history. Some, the Anthenes in particular, rejected the idea that unified mages should be put down like wounded livestock. They believed unified magic was a form of transcendence. This divide actually fed the tension between the Anthenes and the members of the magical Arts. Not only did some members of the magical Arts look down on Anthene magic, but those same magicians also feared that the schools of the individual Arts would lose their value if unified magic was permitted. They feared their loss of power. They vilified Anthenes for their refusal to reject magic that threatened the power structure of Basul.

"The Anthenes did not abandon their conviction after they were exiled. They drew strength from the Prophet's spiritual texts and continued to believe in the beauty and spirituality of unified magic.

"Over time, some at Basul regretted their actions with the Anthenes and engaged with Liat. The effort mended the schism between the two branches of magic and they signed the Treaty Ending the Expulsion. But not all were prepared to welcome back the Anthenes without qualifications.

"A Gaeist named Sheel believed that embracing unified magic would lead to the end of Basul. Reunifiers posed a threat so Basul needed to prevent unified mages from coming into their Art even if Basul had to employ lethal force. To appease those welcoming back the Anthenes, Sheel reached a compromise with Liat. They created the Chamber to trigger a Reunifier's magic in a time of need. But that magic could only be realized by someone who had a basic understanding of unified magic and only Basul would teach that. Basul held the key to unlocking a Reunifier's potential.

"Sheel never intended to honor this compromise and broke the spell so it could never be used. Somehow, you have done what he thought impossible. Without Basul's guidance, you repaired Sheel's sabotage and restored the spell.

"Unfortunately, that is the limit of my information about Reunifiers. Sheel destroyed all books discussing unified magic and how to develop the skill in one who possesses the ability. For you to understand your power, we must go back to a time before Basul, and consult the Prophet's original texts."

"There are only two places that house the complete teachings of the Prophet. One is in Tushman, in the Prophet's Cathedral. We know the Emperor will not grant any of us access. Basul also holds a sizeable collection of works that pre-date its founding in the Archmage's private armory. The Keeper of the Armory has the arsenal to prevent anyone without authorization from reading that material. The Archmage has permission to study the collection but cannot give access to others without permission of the Council. They will only grant that permission during a Time of Crisis."

Merle said, "This is definitely a Time of Crisis!"

Ba'al smiled at Merle, appreciating her exasperated assessment. *Even in this moment, she is unbridled by convention. Tuac picked a good mate.*

"I agree," Ba'al said. "Tuac, be prepared. You will have to convince the Council. I will provide you with the opportunity, but it will be up to you. Please be at the Council chamber in one hour."

Esa stood at attention behind the pile of books that she had obtained from the Vault.

"This is what that fool Gershawn was trying to protect?" the Emperor shouted. He paced the throne room, slopping wine from his goblet.

He's in a foul mood today, she thought.

Esa had hoped that gaining access to the Vault would put the Emperor in better spirits, but that was not the case. In fact, little satisfied Hahook. Since the destruction of Liat, he had been more volatile and brutal. He lashed out at anyone within reach. He had dispatched servants to the gallows for minor and even non-existent infractions.

Esa had rarely considered the Emperor's moral shortcomings. Esa believed in law and order and had viewed her position as a necessary evil to keep commoners from hurting themselves. When she was promoted to this assignment, she felt that she shared many of the Emperor's goals. He rewarded her for her service. But Esa was not cruel by nature and Hahook's degenerating behavior troubled her.

"Emperor, this is everything they have—records from the convention on the founding of Basul, some discussions of the Journey, and early writings of The Prophet. Given when they were written, I think there may be things that can help us fight Nabes. There is also some mythology that pre-dates the Prophet. Largely stories of Mia and a consort called Platt."

"Nabes?" Hahook snorted. "That is a ploy by Basul to frighten the citizenry. Basul controls us with the fear of another battle with Nabes." The Emperor refilled his cup with a shaking hand. He waved it at Esa. "It is all lies. We will deal with whatever is going on near Shalla in due course. Right now we focus on erasing Basul from the face of the planet.

"As for the mythology, I see no reason to keep the ramblings of heathens. They must be forgeries. Mia's mate was Aced. Burn those texts. They keep us in chains. Enough is enough." The Emperor strode toward the door.

This is not a time for the burning of the Prophet's words, Esa thought. *Even if I don't value them, Mia's citizens do.* On behalf of the people, Esa dared to engage Hahook again.

"Your Majesty, perhaps we should wait before destroying historic texts. I agree that they are not for the uneducated. But many value them, and might think we are the enemy if we burn the Prophet's words or stories about Mia without explanation. Maybe they would turn to Basul. Shouldn't we wait until we've liberated them before we enlighten them?" Esa held her breath.

The Emperor glared at her. His eyes were entirely black and he was deathly pale.

He is seriously ill, she thought, *but with what ailment?*

"I do not appreciate you second-guessing me, Esa, but timing is everything. Restrict all access to the Vault. No one in or out. We will deal with the Prophet's teachings when we have cleansed Mia. Now, let us prepare for war."

Ba'al convened the Council. They had elevated Eis to Acetos of the Fire Walkers. In addition to the Acetos, Ba'al invited Rea, Merle, Maeva, Tuac, and the Keeper, who could explain the characteristics of a Time of Crisis. Ki'lel, now Ba'al's second in command, also attended. A few grumbled when Tuac and Rea took their seats, but no one challenged them.

"Thank you for attending. We are caught between an insane Emperor and Nabes. Tuac's unique magic offers us a valuable resource, but only if he can understand it. We must study the Prophet's texts to help Tuac. I exercise my right to declare a Time of Crisis and grant him access to our most secret texts.

The Acetos of the Air Riders grumbled, "There is no basis in our history for this." Eis pounded on the table in agreement. Before Ba'al could answer, Chorra spoke.

"Silence. Ba'al is the Archmage and deserves your respect. We will hear her out and make a decision." Ba'al was grateful for Chorra's support.

Ba'al said, "We have all devoted our lives to protecting Mia. But Basul did things in the name of the greater good that were wrong.

"Our failure grew out of our arrogance. We believed that we should not have to answer for our decisions. We insulated ourselves, numb to the hurt that we caused. We lost our empathy. We rejected the moral imperative that the ends never justify the means. We created and maintained a system that used fear to oppress and control, all to keep Nabes at bay.

"We failed not only in our goal but also in our charge to safe-guard Mia. Our greatest enemy has returned. We must own the consequences of our actions and correct our path. We must call a truce with Tuac and embrace him as the Reunifer. He will lead us in our battle and to do so he needs access to all of our records. I hope that we are not too late."

The Council erupted. The Acetos and Ki'lel yelled. Accusations of treason and treachery flew. Tuac and his group stayed quiet. After a minute, Kira the Keeper cleared his throat.

"Ba'al, as custodian of the records you seek I know the hallmarks of a Time of Crisis. I agree that we are living in perilous times, but I find your position curious. Please explain these failures and why you think Tuac can help us."

The room fell silent.

The Keeper is extending a hand to me, Ba'al thought. "That is a fair question. I should tell you the hidden history of the Great Destruction, unified magic, the Prophet's warnings, and the Journey. This knowledge has been passed down from Archmage to Archmage in an unbroken oral tradition." Ba'al told her audience everything she had told Tuac earlier. She included his miraculous evolution into a unified magician despite Sheel's sabotage of the Chamber. She finished and sat down. She nodded to Tuac.

It's up to him now, she thought.

Tuac stood. "Members of the Council. I am not here seeking retribution for what you did to me. I am focused on the future, *our future.* I have looked into Nabes' eyes and I know that if we do not stop Nabes, it will destroy all we love.

"The Prophet defeated Nabes once, but that victory was not complete. I suspect that the Prophet was faced with a difficult choice. One avenue would have vanquished Nabes forever, but it would have come at a tremendous cost. The Prophet did not choose that path, but instead created a system that he believed would suppress the magic that had ushered in Nabes' terror. The Prophet made the wrong choice.

"We must discover what that other avenue was and its costs. Only then can we determine if there is a different solution. I come not as an enemy demanding that you submit to me, but asking you to ally with me. Our union provides the best opportunity to defeat Nabes. But mark my words, I will face Nabes with or without you. I leave you now to deliberate and I hope you choose to join us."

Tuac motioned to Merle, Rea, and Maeva and they left the room together. Ba'al waited until the door closed behind them.

She said, "Kira, you have your answer. Nabes has arisen. A unified mage has come into his power, albeit without any training. Only the Prophet's words can save us. We need to understand Tuac's potential and how the Prophet defeated Nabes. If we succeed, we can consider how Mia should be governed in a new age. If we fail, we will all die.

"Ba'al, Tuac is the threat here!" Ki'lel said, his voice fierce. "We don't need him to defeat Nabes. How can you reject the warnings about unified magic and suggest an alliance?"

Her trusted advisor's tone surprised Ba'al. She wondered what had changed in the man who had once advocated for the boy. She resisted the urge to escalate.

"Ki'lel, we need to recognize the limits of our knowledge. It is also possible that the motives of those that founded Basul colored their interpretation of the Prophet's teachings. We can hold on to the old ways, but the return of Nabes suggests that we should consider alternatives.

"Reviewing the Prophet's teachings will not dictate the conclusion, only give us the unfiltered truth of what happened and why. I cannot do this alone, there is little time and so much material. Tuac's growth as a unified magician also may give him unique insights into those writings."

The debate continued for a while longer, but the voices supporting her outnumbered those rejecting her proposal. She, and Tuac, had won the day.

Tuac waited outside the meeting room. He heard Ki'lel shouting and Ba'al's measured response. Finally, the door opened. Tuac expected Ba'al to deliver the Council's judgment, but it was Kira who appeared.

"Let's go, Reunifer. Your request to explore the Prophet's words has been granted."

Only Ba'al and Ki'lel joined Tuac's group as Kira led them to the Archmage's armory. Tuac sensed Ba'al's excitement, touched with anxiety. To his sorrow, he felt Ki'lel's smoldering anger.

Kira opened the door and Tuac marveled at all the weapons. He stood examining a wand. He caressed it in its case and felt its power. It had several markings similar to those on the one Ki'lel had given him. Ki'lel stopped next to Tuac and picked up the wand.

"I wish I could find my wand. It would be useful right now."

This startled Tuac. He thought that Ki'lel had left him the wand but apparently it was someone else. Tuac reached inside his tunic and presented the wand to Ki'lel.

"I found this in my room when I was packing to leave Basul. I did not realize it was yours." Ki'lel stared at the wand, then plucked it from Tuac's hand. For a long moment, grief stained Ki'lel's turbulent aura. *He's missing Meiach.*

They gathered in stood in front of the yellow oak door and raised her hands. "I am Ba'al, Archmage of Basul. In the name of all the Archmages of the past, I claim my right to enter this chamber. Let the Prophet's words guide us and lead to our salvation."

With a click, the door swung open.

This reminds me of the Chamber, Tuac thought. *It must have been built to echo this room.* He saw a desk covered in dust and an unlit candle. There were two bookshelves, each with four levels. There were about one hundred books. The group surged forward, but Ba'al held up her hand.

"Tuac," she said, "you should select the first volume."

Tuac's family smiled at him and he could feel their warmth and support. Ki'lel scowled and would not meet Tuac's eyes.

Tuac ran his hands over the sacred texts starting at the top left shelf. There were a dozen books that appeared to be early religious texts of Mia, followed by twenty books that had the words *Curiosity Log* and a number on their spine. One book appeared to be missing. The books that followed looked different. The bindings were made of animal hide and they were unmarked.

These must be the Prophet's teachings.

Tuac picked up the first *Curiosity* log and read, "We left from Earth on a clear day. Our mission is to find other planets that will support life, as we have outgrown the resources on our home planet as well as the Moon and Mars."

Tuac leafed through the pages. The handwriting was Orris's but the log was dry and technical. The book Tuac had must have been Orris's private record.

Tuac skimmed discussions of the ship, noticing references to things called computers, life support systems that allowed them to breath and grow their food, and strange weapons. Most of the *Curiosity's* passengers had slept as the ship traveled from Earth to a planet called 55 Cancri E, a distance Orris described as forty-one light years. The rest of the book detailed how they had veered off course and arrived at Mia.

Tuac put the log down and examined other volumes that appeared to be writings of the *Curiosity's* crew. One was called a *Journal of Local Flora,* and it contained detailed descriptions of Mian plant life with beautiful drawings, so precise they seemed alive on the page. Another cataloged Mian animal life. The texts noted similarities between vegetation and animals of Mia and those of Earth. Tuac saw a hursa beside an Earth creature called a "horse" and he could see the resemblance. Another book was titled Linguistics, which started with columns of strange symbols and a second column of Mian letters. The next section featured groupings of the symbols next to Mian words.

As he studied the text, he realized he had this backwards. The symbols were early Mian letters and they had been translated into a language from Earth. Tuac had wondered why he could read the texts of the *Curiosity* crew but now he understood. Mians now read and spoke the language of these visitors. He wondered what else these people had done to Mia's culture.

Finally, Tuac came to unmarked journals. He picked up the first one, and started to read aloud.

This is the story of my life. I live in the Shalla Colony, founded where Curiosity crashed. This is home to some of the families of the crew that survived.

My parents died and I am being raised by my grandfather in this safe haven. We are a mixed-race community—colonizers from a planet I've never seen called Earth and the local inhabitants of the only planet I have ever known, Mia. There are others who fathered or mothered children with Mians that are not part of Shalla. They chose to leave the safety and rules of our community.

My grandfather, captain of the Curiosity, does not speak kindly of those who have left, claiming that their intentions were nefarious. Although he has never explained exactly what happened, others have told me the exiles were responsible for my father's death.

My grandfather does his best to raise me. He is full of love, justice, and service. He tells me stories of Earth's history and culture.

I asked him if I should write down Shalla's history. He agreed, and gave me one of his empty books so I could start my own journal.

I am starting today on my 10th birthday. My name is Elijah Orris. In Shalla, we name our children after Earth's historical figures to keep their stories alive. For me it is annoying, because they call me Prophet.

Tuac put the book down. Elijah, the Prophet, was the grandson of Sam Orris. *First, the hidden agenda of the Journey and now the truth about the Prophet. What else will we learn?*

After several hours, the group left the Archmage's armory. Tuac and his group took the Prophet's journals back to their quarters to study them.

When Ba' al and Ki'lel were alone, Ki'lel's anger erupted.

"The Prophet was a descendant of the *Curiosity's* crew? We have all heard the stories of what happened—they landed, killed almost all the Mians before dying out. Despite years of efforts to try to find them, other than a few random pieces from the shipwreck, nothing was ever located. I do not believe one word of this!"

"Enough," Ba'al said, her tone calm. "We have guarded these books since Basul's founding. Whether we like it or not, they are the truth. Our job now is finding what they can offer in the battle against Nabes." She laid a hand on Ki'lel's arm. "It's been a long day."

Ki'lel pulled away from the contact and glared at her.

The boy attacks all of us. He stole my wand. He is arrogant and has no morals. This is not a person we should trust, Ki'lel thought. "This is heresy," he hissed at Ba'al, then he left.

He stewed over his options on the way to his quarters. Basul needed to focus on marshalling all forces against Nabes. Tuac was a distraction, an obstacle that undermined their preparation for war. Either Ba'al would come to her senses or Ki'lel would need to act.

As Ki'lel strode through the hallways, he muttered to himself.

"I will show Ba'al that she's being a fool." His glower warned everyone to stay out of his way.

The Watcher observed him. The altercation between Ba'al and Ki'lel was an outcome that the Watcher had anticipated but had hoped to avoid. When the Watcher started down this road, there was a narrow range of options available given restrictions on direct interference. The Watcher recognized there was a risk that Ki'lel would react badly when he discovered that Tuac had Ki'lel's wand. The Watcher had run through countless simulations to find the strategy with the highest percentage of success. The conclusion always was the same—Tuac had needed both enough information to heighten his chance of discovering the truth and enough magical firepower to bridge the gap until he had unlocked his true power.

The Watcher had given some information to Tuac, but the Watcher had also needed Ba'al. The Watcher had planted images of Nabes' contagion in her mind while she slept. The Watcher knew it would heighten her anxiety and drive her to the inner sanctum of revered texts in search of answers. Stress, exhaustion, and sleeplessness kept her from remembering her late night wanderings. He had nudged her to remove *Journal of Sam Orris* from the collection and take it back to her room to read. It was a simple matter to plant the suggestion that she should leave the book in Tuac's quarters. Tuac had not read the entire journal yet, and there was still more he needed to learn from it.

Ki'lel had been a tougher case, but the Watcher needed to ensure that Tuac would have a weapon until he came into his power. Ki'lel was stubborn and arrogant, and those characteristics created walls around his mind that the Watcher found hard to penetrate. But Ki'lel's grief over Meiach's death at their battle with Nabes wore down Ki'lel's defenses. The Watcher had distracted the magician, causing him to drop his wand in front of Tuac's room. A housekeeper helpfully moved it onto Tuac's desk. Tuac had an emotional connection with that wand which had allowed it to channel his latent ability. Tied to what created magic on this planet, the wand enhanced Tuac's skill so he could protect himself until he unlocked his real power.

The Watcher's observations of Ba'al and Ki'lel revealed their true characters. The Watcher could see their commitment to the survival of the magical order. But they differed on whether magicians should exercise restraint and empathy. Ba'al struggled with the moral balance between the needs of Mians and the rules of her office. Ki'lel believed that magical power created moral superiority.

Ba'al's dilemma had played out many times, even between the Prophet and his mate Luina. Nabes' return demonstrated to

Ba'al that neither she nor her predecessors were infallible. Basul's governance was a mission of service and the magicians had failed in their duties. Ki'lel, on the other hand, clung to the belief that Basul ruled because it was entitled to do so.

The Watcher had gambled that Ki'lel would be persuaded by the threat Nabes posed and the potential that Tuac offered. Unfortunately, Ki'lel's arrogance was fertile ground for his inner demons. Nabes might take advantage of that.

Things were coming to a head. Nabes' power had peaked and Nabes had acquired formidable players. The Watcher had done all that was permitted and now the debate between right versus duty would play out again.

Twenty-Six

My grandfather taught me the history of his world. He told me that evil repeatedly pushed Earth to the brink of annihilation. Over time, the weapons became more destructive and the loss of life more horrendous. One battle would lead to another, greater one, all in the name of power.

My grandfather's stories were not tales of despair, though. They were tales of hope. Each time his world reached the brink of annihilation, a group of champions rose to fight those seeking to subjugate the rest of their planet.

My grandfather wanted me to know his planet's history because he feared for Mia. And here I am, embroiled in a conflict brought about by the consequences of Curiosity's arrival.

I am Sam Orris's grandson, Elijiah. And like the champions of Earth, I swear I will stop the plague Mia now faces or die trying.

The Teachings of the Prophet, 1:1

When they got back to their private quarters, Tuac called a meeting. Tuac placed the *Journal of Sam Orris* on the table.

"This is the *Journal of Sam Orris*. It contains the personal thoughts of the captain of the *Curiosity*—the Prophet's grandfather. Someone placed this in my room shortly after I arrived at Basul. It must have come from the Armory but only Ba'al had access to it. She has never mentioned it to me and I'm not sure she realizes I have it. I can't explain that.

"I have read only a few passages. I didn't have a lot of time to delve into it. I think this," Tuac said, fanning the pages of the tome, "contains information we need."

Tuac studied the faces of his family as they looked at the *Journal*. He felt from his bonds with Merle and Maeva that they were afraid of opening it. They, too, wondered how the journal had arrived in Tuac's room. Finally, Merle reached for the book.

"We only live once," she said. Merle's courage lightened the mood. She leafed through the pages and then stopped roughly three-quarters through. "Oh my. I think this is what you were looking for," and started reading aloud:

4072 SY

The last thirty years have been challenging for us. Most of the *Curiosity's* resources are gone and we have been forced to create a colony at our crash site to live off the land. We were able to cannibalize our solar array to power our most critical computers, including ACED, our Artificial Cerebral Enhancement Device and our amplification tools. Our communications are fried but our distress beacon still works. We can use our medical facilities and we have started hard copy logs of our research.

The locals call our home Shalla. They no longer fear us, and we have developed a barter system to help us survive.

Many of us have found lasting friends and even partners among the locals. I found my beloved Srah here. She was the emissary of the locals, and helped establish the fair value system that we use for trading, a fine piece of negotiation. Srah is also the best hunter in Shalla, and introduced me to the challenges of an art I have never practiced. It was not long before she captivated me, the intelligence in her crystal green eyes, quick smile, and blonde hair soon haunted my dreams. It took quite a while for her to return my favors, but I won her over. It has made my life here not only bearable but rich and rewarding. In time, I found myself in love with her and with Mia. After the crash, I had not envisioned myself finding a home.

Srah and I have a young son, whose name is Plat. He has warm brown eyes like mine, and the blond hair of his mother. We named him after the mate of the goddess Mia, whom the locals worship as the source of all life on the planet. The love story of Mia and Plat reminds me of some of Earth's creation myths. They created the stars and the planet. Srah wanted our son to have a name regal enough to lead.

Plat is my everything, although I am still trying to cope with his enhanced abilities. Our scientists have concluded that the Mian cerebral cortex is close enough to human to be enhanced by ACED but has qualities that magnify the effects of the computer. We built ACED to enhance human senses, allowing ordinary humans to access more acute senses of smell and touch, and if focused properly, move small objects. The children of Mian and Terran parents can do even more, like shaping fire into small balls and more advanced telekinesis. The blended genome makes ACED's effects more pronounced.

Merle stopped reading.

"ACED was a 'com-puuuter'? Whatever that is, it doesn't sound right. We all know Aced and Mia created all that we are and see. And Plat is the white metal we find in the ground, not Mia's mate."

Tuac considered what she had read. *Just like our language, magic is yet another way that the Terrans changed us. Why don't we know this story? Is that why I have this journal? I hope there is something here about Nabes, too.* He took the book from Merle. She was pale and her eyes were anxious.

Tuac flipped through the pages. A reference to the Prophet caught his eye. He started reading aloud.

4107 SY

Today is my grandson's 10th birthday. I look at Elijah and I see his father and mother in him. And he has green eyes like my beloved Srah.

Elijah's life has been filled with tragedy, yet he is not bitter. His mother, who was also of Mian-Earthen blood, died in childbirth. His father Plat was taken from us by the Renegades three years ago. It should have been me, but Plat wanted to negotiate with them instead of attacking. I warned him that they could not be trusted. Tempers flared, and they killed him. They said it was accidental and left without further violence, taking all of our plasma weapons. I do not believe it was an accident.

I have raised Elijah, hoping to instill in him my values, helped by my fellow Shallans. Because of my connection to the *Curiosity*, they consider me their leader. I view myself as caretaker of our Terran technology and I am one of the few people that can keep the solar array working. But the panels are failing, and we will need a new power source.

I have tapped into a geothermal vent I found in a cavern under the hill where we established our camp. We have built a larger generator using salvaged parts, and the heat powers it. I have moved several invertors from the solar array and we now have a strong, constant source of electricity to power ACED. I also connected the distress beacon to ACED to preserve its signal. With the improved power, it also bounces off the ionosphere and blankets the planet. Sadly, our medical systems have no more supplies, and critical parts have aged and failed.

Srah and I have tried to be parents to Elijah, so he would not feel orphaned. He is a handful! Every time I turn around, he is moving something or talking to the livestock. His ACED-enhanced powers are exponentially stronger than those of his father. And while I am continually astounded by his abilities, for him they are very natural. I think that is why he is so strong.

I am lucky that he is guided by love and justice, and not greed or power. He gets his empathy and commitment to our community from Srah. A mother's love can temper a male's natural aggression.

I fear for this world and Elijiah's future. I tried to create an environment where these new-found powers would only be used for the right purposes, but the Renegades rejected my views and are using their ACED-enhanced abilities and the amplification tools they stole from us to rule over other communities. I am worried we will have to confront their abuse of ACED.

Every night I tell Elijah stories of Earth. His favorites are of mythical battles of knights and dragons. I also try to teach him of the science that brought us here, but that is difficult since our reference materials vanished when our central computers were destroyed in the crash. I tried to explain his enhanced skills, but he could not understand ACED's effects on brainwaves or why his genome is more sensitive than mine. He described his abilities as magic like that in the stories. I did not correct him, because science is but magic of a different form.

We also talk about good and evil, and invariably that turns to a discussion of the Renegades. He does not understand why some in our community would use their enhanced abilities to rule over those without. I had the same conversations with his father. Plat believed in the inherent goodness of people, a trait he got from his mother. His unshakeable devotion to the greater good is what got him killed. He underestimated the potential for evil and that sometimes it is necessary to stand against oppression. Force should never be the first resort but sometimes it is the only resource left.

I wonder whether we brought injustice to this world or whether it is present in all civilizations. Is lust for power one of our genetic characteristics? Earth almost did not survive our violent nature. I wonder if Earth's civilization still exists, as well as what will come of this planet. The carnage wrought by the nations of the 21st century left the planet mostly uninhabitable, we had to reach out into space seeking new homes. At what cost?

This was the last entry of Sam Orris. The rest of the journal had been torn out.

His family sat silent when he finished reading. Maeve dabbed tears from her eyes.

"Are we to believe that magic was created by Terran technology?" Rea said, "that giftedness is connected to one's ancestry?"

"No wonder this journal was hidden," Tuac said. "I was meant to find it, but it only leads to more questions."

Merle grasped his hand and squeezed, and he squeezed back. They left the table to sit in front of the fire, leaving Rea and Maeve to their thoughts.

Esa assembled her provisions for the march. She would be leading the troops in procession past the balcony after the Emperor's speech to the citizens of Tushman. They were marching for Basul immediately. Hahook had made clear to Esa that he wanted to limit the time the magicians had to prepare a defense.

Preparation for the Emperor's war had happened at a dizzying speed. Esa had cautioned Hahook against this assault, but he rejected Esa's Council. The former Charge Gershawn, who had become a sniveling toady, did not support her desire to avoid all-out war with the mages. His obsequious platitudes made her want to retch. He had gone from preaching the words of the Prophet to directing the faithful toward the Emperor's vision.

The Emperor had whipped the masses into a lather with daily speeches of divisiveness. He knew Tushman's poor wanted a scapegoat for their troubles, and the magicians were perfect targets. His favorite technique was to go to the markets and complain how the magicians had not helped this year's crop.

He would stand and shout, "Where are they when it gets too hot or there is a flood?" or "Couldn't they use their Earth-moving skills to enrich the ground?"

Soon the people believed that the University was responsible for every problem anyone had ever had. Gershawn's clerics reinforced the Emperor's attacks. They harped on the perils of magic and how, but for the courage of Cedric, all would have been lost in the Great Destruction. The Prophet was no longer their savior, the Empire was. Esa had to admit that co-opting the Church was genius.

Today was the Emperor's final step before launching his war. He declared a holiday called Deliverance Day. As this was a new holiday, the people crowded into the main square of Tushman waiting for an explanation. Esa's troops were ready to march, and could manage the masses during the speech. She moved to a good vantage point so she could watch the Emperor speak from his balcony.

"Fellow Mians! I stand before you as a humble man, whose only desire is to serve you. The Empire defeated Nabes and we built a great nation here. But for all we have done, there is one group that stands apart from us. One group that believes they are better. One group that could do more to help all of us, yet they choose to do nothing. One group that has never acknowledged its role in the Great Destruction."

The Emperor paused.

Esa heard shouts of "Down with the mages!" and "The magicians only care about power!"

Hahook smirked.

I'm growing tired of his arrogance, conceit, and lies, she thought.

Hahook raised his hands and the crowd quieted.

"Mians, enough is enough. The magicians were invited to be part of our society and chose to remain separate. They have defended their withdrawal from our society as necessary to protect their power from unnamed enemies of Mia. Even now, despite all the poverty, famine, and drought, they devote their attention to the rise of Nabes.

"We know the truth. Nabes is long gone. They are trying to preserve their power so they can use it against the Empire! But fear not, my fellow Mians. I will protect you against their evil."

The crowd roared and shifted, waves of angry energy flowing across the square. Esa's retinue closed ranks around her, and she signaled her commanders to watch for those who might incite a riot. The Emperor waved his arms, encouraging their rage to grow. The crowd's noise reached a crescendo, then Hahook skillfully subdued them for his final statement.

"Today we take back Mia from the magicians. Cedric knew better than to trust them but he did not have the resources after the Great Destruction to deal with them. I do. I will finish Cedric's task. I will deliver us from this evil and erase the magicians from this planet once and for all. Who stands with me?"

The crowd roared so loud that Esa wondered if Basul could hear it.

I realize they are ignorant, but can't they see they're being manipulated? Esa thought. Esa believed that the Empire needed to protect its people, but not like this. Her chosen standard bearer was a raving lunatic.

The group debated what to make of the information they had discovered from the *Journal of Sam Orris.* Rea wanted to let Ba'al know since the information could lead to a greater understanding of magic as it now existed. Maeva resisted. She did not trust the magicians and argued that disclosing what they had uncovered would be met with incredulity, and perhaps accusations of heresy. Maeva acknowledged that Basul had never embraced the mythos of Aced, but disclosing that the magicians' gift was an effect of alien machines would not be well received. Tuac let the argument play out, fatigued by the sensation that he was living in a story that had spiraled out of control.

At one particularly heated moment between Rea and Maeve, Merle interrupted.

"Stop! We will need to talk to Ba'al but we are not ready. Orris' story was only part of the puzzle, but it does not shed light on the reason for the Journey or Tuac's role in defeating

Nabes. All we know is that these aliens corrupted Mia and we are all now paying the price for it. If we go to Ba'al with half an answer, it will serve no purpose and may do real harm. The mages might reconsider whether they view Tuac as a threat."

Tuac looked at his beloved.

How lucky I am to have you as my mate. He needed to refocus his family and also create a bit of space between Rea and Maeva. He loved and needed them both. Then he spoke.

"Merle is right. We shall divide into two teams. Rea, you and Merle will review the Prophet's journals to see if there is any more information about how the Prophet defeated Nabes. Maeva, you and I will see if we can learn more about this computer called ACED and how magic works.

The groups dove into their research and, over the next two weeks, they uncovered a great deal. They met nightly to report, allowing their discussion to sharpen their research. Tuac and Maeva learned that ACED was designed to assist in the *Curiosity's* long space journey by a group that Orris called *scientists*. But the machine's effects on the crew were nothing like the magic Mians used now. On the ship, ACED amplified senses, enabling *Curiosity's* crew to do things like notice slight changes in body heat as a warning about infection or to read emotional auras.

Early in the voyage, the *Curiosity* crew had experienced an unintended effect of ACED. An object pierced the ship causing what Orris called decompression. To contain the emergency, they had to repair the damage or they would all die. But the crew could not maneuver to patch the hole. Facing certain death, Orris focused on a metal sheet near the breach. It moved. He shouted at the rest of his crew to do the same and, working together, they were able to move the sheet and plug the hole.

Telekinesis! I could do that without any effort, thought Tuac.

Tuac knew they were on the right track, so he told Maeve to

look for anything discussing how ACED's effects grew. They learned that the *Curiosity* crew experimented with their new-found skills. They learned focus and control, but individually their abilities were limited to moving small objects. They used telekinesis for small tasks and repairs, but it was not the magic of Mia.

ACED's effects increased among the children of Mian and Terran parents. Some of the stories of these children were comical. The youngsters inadvertently caused problems—fires grew out of control, they flung objects during tantrums, and had scary, but benign, interactions with local fauna. The Terran parents tried to explain how ACED caused these strange developments in the children, but the Mians did not understand. The Mians believed that Mia had blessed them with powers.

Orris speculated that ACED's effects were caused by the differences and similarities between human and Mian minds. Tuac struggled to read and re-read these confusing passages, because Orris used words like genetics and DNA. Although he was not quite sure of their meaning, Tuac concluded that these terms referred to the reason why children look like their parents, having similar eye color and build. Based upon Orris' descriptions, DNA was the magic behind the physical characteristics of a person. Orris believed that Mian DNA was almost like human DNA, so ACED affected Mians. But their DNA was different enough that the effects were larger.

Orris observed that those with enhanced abilities excelled in particular tasks or working with specific materials. These echoed the child's personality. For example, those who could shape fire were volatile, with fierce tempers and deep passions. Certain personality traits aligned with each skill, the Arts as Tuac knew them. Those who did telekinesis were more cerebral, those who practiced healing were empathetic, Gaeists were drawn to animal life, early Air Riders were mischievous and playful, and early Stone Movers valued structure and order. Orris named the Gaeists and Anthenes after gods of Earth. Orris noted that a rare few could access all of the abilities. Those persons sought balance in the universe. Orris called them Unifiers because they believed that all things are connected.

Merle and Rea found useful details in the Prophet's personal journals. His full abilities had appeared later in life, after his grandfather had died. Sam Orris was the last of the *Curiosity's* crew, and his death had changed his grandson Elijiah. The Prophet had realized that his grandfather had prepared him to be the protector of Shalla. Sam's stories had been lessons that had taught Elijiah how to lead and what to value.

Sam Orris had seen a growing darkness on Mia, and the Prophet had felt it was his mission to continue his grandfather's fight against this evil. The Renegades had used their ACED-enhanced abilities to enslave Mians. They had wanted control of the entire population and fought amongst themselves as well as against the community of Shalla.

The Prophet's journals describe how they pushed the Renegades back when they attacked Shalla. Once the community was safe, the Prophet journeyed to help other communities. His records detailed an increasing level of depravity and aggression. Rea found references to Nabes being the source of this evil, and suggestions that it was related to ACED's effects on Mians. She also found references to the Prophet's early efforts to organize a resistance.

"On one mission, the Prophet met a woman named Luina." Rea recounted. "She was defending a village from Renegades and had circled them in a ring of fire. The Prophet stepped into the battle and quieted her flame, and then put the attackers to sleep so they could be captured."

"He used two different types of magic?" asked Merle.

"I hadn't even thought of that as I was too enthralled by the story. How is that possible?" Rea said.

"He must be like me, able to use more than one Art. What else did you find out?" Tuac responded.

"The Prophet described how furious Luina was at the Prophet's intrusion but calmed down after the Prophet explained he was equally motivated by protecting the innocent. They debated approaches into the night. The Prophet said Luina's spirit and passion for justice astonished him. In passage describing the interaction, he said 'Luina's fire burned bright white like the sun, reflecting the purity of her spirit.'"

Rea said the Prophet and Luina did not appear to ever agree upon on the role of enhanced people in Mian society. The Prophet wanted to restrict the enhanced because the Renegades were using their abilities to enslave others and damage the planet. Luina, who had grown up outside of Shalla and was unaware these abilities came from ACED, saw her power as a divine gift. Like any gift, it could be used for evil or by the righteous. The Prophet tried to explain to Luina the origin of her talents, but she refused to accept his explanation. Like his grandfather before him, the Prophet described Luina's power in magical terms. Luina, and others who followed the Prophet, adopted *magic* to describe their abilities of the gifted.

They often argued, but their love for each other saw them through, and conflicts usually ended with a night of passion. In time, their pairing produced a daughter. After Luina's death in the Great Destruction, the Prophet decided that Luina's parents should raise his child because the demands of the new order prevented him from giving her the attention she deserved. The news that the Prophet had a child startled all of them. They had never heard this. Her name did not appear in any of the writings, and they did not know if she survived to bear children of her own.

The Prophet agreed with Luina on the need to focus on the fundamental difference between good and evil. The Prophet, Luina, and their followers sought justice, morality, empathy, and equity. The Renegades only cared about power, wealth, and control. The Prophet wrote about his efforts to secure allies, including Cedric.

At the end of their period of intense study, the group discussed their findings.

"Nothing! There is nothing here to explain Nabes," Rea said. "And we are no closer to understanding your role, Tuac."

Tuac poked at his food. "I would say that we have a better idea of what magic is, and it still falls into the categories identified by Orris. Fire Walkers are definitely still volatile." Tuac winked at his sister. "And we know that the Prophet was able to use more than one Art. But you're right, we still haven't found more about how the Prophet defeated Nabes. Perhaps tomorrow we should—" A pounding on the door startled them.

"Come in," Tuac said.

Ki'lel barged into the room. "The Emperor has arrived with his army. They're going to attack tomorrow. Whether I like it or not, we must fight as allies."

Rea bolted from the table, followed by Ki'lel and Tuac. The Dragon Squad was assembled at the gates when Rea, Ki'lel and Tuac arrived.

Ba'al stood in the opening between the gates. Ki'lel stopped beside her and Rea stood behind him. Tuac stood at Ba'al's other side. Rea surveyed the Emperor's forces and felt as if she had been kicked in the gut. Campfires extended as far as they eye could see. She did a rough count, guessing at the number of the troops associated with each fire, and determined that thousands of soldiers waited on the field. The Emperor had prepared for this war.

Ba'al barked orders. "Ki'lel, tell the Stone Movers to reinforce the gates, and see if the Gaeists can direct thorny vines up the walls to make them harder to climb. Call the Water Sculptors' fire brigade and send the others to their positions on the wall. The Fire Walkers and Air Riders should ready their battle magic. Your telepaths will shield us. Remember to use the rotation we discussed to keep each division strong."

Ba'al turned to Rea. "I do not want to kill anyone if we can avoid it. Our biggest concern is Nabes. Whether we destroy the Emperor or he destroys us, Nabes wins. The only way to keep this from strengthening our true enemy is to prevent the battle from happening. But if we need to defend ourselves, we will.

"Ready your Dragon Squad and be prepared to act. But wait for my order."

Rea saw three riders approaching from the camp. The Emperor rode in the center, flanked by a cleric and a woman in armor. Rea guessed that she was Esa, the Emperor's general. Rea had heard that Esa was a brilliant tactician and formidable opponent.

"Let's see what all this is about," Ba'al said. With Rea, Ki'lel, and Tuac at her back, she walked down the hill. Rea's fire burned bright. She started to glow. She would protect her brother.

"Calm yourself," Ba'al said. "This isn't the time. Perhaps we can avert this war."

Rea subdued her magic, though she kept fire at her fingertips so she could react instantly to any treachery. But she would not attack without provocation.

Why is he doing this now? Rea wondered. Ba'al stopped close enough to the riders that they could converse without shouting.

"To what do I owe this visit?" Ba'al said. "Are you offering to protect Basul from the coming onslaught of Nabes?"

"Ba'al," the Emperor sneered. "I am here to deliver the terms of Basul's surrender. The magicians of Basul, like their Anthene brothers, are a blight on Mia. You have used your power with impunity, showing little concern for anyone else. Every day Mians starve, struggle, and die, and you do nothing to aid them. Today that stops. Either Basul submits to the authority of the crown in service to Mia, or I will disband your little magical school. With force, if necessary.

Rea's hands burned hotter. *It is time to incinerate this fool.*

Ba'al said, "Emperor, the Prophet created the triumvirate to ensure peaceful coexistence between the magical, spiritual and civic realms on Mia. The Prophet gave each of us a flock and our duties. That structure allowed us to crawl out of the abyss created by the Great Destruction.

"I am not about to change that structure with the looming threat that Nabes presents. Although I am willing to discuss new ways for Basul to assist the people since you believe we are not doing enough."

He makes me want to puke, thought Rea. *But I respect Ba'al for giving the Emperor a way to step back from all of this.*

"Fool!" the Emperor barked, "You invoke the Prophet to save your skin? I am now the Charge of the Church. The Prophet will not spare you from the punishment you deserve. And using the specter of Nabes to frighten the people is a pathetic distraction. You have until sunrise tomorrow. Surrender or die. Those are your choices." The Emperor reined his hursa around and galloped away.

Twenty-Seven

NABES has infected the Renegades. We knew ACED creates NABES in all humans to a varying degree. For some, it becomes debilitating. But with all that has happened since we landed on Mia, I never once considered NABES' effects on these people. I should have anticipated that, just like ACED, NABES would have more pronounced effects. ACED amplifies the cortex of the genetically mixed, and now the genetically mixed amplify NABES.

It is now alive.

From the lost pages of The Journal of Sam Orris

Ba'al presented the Emperor's terms of surrender to her war Council. All but Rea, who was readying the Dragon Squad, were present. Tuac watched the Acetos shout at each other.

Chorra preached calm. "The Emperor is bluffing and will back down."

Tuac was not convinced and, looking at the faces of the other Acetos, he did not believe they were, either. Tuac suspected a show of force would be necessary, but he worried about the consequences. Before Tuac could speak, Ki'lel stood and addressed the Council.

"Basul's charter restricted our involvement in Mian society because Basul's founders feared we would wield power incorrectly. But we have been removed from affairs of state for too long." Anger tinted Ki'lel's voice. "Basul's founders were wrong. Because we took no active role in governing, Emperor Hahook has become a tyrant. Now he threatens us. Basul must assert its divine primacy. It is our right and destiny."

Ha! Magicians have the moral authority to rule? Tuac thought. *If only Ki'lel and the rest of them knew that they owe their power to alien explorers.* As tempting as it was to chastise the magicians, Tuac knew any disclosure of what he had discovered from the *Curiosity's* journals would divide them further. Nabes was behind this acrimony. They needed to overcome their division and create a unified response.

Tuac waited for the right moment to intervene. After an hour, the arguments became repetitive. Tuac appealed to both sides.

"The real enemy is Nabes," he said, "and we will be at a disadvantage in the war to come if we decimate the Emperor's forces. I also agree with Ki'lel that we need a show of force. I believe the Emperor will back down, and we need to encourage that decision.

"I suggest that, rather than attacking, we present a dramatic, visible defense. We should have the Dragon Squad deploy their arsenal of dragons, stone giants and the like. Their presence will give the Emperor's forces pause. It is a reasonable gamble, and we are prepared if it doesn't work."

Tuac studied the Council members and hoped his approach

struck the right balance. The show of force would satisfy those demanding that the Emperor pay for his impertinence. The Dragon Squad's defensive display would satisfy those seeking de-escalation.

"A sound approach," Ba'al said.

Ki'lel nodded and, one by one, the other Acetos agreed. Tuac had won the day.

"We have an accord," Ba'al said. "Ki'lel, you are in charge." The meeting adjourned.

"Tuac, a moment," Ba'al said. They walked to Ba'al's chambers and stood together on the balcony. The first sun of Mia was rising and, on the horizon, he saw the thousands of troops massing outside of Basul.

"You restrained your words back there," she said.

She is perceptive, Tuac thought. He noticed for the first time how exhausted she was. She looked pale and her shoulders hunched.

"I didn't say everything because I'm afraid of what will happen when I do. It has nothing to do with my opinion about the Emperor's arrival. For that, we need a measured show of force. But if I spoke about all we have learned, we would be unable to respond to the present emergency."

"What aren't you telling me?"

"The journals show that Basul was built on a lie and magic is not what we believe it to be. Magicians are not the chosen of Aced and Mia. Their power comes from alien science, the result of a device brought here by the *Curiosity.* Somehow, it still affects all of our lives."

Ba'al's eyebrows shot up. "Tell me what you found."

Tuac relayed all that they had discovered. "We still don't know how the Prophet defeated Nabes. What we do know is that the Renegades used their magic for evil and the Prophet stood against them. We also know that the Prophet could use more than one Art. Despite his power, Nabes survived and we are seeing his evil again.

"Well, that is news." Ba'al said. "The Prophet's concern about preventing the rise of this kind of magic makes so much more sense now. It wasn't just a theory, but rather based upon his experience in the Great Destruction."

"And despite all of the Prophet's efforts to dilute magic through the Journey, I am a unified magician like the Prophet. My magic must be the key to stopping Nabes."

War had come to Mia like it had on Earth, and Tuac knew that the battle was not just against Nabes. He needed to deal with the computer, too. The Watcher had spoken about a moment when the Prophet had to choose between two futures. Tuac now believed the choice was whether to allow magic to exist or not, and the Prophet had chosen to retain magic and build a society that suppressed evil. He had made the wrong choice.

Tuac would make the right choice. Even though the Prophet's magic had defeated Nabes, eliminating the computer would deprive evil of the weapons that magic provided. Tuac would be Mia's champion even if it meant the end of magic.

* * *

Ki'lel had followed Ba'al and Tuac to her quarters. He wanted to hear what Tuac would say to the Archmage. As Ba'al's second, he believed that he should have been included in that conversation. When he heard Tuac's heretical revelation about the origins of magic, followed by his conviction that he alone could defeat Nabes, Ki'lel bristled.

Why has Ba'al accepted this boy and his perverted magic? She should have eliminated him as required by the charter. The other Acetos need to know. Basul needs a new Archmage. I will put down the boy and we will deal with the Emperor.

Ki'lel gathered all of the Acetos except Chorra. Ki'lel knew they would be outraged by what he had learned. He whipped them into a lather and they had agreed that Basul needed new leadership. Sunrise would herald in a new order for Mia, one that would see the planet ruled by those with the knowledge and power to usher in a new golden age.

———

Rea was up at first sunrise. She had misgivings about Tuac's choice and, while she understood the goal of a peaceful resolution, she did not believe that the Emperor would back down.

Despots do not care about the lives of their followers, only victory, she thought.

Rea had to choose between following her head or her heart. She could abide by the Council's decision or side with Ki'lel. She believed in her brother. Rea avoided taking sides and would be prepared regardless of the outcome. She would not be the first to attack, but if the Emperor refused to stand down, Rea would be ready to eliminate the threat.

She assembled her Dragon Squad on a raised platform built to give them a view over the walls to the plain. Several fire dragons rose above Basul and gigantic stone giants towered in front of the gates. Although Ba'al had directed Rea to focus on defensive measures, the other members of her Dragon Squad prepared their battle magic in case they were needed.

Secondrise glimmered on the horizon. Rea surveyed the plain before the gates. She had never seen so many people. She saw four distinct groups. The first were foot soldiers. The front line of each group carried a large stick on their backs but had no swords at their sides. None of the infantry carried shields.

I wonder if those sticks are the weapons they used against the Anthenes?

She saw soldiers mounted on hursas, then archers, and behind them teams of soldiers manned their catapults. None of these could harm Basul as they could not penetrate the magicians' forcefields.

They must think that the front lines of infantry will do the greatest damage. I will focus on them.

Rea spread word to her Squad to aim at the foot soldiers if they attacked. Ba'al addressed the inhabitants of Basul.

"We face an unparalleled evil." Air magic amplified the Archmage's voice. "Today, it strikes at us through the Emperor, but he is only a tool. The puppet master is Nabes. He has returned and wants to tear apart Mia. We must resist. We must restore balance. We are the protectors of this world, and we will restore what the Prophet created."

Rea and the others all shouted their agreement. She looked at Tuac, expecting to see his joy that Basul was standing against Nabes. But he looked troubled. Then, through their bond, he said,

"Stay true to yourself. This is only the beginning."

The alarms pulled Esa and the Emperor away from their breakfast. She looked out over the battlefield and saw huge beasts of fire rising above Basul and large giants made of stone lining the gates. She saw fear on her troops' faces but they held for now.

"Foolish magicians. They are so arrogant." Hahook said. "They think they can scare us into surrender. We will show them. Esa—ready our forces. It is time to introduce the magicians to an even greater force than their precious abilities."

Though Esa doubted that the magicians' magical show was just theatrics, she followed instructions. Even if attacking the magicians was courting death, disobedience to the Emperor was certain death.

Esa sought out the generals in their tent. On their camp table they had spread a map of Basul with figurines representing the various forces of the Emperor. They believed the front line was the one that would break Basul.

Esa studied the map and shuddered at the pending slaughter. She was afraid and did not feel guilty about that. She also felt numb as she stared at their strategy. She remembered what had happened at Liat. This would be worse.

Her chest constricted and she struggled to breathe. She closed her eyes and composed herself.

"So it begins," she said. They saluted one another and Esa left. She ducked behind a tent and vomited. Wiping her face with a sleeve, she pulled herself together. She strode to the high point where she would watch the carnage with the Emperor's party.

Runners from the generals darted across the field. The infantry began its advance. The forces marched in unison and showed no fear. Those with plasma weapons led the rest. The foot soldiers would inflict a fatal blow on Basul's gate and defensive walls. The rest of the Emperor's forces would eliminate all who remained. The magicians had power, but Esa had numbers.

The Emperor said our infantry would be slaughtered like livestock,

Esa thought. *He does not care. But they aren't animals. They're conscripts forced to fight in a madman's war.*

Esa watched the foot soldiers advance. After taking fifty or so paces, the plasma wielders broke into groups of six, creating forty teams. The first men dropped flat on the ground, the next two dropped one knee, and the last two stood, as they were trained. In unison, they aimed their plasma weapons.

Disciplined. Precise. Deadly.

Esa had anticipated that the magicians would deploy a force-field to deflect arrows, javelins, and trebuchet stones. But the magicians could not have planned for the plasma weapons' power.

The lead commander ordered them to open fire. Blue-white bolts, too bright to look at, splashed against the forcefield, creating ripples in its shimmering surface. Then the shimmer vanished. Before the magicians could restore the wall, her troops fired another volley. The blasts hit the unprotected walls and obliterated them, together with the mages stationed on the ramparts. The great gates of Basul collapsed into molten metal pooled on the scorched ground. Swaths of the wall had vanished. When the plasma fire ceased, eerie silence covered the battlefield. Then she heard screaming.

The Emperor's forces had spent their plasma fuel, but they had cracked open Basul like a nut without losing a single man. With a great shout, the infantry charged Basul.

Rea's ears rang from the explosion that took down the walls and melted the gates. She could not understand what had happened.

What magic is this? If Nabes did this, we are doomed. Everyone on the walls is gone. Just gone. Her knees shook and for an instant her fire faltered.

Rea thanked Mother Mia that she had stayed back with her Dragon Squad. Her team bunched close around her, clutching one another and sobbing as they surveyed the damage.

Everything had been calm until the the infantry had destroyed Basul's walls and gates and those defending them. Bodies lay sprawled where they had fallen, and there was nothing left of those who had been on the walls. Others had been caught in the collapse of the ramparts and stone, or were impaled on the defensive thorns, their bodies hanging limp. Some magicians had been hit by the strange fire. They were missing limbs, or had cauterized holes through their bodies. Few survived those wounds, but those who did screamed in agony.

We've lost so many.

Rea realized her bond with Tuac was gone, and she panicked. She looked for him and Ba'al in the chaos. She saw only Merle and the other Anthenes helping the wounded.

"Move now!" Tuac's mental voice rang in her head. *He's alive!* Relief made her dizzy. She called forth her fire, and her dragon roared above the field.

Though it was made of fire, it had contour and depth, a menacing face and shining eyes. Her rage fueled the beast. It swooped beneath the platform where Rea was standing and she vaulted onto its back. Soon, other dragons with riders filled the skies. The stone giants lumbered forward and the clouds crackled with lightning. Volleys of ice javelins swept down on the Emperor's troops, and barbed vines rolled among them, binding their legs and bodies, pulling them down.

Rea flew her dragon over the advancing infantry and cavalry. The other dragons followed.

"Burn them!" Rea shouted. Her rage had taken control of her. *I will punish the Emperor for all he's done!*

Her dragon exhaled a plume of cleansing fire, erasing many of the soldiers rushing toward Basul's breached gates. The other dragons followed. Below them, the giants hurled massive balls of clay, flattening whole squads. Soon, the Emperor's infantry were no more.

"Kill them all!" she cried. The Dragon Squad leapt to obey, targeting the rest of the Emperor's forces. The imperial archers had regrouped, firing volleys of arrows toward Rea's advancing forces, but their efforts were futile. Arrows ignited before they reached the dragons and could not harm the earthen giants. Dragon Squad Gaeists unleashed vines that strangled most of the archers, and lightning struck down the remaining ones. The battlefield was blood-soaked and littered with bodies.

Rea flew deeper into enemy territory, seeking the royal encampment. Only the Emperor's death would satisfy her. She spotted a huge pavilion surrounded by soldiers and directed her dragon to land. She wanted to face the architect of all this death and kill him herself.

She dismounted from her magical steed and strode toward the Emperor's tent. Behind her, the Dragon Squad riders joined her. All of their steeds hovered low above them.

Rea's flame encompassed her entire body. It burned white, like Luina's flame.

I want Hahook's last moments to be filled with terror, she thought.

Her Dragon Squad companions also cloaked themselves in the forms of their Arts: warriors armored in ice, or fire, or storm flanked her.

A few of the guards reached for their wand weapons and Rea incinerated them. All that remained were those with swords and spears. They rallied to defend their Emperor.

The tent flap opened and the Emperor stepped out, followed by his second in command.

"You cannot defeat me!" The Emperor screamed. "You think that your brother is strong enough to stop me? I was there when the Prophet thought he had won. But he never understood the sacrifice he needed to make. You are no different. Your rage fuels me. Soon I will own this world."

Rea stepped back. She recognized him. "Nabes."

As she named him, everyone looked at the Emperor. The Emperor's second in command backed away, revulsion on her face.

Rea studied her enemy. His skin was sickly pale and his eyes were completely black. Nabes' poison had sucked the Emperor dry.

"Now you know who you are dealing with," Nabes cackled with Hahook's voice. "This fool made an excellent host. It was easy to bend him to my purpose, as he was already tainted. His followers obeyed without question. Look at all he has given me with his hatred and envy." He waved his hand toward the battlefield.

Rea shivered. For the first time, she felt afraid. All this time she had believed her enemy was a person. But she faced a monster fed by the darkness that lived in everyone.

How can we defeat this being? All of us fuel his power. Her heart raced and she realized Nabes had shattered her control. *I came seeking revenge and my rage fed this horror. I must regain my control.*

We must stop the bloodshed or we all die here and Nabes wins.

She shouted at the Emperor's guards. "Your Emperor is no leader. No savior. He is a pawn of the evil that is Nabes. He has sacrificed your comrades and goaded you into slaughtering innocents, all to feed his hunger.

"Now you know who commands you. You have a choice.

You can continue to follow Nabes and sacrifice your souls. Or you can lay down your arms. This was never about what was best for Mia. This was always about hate." Rea subdued her flame to indicate that she offered them safety if they chose peace. Her Dragon Squad did the same.

The Emperor's second and the guards eyed one another. Then they threw down their weapons.

Good. We have deprived Nabes of that victory, Rea thought.

Nabes laughed. It was harsh and ghastly. "Foolish girl. You think you have won the day with a moment of charity. But I am victorious." The Emperor spasmed and collapsed. His body exploded into dust when it hit the ground.

As the Dragon Squad remounted, Rea felt a wave of horror from Tuac. Something had happened at Basul.

***

Ba'al reeled when Basul's walls fell.

What magic had the Emperor used? How could they have destroyed the gates?

Ba'al had been confident in her strategy but now realized how wrong she had been. She would have died if she had not left the entrance to discuss things with Ki'lel. Pools of slag from the melted gates spread where she had stood. The Emperor's forces now rushed through the gap.

"Ki'lel, send half of our magicians to cover the breach in the walls and half to stop the soldiers!" She yelled, hoping her voice could penetrate the chaos.

Ki'lel barked orders. The magicians, though shaken, responded. They leapt into the broken places, deploying every magical element they could. But the Emperor's soldiers had overrun the courtyard. They out-numbered Basul's forces, and magicians and students died defending their home.

"We're losing too many!" Ki'lel shouted. "Retreat to the infirmary!"

Ba'al gathered the remains of her entourage around her. A soldier aimed a crossbow at Ki'lel, but Ba'al flung up a wall of sand to block the shot. Ki'lel thanked her telepathically. She sensed his appreciation but also a sadness unrelated to the attack.

Ba'al saw Merle usher dozens of mages to the makeshift triage area. Many still fought outside. Ba'al did not hear the strange sound emitted by the Emperor's wands, but she knew the Emperor's forces had crossbows and swords.

The clamor of battle moved closer to the infirmary. In moments, heavy blows splintered the door.

They have won. We are all that is left.

Ba'al looked at her fellow magicians. They huddled together, wounded and exhausted. Ba'al raised wall of clay and stones to brace the door.

That won't hold for long.

"Be ready!" she barked, "They will breach this soon. Focus on the archers." Spear points penetrated the mud wall, breaking apart their defense. Clods of rock tumbled into the room, and swords appeared through the crumbling barrier. The swordsmen pulled back and archers aimed into the room. They released a volley of arrows, but Ki'lel deflected them.

This is how it is going to end, Ba'al thought. *Trapped liked animals,*

The archers released another volley, but Air Riders blew them down, skidding across the floor.

This is how I die. I will take as many with me as I can. She readied herself.

As the soldiers swarmed over the threshold, a gust of hot wind buffeted them and flames roared across the soldiers' backs. Ba'al could feel a tug from beyond the breach, yanking the intruders back.

That's not from my Air Riders. It must be Tuac! As they were pulled back, the hole filled with a mixture of mud and metal. Ba'al panted, her hands on her knees. *He's saved us!*

Ba'al heard screams. Whatever Tuac was doing was painful. Then silence fell. A door took shape in the repaired wall. It opened, and Tuac stumbled in, covered in blood. Merle caught him. He clutched her and grinned.

Ba'al strode to them, and reached out to hug the boy. "Tuac, you're amazing!"

As she spoke, pain seized her arm and chest. She could not breathe. Her legs shook. She gasped for breath but Merle was occupied with Tuac. No one else could heal her. Ba'al saw Ki'lel staring at her. His eyes were entirely black. Then she collapsed.

I have won! Nabes thought. *The magicians are decimated, and I control another lackey. No one can stop me. How foolish they are. How easy to manipulate. Now that I know where the* Curiosity's *records are, I can find the distress beacon and use it to lure off-worlders here.*

I will devour all the other planets. I will return to the home planet of the Curiosity, *where it all began. Where it will all end.*

Twenty-Eight

After we won, we gathered to discuss what would happen next. Some of us worry about the next tyrant and believe we need stronger leaders to protect the masses. Others argue that the Renegades only rose to power because they used our fear and envy against us. They argue that we need love and empathy, not emperors and armies.

The Prophet has not aligned with any side yet. We all await his wisdom. He is the last of those who remember the ways of the Terrans, and we trust him to lead us into a golden age.

Records of the Conclave after the Great Destruction

Tuac felt groggy. The last thing he remembered was Ki'lel using his magic to stop Ba'al's heart. Tuac had tried to save the Archmage, but some force had prevented him.

No, someone. Telepaths attacked me while my guard was down.

He looked for Merle. Tuac realized that he was no longer in

Basul. He was not even in his body. The situation felt like the vision he had experienced in the Chamber. Tuac was observing someone else's memories.

In his mind's eye he saw a courtyard. A figure in dark robes loomed over a man on the ground who was shaking his head as though recovering from a blow.

"Had enough, Elijah?" said the man, his voice laced with venom and contempt. His skin was sickly white and his eyes gleamed black. "Get up and fight me. You've come all this way. Let's finish this."

Tuac saw bodies strewn everywhere. Some wore black and others bore Cedric's crest on their tabards. The courtyard seemed familiar.

This is Shalla, before it was ruined. This must be one of the battles in the Great Destruction. Where is Nabes?

The man on the ground struggled to his feet. "Alexander, stop this. There's no reason for this to continue. We've defeated your renegade forces. We must find a way to regulate ACED's magic so this world can grow in peace."

"No reason to do this, Elijah?" Alexander sneered. "You and I are all that is left of the *Curiosity*. Your grandfather ordered us to rein in the Renegades, but we never asked why. They captured me and you never came for me. They tortured me, but when they saw my strength, I won their trust and became their leader.

"Your grandfather was wrong. We cannot co-exist with the Mians. These people are primitive. They worship their foolish gods. This is our world to conquer!

"If you join me, we can rule this planet together. Otherwise, I will end you. You are no match for me as you have never accepted all the power ACED grants us."

This doesn't make sense, Tuac thought. *The Prophet fought Nabes, not this Alexander.*

Then the Watcher's familiar voice spoke in his head. *"I have brought you here to learn the truth about Nabes. We do not have much time. You will wake soon and return to the present. But you must know the nature of your enemy. Watch them."*

"Please, Alexander," the Prophet said, "we were friends. We grew up together. You know I tried to save you. But your pain and despair left you vulnerable to NABES, which blinded you. You rejected my love and now NABES controls your thoughts. Your hunger for power emanates from ACED's unintended consequences, not your nature. Fight it. You are strong enough to resist NABES' effects."

What unintended consequences? Tuac wondered.

"You ask the right question," the Watcher said. "Nabes is not a thing or a person. The term NABES is what Terrans called the Nascent Antisocial Behavior Emergence Syndrome. It is difficult to explain. None of you are pure evil or good. When ACED interacted with the human brain, some users experienced a desire to engage in destructive acts. Think of it like a warped echo. Good people were overwhelmed by amoral urges. These users would lose their inhibitions for destructive behavior. Terran minds could usually control this.

"But on Mia, ACED's effects were magnified. And because Sam Orris amplified ACED's signal to cover the entire planet, it reached some people who should never have had access to it, people who lacked the moral strength to resist their inner demons. The combined effect of ACED's reach and intensity had a improbable result. NABES took on a life of its own, able to feed off of life and negative emotions, able to act on its hungers. The Terrans said it became sentient. There is still more for you to learn." The Prophet's voice rose and captured Tuac's attention again.

"Don't make me hurt you," the Prophet said. "I will if I have to, but I don't want to. We can fix this. We can heal Mia together."

Alexander rushed the Prophet. "I could crush you with my ACED abilities, Elijah. But I want the satisfaction of wringing out your last breath with my hands on your throat." The two men grappled with one another.

"You are a rabid animal. I have no choice," the Prophet gasped.

The ground beneath Alexander melted, capturing his legs. Vines flared upward and encircled Alexander's hands. He belched a cone of fire, but the Prophet deflected it.

The Prophet touched Alexander's head. "Hush, my brother. Return to me. I can erase the evil that clouds your mind."

Alexander's body convulsed then went limp. His pale skin warmed to a healthier color and his eyes faded to hazel. The lines of tension and rage left his face.

The Prophet's magic cleansed him, thought Tuac. *This is how I can defeat Nabes. I will deprive him of his puppets.*

Abruptly, Alexander's body stiffened. His eyes rolled up, showing only white.

Something is wrong.

The fit passed. A tear rolled down Alexander's face. "I'm sorry," he said, his voice faint. Then he died.

Tuac flinched. *The Prophet had cured his friend. Watcher, why did he die?*

The Watcher did not answer.

The Prophet wept. "They're all gone. My beloved. My best friend." He laid Alexander's empty body down. "Grandfather was right. ACED does more harm than good. I will finish Grandfather's mission and turn it off. Mia will be healed and magic ended, even if it means the history of the *Curiosity* is lost."

Tuac followed the Prophet as he walked through Shalla's courtyard. He opened a door opposite the main gate and started down a stairway. Dim red light stained the walls. The stairs ended in a cavern. Glowing stones lined a channel of steaming water. A massive metal container loomed beside a smaller one. Strands of dark material disappeared into the water on one side of the large container and smaller strands connected it to the second box. Tiny lights glinted on the smaller box's surface.

Is this ACED? Tuac wondered. Sweat drenched the Prophet. His hands blazed as he approached the smaller container. He was going to melt ACED.

A shimmering figure appeared. Tuac could see the computer through the bright form.

"Greetings, Elijah. I am Haci. How can I help you?"

The Watcher!

Yes, Tuac, the Watcher said. *I was there. I saw the battle. These are my memories. You need to watch a little longer. We are not done with this story.*

"Haci," The Prophet said. "I don't need your assistance. I am here to destroy ACED. Get out of my way."

"Why do you wish to destroy ACED and me?"

"Because of all the death ACED has caused. We cannot control our destructive tendencies. Now NABES is too powerful. My grandfather warned me this could happen."

"My job is to guide ACED's users," Haci said. "If you explain the problem, I can develop an alternative solution that preserves ACED. It is your choice.

The Prophet's hands faded and he sat down. The vision went dark.

That is all I can show you, The Watcher said. *We have no more time. I will tell you what happened.*

Why did you stop him? Tuac asked.

My nature requires me to give assistance. The Prophet felt conflicted. He wanted to keep magic if possible, and magic can only exist if ACED is working. Its signal—think of it as an invisible mist that covers Mia—is what gives you the ability to do the things you do. The mist, and magic, would disappear if ACED was turned off. We discussed a range of possibilities to dilute ACED's effects and devised ways to suppress those with ill intent. That is where the Journey and the three parts of Mia's governance came from. My calculations were correct, but there was a possibility NABES would return. I explained the risk to the Prophet and he chose. He believed good would overcome evil.

The Prophet did not even tell his daughter about the source of their magic. She grew up believing the lie of its source. I have followed each of the descendants of her bloodline who were gifted, waiting for one would be able to reunify the Arts. You and Rea are the last of that bloodline.

You take no responsibility for what you did? Tuac was incredulous.

I cannot feel as Mians do. But I admit what is happening now is because I intervened. That is why I have intervened again. I am permitted to give advice and to fix problems. I can tell you that NABES will exist as long as ACED exists.

Unfortunately, there is one more lesson. You must learn to reverse the effects of NABES in others. The human experience is beyond me so I cannot help you with that. If you do not solve this problem, many more will die. The loss of life may weaken your resolve and you will not win this battle.

Before Tuac could ask for guidance he felt the Watcher leave. Tuac opened his eyes, and saw Rea and Maeva.

"Where is Merle?" Tuac asked.

Maeva put her hand on his shoulder. He could feel her warmth but she was also restraining him.

Through their bond, she said, *"Breathe, Cub."* Then she said aloud, "Ba'al is dead and now Ki'lel is in charge. He is holding her hostage. He said if you do anything, she will perish. We're confined here awaiting your trial for heresy."

Tuac tried to rise but he was too exhausted from his battle with the Emperor. Several hours passed before Tuac was able to get out of bed. Ki'lel had isolated them in visitors' quarters away from the main buildings in Basul, guarded by mages from each school.

Rea explained that the Acetos had elected Ki'lel as Archmage and she was no longer head of the Dragon Squad. He had forced Chorra into retirement. Ki'lel controlled all of the Acetos and the Dragon Squad. Tuac fumed at this, but he needed to control his anger if any of them, including Merle, were to survive. Even with his powers, Tuac and his companions were out-numbered.

When he was strong enough to stand, Tuac joined his family at the table. A plate of food waited at his place. Tuac sat down and took a bite. His anxiety for Merle made him queasy, so he just picked at his meal. He wanted to tell his family what he had learned from the Watcher but he heard the door latch click.

"I see you're up," Ki'lel said. He was dressed in the Arch-mage's robe and flanked by guards from each of the Arts. Everyone at the table stood.

He's flaunting his new authority. If he didn't have Merle, I would rip his throat out with my bare hands.

"Come, Tuac, we need to speak privately. Perhaps we can reach an agreement and avoid any more loss of life."

Ki'lel put a hand on Tuac's shoulder to steer him into the hallway. At the Archmage's touch, Tuac felt a wave of arrogance and hostility—NABES. Tuac stepped away.

"Now, now, *boy*. That is no way to start a conversation."

Tuac wanted to name his true enemy but he was not sure he

could convince those following Ki'lel that he had been tainted. There would be a time to confront NABES, but it was not now.

"We can talk right here," Tuac said, "Maeva and Rea have a right to be involved."

Ki'lel straightened his collar and smoothed his robe. "You and your rogue magic threaten Mia's existence. If you spread those vicious lies about the origin of magic, what is left of Mian society would crumble. We have to rebuild the Empire and we cannot afford unrest among the people. So how do we solve this situation?

"In a perfect world, you would see the folly of your ways, Basul would install a puppet on the throne, and Rea would be reinstalled as the head of the Dragon Squad. When we are strong enough, we would join our forces to vanquish NABES. This time we will make sure he is destroyed."

NABES means to thwart us, Tuac thought. *Ki'lel's delay will only make it more powerful.* He remained silent as he assessed his true enemy.

"But we do not live in a perfect world," Ki'lel continued. "Since I know I cannot count on your voluntary cooperation, I am faced with the two options. First, I execute you and Rea for heresy, and Merle and Maeva for their complicity. I am prepared to take that step, but it will deprive Basul of the loyalty of those who believe in you. Alternatively, you and Rea publicly swear your allegiance to me. After you do that, you and Merle can be reunited. She will work in the infirmary with Maeva. If everyone cooperates, after we've defeated NABES, Rea will be given a teaching position. And we might let you research and experiment with your rogue magic.

"All of you will be supervised and required to support the hierarchy of Basul. Any insolence will meet a quick, fatal response."

Ki'lel turned to leave. "The choices are not subject to negotiation. You have until the end of the day to swear your allegiance. If you don't, tomorrow I will announce the verdict that you and your family are guilty of treason. Your deaths will be merciful and quick. While I certainly hope for the first option, I expect you will give me no choice but to execute all of you." Ki'lel walked out, followed by his guards. The door's lock clicked.

"Tuac, you can't surrender," Rea said. "I saw what NABES did to the Emperor. You are the most powerful amongst us and we cannot survive NABES without you. Only you can save Mia. We must convince the Council to overrule Ki'lel. If that does not work, we should fight. I'm sure some of my Dragon Squad remain loyal."

Tuac saw the anger and frustration in his sister's eyes. He knew she was prepared to lay down her life for him. He worried what she and the others would do if he revealed that Ki'lel was possessed. Yet a civil war with Ki'lel was not the answer.

"Unfortunately, Ki'lel has a point. I am a heretic. I know that our powers come from an alien source. While I was resting, I had another vision of the Watcher. I now understand NABES comes from that same source as our magic. NABES is not a person or even a god. NABES lives in all of us and the only way for us to defeat it once and for all is for us to destroy that source.

"For a while now, I have thought to end magic. At first, this was because it was being used to oppress people. However, like the Prophet, I was torn by that decision given the good that magic can do. Now I understand that the evil brought by magic is a symptom of a greater disease. To stop NABES, I must end magic. There is no other way. This is the choice the Prophet should have made."

He could tell from his bond with Maeva and Rea that they were considering what their futures would be like if they no longer had their Arts. Tuac could not blame them. It was a daunting prospect, giving up so much in order to save their world. But there was no alternative. As long as hate, greed, and lust for power lived in everyone, NABES could be reborn.

First, I have to break NABES' hold on Basul, thought Tuac.

He hugged Rea and Maeva, not to console them, but to say good-bye. He had a plan, but was not sure his gambit would work. He wanted them to know how much he loved them. Then he pounded on the door.

"Take me to Ki'lel and the rest of the Acetos."

Behind him, Rea and Maeva gasped.

Rea shouted, "Tuac, you shouldn't go alone!"

Then Maeva spoke to him through their bond. *Cub, I am not sure what you plan, but I am sure it is dangerous. Be careful.*

I go into the uruh's nest, but I am a Brea. Yes, I play a dangerous game. But I have the one thing they lack: family.

The guards ushered Tuac to the Council room. Ki'lel was there with all of the Acetos, including the new head of the Gaeists. A lieutenant represented the Dragon Squad.

Tuac subtly touched all but Ki'lel and felt their shared desire to dominate ungifted Mians. He also felt NABES' poison. Tuac's knees trembled and his stomach clenched.

It will be hard enough to wrest Ki'lel from NABES' grip. Am I strong enough to deal with all of Ki'lel's court?

He probed Ki'lel and was horrified at what he saw. Ki'lel had killed Ba'al and now he planned to kill Tuac and his family. Ki'lel sensed and ejected Tuac. The corrupt mage smiled at him. Tuac shivered at the malevolence he felt. He reinforced his own mental shields against Ki'lel's telepathy.

"You surprise me," Ki'lel said. "I did not expect you to come to us so soon. You must miss bedding your little healer." Ki'lel cackled and others on the Council smirked. "Rea has more spine. She would never beg for her life. I always thought she had more potential than you did."

Tuac's pulse pounded in his ears. He reconsidered his gambit, tempted to kill Ki'lel now.

What if I launched a blast of psychic power? I could incapacitate everyone in the room, and then incinerate them. By the time Ki'lel's troops find out, I could reinstall Rea and take control over Basul. Tuac's hands crackled with power. He wanted to release his rage. He wanted revenge for what Ki'lel had done to Ba'al. *I could end this. I would be the one true Prophet. I could lead Mia to new heights and maybe even to build ships like the* Curiosity *to explore and conquer other worlds.*

Before he launched his attack, Tuac saw Ki'lel's knowing smile.

NABES is baiting me. Tuac closed his eyes and took a deep breath, centering himself.

If I attack, NABES wins. It must be afraid that I have learned how to defeat it.

Tuac let go of his anger and hurt and summoned the burning light of his love for Rea, Maeva and Merle. He let their love cleanse him.

"Ki'lel, you gave me choices. You said I could align with you, or I could choose to sacrifice myself. Are you a person of your word or were those just idle promises?"

"You know I don't intend to honor those choices," Ki'lel snarled.

Tuac said, "Despite your duplicity, I am here to align myself to Basul. Are you really willing to discard my magic because you fear that I will tell the Acetos the truth? I demand my right to speak."

"You come to swear allegiance and then demand an audience?" Ki'lel scoffed. "You arrogant whelp! If you intend to swear allegiance, do it now, on your knees."

"You are no better than Hahook, a despot manipulating those you consider inferior. I'm not surprised given the way you murdered Ba'al."

The Council erupted.

"You killed Ba'al?" asked the Acetos of the Stone Movers. "This is not what we discussed. We agreed she would be peacefully removed."

"Wait!" shouted Eis. "How did the boy know that you killed Ba'al? I thought you only discussed this with me! We were going to act together."

Excellent, thought Tuac. *They were united in overthrowing Ba'al, but weren't informed of Ki'lel's plan. I can drive a wedge into that rift. While they're distracted, I can play my last card.*

The Acetos of the Air Riders, Water Sculptors, and Gaeists stepped away from Eis and Ki'lel. The head of the Stone Movers shouted at Eis. The Dragon Squad lieutenant stood frozen in shock. The Telepath Acetos moved behind Ki'lel, and Tuac sensed the man's magic rising to shield the Archmage.

Now is the time. Tuac smirked at Ki'lel.

"How dare you!" shouted Ki'lel. The Archmage vaulted the Council table and seized Tuac's throat.

Just as Alexander had done, thought Tuac. He stayed calm. Ki'lel's blinding rage disabled his magic. This was the opportunity Tuac needed.

Tuac closed his eyes. He focused in spite of Ki'lel's savage grip. His inner light bloomed. He recalled all the times his sister protected him from the bullies at school. How her hugs comforted him. Her love was his shield. Tuac's skin hardened.

He thought of Maeva's spiritual guidance and her encouragement. She fed his hunger for knowledge and accepted his weaknesses. She was his soul. His body glowed white like Luina's flame.

Then he thought of Merle's love for him. Of her touch and her laughter. She was his heart. With that final piece, his flame became a cleansing fire.

He touched Ki'lel's brow. They spasmed. Tuac transported them both ethereally to the Chamber at Liat.

It worked.

"Where am I?" Ki'lel demanded.

"You are in my mind, or perhaps I am in yours. I'm not quite sure how this works. But we are together. You must see my memories in order to understand the path forward."

"You've joined with me? Do you realize how dangerous that is for both of us?"

"I had no choice."

Tuac showed Ki'lel the Watcher's memories of the Prophet fighting Alexander, of the computer that created magic and of Tuac's interactions with NABES.

"Lies!" shouted Ki'lel. "These never happened. You are trying to confuse me to weaken my resolve. I will purge you and your allies from this planet!"

"Telepathy can see through dishonesty. You can tell if I'm lying or telling the truth. Find yourself and reject the darkness. If you do that, you will know these memories are history, not lies."

Ki'lel probed Tuac's mind and memories. Tuac felt Ki'lel's clarity return.

"I murdered Ba'al." Ki'lel's regret flowed through their bond. "I believed she had lost her way and was a threat to Basul. I convinced myself that you were a heretic or an agent of NABES. You needed to be destroyed. How could I have been so wrong?"

"That was not you. That was NABES. That is what it does. It feeds on our darkest fears and emotions. It turns us against each other. Your telepathic abilities and devotion to Mia made you vulnerable. NABES clouded your judgment. What will you do now that you know the truth?"

Ki'lel stiffened. "NABES must be stopped. Can you rid me of this poison? I will fight by your side if you will have me, and when the battle is done I will pay for what I did to Ba'al. Please, help me."

I have reached him. Now I can only hope I learned from the Prophet's mistake.

Tuac returned their spirits to his inner sanctum. They stood before the mirror and Tuac turned Ki'lel so he looked at his reflection. Tuac remembered the words Maeva said to him over and over.

Out of darkness comes light, confusion leads to clarity, chaos turns to order. This was the truth that the Prophet never understood. Neither can live without the other. That is why Alexander did not survive. The Prophet erased all of Alexander's darkness, not realizing that some must remain to balance the light. The Prophet failed to recognize that Alexander had to heal himself.

Tuac had come to this Chamber to accept who he was— passion, love, and justice as well as insecurity, anger and volatility. Each part fueled the others. He could only be his best by accepting all of himself. Ki'lel needed to do the same thing.

Tuac said, "I will stand by you and support you, but only you can restore your balance and accept who you are. Look into the mirror, see all your strengths and weaknesses, good and evil. By embracing all of these, you will become whole and NABES cannot manipulate you."

Tuac hoped Ki'lel was capable of this difficult work. Tuac did not know if there would be a physical cost Ki'lel must pay to cleanse himself of NABES.

Ki'lel focused on the mirror. His ethereal body seized. Tuac caught him and eased him to the floor. Through their bond Tuac felt Ki'lel fighting his internal battle. He pushed out NABES' poison and regained control. Ki'lel's light returned, and his darkness balanced it. NABES was gone.

Ki'lel took a deep breathe and sat up. "I'm whole. I don't like what I became, but I cannot change what I have done. All I can do is recognize my failures, and focus my light and love to make amends."

Tuac said, "Let's reclaim Basul and banish this evil." He returned them to the physical realm. Ki'lel teetered as he pulled the punch he had aimed at Tuac. He snatched his arm back and released Tuac's throat.

"Enough!" barked the Archmage. "We stand down, now!" The other Acetos, confused by this sudden shift, rushed toward them.

Eis shouted, "Tuac has done something to the Archmage! Destroy them!"

Tuac felt the magical energy surging in the room.

I need to finish this now, and unfortunately do not have the time to be gentle. Beams of warm light shot out from Tuac's body and froze each of the other magicians.

Tuac tried to displace NABES' effects but he was drained from helping Ki'lel.

"Take my energy," Ki'lel said. An infusion of magic reinforced Tuac's hold on the Acetos. His magic touched each magician, attacking NABES' effects. Tuac's challenge was to eliminate NABES' infection without destroying the host. He nudged out NABES' evil, hurt, contempt, greed, and lust for power. He did not remove their natural darkness, instead he isolated and banished the poisons NABES had grown inside each magician. He worked carefully so he did not injure the inner complexity of each person that gave them their uniqueness and purpose.

One by one, he returned each magician to their center. Except for Eis, the Acetos were like Ki'lel, essentially good but misguided. Eis' inner light smoldered under the weight of his darkness, so far out of balance that Tuac could not heal him. That would fall to Ki'lel or the next Archmage. Tuac's light faded as he released the magicians other than Eis, whom Tuac put in a deep and lasting sleep.

Tuac staggered, leaning hard on the Archmage.

"Get this magician to the infirmary," Ki'lel shouted. "And release his family."

Tuac awoke to Merle holding his hand. Rea and Maeva sat beside his bed.

"He's awake!" Merle said. Before Tuac could respond, she tapped his chest. Tuac winced. He had not hardened his skin fast enough when Ki'lel lunged, so the mage had cracked a couple of Tuac's ribs. He could sense that they had been healed by Maeva, but he would still be sore for a few days.

"Why did you do something so stupid?" she said.

"It worked," Tuac said, smiling at her.

"Barely," Merle said. She kissed him. "Don't ever forget that you have us. You don't need to act alone anymore." Merle's hug hurt, but Tuac appreciated it anyway. He held her close with weary arms.

Maeva said, "I feel the difference within you. You're more accepting of who you are. Does this have something to do with what happened to Ki'lel and the other magicians?"

Tuac explained what he had done. "The Watcher was telling me I had to kill the disease without killing the host. Your words, Maeva, were the key. The love of all of you gave me the strength and power to heal myself and then the others. I wasn't sure Ki'lel would survive facing his demons given what he had done to Ba'al. I believed I could reach Ki'lel once I connected with him in the spirit world. I needed him to lose control and come close enough for me to grab him, so it was risky. But it worked. The others were easier once I had figured out how to rebalance them. All except Eis, who has darker issues. Ki'lel helped me."

"I'm so proud of you," Maeva said. "The Anthenes believe true enlightenment comes from acceptance, not perfection. It's hard for us to see our flaws, but it is those failures that sculpt us and empower us to improve. You're amazing, especially for one so young."

"I had a good teacher," Tuac said.

Maeva kissed his forehead. "You have taught me a few things too, my Cub."

They heard a knock on the door.

Ki'lel entered. "I see you're doing better. I came to thank you and to tell you I've stepped down as Archmage. Chorra is Acetos for the Gaiests again. Rea, are you are willing to resume leadership of the Fire Walkers and the Dragon Squad?"

Tuac could tell that Rea felt conflicted. He said, "You should do this. It will help Basul heal."

"Yes, Ki'lel. I accept." Rea said.

"Who is the new Archmage?" Tuac asked.

"We'll hold a conclave to pick the new Archmage. Chorra believes it should be you. I've asked the Council to postpone my trial until after NABES is defeated, so I can best help the resistance. They agreed."

"We'll need your strength in the coming battle," Tuac said. "I'm glad you'll be fighting on our side." The suggestion that Tuac take on the mantle of Archmage surprised him. *All I want to do is sleep. I guess there is some logic in this though. After all, I defeated NABES and returned all the Council members to balance. I really should be recognized and honored for what I have done. Then I can lead Basul's forces against NABES! And once it is defeated, I can create a new Mia—one that rewards justice and not greed. Maybe I can figure out a way to keep ACED on, and not just heal Basul but restore the Anthenes.*

Tuac studied the faces of his family, looking for guidance. They knew what he was thinking and he felt their distress.

They don't believe in me. How many times do I have to prove my worth and judgement? How can they have so little faith in me?

Maeva broke into his mental tirade.

Cub, center yourself. This is not you. She sent him warmth. Tuac turned to Merle and saw she was upset.

What, my love? he asked.

Your eyes are turning black, she said.

Tuac shuddered. NABES had targeted Tuac's greatest weakness. *It's making one last effort. How easy it is for NABES to manipulate us!* He lacked self-esteem and needed to feel valued. *No! This is not me. I do not need fame or glory, money or wealth. I only need the love of my family.*

Tuac closed his eyes, took a breath and found his center. He was who he was, and he would rather have love than power or a title. He wanted to live a moral life. As Tuac reclaimed who he was and who he wanted to be, he felt an inner shift, as if a heavy weight left his body. He was whole again.

He said, "Thank you, Ki'lel for the opportunity, but I am not the right person. I suggest Rea. She is smart, knowledgeable, and showed fine leadership with the Dragon Squad. I think she would make a better leader than I would once we've defeated NABES." *And she will be a better person to figure out Basul's role in a world with no magic,* he thought.

"I'll convey your wishes to the Council," Ki'lel said and left.

Rea asked, "How can I lead magicians with no ability? Once you turn off ACED there will be nothing for us to do." Tuac heard the sadness in her voice.

"We must all accept our roles, Rea. My legacy will be to usher in new age without magic. Your legacy will be measured by our success building a new society in the face of that loss. We have learned many things over the Turns, and someone will need to lead Mia while we figure out how to replicate our achievements without magic. The Anthenes will provide us guidance as they have excelled at non-magical healing. I can think of no better person than you to steer Mia through this great change."

Rea beamed.

She needs my faith in her as much I need hers in me, he thought.

Rea hugged him and he grimaced in pain. "You might start with bedside manners."

Everyone laughed. The moment of shared joy braced them for what they were about to face.

Twenty-Nine

I pray. I am not sure why I do it. My grandfather believed in a higher being, and I was even named after one of his religion's heralds. But looking at my life, at what evil my ancestors brought to this planet and the death it caused, it is hard for me to believe. Why would a benevolent divine being have brought the Curiosity and all of its evil here to Mia? Why would it have let so many people die?

It would be easy to reject the ways of my family in the face of an omniscient but uncaring god. But then I realize why I continue to believe—hope. Without hope, evil wins. And if there is a higher being, may she answer my prayers.

Elijah's last words, transcribed at his deathbed

They had defeated NABES at Basul, but true victory could only happen once Tuac turned off ACED. To do that, everyone needed to understand the endgame. Tuac and his family discussed how they would explain the nature of magic to all of the magicians, and how the source of their power was also the source of the evil that was destroying Mia.

The night before Basul's forces planned to leave for Shalla, Tuac and Rea convened the Council and summoned everyone at the University. The Council had been touched by NABES and knew the rest of Basul needed to understand what they would face.

The magicians gathered in the great hall. Tuac looked out at the survivors, sat scattered in small groups on the first few rows of pews. Before the conflict, over two thousand magicians and guests had lived at Basul. The great hall could seat about half that number. Now, a mere hundred and fifty mages survived.

Tuac, Maeva, Merle and Rea sat on the raised dais. Rea addressed the gathering as Tuac, though respected, was an outsider.

"Greetings, my brothers and sisters," she began. "Tomorrow, we will march on Shalla. Many of us will not survive. But I hope and pray to Mother Mia that we will succeed. If we are to win, you must understand NABES' origin and its connection to our magic." Rea explained all that they had learned about the *Curiosity*, ACED, NABES and the Prophet's choice to leave magic in place.

"The Prophet hoped our better nature would withstand evil, but he underestimated our inherent flaws and complexity. His decision to allow magic to exist was flawed. And now, we face destruction. If we do survive, if we defeat NABES, we will have to face the same choice. Tuac and I believe that we can only end NABES if we turn off ACED, even if it ends our magic."

Shouts of "Heretic!" erupted in the crowd. Chorra stood up and raised her hands to quiet them.

"Hear her out. She has earned your respect," she said, and the crowd settled.

"I can't blame you for your outrage" Rea said. "It is difficult to accept what I have told you. But look at the damage that NABES has already caused. Is our precious magic worth all this loss of life?

"Yes, Mia will change. But we are more than our ability to control the elements. We will survive and the world we build will be the one Mia promised us *before* the Terrans crashed here and interrupted Mia's plans for us."

Rea gave the audience final instructions for assembling in the morning then she sat down beside Tuac. The audience's anger did not return. The magicians spoke among themselves in hushed voices and drifted out of the great hall in small groups.

Tuac said, "Give them time. You gave them a lot to think about. They will realize the truth of your words."

"I hope so. We will only win if all of us commit to ending NABES once and for all."

"You were brilliant. You spoke from your heart. They knew how important magic is to you. You were the perfect person to explain to Basul what we must do."

The next morning Tuac and Rea led their small army out of Basul's shattered gates and across the battlefield. The Emperor's troops had long since collected their dead but debris still littered the blood-soaked ground.

"We have not seen the end of these soldiers," Tuac said. "I suspect most of them have marched to Shalla."

"That worries me, too," Rea said.

Merle walked beside her soulmate and squeezed his hand. Her love flowed through their bond and warmed him. He also felt her fear. Tuac smiled at her.

"I will not let anything happen to you, my love. We will win, and then we will have a life in the country together," He squeezed her back.

It took a month to reach Shalla. They marched through a blighted landscape, passing abandoned hamlets and farmhouses. They had carried supplies from Basul and shared what foodstuffs they found. The Gaiests coaxed some edible plants from the wounded soils, but the results were meager.

Every night they camped just off the road. Since there were not many of them, they did not need a huge place to set up for the evening. Tuac wanted them all as close as possible in case something happened. A week out, his caution paid off when they were surrounded and attacked by a group of Hahook's soldiers in the middle of the night.

Tuac and Rea, along with a few of her Dragon Squad, had been on guard when Tuac heard the first sound of the attack. A Stone Mover died with an arrow in her throat. He raised a force field to protect the entire camp from the attackers. A platoon of soldiers circled their camp. Their bodies were withered.

Tuac summoned his fire and his eyes stared to glow. In moments, the attackers burst into flame. As Tuac defended his people, he struggled to control his anger.

Even if NABES controls them, they are complicit in all of this, he thought. As his fury grew, the flames darkened. Tuac wanted to inflict pain on the soldiers, as they had inflicted pain on countless others. He relished their screams and thrashing.

Cub, NABES is trying to control you! Maeva said through their bond. *If you cannot control yourself, we will never have a chance when we confront NABES.*

Tuac shuddered and centered himself. He snapped the soldiers' necks and immolated their bodies.

I am not here to judge or punish them, he thought. *That is for Mia to do.*

When the camp had settled, Tuac crouched by a fire and stared at its flames. *Every time I think I'm strong enough, I fail again. I fall into old patterns. I give into bad habits.*

Merle sat down beside him. Tuac said, "I'm sorry. I should be better than this."

"Stop! Of course, you're not strong enough by yourself. But you're not alone. You have Maeva, Rea and me. Together, we will not be defeated."

Tuac hugged his mate.

Maeva came up and put her hands on the two of them. "Merle is right. We will do this together." There were no more attacks by soldiers that night. But when Rea woke them at first sunrise they learned that NABES had struck them in another way.

"NABES got to our forces!" Rea shook her brother. Tuac stood and surveyed the camp, Almost a third of their mages had left.

"Cowards, the lot of them!" Rea spat on the ground. "NABES must have fed their fears. Now we don't have the forces to defeat him. I'm going to marshal my Dragon Squad and drag those spineless magicians back."

"Rea, stop! Don't let NABES get to you, too. He wins by dividing us. If you go after them, we'll be weakened even more. Those magicians are dangerous to you and the Dragon Squad. Yes, our forces are depleted. But if you leave here now, we will fail."

He could feel her seething. Long moments passed as she struggled to regain control.

At last she sighed. "Fine. I'll stay with you. But from now on we arrange the watches so that either you or I are awake. We cannot afford to lose anyone else."

They broke camp and continued their journey to Shalla. As

they advanced, they met with a variety of attacks. For the most part, they were more annoying than dangerous. The mages were able to defend themselves against the attackers. Unfortunately, one Fire Walker died in an ambush.

After that loss, Tuac divided the remainder of magicians into groups of at least ten, rotating who was on point. The new tactic detected ambushes well in advance, so NABES' minions changed their strategy as well. Archers fired at them from a distance, and Tuac lost another ten magicians. He deployed forcefields that stopped the new onslaught, but NABES was playing a game of attrition and winning. Tuac had neither the time nor the forces to win a prolonged battle. They marched faster toward Shalla.

The direct attacks stopped when they were a week from Shalla. Instead, NABES resorted to nightmares and mental assaults to weaken the liberators' resolve. Despair rose among Tuac's people as they passed through a blackened landscape devoid of life.

"It feels like the entire world has been poisoned," Merle said.

Tuac looked at her and the rest of the troops and sensed their struggle to remain focused. He touched them all with his magic to insulate them from NABES' effect. Using that much magic weakened him but he needed to cloak the liberators against the contagion or they would not reach Shalla.

There was no animal life. Nothing. Even the insects had vanished. Apart from the noises of their group and an occasional gust of wind, the landscape was silent.

Tuac had always enjoyed those moments in the night when everyone was asleep and everything was quiet, but he had never imagined a world without any sound. It shook him to his core, and he was sure the others felt the same way.

"How can we defeat this?" Merle said.

Maeva said, "We defeat this by giving Tuac our love to strengthen him so he can restore the natural balance between light and dark. NABES dismisses the power of love. That is how we win. We use NABES' arrogance against it."

They all stared across the barren wasteland. Tuac could hear his companions' heartbeats. He was proud to be their leader, but his doubts lingered. He was barely of age but, somehow, he was supposed to defeat an ancient foreign influence that had planned this battle for hundreds of turns.

How can I defeat NABES when the Prophet could not?

His anxiety rose. Tuac decided they should stop for the day. He needed to meditate. Tomorrow, when they reached Shalla, would be their hardest day yet. There would be no rest once there, so they must take this opportunity. No one complained when Tuac set up camp. They all put out their bedrolls, but Tuac knew few would get any sleep. Merle came to bed without saying a word. He held her close and listened to her breathing, a comforting sound in the deathly silence.

They faced no opposition the next day. NABES was inviting them in for the coming battle. Their number had diminished to eighty-eight, including Merle, Maeva, Rea, Ki'lel and himself. This seemed like such a small group of gifted individuals against evil incarnate, the remnants of the Emperor's forces, and the magicians who had joined NABES. Tuac's concern that he was not up to the task grew, but he anchored his resolve in hope.

As they trudged along, Tuac ruminated on his inadequacies.

I don't have enough training. My power has limits, but I don't know what they are. Yes, I can unify the Arts, but will that be enough? Rea's Dragon Squad amazes me. Can I ever match their power in battle? What will happen to Merle or Maeva if I fail? They believe in me. They love me. They should be following a real leader like Rea.

At first sunset they reached a hill that overlooked the valley of Shalla. Tuac surveyed the bleakness below, ruled by the jagged ruins of the black castle. Arrayed around it were the remains of the Emperor's army, about a thousand men. Tuac was surprised there were not more.

This is impossible. We can't do this.

The utter blackness of the landscape made it difficult to see details of the topography. By the low angle of the evening light he could make out trenches and stoneworks. Siege towers dotted the valley in front of the walls. Tuac sensed magic. He used his telekinesis to fling stones at the castle, but a forcefield deflected them before they reached the castle's walls. This confirmed Tuac's suspicion that rogue mages had aligned themselves with NABES. They would face battle magic tomorrow.

Tuac gathered his advisors in one tent and set up a telepathic shield that he hoped would keep NABES from eavesdropping. Rea had also invited two of her Dragon Squad—a Water Sculptor named Heron and a telepath named Mergo. They set up a battle map so they could assess the enormity of their task. They had to defeat all of the ground troops, disarm the magicians and carve a path for Tuac to get into Shalla. Once there, Tuac had to find the Terran computer and turn it off. Tuac related his vision of the Prophet's encounter with the Watcher in the cave that held the ACED. Tuac thought that cave must be deep under the castle.

They debated tactics.

Rea said, "The Dragon Squad can destroy NABES' magical defenses. We can eliminate the telepathic shields and send our dragons against the troops. We are more skilled in battle magic than they are."

"I agree. Our telepaths can take control of any archers in the siege towers and turn them against the Emperor's army," Ki'lel said.

"Your strategy would kill all of them," Merle said. "We are better than this. A victory built on the lives of others would be hollow."

"We have no choice." Rea said. "We are outnumbered, and must use our resources to ensure victory. It isn't that their lives don't matter, but they chose to join NABES."

"These were not choices freely made," Tuac said. "NABES manipulated their doubts and insecurities. Many of them feel we are the threat to Mian society. Some are soldiers following orders and have no ability to resist. I want to spare them if we can."

We are reliving the debate from the Great Destruction, he thought. *What is the right measure of force to combat an enemy that does not care about life? But maybe Rea is right and we should destroy it all and rebuild. These people hurt Mia and need to be punished. We can kill them all and succeed where the Prophet failed. Then there would be no need to turn off ACED. We can save Mia without throwing away magic.*

Cub, I feel you giving into bloodlust, Maeva said through their bond. *Merle is right, we cannot heal our society by spilling the blood of the innocent.*

Tuac flinched. *NABES is in my head again. And again, you save me. Thank you. I have to find a third road—defeat NABES' forces without punishing those that can be redeemed. We need to win with the same justice that we hope to use after the battle.*

Tuac said. "You both have valid points but neither is the best solution. That's because we are letting NABES dictate our choices. NABES knows if we show too much compassion, we will fail because we did not use enough force. NABES also knows if we use overwhelming force, we lose our moral authority even as we win this battle. And either way, NABES wins because death and despair strengthen it.

"We need to distract the forces long enough to disarm them and eliminate those who are truly complicit. This will give me the opportunity to shut off ACED and end NABES without further bloodshed."

"That's a good idea, but how do we do it?" Ki'lel asked.

They studied Shalla's defenses. A scattering of archers patrolled the walls, enough to make flying over them risky. The Emperor's soldiers were divided into five battalions of two hundred and positioned within the forcefield that protected the castle. The siege towers stood between the groups to provide support.

"There," Rea said, pointing at the gates. "If we take down the telepaths and launch a concentrated attack at the gates, we might get inside without many casualties. There aren't enough archers on the parapets to repel a ground force attack. The battalions are too far apart to help each other. We just need to eliminate the siege towers and use our magicians to counter theirs."

Tuac said, "An excellent idea. In NABES' efforts to protect the castle from all sides, it has spread its forces too thin. But I think it would help if we deployed some smaller attacks along the walls so NABES thinks its strategy is correct."

There was a disturbance outside the tent and Tuac turned to see what it was. The flaps opened and one of the Dragon Squad that was on guard outside, an Air Rider, walked in.

"Excuse me for interrupting" the magician said. "There is a soldier here who says she must talk to you. She says it is urgent."

Tuac looked at Rea and raised his brow. "This could be a trap, but we should hear her out."

Rea responded "Show her in." Tuac noticed that Rea's hands started to glow. *She will take no chances.* Tuac readied himself too.

The tent flap rustled again and the newcomer, wearing full armor, walked in.

"My name is Esa and my forces are at your disposal. As I was waiting outside, I heard some of your debate and your tactics. I have already sent scouts to the castle and believe you are being baited by NABES. Based upon what I've confirmed, your plan will fail. I have a better idea."

"Esa?" Tuac said. "What are you doing here? We released you after we defeated the Emperor's army. I'm surprised you aren't with NABES."

"Yes, you did release me. For the first time in turns I had a choice. I could go home, I could follow you, or I could join NABES. As I thought about this, I realized how far I had fallen. I love Mia and thought the Emperor did, too. I followed Hahook believing he would protect Mia. As I rose in the ranks, my fear of losing power overcame my devotion to the people. I lost myself.

"Hahook's vilification of magic mesmerized me. I convinced myself that the magicians were a threat to Mia, having neither loyalty nor morals. They needed to be controlled or put down, along with their supporters. I never considered the cost.

"Yet I felt guilt and horror at the massacre of Liat. I denied those feelings until you gave me back my free will. I cannot take back the decisions I made and, if we win, I expect to be punished for them. But for now, I swear allegiance to you and your cause. And I have three hundred battle-hardened soldiers who feel the same way."

Tuac was speechless. He could not imagine what Esa had gone through, the guilt she must feel after being complicit. Good people can contribute to bad events. They do not always see the implications of their choices, or they are manipulated by those in power into believing that justice can come from unjust actions.

But here stood Esa and three hundred soldiers willing to risk their lives to fight back and reclaim their souls. He probed her softly and confirmed there was no taint of NABES. Esa's rejection of evil at Basul had insulated her.

Tuac said, "We all have had moments where we failed to resist evil, Esa. I am not here to judge. I am here to stop NABES. I accept your service. If we win, we can discuss your redemption. I would like to see your troops, and then you can help us refine our strategy."

The war Council walked out of the tent, and three hundred well-equipped soldiers stood in perfect ranks before them. These were seasoned warriors from the upper echelon of the military. As Esa introduced her commanders, she explained that these troops had sworn to protect Mia, but, like her, had been blinded by the Emperor. They were embarrassed and ashamed that they had participated in Hahook's attacks, and many asked Tuac for his forgiveness as they were introduced. Several knelt on one knee as he passed. They had a common bond, sickened by their participation in the massacres.

Esa explained that they had stayed nearby when she had been captured. When NABES summoned the Emperor's army to Shalla, these soldiers had resisted. Their loyalty to Esa and Mia was stronger than NABES' promises. When Rea released Esa, these troops rallied to their new leader, calling themselves the Protectors of Mia. Esa had decided to join Tuac, and the Protectors swore to follow her into the coming battles. It had taken them time to catch up to Tuac's group, and they had skirmishes with NABES' forces along the way. But now they were here, and they were ready.

"NABES has approximately four thousand foot soldiers and fifty archers. The siege towers are empty and just a distraction.

NABES has left its gates undermanned to draw you in, then you will be trapped by the troops waiting here and here—" she pointed to two large berms flanking the castle. Tuac, having no experience in warfare, had not seen them as a threat. Stone Movers must have created them.

"Once you are close enough, they will rush in behind you and trap your people against the castle wall. Their archers are in the back, opposite the gate, and will pick you off one at a time. The flanking troops will clean up the rest."

Without her help, we would have been slaughtered, Tuac thought. "What should we do?"

"The key to any battle in which you are outnumbered is to let the other side think you're doing what they want. We let NABES believe you are storming that gate. But he did not expect the Protectors, nor does he have a professional strategist on his side.

"I propose that we split my troops into to three groups. The smallest will go with you. The other two will infiltrate NABES' forces behind the berms.

"You attack from the front as NABES expects. When its troops move to trap you, the Protectors seeded among his troops will attack from within their ranks, disrupting their maneuver. There are fewer of us, but we have superior training. If your mages can target theirs, and the archers, we have a chance. The only thing we need to do is hide our true strategy."

Tuac studied the plan, impressed with Esa's thinking. They now had a strategy that might work.

"We'll divide our magicians," Tuac said. "I will take half of the Dragon Squad with me. I need the best of the Fire Walkers, Air Riders, and Stone Movers. All of the Telepaths will stay here and search out NABES' magicians. Our Telepaths will also shield our forces. The rest of the Dragon Squad and mages will form smaller groups to attack NABES' forces along the foundation.

"I see one problem," Rea said. "We will have to disseminate our plan to our magicians and Esa's troops. Once we do that, NABES will know we are coming."

"I have an idea about how to keep this from NABES," Tuac said. "But you won't like it."

Tuac explained his plan to his trusted advisors. They agreed that while it was not ideal, it might work. He ended the meeting and Tuac told everyone to get some sleep. He knew that, regardless of who won the day, Mia would be fundamentally changed. As he held Merle close, he hoped it would not be for the last time.

Several times NABES had felt Tuac almost succumb to his inner demons. NABES needed Tuac to surrender to despair. This would grant NABES access to Tuac's innermost thoughts, and it could thwart whatever the resistance had planned.

But every time Tuac came close to that surrender, he was pulled back by *love*. This was the only emotion that baffled NABES. Other emotions could be twisted into snares for its prey. It was easy to turn a sense of honor into self-righteousness or a commitment to fairness into prejudice. But love was challenging. Many claimed to act from love when their choices were driven by other things—insecurity, fear of abandonment, and lust.

But true love was a different story. Willingness to sacrifice oneself for the good of another, without hesitation, glory, or reward, might be the one thing that threatened NABES. It wondered if Tuac was more of an existential threat than it had originally believed. NABES discounted that possibility—all Mians were weak and struggled with their darker natures. And where there was darkness, NABES could enter and take control. Its trap had been set. Their foolish optimism would blind them to the danger. It was only a matter of time before NABES won.

THIRTY

The silence of the morning is my sanctuary. Before first sunrise, before people stir, before the day's busyness. It gives me a moment of peace to consider decisions I've made and choices to come. The soldiers outside my tent are mustering and my love stirs beside me. Soon I face my destiny. My family is depending on my judgment, not knowing it is undermined by self-doubt.

I never asked for this and I am too flawed to be anyone's savior. But this is my journey and, even though it is not easy or fair, I will not run from my duty. I will finish this and hope I do not fail.

The first page of the Reunifer's Journal

"What are you doing, my love?" Merle said as she rolled over.

Tuac had been awake for hours. "I started a journal today. If I survive, I want people to know what we did and why. I want those who follow us to understand all the damage caused when we forget our history."

Merle stroked his face. "You have a future, my love. Never give up on that. I need you, more than you will ever know. You have inspired so many with your willingness to fight this evil. There is a reason why we believe in you. Give me that journal and I will hold it until you return."

She smiled the warm smile that Tuac cherished. If anything would get him through this day, it would be Merle's love for him. Tuac handed her the notebook. "I'll do my best, and I'll carry you with me as I confront NABES." He gave Merle a kiss on her forehead and left the tent.

He knew she would read what he had left behind. He thought he heard a muffled cry but did not turn back. He was thankful she chose not to follow. They both would need the strength to get through today.

As planned, Tuac met Rea and Ki'lel right before firstrise. They found Esa.

Esa said, "We are ready. My forces will march with you and your team to the main gate."

Rea added "The Dragon Squad is ready to distract NABES' forces as you advance."

Tuac came up to Esa. "Yes, but first we must do something." He touched Esa's head and her eyes fluttered. At the same time, Ki'lel touched Rea's shoulder and she shook her head.

"What happened? I'm confused. Why are attacking the main gates?" Rea said. "The last thing I remember was discussing Esa's battle plan and how NABES had set a trap for us."

"That is because we put a spell on you." Tuac responded. "The only way for our plan to work was for you and Esa to forget our strategy. Ki'lel and I were strong enough to keep NABES out but the two of you needed to be shielded. We deployed small groups of your forces, each with a telepath to protect them, last night. But none of those who remained in camp knew our battle plan. Not even Merle or Maeva know what we have planned."

Tuac waved his hand and cast another spell. This time he insulated his three companions. It took considerably more energy than his psychological suggestion the night before, but it was necessary to keep their plan hidden. He would only need to keep the shield active until Esa's forces sprang into action.

What was left of camp readied for war. Half of the Dragon Squad, including telepaths to protect them from NABES' probes, split up into smaller forces to attack along the gate. The remainder of Rea's Dragon Squad mustered to Tuac, Rea and Ki'lel. Esa was with them, along with twenty of her soldiers, enough to make it look like they were following their weak original plan. None of Tuac's assault group knew that Esa's troops were secreted in NABES' forces.

Tuac's forces started on the road to Shalla. They marched in the open. As soon as they got within range, the Fire Walkers sent out blasts that ignited the siege towers. Tuac's forces released a joyful shout. The resistance continued their assault. Ice javelins and huge balls of mud pounded NABES' defensive forces, pushing them away from the gates.

Good. Basul's magicians are following NABES' script, thought Tuac.

Tuac led his attack. Rather than using deadly magic, he reached out to clear a path to the gates. Waves of wind and water and shifting ground unsettled the enemy. Walls of fire pushed the lines back. NABES' soldiers tested Tuac's defensive measures, and they were repelled. Tuac left his forces open to magical attacks so Tuac's magicians could track the magical source. With each volley, Tuac's telepaths disabled those mages who had bent to NABES' will. Soon, the magical attacks ended.

A modest victory, Tuac thought as he surveyed the battlefield. *We still have to defeat the legions of NABES' soldiers. Now we have a chance. But at what cost?*

Tuac's assault on Shalla proceeded in a calculated and methodical way. When they got within a few hundred paces of the gates, NABES sprang its trap. Soldiers yelled from their hiding places behind the berms and charged. Tuac felt Maeva through his bond.

Be careful, Cub. NABES is trying to trap you!

NABES is not the only one who can snare prey, he replied.

In the midst of the chaos, Tuac stopped. He closed his eyes, released the telepathic shield on his fellow magicians, and summoned all his magic. He needed a vehicle for magic that would counter NABES' attackers. He could have chosen a dragon like his sister and the Prophet had done. But Tuac had something different in mind. His body glowed and a translucent figure coalesced beside him.

I am not a Cub. I am the Brea. And I will protect my family!

A shimmering giant Brea stepped in front of Tuac, outlined by flowing fire and gleaming with every color. It howled, releasing a gust of fierce wind. At first Tuac's troops stepped back, but it waved its mighty paw and brushed aside NABES' advancing forces. The huge creature roared again.

NABES' forces hesitated, then regrouped, racing to encircle Tuac's people. The Brea and his magicians kept them at bay but the enemy tightened its noose. Tuac's mages followed his orders, deploying lethal magic only if necessary.

Now! Tuac thought, reaching out to Esa's troops. Chaos erupted behind NABES' charging forces as they were cut down by the Protectors. Tuac sensed row upon row of NABES' troops dying. Despite their casualties, their front line advanced.

NABES controls their minds. They will not stop as long as we still breathe.

Twenty paces from the gate Tuac's squad halted, surrounded and fighting for their lives.

Even with his great beast, Tuac was losing. His troops inflicted severe damage on Shalla's forces, but as each soldier fell, another stepped forward. Tuac's squad also had casualties. His magicians could do only do so much to protect their brethren, and their opponents' superior numbers were winning.

We cannot win a war of attrition, thought Tuac. *I must do something.*

Tuac reached out to all his magicians.

"To me!" All of his mages fought their way through to join him before the gates. Dragons swooped over the magicians, protecting them with fire and ice. They pushed NABES' forces back but it had focused its forces on defending the gate. NABES could afford to play the long game but Tuac was running out of options.

Enough is enough. Tuac thought. He shouted to Rea, "You were right. There is a time for peace, and a time for war. Do whatever you need to do to get me inside."

Released from Tuac's directive to spare life, Rea's Dragon Squad unleashed their wrath. Plumes of fire seared NABES' troops as they advanced. Giants hurled rocks. Archers collapsed as Water Sculptors crushed their hearts and Telepaths attacked with waves of psychic energy. In minutes, NABES' dead covered the field, but the survivors rallied and pressed forward, stomping over the corpses of their comrades.

In the space created by the turning tide of battle, Tuac did the one thing that he believed could end this war. He reached out telepathically to the source of evil in Shalla.

"Enough!" he said. *"This battle comes down to you and me. If this continues, neither of us will survive. Even if I lose, there will not be enough life left on this planet to sustain you. Let's end this."*

NABES' forces faltered, backing away from their opponents. They opened a path to the gate wide enough for one person. Tuac's forces pursued them, so he sent them a message to stand down. They regrouped, strengthening their defensive formation around Tuac. The dragons circled overhead.

It believes it can defeat me, he thought.

Tuac stepped forward. Rea grasped his arm.

"No," Tuac said to her. "It has to happen this way. Send our wounded back to camp to Merle and Maeva. You and the other troops must watch these gates. It could be a trap. If I lose, you are our only hope."

"I could end this right now, Tuac. I could incinerate all of their forces and melt Shalla."

"You could, but there's no guarantee that would end ACED or NABES. You may be one of the greatest Fire Walkers Mia has ever known, but resisting NABES requires more than brute force. I wield Merle's love, Maeva's balance, and your fire, and I unify all the Arts in myself. The Watcher sent visions to show me what must be done. I am the vessel that ends NABES."

"Little brother, how you've grown. Mia needs a champion, and you are the one. I believe in you." Rea hugged Tuac and whispered into his ear. "Go forth, Brea. Your family needs you." She released him.

Tuac turned toward the gates, and his defenders parted to let him through. The final battle had begun.

He stepped into Shalla's darkness. As he crossed the threshold, he drew upon his family's strength and surrounded himself in a sphere of white light to push back NABES' disease. In the courtyard, Tuac saw the desiccated bodies of the Emperor's soldiers and the mages it had corrupted strewn about like rag dolls. Some still twitched. Their eyes had rolled back to show only the whites, and their faces had frozen in expressions of despair and anguish. NABES had fed on their evil, greed, and contempt for life, and then drained their bodies. It was a terrible way to die even for those that had chosen NABES.

"That is your weakness," NABES said. *"You're too empathetic. You have sympathy for those that turned on you. Why? You should not be wasting your energy on them. Rea would have been a better champion. She is not distracted by petty compassion.*

"The Prophet also believed in love and justice. The Terrans called it humanity. But I exist because humanity is a lie. Mians, like their cousins from Earth, are driven by hate, not love. And just like the Prophet, you are not strong enough to make the ultimate sacrifice. Whatever happens today I will return, tomorrow or a thousand Turns from now. I will succeed, I will take over this tiny outpost of a planet, and then I will leave and feast on others throughout the stars."

Tuac knew it meant to weaken his resolve. *What if NABES is right?* he thought. *Am I strong enough? I could stop here and call for Rea—* Tuac paused and recentered himself.

No. NABES knows that Rea will make the same mistake the Prophet did, believing that her magic will be enough to protect Mia. It knows I will succeed, so it's attacking my confidence.

Tuac walked across the courtyard, skirting the piled bodies. He sent a prayer to Mother Mia for the souls of those NABES had killed.

"Ha!" NABES cackled. *"You think your god will help you now? What has your god ever done for you? She allowed me to thrive. She allowed me to feed off these pathetic lives. How could a benevolent god allow me to destroy Liat and kill Ba'al?"*

Tuac braced himself against the attack. He did not blame Mia for the massacre at Liat or for Ki'lel's brutal actions. Those were acts of persons controlled by NABES, not acts of free will.

I will not blame Mia for those crimes, he thought. *We are responsible for our own peace, our own justice.* Tuac did not dignify NABES' rant with a response.

He entered the castle's grand hall. Once it had been splendid, but now it was a toxic ruin. His bright shield had contracted as his energy faltered under the pressure of resisting NABES' evil. Tuac knew he had little time and needed to find the entrance to the stairs. At the opposite end of the room, he saw an arch and felt a warm breeze. He followed that heat.

The arch opened into a long hall that sloped downward. Unlit torches in sconces lined the walls. Tuac touched them with his fire. They burned low in the foul air, but they guided Tuac. As he hurried forward, he fought his fear.

What if NABES stationed troops to ambush me? My magic weakens. I cannot survive. I should turn back and get reinforcements.

"Yes, boy. You cannot win. You're too weak," NABES' voice reeked with contempt.

Tuac flinched but kept walking. NABES would not win using a physical attack, it would win by manipulation and intimidation. It would twist his strengths and weaknesses against him. *It cannot harm me if I stay focused,* he thought.

Tuac steeled his resolve. The hot, stinking breeze was stronger now. He reached a circular stair going down. This must be the entry to the cavern where he would find ACED.

Tuac took the stairs, turn after turn, deep into Mia. An oppressive wave of sticky heat hit his face and soon his clothes clung to his skin. The stairs ended in a path carved into the stone. Wiping his brow, he followed the path. His shield was dim now, but it lit the way a few paces ahead. He ran his hands

over the walls. They were smooth as glass and filmed with moisture seeping from the stone. Not even Stone Movers could make
such tunnels.

*The Terrans must have created this. Somehow, they cut into Mia's
core.* He wondered what tools Orris had used to create this
passage. Tuac knew what he would find at the end.

Breathing was difficult in the oppressive air. Sweat dripped
down his face and his legs shook.

The air is tainted here, he thought. *I am so far from the surface
there is no fresh air coming in.*

The tunnel opened into a huge cavern. The texture of the
walls looked natural and columns of rock reached down from
the ceiling and up from the floor. There were steaming pools of
muddy water beside the path. Some of them boiled, slow
bubbles popping, releasing smelly steam. To his right, he saw a
large pool of clear water in a natural stone basin. He walk up to
the rim. It did not stink and it was cooler than the air in the
cavern.

That water must come from a spring closer to the surface. He
scooped up a handful and took a tentative sip. It was good. He
drank his fill and felt refreshed. As he splashed water on his
face, his hand brushed against a metal opening in the basin
wall. He focused his shield light and saw where the floor had
been cut and then refilled and sealed with the same smooth
material as the tunnel walls. He followed the seam with his
fingers.

Despite the heat of the room, this felt cooler than the rest of
the floor. He followed the seam across the cavern. His eyes
detected a faint blue light from the walls. Clumps of fungus
glowed against the stone.

All the way down here, Mia supports life, he thought. He walked
along the seam, stepping around columns of stone that had

formed on top of it. Past one of these he saw a glowing river of deep red lava.

Near the molten river, he saw the huge metal cubes of ACED, its tiny colored lights winking just as they had in his vision. The seam in the floor ended in front of the largest cube.

"Beautiful, isn't it?" NABES said. *"The Terrans were quite creative. Fortunately, they did not consider the consequences of their actions. When Orris gave ACED enough power to cover the planet, he gave me a way to touch all its inhabitants. The Prophet tried to contain me, but he only delayed my victory."*

Tuac considered NABES' words. *Why now? The Prophet had contained NABES, but something changed that released it to grow. The Journey has not changed. There has always been an Emperor. Basul is strong. The only schism was—*

"The Anthenes," Tuac said.

"Yes! They kept the magicians in balance. When Basul expelled them, my prison cracked open. The Anthenes were too far away to protect the magicians. It was only a matter of time before I regained my strength."

"That's why you massacred them."

"Yes. They were a greater threat than you are. They could imprison me by depriving me of sustenance."

"I can end you."

"That would throw Mia into chaos. Is this what you really want? They call you a heretic. Do you also want to be known as The Destroyer?"

This was the Prophet's dilemma, Tuac thought. *But NABES has shown me the key. I could rebuild the Anthenes and restore the balance. We would teach our true history. We can drive NABES back into its prison.*

"Yes, Tuac, there you have it. The Anthenes can keep me in check. I can wait."

No, Tuac thought. *This is not the solution. As long as ACED exists, NABES will too. As long as NABES exists, Mia is threatened. NABES is immortal and one day we will falter and it will escape again. This is what Sam Orris wanted Elijah to learn from the stories of Terran governments. There will always be good, but there will always be evil.*

Tuac studied ACED. *How should I destroy it? As soon as it is broken, I will lose my magic. I have to do enough damage in a single blow that it cannot be rebuilt.*

"Tuac, is this really what you want? What about your precious Merle? Once you turn off ACED, you will lose her. There will be others more attractive who have wealth, skills, and status. You cannot keep her happy if you give up what she values—your power."

What if Merle only wanted him because of his magic? Tuac wavered.

"Yes, Tuac, that's right. How could a beautiful girl like her want someone like you? You are nothing, you came from nothing, and you will die as nothing if you turn off ACED. You will be weak and she will want a powerful man."

Tears joined the sweat on Tuac's cheeks.

NABES continued, "What will Rea and your family think? Rea was always favored by your parents. If you destroy her power, she will never forgive you. Your parents, who did so much to provide for you, will be ashamed that you were so envious of her that you brought down Mian society just to deprive Rea of her magic."

He screamed, "What do you know about love and family? If you really want to stop me, come fight me!"

NABES' laughter filled Tuac's head. He could barely think. His rage burned hot and deep.

I'll destroy NABES, and then I'll deal with ACED. The Prophet failed. But I will cleanse this place and then all of Mia.

Tuac's shield flared brighter and his hands glowed. NABES' laughter fed Tuac's lust for battle.

I will protect Merle and Maeva, he thought, *and they will love me forever.* Then the image of their faces cut through his anger. He caught himself. Took a breath, and restored his inner balance.

That was its last attempt. If I give in to my rage, NABES will control me. I must keep believing that I value life and love more than power, and duty more than titles. I have to finish this.

Tuac examined the cubes, looking for vulnerabilities.

"*NO!*" NABES screamed.

Tuac focused his will into a mental shield to keep NABES out. The voice vanished.

Tuac walked around ACED. He kicked at the pipes coming up from the floor seam and the ones in the lava. They did not move. The walls of the cubes had no joints. He shoved it, but it did not budge. He had to use magic to destroy it. Tuac needed to set a process in motion that could continue without magic, as his skill would vanish as soon as the machine failed.

The heat from the lava oppressed him, and that gave him an idea. ACED sat on a plateau beside the molten river. He could use his stone moving magic to shatter that plateau, the debris and ACED would fall into the lava. He realized that the amount of force he intended to use might throw him into the chasm as well. Tuac backed away from the cubes toward the passage.

He summoned his magic and the stone hummed with it. Cracks appeared. Tuac directed the fractures around the cubes. Steam shot out of the floor seam and ACED's lights flashed faster. He heard a pulsing squeal from the cubes. The floor beneath them shifted and sank a handspan.

A wave of dizziness passed over him. He had wounded ACED. He concentrated for a final, powerful push through the broken stone and the floor heaved. The cracks separating ACED from the rest of the floor widened and glowed deep red.

His vision went gray.

Tuac stumbled behind a stone pillar to watch. Nausea flared and he felt his magic drain away. The cracked stone slabs tilted, sliding into the river beneath them. ACED's lights blinked out and the squealing noise stopped. The cubes settled deeper into the lava. Steam filled the cavern so Tuac could not see the destruction, but he heard the stones grinding and the floor of the passage trembled. Behind him, he heard the bubbling mud pools gurgle. A stream of steaming, stinking mud flowed past him in the passage, scalding his left foot.

He ran for the stairs. His legs trembled and his head pounded. Climbing the stairs took all his concentration. At the second turning, he vomited. He looked down and the mud had reached the stairwell. Tuac pressed on, turn after turn. The stairs shifted and his dizziness made each step harder.

Just as he reached the sloping tunnel, the stairs came loose from their anchors in the wall. He leapt onto the smooth floor, panting and terrified. The air in the tunnel was hotter than it had been, but it was still easier to breathe here. He gasped and staggered upward toward the dim light of the entrance in the great hall.

ACED was gone. The battle was over.

EPILOGUE

When Tuac limped out of the ruined tunnel. Rea, Merle, and Maeva hurried toward him. Tuac felt numb and disoriented from the loss of his magic, and trembled with exhaustion. The pain of his scalded foot was almost unbearable. He started to ask Maeva to heal him, but caught himself.

No more Anthenes. We have to treat injuries and illness another way now. Merle embraced him. Her touch warmed and steadied him. In spite of the pain, he wanted this moment to last forever.

Maeva laid a hand on his back. "You are the Brea, but you are still *my* Cub."

Rea said, "Well done, little brother. I never doubted you."

Tuac laughed. "Well, that makes one of us." Keeping an arm around Merle for support, he surveyed the remainder of his troops. Ki'lel and Esa moved among the surviving Dragon Squad and Esa's forces praising each soldier. Across the field, NABES' troops lay where they had fallen or huddled in the mud, eyes blank and staring. As he watched, several slumped over to join their fellows, too drained to live.

He studied the former magicians. Tuac could see their discomfort. They stood in pairs or trios, speaking softly or holding one another.

They are mourning the loss of their magic, he thought. *They will have to learn who they are without it, that they were always more than their gift.*

Merle pushed something into his hands. He looked down and saw his journal.

"Now you need to complete your story. Please change the opening paragraph. You are not flawed. You are just you."

They walked to the base camp. As they moved among the survivors, the soldiers thanked Tuac for his courage. The magicians watched him pass with tear-streaked faces. He wanted to console them but had no words. His family guided him to his tent.

Soldiers guarded the entrance. Inside, he found a tub with hot water.

"You may be a champion, but you stink." Merle said.

Tuac peeled off his filthy clothes and settled in the warm water. He fought to stay awake as Merle scrubbed him. Her caresses washed the evil of NABES from his body. When she was done, he stayed in the water, relishing the end of his obligations and his new freedom. When the water cooled, he got out, dried himself, and lay down next to Merle. Her naked body warmed him. As tired as he was, his soul needed to be fed and Merle's was just as hungry. Their passion was both urgent and new. This was the first time they had made love when they were not affected by ACED. They rebuilt their bond with touch and soft words. He did not need telepathy to know how much she loved him.

When he awoke, he was famished. Merle was seated at a small table.

"You had me worried," she said. "I thought maybe NABES had hurt you. But Maeva told me it was just exhaustion. I kept watch so no one disturbed you."

"How long have I been asleep?"

"Three days, my love."

Tuac was still groggy from the loss of his magic. It took him some time to process what Merle had said. He rubbed his face, trying to clear the fog.

Merle helped him stand and dress. His burned food and every muscle ached. He faltered, and Merle steadied him.

"Even now, you are here to catch me when I fall." Tuac said.

"Yes, and I always will be. Come, see what you have done."

Tuac could walk, but he did not let go of Merle. He was not used to relying on others, but Merle's support felt comfortable and right.

"I was told to bring you to the main tent once you were ready."

On the way there, Merle explained that the Protectors' ranks had thinned. Most of the former magicians had gone back to Basul. Esa had remained with a small force to guard the camp.

Rea stood outside the tent.

"I heard you were up!" she hugged him.

"Good morning, Cub," Maeva said. She eyed him from head to foot and nodded. "Headache? Any dizziness?"

"Definitely dizzy," Tuac said. "And the world feels different, more distant."

"All of us who lost our gifts feel disoriented," she said. "But it will pass."

"Come, Tuac." Rea said, tugging at his arm. They walked to the edge of camp where they could oversee Shalla. There were huge pyres for the dead. Esa and Ki'lel were lighting the fires and speaking words of benediction. As Tuac and his family walked down to pay their respects, Rea explained how everyone had felt ACED's destruction. Most of the magicians had retched and trembled when their magic had disappeared. Esa's troops also felt different.

"Esa described it as being able to breathe freely for the first time," Rea said. "It felt as if a great weight had been removed, one we had always carried and didn't realize it until it was gone

"ACED has affected us for hundreds of Turns," Tuac said, "even those without gifts. The Journey was intended to dilute ACED's influence, but it also spread the Terran blood across Mia. All of us were touched by the machine's influence."

"Where should we go from here?" Merle said. Tuac had never thought beyond the battle with NABES.

"Some of us discussed this while Tuac was sleeping," Rea said. "Esa felt strongly that we should direct the rebuilding of Mia from Tushman. While the presence of the Church will be awkward given what we now know about the Prophet and ACED, the city has a civil structure that we can use. There are people skilled in all the tasks a government needs to do for its people. It will be the perfect place for Tuac to lead us into a golden age."

"No," Tuac said, "that is not my role or destiny. Mia needs people who know how to lead. You should do this—you have so much experience from forming the Dragon Squad. And I recommend that Ki'lel and Esa assist you. They were affected by NABES but recovered. They have valuable experience to offer.

"I have fulfilled my destiny. I was the Unifier born in this generation. I have done what was needed to give Mians a future without Terran influence. Now it is your turn to take the lead. I will be an advisor for a little while, but then I want to build my own life with Merle."

Rea opened her mouth to say something, then stopped. She nodded and walked over to Ki'lel and Esa.

They knew my answer before she asked, he thought.

Tuac started toward the three to explain that he was not abandoning them when Maeva put a hand on his arm.

"It's okay, Tuac. You have done enough. This is now Rea's path to walk. She's annoyed because she would rather be exploring new paths to knowledge than governing. Just give her time."

The next morning they broke camp and started toward Tushman. Each night Rea would convene a leadership Council with Tuac and his family, Ki'lel, and Esa. Rea grew into an insightful leader, willing to debate complex possibilities and also make firm decisions. There were moments when her pursuit of justice blinded her. Tuac resisted the urge to soften her self-righteousness, letting Ki'lel and Esa grow into their roles as trusted advisors.

Over the weeks of their journey, Esa, who had the most experience with the structures of government, became the architect of a new civil order—one anchored in justice, not power. She assembled her soldiers into small squads who would maintain order in the towns. Those that led with empathy would be promoted, those who exploited their positions would not, and they would be punished. Esa would judge her success by people's health and happiness.

Ki'lel focused on rebuilding Basul. Without magic, it needed a new mission. Tuac remembered that he and his family had found books in the armory that contained what the Terrans called science. His family shared their discoveries with Ki'lel, and the group realized that the subjects overlapped with the Arts.

A skill called engineering approached the marvels of stone

moving. Books on metallurgy and physics would suit the Fire Walkers. Maeva noted that there were books about medicine and healing that the Anthenes had studied in Liat and volunteered to continue that work. The Anthenes had also explored the many kinds of life on Mia, which the Terrans called biology. She offered to give those books to Basul for the Gaeists. The skill called psychology described methods similar to the ones used by telepaths to explore the mind, and the books on weather would appeal to the former Air Riders. Although the Journey had ended, Basul would still recruit Mia's best minds to study and teach.

Rea would be the bridge between old and new, and that was not an easy task. Many of the former magicians were distraught about the loss of their power. She was concerned that they would withdraw from Basul and might even take their own lives. She and Maeva spent many hours talking about ways to make the transition easier for these people.

They arrived in Tushman a month after the battle at Shalla. Esa had sent groups of her peacekeeping troops ahead to restore order and to calm the populace. When they crested the ridge above the city, throngs of people waited for them. The stories of Tuac's valor had spread. Even from this distance, Tuac saw huge banners draping the city walls. They featured a dragon encircled in concentric rings of white and black.

Rea said, "I hope you don't mind, Tuac. Esa suggested that I draw up a family crest that represented both of us. She sent the design ahead so the banners would greet us."

Tuac smiled. "It's perfect".

When they entered the city's gates, Esa's soldiers met them. The commander explained that they occupied the Emperor's palace and had clean quarters prepared for all of them.

After a few months, things settled into a routine. Rea would convene a meeting with Esa, Ki'lel, Maeva and Tuac every morning. Merle was invited but she was already feeling the need to leave. The battle was over and she pined for normalcy. Esa presented reports from the security forces and emissaries. Regular messengers between Basul and Tushman kept Ki'lel informed. When his chosen emissary from among the former magicians arrived to take his place in Tushman, he set out for Basul.

Maeva left next. Anthenes were now welcome at Basul, but she wanted to rebuild Liat. She asked Tuac to come with her, as she valued his ideas about the library in The Chamber and how it could be shared with all Mians. As much as he wanted to help her, he knew that if he went to Liat he would be seen as the leader of the new Anthenes, a position he felt belonged to Maeva. She had been his mentor, teacher, and friend, and when she left his heart ached at her absence. But he longed to establish his own life with Merle and start their family. Perhaps one of their children would one day enroll in the school at Liat to become a healer.

When Tuac had arrived in Tushman, he sent a letter to his parents telling them about Merle, and how he wanted to return and settle in Starra. He wanted to start a family and open an inn for weary travelers. His parents wrote back, ecstatic that at least one of their children would return home.

Despite his desire to leave, he remained in Tushman for another month, helping Rea plan a new library that housed the Church's collection of ancient books. It would be open to all who wanted to study the history of their people. With each day his longing to be free intensified.

Whenever he broached the issue with Rea, she changed the subject to avoid the inevitable parting. It came to a head one night.

"Rea, I'm leaving tomorrow. I've given you and Mia everything I can, and now I want to begin my own life."

"But—"

"No. This is not a discussion. You don't have a vote in this matter. Merle and I set out for Starra tomorrow. It isn't far from here. I can return if I am needed. And you can come visit us. Your new message routes can carry our letters."

"You're needed here, little brother. Please. I need you." Tears streaked her face.

"You don't know your own strengths. You think it is only your intellect, but it is so much more. You won't realize all your gifts as a leader while I am still here. You have built a wall around yourself. You feel like you need me because you left a door in that wall for me. Rather than keeping that door open for only me, take down those walls completely to let others in. I believe in you."

He gave her a long hug. Tuac cried, too, as he had with every goodbye. Tuac sensed she was beginning to open herself. She needed this moment, so he held her until her tears were spent. After a time she pulled back, and then punched him in his arm.

"If you ever tell anyone that happened, I will hunt you down." They laughed and hugged again.

The next day, Tuac and Merle left for Starra. There was no need to hurry. They traveled as far as they wanted each day, often taking a day just to rest and enjoy each other.

They arrived at his parents' shop late one afternoon.

"Are you ready?" Merle asked.

"Are you? My mother can be a bit overwhelming, and my father will hug the breath right out of you." Before he could say more, she knocked on the door.

Cisrena opened the door. His eyebrows shot up and his jaw dropped. From the depths of the house, Loree called to ask who had come. When Cisrena did not answer, she hurried to the door, wiping her hands on her apron. She gasped, shoved past her shocked husband, and hugged her son. Tuac was taller than her now. Cisrena wrapped his arms around the two of them. To Tuac's surprise, his parents seemed smaller. He could see signs of age in their faces and bodies.

"We did not know when you would arrive," Loree said into Tuac's chest. "Come in and eat. Tomorrow we have something to show you."

Loree released her son and turned to Merle. "My dear. I am so happy to meet you. Welcome to our family." She opened her arms and Merle stepped into her warmth and kindness.

"Papa, run to the market and buy what we need for carabasch, and get some of those honey cakes he loves. We are not feeding our children leftovers!"

Cisrena smiled at Merle, stroked her shoulder, and set out to fetch the dinner ingredients. Loree showed them to Tuac's room, which had not changed since he had left it.

"I'm sorry it's so small, but we'll sort this out tomorrow. I'll put water for baths on while I cook." She eyed their scant packs. "Is that all your things? You must have laundry."

Tuac and Merle sorted their dirty garments and passed them to Loree. The journal of Sam Orris slipped out of Tuac's pack.

"What's that?" Loree asked around the armload of clothes.

"The beginning of a very long story," Tuac said. "I promise to tell you all of it."

That night they ate and laughed. Tuac and Merle gave them a short version of all that had happened since he left. Merle interrupted him often to emphasize something Tuac had done but which he had excluded in favor of the contributions of others, especially Rea. He focused more on NABES' awakening and defeat than on its true nature. They were not ready to learn the real history of the Prophet and the Terrans.

The following morning, after a robust breakfast, Cisrena got up from the table and said,

"Let's go!"

"Where?" Tuac asked.

"We have a surprise for you," Loree said. She tucked the left-over honey cakes into a parcel. The four of them set out, and though Tuac's parents kept a brisk pace Tuac walked slower, pointing out landmarks to Merle and telling her stories of his exploits with Rea when they were children. He did not pay attention to where they were going.

On the northern side of Stara, just off the main road to Shi'bo Coula and Basul, Cisrena stopped.

"Here we are," Loree said. She and Cisrena were beaming.

A massive building, set back from the road, featured a bright carved sign: *The Brea's Lair.* Beside it stood several smaller buildings. Workers moved in and out, carrying lumber, buckets of whitewash, and tools. Other supplies lay stacked in the yard.

Loree said, "When finished, this inn will have ten guest rooms, a tavern, and a kitchen. The stables are that smaller building. It will be the finest bed and breakfast in all of Mia. You can't see it, but in back there is a house for you and Merle, already completed. It has five bedrooms."

"They had this built for you," Cisrena said, handing Tuac a letter. The seal featured a dragon in two circles. Tuac opened it and read:

Dearest Tuac, I started this project the moment you told me you wanted to leave Tushman. I knew this time would come. My words cannot do justice for all you have done for me and for Mia. I know we

have talked about all the times I failed you—not because I didn't love you, which I did and do, but because I didn't believe in you. And despite that, despite all that you have faced, you have grown into a warm-hearted man. I wish I could have your empathy, your optimism, your never-ending love. At times, I see my own limits and I wonder why I am not more like you. But then I remember the lessons we have learned together, and I realize I am who I am and there is balance in me as well.

I thank you for that—for teaching me to find my own balance, teaching me to embrace all I am not just the parts I like. And most of all, thank you for never giving up on me.

I love you more than life itself. I am so proud of you.

Rea

Tuac passed the letter to Merle, blinking back tears. She read it and gasped. Then she hugged him hard.

"Let's go see the house," Merle said. "We need to prepare two bedrooms."

"Two?" Tuac said.

"We have a few more months, but yes."

Tuac's mother whooped with glee as Tuac looked at Merle, confused. Then he understood and he clasped her to him.

A family, a future, a new beginning. His father joined the hug.

"Easy, now!" Merle exclaimed. "Don't hurt her."

"You already know it's a girl?" Loree said.

"Of course she does," Tuac said.

As his parents gave Merle a tour of the grounds, Tuac went into his new living room to start his home's first fire. The room was bright and inviting. It would be a good place to write his journal and tell his daughter about the story of how her father was once a Heretic, a Destroyer, the Reunifier, and a Brea.

He arranged the wood in the fireplace and looked for a flint to start the fire, but could not find one. Tuac checked to see that he was alone. He reached for the wood and a spark jumped from his finger to ignite the tinder.

Merle is not the only one with residual magic, Tuac thought. When the blaze was going strong, he walked out to invite his family inside.

High above Stara, Shalla, and Basul, the Earth starship *Explorer* orbited Mia. The *Explorer* was the latest of many ships to visit Mia since the *Curiosity* had crashed on the planet. Each ship observed the edicts of Earth's Command Council: observe but avoid contact with the local population of Mia. Earth CC had abandoned the ACED program. It had caused multiple instances of violence on Earth colonies.

ACED's impact on the native Mians had been unique. When Commander Orris had extended ACED's field to the entire planet he had created the conditions in which an artificial intelligence had emerged. Orris' ingenuity had saved what was left of the *Curiosity's* crew but had subjected Mia's populace to a sentient being composed of the darkest elements of the population's emotions.

Earth CC had ordered the monitored isolation of the planet. Mia's observers would not allow that sentient being to escape. For centuries, visiting ships had watched and hoped the entity would expire on its own. They would intercede if necessary, regardless of the turmoil that would cause.

The arrival of *Curiosity's* crew and ACED had disrupted the evolution of the native population. Those swayed by the AI had set out to conquer the world, but had been defeated by people who had not been tainted by that darkness and who had fought for a more equitable culture. Sam Orris's grandson Elijah had led the defenders of the planet. He had learned enough basic science from his grandfather to identify the effects of ACED and the emergent artificial intelligence, and he had designed social systems to keep the AI in check.

Elijah's strategy had diluted the gene pool so that those most affected by ACED were spread widely and their numbers had dwindled over time. Unfortunately, while this had lessened ACED's effect, it did not eliminate the AI.

The *Explorer* had arrived before the AI had assembled an army and begun to feed off the population. The speed of the malevolent being's spread concerned Earth CC. If the AI had succeeded in its conquest, the *Explorer* had been ordered to destroy the planet. Then a boy with recessive genes that gave him unique access to ACED's benefits had gathered his own forces to protect Mian civilization. He had confronted the AI and had destroyed it by eliminating ACED.

After ACED no longer influenced the population, the Earth CC directed the *Explorer* to evaluate the culture's new direction. The captain discussed the situation with the ship's HACI.

"Are ACED's effects gone?"

The ship responded, "Yes, but Sam Orris's records mention that the local population had already evolved telekinetic brain patterns. This is why ACED had such a pronounced effect and why the AI emerged. My scans confirm that ACED no longer impacts the planet. All Earth technology is inactive."

"Should we be concerned about the Mians' innate abilities?"

"We cannot completely undo what the *Curiosity* did. If we had not interfered, Mians might or might not have learned to control their telekinesis on their own, we cannot know. But after *Curiosity*, their evolution changed. Now they will explore their natural abilities. We cannot predict where that will lead."

"HACI, will they be a threat?"

"I lack data to calculate that outcome. They are building a government that values justice. The AI will be folded into their existing mythos as a warning."

"Thank you HACI. Lieutenant, send Earth CC the following:

"SY 5107, Captain William Emory of the Starship *Explorer*. After 1,000 years, it appears that the local population of the inhabited planet called Mia have been relieved of the adverse impact of the Artificial Cerebral Enhancement Device carried by the *Curiosity*.

"Mians will now choose their own direction, untainted by Earth influence. They are developing a benevolent government. Time will tell if they survive. We suspect that the *Curiosity's* influence will affect how they harness their innate telekinetic skills, but we see no reason for concern. Telekinesis is not intrinsically bad, so I recommend that the Mians be allowed to grow. Mia should have the choices that all our member societies have had. We should not interfere unless they become a threat, which I do not anticipate happening.

"Emory out. Helmsman, take us home."

The End

Afterword

Thank you for sharing Tuac's journey with me. I hope you liked reading it as much as I liked writing it. Tuac's journey started over 25 years ago. I was in a bad point in my life, feeling abandoned and scared. I had tried journaling without much success, but I felt that I needed to write myself out of my mental abyss. I decided to write a story about an overlooked boy who would rise up to save the world. It had to be fantasy, since that is all I read and still resonates with me.

Deciding to write a story and actually writing one are two very different things. The overall arc of my story—a boy, magic, defeating evil—came to me easily. Of course, that is also the story line for *King Arthur*, *The Hobbit*, *Harry Potter* and so many others. I wanted my story to be different. As I thought about all the stories and authors I have loved, I realized I never really asked myself questions about those books, I just became engrossed in those tales. And that was when I realized how I could try to make my story more unique—it would not only be about magic, but about where it comes from and why evil exists.

My choice to tie magic to AI and science was rooted in my education and the world we live in. Once I set my story on a distant world that had been tainted by Terran colonizers, the rest flowed easily. I did not anticipate how much I would change in the course of writing this book, and how much those changes would become part of *Reunification*. Inner healing, global events, and my yoga journey all added depth to my story.

I need to thank many people. First is April White, a family friend and an author. Without her sage advice to "Just write it" I would never have gotten past the endless loop of rewriting the first 50 pages. April explained that the story comes first, then refinement. Andrew Robinson, my dear friend from college, gets a big shout out, too, for convincing me to secure a great team to sharpen my story. Thanks go to Stephanie Crochet and Jocelyn Solomon for bringing the joy of yoga into my life.

As for my team, I am so appreciative of the work of Mia Kleve and Anne Larsen. Andrew recommended Mia to me and she read this book before anyone else did. I was scared when I sent her my first draft. The whole project was suddenly *real*. She told me there was a story here that needed to be told, and my heart swelled. She introduced me to Anne. Anne's tireless hours of editing and re-editing, and a ton of formatting, were instrumental to this book. And after a year, she was very much my friend.

My team was rounded out by Sean Inoue, Steve Wilner, Eileen Ansel, and my wife, Francie. The read galley proofs and I learned that, despite five rounds of drafting, editing, redrafting and more edits, the manuscript was not as finished as it needed to be. All of their careful corrections and insights have made *Reunification* a better book.

www.ingramcontent.com/pod-product-compliance
Lightning Source LLC
Chambersburg PA
CBHW061113100726
47911CB00013B/518